ANNA'S MISSING MEMORY

ROBERT MURDEN

proving
press

Book Design & Production:
Columbus Publishing Lab
www.ColumbusPublishingLab.com

Paperback ISBN: 978-1-63337-975-6
E-Book ISBN: 978-1-63337-976-3

Printed in the United States of America
1 3 5 7 9 10 8 6 4 2

Also by Robert A. Murden

It's a Bob's Life:
A Memoir of Robert A. Murden, MD (2023)

ANNA'S MISSING MEMORY

CHAPTER 1

WEDNESDAY, WEEK 1

A nna slowly entered the psychiatry offices in the late afternoon. She walked gingerly, as if she were trying to avoid broken glass. She barely noticed that the brightly lit reception area displayed calming portraits of forests and landscapes on the off-white walls. Anna crept past the two other patients waiting and presented to the registration clerk. Signs above the desk noted that the clinic specialized in eating disorders, PTSD, and blocked memory therapy. The clerk checked Anna in and asked her to take a seat.

Anna sat apart from the other patients, in one of the gold-colored cushioned seats that were arranged so that those waiting would not have to look at each other. As she waited, she contemplated whether either of the other patients was there for a similar reason as she was, or if either one felt anywhere near as anxious as she did. She waited for several minutes with her right leg mildly shaking the entire time.

Finally, her first name was called, and a pleasant, dark-haired female aide escorted her down a short hallway. Anna passed more portraits, this time of flowers, that were clearly meant to be soothing.

The aide ushered her into a medium-sized room with cream-colored walls. The walls to the left and right sported matching dark-stained chests of drawers. Narrow bookshelves extended from the chests to near the ceiling. A small sink and a

2 | ANNA'S MISSING MEMORY

mini refrigerator were next to the bookshelf on the right. Framed diplomas and certificates were displayed on the walls next to the bookshelves. The wall opposite the entry door boasted a large window with brown curtains that were almost completely closed. The floor covering was thin, light-tan carpeting. The room held two comfortable-looking camel-colored upholstered armchairs situated well away from the left wall and facing to the right. A separate large burgundy leather Queen Anne-style chair was positioned on the right, facing the two seats. In that chair sat a man whom Anna presumed was to be her psychiatrist.

He wore a dark brown blazer, a light-yellow dress shirt sans tie, and brown dress slacks. He appeared to be in his late thirties. He was clean-shaven and had medium-length dirty-blond hair, which was neatly trimmed. Anna attempted to read his expression, but she couldn't tell if it was open, neutral, or professionally nondescript.

The doctor studied his new patient as she entered the room and stopped. His initial impression was that she was quite subdued. She pointedly turned and watched as the aide exited the room and closed the door, then she slowly turned back in his direction.

She was a thin and relatively attractive young woman who was fair skinned but with a mild tan. She wore a short-sleeved white linen blouse and beige dress slacks. Her short brunette hair was done in a sleek straight bob. Her expression was blank. The doctor rose from his chair, crossed to his patient, and offered his hand.

"Hi, I'm Dr. Ellis. It's very nice to meet you. Would you like me to call you Anna or Ms. Jones?"

"Either one is okay," she replied, while providing a limp handshake.

The doctor pointed to the sitting chairs. "Please make yourself as comfortable as possible. I hope you'll find this to be a safe place to express your thoughts. My patients usually call me Dr. Ellis, if that's okay."

Anna nodded and took a seat. She hadn't made much eye contact to that point. She held her legs tightly together, and her hands were grasped stiffly in her lap, giving her the overall appearance of a woefully insecure job applicant.

The doctor returned to his chair. "Thank you for agreeing to meet at the end of usual hours. My notes say that you requested an urgent session to deal with a memory disorder. I'm the only psychiatrist in town who specializes in that area, and this is the only time I could meet this soon. Can you tell me briefly why we're trying to regain a lost memory for you?"

That's when Anna's thoughts started racing. This was her initial appointment in this clinic, and many steps had led to this point.

It was her first appointment since the police had informed her of the two other women who were savagely attacked in a fashion similar to her prior assault. The first one since she informed the police that she had no actual memory of her own attack. The first one since the police asked her to help their case by seeing someone at this clinic, in hopes of recovering her memory. The first one since Anna realized the possibility of unleashing the unspeakable horrors that might reside in her blocked memories.

"It's really hard to talk about."

"That's okay. Take your time."

Anna knew she had to speak eventually, but she was aware of the likely stress inherent in this process. She really had no idea what to expect. Even though she'd agreed to the therapy, she felt a little like a mouse who had to avoid a very dangerous trap if she wanted to reach the goal of identifying her attacker. She replied in a meek voice.

"I was attacked two years ago behind a bar one night. I had head injuries and got a concussion. After I recovered, I had no memory of the attack, and I haven't gotten any memory of it since. The guy was never caught.

"Apparently since then, two other women have had attacks nearly identical to mine, and last week the police interviewed me. When I told them I couldn't give them any details about my assault or my attacker because I had no memory of it, they asked me to have memory therapy. They're hoping I can remember something that will help them identify and catch the guy who they think is committing these attacks. They said they have almost nothing to go on now."

Dr. Ellis was not expecting that answer. It suggested that he would be in for a complex and possibly prolonged process if he were to help her. He paused briefly to collect his thoughts.

"Okay, Anna. So that we can approach this in the best way for you, let me ask you first about your concussion. Did the doctors ever mention a diagnosis of TBI, or traumatic brain injury?"

"I don't remember any term like that."

"How severe was your head injury?"

"I briefly lost consciousness from the attack, but I didn't crack my head open. I only had to stay in the ER for a few hours, as far as I remember."

The doctor nodded. "Okay, that's helpful information. After an attack with a head injury, there are two types of memory loss, or amnesia, which can develop. One is from physical damage to the brain. The other is from psychological trauma from the attack. There's no therapy that reliably helps amnesia from brain injury. It either resolves or it doesn't on its own. The therapy I can offer could only help if psychological trauma was causing the amnesia. Do you think it's worthwhile to pursue therapy for that possibility?"

Anna hadn't really thought of her absence of memory for the attack in these terms. She hadn't wondered why she had no memory; she'd just accepted it. She'd previously sometimes wondered what had actually happened to her that night, though that uncertainty didn't consume her. But ever since the police recently asked her to seek memory therapy, she had hardly been able to stop thinking about it.

She knew there were many possibilities of what could have occurred, several of them quite ugly. If any of those awful possibilities were true, she would understand a traumatic reaction. She also presumed that the degree of physical trauma she'd suffered that night likely wouldn't have caused enough damage for permanent memory loss. She reluctantly decided that if she wanted to help the police, she would have to consider the therapy for traumatic memory loss, as worrisome as it sounded.

She replied with a large sigh. "I guess we can try the therapy you mentioned."

Dr. Ellis leaned forward with a hopeful expression. "Now, usually in a first session with a patient, I would begin with gently spending time getting to know you in a non-threatening way. But if we're going to help your situation, I want to first try an exercise that could help us find out if this is truly psychological traumatic memory loss or not.

"This is jumping in rather fast, but if you're okay with this, I'd like to try some brief hypnosis. This method could help you recall memories that were suppressed by emotional trauma, but it's very unlikely to help recover memories from traumatic brain injury. The results can help us decide how to proceed."

Anna replied while her eyes darted around the room like jackrabbits running through a field and didn't hold the doctor's gaze. "Hypnosis is a really scary idea. I wasn't expecting you to suggest anything like that. I want to help the police and the other women if I can, but I'm really frightened about reliving any trauma."

"I can't reassure you that this won't be frightening, but I'll be here to support you. Why don't we start and see how it goes? Do you feel you're able to try it?"

Anna fidgeted and wrung her hands back and forth, but she replied that it was okay.

"I want you to try and relax as much as you can. Sit against the back of the chair and close your eyes." Anna slowly assumed the suggested position. She bowed her head, slumped her shoulders forward, and held her hands very tightly together, almost as if she were praying.

Dr. Ellis noticed her stiff posture. "For this to be effective, you need to relax your body and your hands as much as possible, please." Anna relaxed minimally.

Dr. Ellis stood and dimmed the lights. He returned to his seat and began, in a voice that was commanding yet soft, slow, and gentle.

"Now clear your head and listen to my voice. Imagine you're at the beginning of a very long hallway that slopes downward. You're going to walk down this hallway very slowly. Begin walking down the hallway. As you walk, your head will lose any other thoughts, and you'll start to feel sleepy. Your shoulders loosen and you have no tension. You continue the long, gradual descent slowly, slowly.

"You're becoming sleepier and sleepier. You don't have a care in the world, and you're feeling more comfortable. Keep descending and keep getting sleepy. You're going down, down, down, and becoming more and more sleepy. You can hardly hold your head up. It's darkening around you, but you can still see. You're intensely sleepy. You reach the end of the hallway. There's a dark opening and you slowly walk through it.

"You're in a darkness, but you can see a dim light that suggests an exit. You walk toward the exit and you feel totally relaxed when you reach it and step into its void. You feel safe and calm, and you're able to think about anything. Now, think about that night two years ago when you were attacked. It's dark and you're behind the bar. What do you see?"

Anna had fallen into a state of profound relaxation in the chair during the hypnosis, but then sat up, with her eyes tightly closed as if she were trying to concentrate.

"I…I'm getting something. A memory. I'm in an alley behind the bar. I'm frightened and confused. A man is behind me, and it seems like he's a little bit taller than me. He's holding me from behind.

"I sense that he's angry, and suddenly he throws me hard at some trash cans. The cans are coming at my face and head so fast, and I'm terrified. I guess after I hit the cans I blacked out. I don't remember anything after that, and I don't remember seeing him at all."

Anna opened her eyes and displayed the terror-stricken look of an audience member at the climactic scene from *Carrie*. Dr. Ellis noticed that she was sweating profusely, and she appeared to have just recovered from a trance.

"I can see that this memory was very difficult for you to experience. I don't want to push you too much, but can you talk about this memory?"

"Honestly, I want to forget the memory, not talk about it. When I came up with that memory, I immediately knew that I didn't ever want to be that terrified again. I don't want to relive the feeling if I can help it."

Dr. Ellis leaned forward and gazed intently into her eyes. "That's certainly understandable. Although this hypnosis exercise today was brief, the fact that it succeeded strongly suggests that there is a traumatic amnesia present. So, further therapy could really be effective. It's a major breakthrough that you were able to remember even that small amount of detail today in this first session. Now, you should try to relax. Take some slow, deep, calming breaths."

While she tried to relax, the doctor went to the switch and returned the light intensity to normal, then returned to his chair.

Anna attempted to change her breathing pattern, but she could feel her heart pounding and was aware of the beads of sweat on her face and under her blouse. She hated this feeling of terror. This made her recall the inexplicably stressful feeling she had noticed when walking past a bar now. "Is this feeling going to get worse if we have more therapy, Doctor?"

"I can't really answer that for you. You might never remember anything else, or you might remember many more details, some of which could be even more frightening. You might learn that you can tolerate these memories surprisingly well, or you could find that some new memories cause even worse reactions."

"Do you think that anything I remembered today will be helpful to the police?"

"It's hard for me to answer that. I assume that anything you remember is likely to be of at least some help, even if it doesn't immediately lead to discovering the identity of your assailant. You'll need to discuss that with the police."

Anna's upper chest was red, her blouse stained with sweat along her underarms, and her eyes flitted in many directions. "I know. When they came to me with the information about the other assaults, we had a long discussion about this. The plan is for me to go to the station after each of our sessions and tell them any details that I remember. I'm really not looking forward to that meeting, but I'll probably go tomorrow. They said I don't need an appointment."

Dr. Ellis decided that he should help Anna to calm down by ending the session on a more positive note. "Let's briefly change subjects. Since we didn't have the usual introductory session talk today, can you just tell me just a little about your day-to-day life and maybe review your plans for the week?"

Anna's body responded by sinking back into the chair, and her eyes brightened. Her speech was steady.

"I love my job. I'm the manager of a primary care clinic. My position is a good fit for me. I really enjoy the people I work with, and I have a few work friends. As the manager, though, I can't get too close to the staff. We have fun work parties on special occasions, and I love arranging them.

"Outside of work, I enjoy being with my dog, Milo. I also enjoy hanging out with my roommate Sonia. We go to restaurants and concerts together, and sometimes we'll see a movie. I love running and exercising, and I regularly run in 5K and sometimes 10K races.

"As for plans this week, since the weather's going to be nice, I'm going to take Milo to the dog park for a long visit with his dog friends tomorrow. On Friday, Sonia and I are going to a restaurant that we like. It has lots of vegetarian options for me, but also plenty of alcohol and artery-clogging red meats and fried foods on the menu for her. Saturday, I plan to go to the gym, and I'll do my runs three times a week as I always do."

Dr. Ellis replied, "All of that sounds very healthy, other than for Sonia, I guess," eliciting a brief shy chuckle from Anna.

Anna informed the doctor that the police were hoping for some answers soon. The doctor indicated that it might take several visits to fully uncover her memory, so he suggested twice-weekly sessions. Anna reluctantly agreed and they arranged a schedule with that frequency.

"I expect that you'll do fine when you talk with the police about today's memories. Let's plan to start the next session with you discussing how the meeting with the police went for you."

"Okay, Doctor. I guess I'll see you Monday for the next session. Will we have to do hypnosis again?"

Although Dr. Ellis didn't want to throw too much at Anna all at once, her question provided a good lead into discussing memory therapy. "Let me answer that by telling you a little about memory therapy.

"We label the issue that you're experiencing dissociative amnesia, a blocked memory. This occurs when there's a massive psychological trauma associated with the event that's in your memory. Your subconscious disassociates the memory from your consciousness in order to spare you the trauma. This causes a form of temporary amnesia.

"People can unearth the blocked memory piecemeal or all at once, and on their own or with help. People usually get back most of it. You might notice that I haven't used the phrase 'recover your memory.' That's because many years ago, there was a scandal involving therapists who were attempting memory recovery. This was used in cases of suspected child abuse long after the fact.

"Apparently some therapists suggested specific memories to their clients. When patients said they'd recovered those memories, it was unclear if they were real. Many people accused of wrong-doing due to the memories had their lives ruined. As a result, the term 'recovered memory' and the practice of trying to recover long-lost memories were discredited.

"Dissociative amnesia, which is what you seem to have, is accepted as a phenomenon and a diagnosis. Several psychiatric techniques are the most effective ones to help the amnesia. These are hypnosis, general psychotherapy, and mindfulness, which is a technique in which you focus your mind on specific thoughts and ideas.

"Next session, we plan to start by reviewing your meeting with the police, then get into some general review of your background. These types of discussions are part of what we refer to as psychotherapy, meaning discussing thoughts, events, and feelings. We can save the other techniques for when it seems fitting. We definitely won't plan for hypnosis next time."

"Okay, Doctor."

It seemed like the session was over, and both Anna and Dr. Ellis stood up. The doctor said, "Oh, I meant to ask this question earlier. Since two other women were attacked by the man who assaulted you, why are the police so anxious to get *your* memories for their case?"

"Because one of them is dead, and the other one's in a coma."

Anna turned and slowly walked out of the office, leaving a stunned Dr. Ellis, who stood staring at her departure with his mouth open. She hurried down the hallway and through the waiting area, as if leaving quickly might erase the unpleasant parts of the session.

She understood now that her subconscious had reacted to the overwhelming trauma she must have felt at the time of her attack by completely suppressing any memories of it to protect her. Having even the minimal amount that she remembered today resurface was an alarming feeling. She wondered if there were a lot more memories to recover, and if so, what terrors they might contain. She also wondered if her memories might actually reveal who the attacker was.

Anna was glad that this session was late so she could delay going to the police station until tomorrow, as that might be another unsettling experience. She'd had enough trauma for today. A thought briefly flashed through her brain that maybe she'd even made a mistake in agreeing to the therapy. It seemed like life was going to get more and more stressful for her if she continued with this process.

But realistically, continuing seemed to be the only way she could go now. And after having learned some of what had happened to her that night, she realized that a part of her wanted to know all of it. She just prayed that this process would have a tolerable conclusion.

CHAPTER 2

THURSDAY, WEEK 1

A nna had planned to go to the police station in the late afternoon. She finished a little early at the clinic and got in her car, a seven-year-old used blue Kia. The front was fairly tidy, but Milo rode to the dog park in the back, and most humans wouldn't want to sit there in its current state. In Anna's defense, however, there were only two dog bones, one very used drying towel, and a modicum of dog slobber on the blue cloth seat.

The weather was beautiful for her trip: summer sunshine with a cloudless sky but a nice breeze to temper the heat. Her mood was not as beautiful, as she was uncertain what to expect from her first visit with the detectives to relay her new memories.

The short drive through the downtown streets was relatively empty of cars and pedestrians, as is common for summer in a college town. She parked in the visitors' area and headed to the station entrance, giving a wide berth to one rough-looking man loitering against a car. The two detectives on the case had initially spoken with her at her apartment, and she now found it unnerving to be entering the police station, though it certainly wasn't her first time in one.

The station had a small lobby containing one long bench, half a dozen chairs with hard plastic backs, and the desk. The only occupants were the desk officer and a young man who was slumped down half asleep in one of the chairs.

Anna explained to the officer that Detectives Williams and Smith had asked her to come in and talk with them any time she had new information on her case. He called back and was told that Detective Smith would come out to the desk. Anna was pleased that Detective Smith was the one available, rather than the nice but older and less comforting Detective Williams.

A couple of minutes later, a dark-haired woman who looked to be in her thirties approached the desk. She had very light olive skin, suggesting a Mediterranean heritage. She sported glasses with Gucci frames, wore an Apple watch with an elegant two-tone steel band, and was wearing a purple scoop shirt with black slacks supported by a wide silver-buckled belt. Anna considered her to be a rather attractive woman.

"Hello, Anna."

"Hi, Detective Smith, I think I've got some information for you."

The detective smiled. "That's fantastic news. Come back with me, and we can talk. Detective Williams is out of the station now, but I can fill him in later."

The two of them headed toward the back of the station, with the desk officer's eyes following the women for an inordinate amount of time. The detective took Anna into a small room where they could close the door for privacy. The room held a small table with three wooden chairs arranged around it. They took seats on opposite sides of the table. "How have you been feeling, Anna?"

"I'm doing okay, but it's uncomfortable to be here."

"That's understandable. What would you like to tell me?"

"I had my first session with Dr. Ellis yesterday, and I remembered some details about the attack during the therapy."

Detective Smith pulled out her report book to make notes. "Go ahead and let me know what you have for us."

Anna was shifting in her seat, and her hands shook a little, but Detective Smith's presence was calming and made her feel mostly at ease. "In the session, I got both a visual and a sensory memory. It was brief, but I remembered I had a sense that the man who attacked me was a little taller than me. He was holding me from behind and he seemed to become angry. Then he violently threw me into the nearby trash cans. After that I blacked out. I didn't see him in this memory."

"You stated you had the impression he was a little taller than you. How tall are you?"

"I'm five foot seven, Detective."

The detective smiled. "That's nice—you're the same height as me. Now you mentioned that he seemed to become angry. Was he not angry before that, or do you remember what specifically was going on before that which triggered the anger?"

Anna was hesitant to continue discussing the troubling memory, but she felt supported by the detective, who was easy to talk with. "I didn't recall anything in the memory before I noticed that he was angry. I'm sorry. Maybe I misspoke when I said he *became* angry. I didn't actually notice him changing to angry, just that he was angry."

"You don't have to apologize or feel sorry for anything that you tell us, Anna. Please understand that," Detective Smith replied, with a voice that exuded empathy.

"Thank you, Detective."

"I also don't want in any way to suggest that you aren't doing your best for us. However, we know that sometimes memories, particularly those recovered with blocked memory therapy, are often not completely accurate. Do you think this was an accurate memory?"

That brought up to Anna a very disturbing incident from her past, and she hesitated at that question for good reason. She hoped that the detective didn't notice and wouldn't inquire about the reason for her significant delay in answering. "It, uh, felt very real—in fact, too real and very terrifying. It could be the terror that convinced me it was real. I saw the trash cans also, but not much else."

Detective Smith responded, while presenting an empathic smile, "Okay. Is there anything else you remembered or wanted to talk to me about?"

"No, that was it."

"As I said before, I'll share this with Detective Williams. How are you feeling in terms of continuing to undergo your therapy?" Anna noted the deep concern in the detective's voice, which further cemented Anna's kindly feelings toward her.

"I still feel really anxious about this, but I also want to help catch this person, particularly after that recent, awful attack."

"We greatly appreciate your courage in doing this. I want you to know that we're very focused on catching the person responsible for these attacks, and we'll continue to work hard to get the answers we need."

They stood, and Detective Smith walked Anna out to the entrance of the station, under the extremely watchful eye of the desk officer. She smiled and thanked Anna for her help.

Anna returned the thanks and went back to her car, feeling good that she might be able to help. She felt anxious too, not only about what uncovering the memories could do to her, but about what horrible images and emotions her remaining memories might contain.

Her upcoming therapy sessions might be even more revealing, and even more terrifying. Then, of course, there was also the recent, more constant fear. The man who committed that awful attack on her was still out there and was attacking again. Who might be next, and was she still in danger?

After leaving the station, Anna went directly home to the apartment she shared with Sonia. It was a small two-bedroom place on the top floor of a moderately large but plain three-story building. Anna changed into shorts and a T-shirt and walked her brown-and-white Boston terrier, Milo, for twenty minutes through their neighborhood. After that, she scanned her phone as she anxiously waited for her roommate on the small sofa in their living area. Anna was ready to run her experiences of the past two days by her friend.

The raven-haired and tan-skinned Sonia, who was both a few years older and a few inches shorter than Anna, arrived at their apartment after she finished work at the spa. She was still dressed in her work outfit that resembled tight-fitting black scrubs, and she had her hair in a ponytail.

She walked over to where Anna sat and immediately began ranting about her last client. Sonia felt that the client, who was unhappy about her facial, had diva aspirations and was under the delusion that she possessed Kardashian-level clout, rather than the George Costanza level that she actually had. This made her complain routinely about even the most perfect results.

Sonia gestured wildly with her hands and didn't even sit during her rant, but when she finally stopped talking, Anna commiserated with her. She then said she wanted Sonia's opinions about her therapy session. Sonia sat on the sofa beside Anna, eschewing the small, cushioned chair, which was the only other seat in the living area.

"You're aware that I started my therapy yesterday, right?"

"Sure, honey."

"Can I tell you about it?"

"Absolutely. I'm always here for you."

This reminded Anna of the night she'd met Sonia and of their immediate bonding. They had met at a loud and crowded bar over a discussion Sonia had initiated about the poor quality of the available men they saw in the crowd that evening. Anna found herself in full agreement with Sonia's observations and her humorous ranking system for men. They found themselves agreeing on the music they liked too.

Anna was pleased with how complimentary Sonia was about Anna's outfit and appearance, which she had always taken pride in. Sonia seemed to enjoy having a companion who agreed with some of her outlandish opinions, but who was also a foil for Sonia's most offbeat thoughts. They made plans to go out together the next weekend and became very close after that.

They planned their activities together, and they had helped each other regularly with dating, work, family problems, and worries. Anna had truly needed a close friend then, as she hadn't had a best friend since Madison back in high school. She tried her best not to dwell on the tragedy of that lost relationship.

"Thanks. You're so good to me." Anna then described her therapy session and the memories she'd unearthed. She told Sonia about her anxious trip to the police station. She relayed her worries about how terrifying future therapy sessions could be. She also told Sonia that she wanted to be strong and be able to help the police and the other victims, but she had reservations. She asked for Sonia's opinions.

"We both know that you've been less outgoing and less confident since the attack. I think this could help you get back to who you were before."

"That would be wonderful, but do you really think this therapy will help with those issues?"

"You've been avoiding a lot in the past two years, honey. I assume that's because of the attack. Addressing it might help you become the ideal, poised version of Anna again. How's the therapist?"

Anna sat back with a very tentative expression. "It's kind of too early to tell. I guess he knows what he's doing, and his mannerisms are kind, though I certainly didn't warm up to him yesterday. It might have been better if I'd gotten a woman psychiatrist, but apparently that wasn't an option. There weren't really any other negatives about him."

"Then I say, why don't you go for it? Just make sure that when you're in his office, you're the one sitting closest to the exit door," Sonia said with her roguish smile.

"Gee, thanks. I really didn't need another thing to worry about."

"Listen, I'm on your side, even if I am responsible for you being in this messed-up situation. But let's go have a wonderful dinner and get our mojo on and not worry about it tonight, okay? I need a fun night out after my day at work, and I know that you sure could use it."

Anna gently replied, "You know I don't blame you in any way, Sonia. I'm so glad that I have you. I don't know what I'd do if anything happened to us, or to you, and I had to live without you."

She knew that Sonia was not aware of just how much she truly worried about that possibility, and why. She'd never told Sonia anything about that difficult part of her life. Anna knew that she couldn't tolerate anything remotely like that happening ever again.

CHAPTER 3

MONDAY, WEEK 2

D r. Ellis awaited his second session with Anna. His office door was ajar, and he sat on his therapist chair with a pad and pen in hand for taking notes. He loved his therapist chair, as it helped him to feel confident, in control, and caring, all simultaneously. He found himself wistfully daydreaming about his job and all of the wonderful things he'd done for people previously while sitting in this chair. These Walter Middy-esque reveries were interrupted by a knock on the door, and the office assistant showed Anna into the room.

"Good afternoon, Anna. It's good to see you again," he said as he stood and they shook hands.

Anna thanked the doctor, who wore a similar outfit to that from their first session. She sat gingerly in her chair, which she realized was the closest one to the door by a small margin. Sonia would be ecstatic.

"How are you feeling today?"

"I guess I'm doing okay."

Dr. Ellis desperately wanted to talk about the dramatic ending to their last session, but he'd promised Anna that today would be easy for her, so he held off.

"We said we'd start today with you letting me know how your visit with the police went. Is that still okay with you?"

Anna remained not at all sure about this experience and about talking with the doctor about anything even approaching a difficult issue. Her expression suggested that she was about as optimistic about this session as someone facing an IRS audit. She knew she should pull herself together. At least there would be no hypnosis in this session.

"Yes, it's okay. I saw Detective Smith, who's the nicer of the two detectives. I told her what we'd uncovered at our last session. She asked me a lot of questions for clarification, and some of them were difficult. She was nice enough to me, but she even directly asked me if I thought the memories were real, and that question bothered me. I guess it wasn't quite as bad as I'd imagined it would be."

The doctor replied, "In terms of what the detective said, you should be aware that memory is unpredictable. We know that memory is fallible by comparing memories that have existed as gospel in people's minds for years with objective documentation of the events. Some long-held, firmly entrenched memories turn out to be significantly inaccurate. It's possible that some memories that you discover through this process may not be completely accurate. But there would be no way to know, and I'm not implying that you're making up any memories."

She replied with an almost hopeful tone. "I told the detective that they seemed very real to me."

"And I'm sure they are real for you. Now, I'd like to spend the session today getting to know you better. This should be more relaxing for you, and it will help both of us to fully understand your responses in our remaining sessions, which will focus on your memory therapy. Can you begin by telling me about your upbringing and background?"

Anna was hoping this question indicated that today's session would indeed be less stressful than the last. She settled back in her chair. "I was raised in the suburbs of Chicago. I have a younger brother who I fought with a little, like normal siblings, I guess. My father's an accountant, and my mother's a nurse who only worked part-time until my brother and I were older, then she went back to full-time. I got along well with them, and I'm definitely close to them, but not like those women who say their mothers are their best friends.

"I had a lot of friends in high school, but I don't keep up with them much now." She paused and had a faraway, melancholy look when she said that. Dr. Ellis wondered what caused that appearance.

"I was a very good student in high school. I didn't really enjoy Chicago that much because my family and friends didn't like to go into the city, and the suburbs seemed bland. I was really happy to get out of there and come here for college. Missouri was close enough that I could get home easily for breaks, but far enough from Chicago for me to feel independent."

"Was yours an unhappy childhood for any reason?"

"No, it was fine. There were no really unpleasant experiences in my early childhood, and my family situation was fairly normal."

Dr. Ellis thought, *How lucky you are, Anna*, then responded, "How did you deal with major disappointment or negative events in other aspects of your life outside of your family?"

Anna instantly took on a pained look. This wasn't at all what they were supposed to be talking about today. This topic was something she didn't even want to think about, much less discuss. She had no idea what to say. She hesitated for an uncomfortably long time before replying haltingly, while avoiding eye contact.

"I guess the worst thing I remember was borrowing my mom's car and having a minor accident when I was looking at my phone while driving. The car was damaged, but I was okay."

Dr. Ellis filed away the striking hesitation in Anna's response. He was certain that there was significantly more that she could have said on that subject of negative events, but she seemed to be holding back. He decided not to push her on it in this session. "What about in college?"

Anna let out a sigh, then reclined comfortably back into the chair.

"I had a slow start to college at Mizzou, but by my sophomore year everything was really good. Overall, I'd have to say that I had a blast in college. I enjoyed Columbia as a town. I had a lot of friends to hang out with. I never was busted for underage drinking. My grades were good. I never was hit on by any of my professors. I loved intramural sports and listening to good bands. I also completed a master's program here, which seemed like a continuation of college. I was sad when my schooling ended."

"You didn't mention any romantic relationships."

Anna visibly withdrew, before answering in a demure voice. "I tend to avoid thinking about that part of my life now. I guess I dated about as much as the other girls. I had a few typical college sexual experiences. I just had one close relationship in college. That relationship lasted several months, but I ended it when he became too possessive of my time. He didn't mind my exercising, but he got upset when I wanted to spend time with my girlfriends rather than him."

"Was it a sexual relationship?"

"Why do you need to know that, Doctor?"

He replied with a soft and kindly tone. "I want to have a deep understanding of your background in all areas that might impact your responses to trauma. This will be helpful to review before we tackle even more difficult issues."

Dr. Ellis noticed that Anna had become quieter and less confident when talking about her relationships. The atmosphere in the room was muted, and Anna was making less eye contact. He decided not to pursue an answer to his prior question, and he asked this next question as gently as possible. "Given the reason you ended it, was there anything rough, violent, or abusive in any way about that relationship?"

"My gosh, no. It was good until just before I ended it. He got fairly upset then and did a lot of pleading for us to get back together, but nothing of a worrisome or physical nature. The pleading wasn't obsessive, and he eventually gave up."

"What about the possessiveness that you mentioned. Was it emotionally abusive while you were seeing him?"

Anna furrowed her brow and stared away as if looking for answers. This supposedly easy session was taking directions that she never expected.

"I never thought of it that way. Toward the end, he tried to tie up all my weekend nights so that I had to be with him instead of my girlfriends, but it was college, so there were the weekdays. I snuck out with my friends while he studied. but he sometimes quizzed me about where I was those nights.

"My friends told me they thought he was too controlling. I guess I never thought I'd have bad enough judgment to be with someone with that character flaw, so I didn't really see it until the end. I certainly never felt that I was in any danger."

"How about since college?"

"As I mentioned, I liked Columbia, and I enjoyed the climate and job opportunities. I enjoyed the outdoor activities like canoeing that the area had. So I decided to stay in town, initially working for the university. I eventually was hired to help administer the clinic, where I'm the manager now."

"Other than what you told me last time about your roommate and your dog, what kinds of things have you most commonly done for fun?"

Anna answered through pursed lips that were almost in a frown, "I used to like going to the bars with my friends, which I did a lot. I enjoyed drinking but not to excess, good food, and dressing up to go out. I liked to wear fashionable and trendy outfits. Instagram posts of my meals, activities, and observations got a good number of likes. I met my roommate, Sonia, at a bar one night. We became close friends and eventually roommates, and I was usually out with her after that, particularly once we moved in together."

"You began that reply with used to. What do you mean?"

Anna lowered her eyes to avoid contact and lowered her voice. "Since the problem two years ago, I've stopped drinking alcohol and I've avoided going to any bars."

"Can you tell me more about that?"

"I didn't remember any details of that night, but I know it was bad. I don't want to take a chance on whatever occurred that night happening to me again, so I don't drink and I stay away from the type of place where the attack happened. I'm a little more withdrawn now and life's a bit less exciting, but it seems safer."

"If you suffered a major trauma that night, I guess I can understand you taking those steps."

The doctor briefly paused. He realized that after his unfortunate experience last year, and the changes he'd made as a result, perhaps for the first time ever he fully grasped what his patient was feeling. He truly did understand her to an extent. The lack of such kindred experiences had never previously kept him from routinely assuring patients that he fully comprehended their feelings and actions, however.

"You haven't talked about relationships since college. What about them?"

"Do you really need to know that, Doctor?" she meekly replied.

"I don't want to cause you to worry, and I'm not wanting to press you too hard. But these kinds of questions are part of what we consider to be your therapy. It's a way for both of us to understand your background and what your baseline psychological profile is like. I would prefer it if you did answer, but you don't have to talk about anything that makes you too uncomfortable."

Anna noted that up to this point, today's session had generally been a mere three on a ten-point anxiety scale. Although she noticed that the doctor's hand had been in nearly constant motion with furious note writing, she hadn't considered what exactly he was jotting down. Now she began to wonder.

Was he just documenting the facts, or was he making opinions as to her psychological profile, as he described it? Was he making judgments about her? Was she speculating now because he was asking about relationships and sex, or for some other reason?

She didn't feel too uncomfortable with the doctor per se. He came across as calm and interested in her well-being. But she did note that even though they were avoiding the hypnosis technique, this session was eliciting increasing discomfort.

"I suppose it's okay, but I want to avoid getting into too many details."

"So just tell me what you feel you can share at this time."

Anna stroked one hand with the fingers of her other one. Her eyes darted between making brief eye contact and looking around the room. "Well, since finishing college, I've had one short fling and two relationships that lasted for a good period of time."

"Can you tell me about the relationships?"

"The first one was sexual and was good. I enjoyed the fact that I had someone to be with and do things with, and I enjoyed the closeness. But we liked different things, and I think that made us gradually grow apart. We'd been together for close to two years when he was offered a job in another state.

"We weren't at a stage then where he would've asked me to move with him. Even if he had, I would've said no. After he moved, we agreed that a long-distance relationship wouldn't work for us, so that ended it."

Anna stopped talking, and Dr. Ellis noted that she hadn't yet offered anything about the second major relationship. He felt she had done moderately well so far in the session, being able to handle most of the questions and not seeming to balk too much. He was hoping he could help her. But it was clear he would have many barriers to break through if this was to succeed for her.

"And the second major relationship?"

She paused briefly before responding in a near monotone, "I never think about it now. It was about three years ago. We'd met in a bar and hit it off. I enjoyed his personality, and we had a lot in common, even our height as he was only five ten. I wasn't physically attracted to him, though. We went out to movies and parties and sometimes to bars together, but I tried to avoid being alone with him in either of our apartments. That's all."

Dr. Ellis could sense that Anna was holding out again and he would need to pull it out of her.

"How did the relationship pan out?"

Anna leaned away as if she were trying to push herself completely through the back of the chair, and she avoided most eye contact. It was several seconds before she slowly responded.

"This is hard for me to talk about. I agreed to go back to his apartment after we went to an afternoon rom-com once. We were somewhat, um, intimate, but when he tried to get me into bed, I stopped him. I don't remember what reason I gave, but he didn't accept it. He was very insistent, and it got unpleasant very fast.

"He wasn't physically holding me down, but he was right up against me in an aggressive manner. That went on for way longer than it should have. I honestly don't remember if I felt physically afraid, like he was going to try to forcibly get his way, or just emotionally afraid of the situation."

Dr. Ellis stopped writing and slowly leaned in. "How did this unfortunate situation end?"

Anna became restless and a tear formed in the corner of her eye. Eventually she replied, "I said a strong 'NO' to him and told him that I was going to leave. He wanted to talk about it, but I told him I wasn't in the mood then. He got very close to me when I collected my stuff to leave, and he held my arm initially, but he didn't actually prevent me from going. When he called later to schedule a time to talk about it, I said I really wasn't comfortable with him anymore, and we needed to stop seeing each other.

"He kept calling. The calls were very frequent, and they went on for weeks. Sometimes on these calls he made really creepy statements, such as he didn't think he could live without experiencing our physical love together at least once." Anna rolled her eyes when relating that comment.

"He even showed up at my apartment once, but I didn't let him in. If he'd shown up at my office, or any other times at my apartment, I would've considered asking for a restraining order; it was that bad. Fortunately, he didn't confront me anymore in person, and the calls eventually stopped."

Dr. Ellis noticed that it took a lot out of Anna to relate that story. He was interested in knowing if Anna had continued to worry about that man even after the calls ended, but he didn't want to further traumatize her by asking. He realized that this would be a good time to begin to close the session. "This has clearly been a lot for you today in what was supposed to be an easier session, and I think we can end now, unless you want to talk about that relationship some more."

"No, I'm totally fine with ending now," Anna said with palpable relief.

"Okay, so if there's nothing else, I'll see you on Thursday afternoon at 3:30?"

"Okay. I'm worried about going after more memories then, but I know I'll have to. The police told me that I'm their only hope."

Dr. Ellis stood and shook hands with a subdued Anna. As she left, he felt encouraged that they had spoken of this difficult relationship that Anna had, and that she was able to open up to a degree. He had some questions about that last relationship, but they could be pursued later. He also needed to further explore, at some point, her significant hesitation in talking about negative issues in her past. And he wanted to ask about the other victims sometime. All in all, he liked Anna and he believed he could help her a great deal.

Anna very quickly left Dr. Ellis's office. She was surprised at what they had discussed today. That relationship three years ago was a traumatic experience for her, and she surprised herself that she was able to talk about it as well as she had.

She reviewed these feelings in her mind, but since that relationship surely couldn't have been related to her attack two years ago, she wasn't going to upset herself further by mentioning any of today's discussion to the police. She felt certain that she no longer had to worry about that man who had treated her so poorly.

She was thinking that this calm psychiatrist might actually be able to help her regain some of her memories of her attack. Fortunately, she also learned during this session that she could deflect some of the doctor's difficult questions, so she wouldn't need to disclose the darkest secrets from her past. She was optimistic that this was going to work.

CHAPTER 4

TUESDAY, WEEK 2

D etective Derek Williams was a living cliché as he entered the station carrying his large coffee in one hand and his small bag of donuts in the other. He didn't need a large box for sharing because his partner's more health-conscious diet completely excluded any foods that he enjoyed. He wore a slightly rumpled brown blazer over a tan dress shirt and dark brown dress pants. He worked out regularly, which kept him noticeably in excellent shape. His prior divorce had taken an emotional toll on him, though, and he looked every bit of his forty-eight years of age.

His kinky black hair was beginning to gray, which added to the aging effect. He regularly participated in community outreach, which provided him a feeling of accomplishment. He derived great meaning in passing on his perspectives learned from being raised African American in this country. He had a lot to share on this issue, and he loved his time with the kids that he worked with. He also deeply enjoyed his job, and knew he was very good at it.

When he arrived at the station, he learned that there were no new cases today that he had to deal with. Therefore, this morning could be devoted to the unsolved case conference review with his partner that was scheduled to begin soon. They had talked about the series of attacks before in a piecemeal fashion, but it would help to review all of the data at one time in detail. The review had the potential to assist them in locating any missing pieces in the cases.

After he finished his morning meal, he went to an open area where a large case board was displayed. He began to review it, and shortly thereafter his partner, Audra Smith, boldly strode in. She wore a blue scoop neck shirt with her usual belted black slacks and her signature gaudy belt buckle.

"Good morning, Derek. Those wouldn't be donut crumbs on your shirt, would they?"

Detective Williams responded while brushing off the crumbs, "Oh, I guess these must be pieces of falling ceiling tile. Morning yourself. Everything good at home?"

She smiled at his need to conceal his eating habits. "Fine, thanks. My husband has a full day of outdoor activities planned with our son."

"You're lucky his teaching job gives him summers off, so you don't have to deal with daycare. I hear that's a big hassle."

"Amen to that."

"Are you ready to look these cases over?" he said as he gestured toward the board.

"Yes, I am, and I haven't seen anything new for us to address today instead of these cases. I'm assuming that since Anna didn't come to the station yesterday afternoon, she probably didn't retrieve any new memories to help the cause."

Her partner replied, "That makes sense. Why don't we start at the beginning? Can you summarize all three attacks, in order, with the details that we know?"

Detective Williams stood at the board, while Detective Smith sat in a chair facing him.

"Okay, Derek. Anna is a brunette who was attacked in the middle of the summer two years ago. She was twenty-seven at the time. She doesn't remember the attack, possibly due to developing traumatic amnesia as a result of it. Some of her lack of memory could potentially be attributed to her associated head trauma, or her alcohol level, or both. Due to the memory loss, we have little to go on.

"We know that she was at the bar and went out the back door to get some air. She frequented that bar regularly and was aware of that door. No one was seen leaving with Anna. Her minimal statement noted that she'd had too much to drink that night. She remembered nothing of the attack, until a few details emerged during her therapy session last week.

"Everything we have in the files on the attack is from bar employees, other patrons, and the police report. A bar employee went out to the alley behind the bar to empty some trash and found Anna unconscious, face down against the trash cans, which were knocked over. The employee reported that her dress was on, but her underwear was down around her ankles. No one else was in the alley. The employee was able to shake her enough so that she started regaining consciousness, then he rushed inside for help.

"Anna was unable to say what time she'd left the bar for the alley, and the people she was with were also unable to provide a specific time. Therefore, we don't know how much time passed from the moment she entered the alley until the time she was found. No cameras were located that could pick up anyone entering or leaving the alley, and none of the few street cameras in the area found any single suspicious men. Anna was taken to the University Medical Center.

"She was found to have significant head trauma along with some arm and upper chest trauma. That was all consistent with having been thrown into the trash cans forcibly as the crime scene suggested. She may or may not have been struck first. The degree of trauma and the evidence at the scene were inconsistent with her having accidentally fallen into the trash cans. She also was noted to have a concussion.

"She was still somewhat inebriated at the hospital and stated she couldn't remember anything that had happened. Due to the finding that her underwear was off, the medical personnel offered a rape kit and genital exam, and she consented.

"The findings showed no vaginal tearing or internal or external genital bruising or trauma, but semen appeared present. A vaginal sample was collected, and when it was eventually tested, it was positive for male DNA. It didn't match any DNA in the database. Anna denied having had consensual sex any time that day to the officers. Due to her lack of memory for what happened, she didn't want to press sexual assault charges. The official report was therefore labeled as a physical assault only. No suspects were identified, and the investigation went nowhere.

"Video from a CCTV camera that showed the front entrance of the bar was examined, but no one of suspicion was noted. The video is still available as evidence. The only other information we have is from Anna's therapy session last week.

"At that time, she regained her first memories. She remembered the attacker as being a little taller than her height of five seven, and remembered that he violently threw her against the trash cans, after which she blacked out. She said she didn't see him, so we still don't have any idea of his age or race."

Detective Williams remarked. "That's a good summary. Tell me about the other attacks, then we can discuss everything."

"Of course. The second attack occurred last year, about the same time of the summer as Anna's attack the year before. I prefer using victims' names since I think we subconsciously try harder to solve cases when we treat the victims as real people. Monica was in her late thirties, a few years older than Anna. She was also brunette, but a little shorter than Anna. She had gone to her gym for a late-night workout, which she said was not unusual for her.

"According to her statement, as she was about to unlock her car door after leaving the gym, a man forcibly grabbed her from behind. She had parked in a dark area far from the gym entrance, and her car was positioned so that the driver's side door was away from the gym and any foot traffic, which was good cover for her attacker. He put a gun to the back of her neck and demanded that she pull down her shorts.

"She tried to talk him out of what he was planning, but he was persistent and very threatening. She reluctantly went along, and he sexually assaulted her vaginally from behind. After that, he beat her about the head with his hand and the gun, then threw her against the car. She fell to the ground and was nearly unconscious.

"She never saw any part of her attacker and didn't see him run away due to her nearly unconscious state. She got the impression from where his head and voice were behind her that he was just under six feet tall. When she regained her senses, she pulled up her pants and went to the gym to get help.

"Officers were called, and she was taken to the ER. No useful evidence was recovered from the scene of the attack. At the ER, she was found to have had significant trauma to her head and neck, and she had a concussion, but it wasn't bad enough to require her to stay there overnight. She underwent a vaginal exam, and there was mild external and internal bruising, with no vaginal tearing. She was swabbed vaginally, and the specimen was sent for DNA tests.

"The officers wanted to get a detailed statement from her, particularly about recent sex partners and men she might be worried about. However, Monica stated that she was extremely traumatized by the attack, and her head was quite fuzzy, making it difficult for her to think. She said that she wanted to retrieve her car, go home, settle down, let her mind and body recover, wash off thoroughly, and see if she remembered anything else.

"She promised the officers that she would go to the station the next morning. A friend picked her up at the ER and was driving her to pick up her car at the gym lot when a drunk driver ran a red light and T-boned the passenger side of the car where Monica was seated. Unfortunately, she barely survived the accident and didn't survive the night in the ICU. The friend who was driving her survived the accident but suffered a severe concussion.

"Since Monica was never able to return for the more complete interview, there is no more information about the details of her attack, or about anyone who might have wanted to hurt her. The rape kit results came back a long time later, revealing male DNA matching that found on Anna's exam. CCTV footage from the area in front of the gym showed a few single males walking by, but none who appeared suspicious. That footage was also saved and is available as evidence. Once again, no suspects were ever identified."

Detective Williams replied as he slowly shook his head, "This entire case, or I guess series of cases, is one huge freaking tragedy."

Detective Smith continued. "Absolutely. As for the third victim, Hannah, she's a medium-height blonde woman in her late twenties. She was jogging through the park in the evening, which is something she apparently did commonly. Friends of hers don't know if she took the same route each time or went at the same time each night that she ran. She was attacked two weeks ago, near to but not on the second anniversary date of Anna's attack.

"As far as we can tell, she was blitz attacked when she ran past a bush. No one reported any screams. She was sexually assaulted and beaten very severely. The damage appeared to be from both a gun and fists and, by the location of the damage, appeared to have come from behind her. She was left behind a bush, and a man walking his dog discovered her.

"We've no way of knowing how long she was there before the dog walker found her, as she was well hidden. Hannah's shorts and underwear were around her ankles when the other person found her. After he determined that Hannah was unable to be roused, he left her with her underwear down, so as not to disturb the evidence, he said. Due to TV crime shows, everyone's a forensics expert now, it seems." The detective rolled her eyes. "He did take off his shirt and covered her before going for help.

"No suspicious men were captured entering or leaving the park on any nearby cameras, though very few cameras are in the area. The man who found Hannah was questioned, as were contacts of his, and he isn't considered a suspect. Hannah was still unconscious when the EMTs arrived, and she's remained in a coma since. Therefore, we have no information from her about her attacker.

"At the university hospital, the notes indicated that she had a small head laceration where she was struck, likely with a gun. Her exam also revealed external genital trauma. At a later time, her family agreed to a vaginal exam, which discovered no internal vaginal tearing, and swab samples were sent for DNA testing, which isn't back yet. The doctors are unable to speculate as to when, or if, she'll regain consciousness. If she does, they can't speculate about how much she might remember.

"No other useful evidence was recovered from the scene of the attack. There were no recoverable footprints in the area.

Hannah's family and friends were interviewed, and none of them could suggest a person who was harassing her or who might have wanted to hurt her. There are still no suspects."

Detective Williams ran his hands through his hair. "Frankly, this is a goddamn mess. Okay, can you go over the similarities in these cases?"

"Sure. There are several. Each of these attacks occurred outdoors at night at a similar time of the year. In all three cases, the woman was presumably raped, and it was apparently done from behind in each case. All three victims suffered significant physical trauma, and at least two of the three were thrown into damaging objects in front of them. Their ages were similar, ranging from mid-twenties to late thirties. All three were fit women.

"Each of these attacks occurred where no cameras were stationed, implying some possible planning. There was also no useful physical evidence found at the scene in any of these cases, other than the vaginal DNA. Additionally, we have statements from two of the women that the perp was of a similar height, taller than five seven and shorter than six feet. The kicker, however, is that the DNA from the semen recovered in the first two cases is from the same man!"

"Good. Now what about differences?"

"They didn't have the same hair color. Presumptive evidence indicates that a gun was involved in the two most recent attacks, but not necessarily in the first. We don't know if any of these women were specifically targeted. There's a mild age variation. Also, in Anna's case, there was no vaginal evidence of trauma. Some vaginal trauma was noted in each of the other two cases, implying a more violent nature to them. Finally, we don't yet have any semen DNA confirmation from Hannah's attack."

"Putting it together, what do you think?" asked Detective Williams.

"As you know, after Hannah was attacked, we noticed the similarities between her attack and Monica's. Then, after digging into more files, we found the records of Anna's attack. When we saw multiple similarities between all three attacks, we postulated that one person was behind all of them. We have DNA evidence that the first two were committed by the same person. There's also evidence that the assailant in the first two attacks was about the same height.

"The last two attacks included presumed use of a gun and included genital trauma, suggesting a violent attack, but Anna's attack didn't contain either of these characteristics as far as we know. It's possible that the assailant evolved with his violence level escalating with time. That would fit with Hannah's attack being even more violent than Monica's, despite a gun being presumably used in both.

"The first two attacks are linked together by the semen and the height of the attacker, and the two most recent attacks are linked by use of a gun and more violent sexual assault. Since Monica's attack overlaps both of these linkages, it's reasonable to dismiss the minor differences noted and conclude that one attacker is responsible for all three crimes.

"The nearly annual occurrence at about the same time of year seems to be a red herring, in my opinion. A psychotic serial killer might have a reason for annual or anniversary attacks, but a serial rapist is unlikely to be motivated in a similar manner.

"Otherwise, the close resemblance of all three attacks also makes the idea of one assailant more likely than not. These specific women were almost certainly victims of opportunity with minimal planning, other than avoiding areas containing cameras. It seems to be a real stretch to think that any of them were specifically targeted. Thus, it's unlikely that the assailant knew any of the three women."

Her partner asked, "Do you have any real questions about any of these attacks?"

"I know where you're going, Derek. I saw that the investigating officers in Anna's attack wondered if there was some initial consensual component due to the lack of vaginal trauma and her claim of memory loss. As a woman, I'm very aware that victims of sexual assault are often blamed or not believed. All of us in law enforcement need to be better in this area. I think we need to assume that this was assault all the way, unless Anna's memory offers other evidence.

"I'm not implying that we have to lose objectivity. There was no evidence for use of a gun or for significant vaginal trauma in Anna's attack as in the others. We have to eventually explain those differences. But we have the same male DNA found in both Anna and Monica, and we know Monica was raped.

"We also have Anna's memory and the evidence at the scene that she was thrown so violently into the trash cans that she lost consciousness. Whoever did this to Anna didn't stay around to help her, or to try blaming her. And if Anna had allowed something initially, why would it have ended so savagely?"

"Well, there are so-called men who get off on violence during or after sex. But I think it's unlikely that some random person wandering through the alley would have appeal to Anna as a sex partner, even in her drunken state. There's no evidence that she left the bar with someone to go into the alley. So where does all this leave us, Audra?"

"With one big question, first. In reading the case files, it seems that the momentum faded quickly in last year's investigation, once Monica passed away from the accident. It seems like no one noted the connection to Anna once the DNA results returned after a long delay. And though family and friends knew of no exes who would have wanted to hurt Monica, other details were sketchy. Would there be any benefit in revisiting the interviews of her friends and family, particularly the person who drove her home from the ER that night?"

Detective Williams said, "That's a great idea. Something might have been missed, or some new thoughts might have come up in the past year. We should talk to some of her contacts and see if we get anything useful.

"Unfortunately, Audra, other than that line of questioning, it really leaves us needing more from Anna. Unless we get anything useful from Monica's friends, we get a hit on the DNA, or Hannah comes out of her coma with some information, we're left with relying on Anna's help. I think that we have to hope for some bigger breakthroughs in Anna's memory therapy."

Detective Smith replied, "I'm with you on this. I hate thinking of some lowlife like this who might go after other women still being out there. Unfortunately, we've nowhere else to look at this time. If Anna doesn't come up with anything else, we might have to consider releasing stories to the media suggesting that there's a serial attacker, both to search for tips and to put the women of this town on alert."

Her partner said, "I've already spoken with the chief about that possibility, and he doesn't want to do that yet. He said that we don't want to alert the perp that we're on to his serial spree. He also said that with a timeline of one attack a year, so far, we hopefully aren't putting more women in danger by taking our time."

Detective Williams followed with a large sigh. "With all of that, let's split up the tasks. What do you want to do?"

"It might be better, since I'm a woman, if I re-interview Monica's friends. That might put them more at ease and maybe make them open up more if they have information that they're reluctant to share. I'm also likely to be closer to their ages than you, which might help," she replied, with a bit of a grin.

"Okay. I'll talk with her family, who are more likely to be closer to my advanced age and might bond with me, given your youthful reasoning?" said Detective Williams.

His partner chuckled. "Yes. I guess as a detective team, we're not nearly as homogeneous as Cagney and Lacey or Rizzoli and Isles. Maybe we should think of ourselves as Holmes and Drew, channeling Sherlock and Nancy, of course."

"So, does this mean you're at last admitting that I'm the smart one, Audra?"

Detective Smith smiled, ignoring the mild sexism in his response. "All kidding aside, let's hope we can get something more significant from Anna this week. I know she's worried about regaining some terrifying memories, but she's our best, and maybe only, hope for developing any valid suspects at this time. I can't tell you how much I really want to catch the guy who's doing this."

"Amen to that. We have to nail the bastard."

CHAPTER 5

THURSDAY, WEEK 2

Anna's meeting finished a few minutes later than planned, so she had to hurry to make it to her therapy session. She remembered that the last session was not too horrible, but that may have been because no new memories were unearthed. She worried that Dr. Ellis would suggest attempting hypnosis during today's session in order to search deeper into the recesses of her mind.

She remained constantly conflicted between wanting to help find the attacker and being reluctant to locate any more frightening images from that evening. As she drove to the office, the rest of her thoughts were as scattered as playing cards in a game of 52 pickup. The work meeting had gone well. She wondered how Milo was doing at home and how work was going for Sonia. She was anxious about the upcoming session. She wondered if her attacker would ever be found.

Anna reached the medical building and briskly took the stairs to the second-floor psychiatry practice. When she entered the office, the registration staff instantly recognized her due to the frequency of her visits. After being registered, she had little time to fret as she was called almost immediately. The walk through the supposedly calming hallway, with its carefully planned artwork and pictures, did not achieve the intended objective. From her earlier, more quiet state, she had transformed into a labyrinth of nerves.

As she was shown into the therapy room, which was rather dark due to the drawn curtains, Anna's gaze instantly fell upon Dr. Ellis. His outfit was similar to what he had previously worn, a fashionable blazer, blue dress shirt without a tie, and slacks to match the blazer. He seemed to be a nice person, and it was not the doctor who worried her so much, but the process and the potential outcome. She knew she needed to find more, likely frightening, memories.

Dr. Ellis noticed that Anna was smartly dressed in a light-gray short-sleeved blouse and a simple black skirt. She seemed a little on edge.

"Good afternoon, Anna, please take a seat," he said in a soothing voice and with a pleasant smile. As she sat, he asked, "How's your day been so far?"

Anna was making some eye contact and sat in a comfortable position in the chair. "It's been fine, Doctor. My meetings went fairly well, and there were no crises at the clinic."

"That's good to hear. Why don't you begin today by telling me how you've been since our last visit?"

Anna recoiled briefly and took time to collect herself, avoiding eye contact while doing so. She finally looked up and said, "I guess I've been okay, but I didn't like discussing my sex life during our last session. I haven't dated in the two years since my attack, and just thinking about dating or sex makes me uneasy now. In fact, even before beginning these sessions, I usually avoided those thoughts."

"Have you spent any time considering why such discussions are still uncomfortable for you?"

"Not really. It seems like I have a block in my mind about it. That subject has a heavy black door in front of it labeled 'DO NOT ENTER,' and the thought of opening that door terrifies me."

"It's sometimes helpful for people to understand exactly what's triggering them. Could there have been something specific about the events of that night that elicited this change in you and placed that block in your mind?"

Anna thought for a moment. She was only aware that she'd been attacked and was injured because she was told that by police afterward. She knew nothing else of what happened that night. "How could that be? My mind is a total blank concerning that entire night, and I have no mental image of it besides what I got from our first session.

"Since my attack, I haven't gone out with Sonia or my work friends to a bar. I guess my mind associates the image or idea of a bar with terror now. If I even walk past a bar, I feel stressed. I understand that feeling since I was attacked behind a bar. But since I wasn't on a date that night, I don't know what might have happened during the attack that's causing me to avoid dating."

Anna noticed that her answer caused Dr. Ellis to appear as if he had just solved a Hercule Poirot mystery on page five of the first chapter. She couldn't figure out what she had said that led to his apparent epiphany. His follow-up didn't provide her with any clues.

"That's helpful to know, and we should definitely talk about this more at another time. For now, let's try to help you in remembering some more details about the attack. I don't mean to leap too quickly into the session, but can we try hypnosis again?"

Anna recoiled slightly. "I knew this was coming, but I hate the thought of it."

"Was that a yes, or at least an okay?"

"Okay, we can try."

Dr. Ellis had noticed that after her initial non-response, Anna had been somewhat less wary today than in her two previous sessions.

"Alright. First, let's have you perform some calming exercises. Take some slow, deep breaths. Hold your arms in front of you and gently shake them. Rotate your neck slowly in a circle. Try to clear your mind of any interferences. Now sit back in the chair and get as comfortable as possible." He stood to dim the lights and then returned to his seat.

Anna sat back and appeared to settle into the chair. She slumped down a little. "Take a few, slow, deep breaths again. Okay, now we can begin. First, close your eyes." She closed her eyes, but the dread she felt seemed like a geyser that was rapidly rising up within her. She knew she needed to make her mind more of a blank.

Dr. Ellis waited a few seconds, then proceeded with leading Anna slowly down the long hallway of hypnosis that he had described for her at the first session. When his calm words reached the end of the hallway, he said, "Now, picture the alley behind the bar that night." Anna's eyelids started to flutter rapidly but didn't open. "Everything's okay, and you can see the alley now. What do you notice?"

Anna's eyes remained closed and the fluttering stopped. She remained reclining in the chair. After several seconds, she sat up straight and said, "It's coming to me. I went out to get some air. I'm really woozy from the booze. I feel the cool air and it helps the wooziness. I really feel like I'm in a fog, though. I'm rocking back and forth. After a couple of minutes, I get a sudden unsteadiness, and I stagger and start to fall backward.

"I'm in heels so I worry that I might have a bad fall, but someone catches me from behind. I remember feeling really surprised but thankful that I was caught and didn't hurt myself. I feel him grabbing me around the waist with one arm, steadying me, and I feel relieved. I lean back into him, feeling supported and safe for a minute."

Anna had visibly relaxed to that point in the memory. Then there was an abrupt change, and she began breathing faster and speaking rapidly. "I feel his other arm and hand move across my chest. He puts his hand down my dress in the front, and he grabs and rubs my boob. For a few seconds, it feels okay, almost like being in a fantasy during a dream. But I feel myself suddenly wondering what the hell is happening. I realize it's not a dream and it's not at all okay, and I start to panic."

Anna began to sweat and fidget. "About that time, he takes his hand off my boob and pulls it out of my dress. That relieves my panic somewhat. I can see his hand and wrist, but it's like looking through a mist. I can only tell that his wrist and hand are white and clear." Anna was sweating more profusely and suddenly sat forward, opened her eyes, and looked around to identify where she was.

Dr. Ellis had been listening intently and leaned forward with great concern in his face and eyes. "Is there anything more, Anna?"

"Just that I felt a sudden sensation of impending doom. Then the memory left me."

"You're back here now and you're safe. I want you to continue to feel safe, so let's take a breather. Can I get you anything, such as a drink of water or a cool washcloth?"

"Actually, both would be nice."

Dr. Ellis undimmed the lights and went to the small sink where he wet a washcloth. He grabbed a bottle of cold water from the mini refrigerator and brought everything to Anna, who was now leaning back in the chair. "Here you are. I hope these help you to feel better."

"Thanks." They both just sat still for a moment, neither talking, with Anna avoiding eye contact.

"Would you like to talk about any feelings that these memories have evoked?"

"This is really unsettling. This is all new information to me in terms of what actually happened. Until these past few days I just had that vague knowledge, without any kind of image, that something bad happened to me two years ago."

Anna stopped, looked directly at Dr. Ellis, then spoke very deliberately, accentuating one word at a time. "Now I have an image, and I do not like what I see." If a crowd had been in the room, her statement would have stunned everyone into an immediate group silence.

Dr. Ellis attempted to take it all in and process what Anna had just said. It was not only the surprising memories she had just regained. It was also that the past, as she understood it, had suddenly changed for her. She was a poster child for the effects of deeply repressed memories on a person.

"Anna, in addition to how frightening this uncovered memory itself might seem, you're feeling the intense effects of suddenly having new dramatic memories. This often happens to people who undergo memory therapy, and it can be overwhelming. We need to discuss how you should proceed at this point."

Anna's expression displayed both horror and anger. "Doctor, how in the world does anyone proceed with being able to process something like this?" she asked, a question that seemed clearly rhetorical.

Dr. Ellis thought briefly about her question. "I'd like to suggest some things for you to try prior to our next session, which might help. I know this is asking a lot. Between now and our next session, please try to work on these tasks if you can." The doctor then leaned forward toward Anna.

"First, examine how you feel about having new memories. Second, think about the specific memory that you uncovered today and how it makes you feel. Think about whether it can explain your reluctance to date. Third, I suggest that you perform one of those mindfulness exercises I had mentioned previously.

"So far, you've uncovered a memory as to how your attack began, and a memory as to how it ended. Those would be common places for your recall to start. But the memory that connects these two hasn't returned to you yet. That could mean that it's the most terrifying memory of all to your subconscious. The mindfulness exercise is to put yourself at the end of today's memory, contemplate what could have taken place next, and decide what you might need to focus on to allow you to find that next memory."

"So, you don't think I've gotten the whole memory back yet?"

"You might have retrieved all you'll be able to, but I highly doubt that was all of your memory. The remaining portion might be where you recognize your attacker, which could be why you're still suppressing that part."

Anna's posture was sagging, and her eyes were unfocused. She sensed that as bad as the previous sessions were in uncovering her first memory of the attack and examining her sexual experiences, this was several orders of magnitude worse. It seemed as if a frightening monster had been released from under the bed, and it was never going back. She realized that these sessions must now continue to their conclusion, even though they could unearth memories that were infinitely more terrifying.

"I realize that I didn't see any part of my attacker except his hand in today's memory, but I'm hoping to get back some memories of seeing more of him. And I know I'll have to think about what I went through today. I'll do my best to work on the tasks you suggested. It's upsetting thinking about them, though."

"Are there any other things that you wish to bring up or discuss now?"

"No, this is more than enough for today. I'll see you next Tuesday, though I'm not really looking forward to it."

Dr. Ellis stood and offered a firm but friendly hand to Anna. "I very much understand and sympathize with that feeling. However, this was good progress today, and I'm optimistic that we will be able to find out the answers you're looking for. Have a good rest of your day."

Anna stood and walked out, neither slowly nor rapidly. She didn't really share the doctor's optimism. So far she hadn't learned much that could help identify her attacker. She'd mostly just been shocked by her memories. She knew that she needed to keep going, despite the risks. But she wasn't sure how she would take it if the memories got much worse, and she still hadn't figured out who her attacker was. She hung her head as she realized that this could get almost as bad as that awful experience in high school, which had devastated her.

Dr. Ellis attentively watched her depart. With each session, he gained a new appreciation for what Anna was experiencing. He wanted to be as empathetic as possible, so he had refrained from taking notes during the more emotional periods in the session. He sat down immediately and began writing so that he would not forget any of the crucial points he had learned about Anna and her memory.

Anna seemed a little stronger today. She showed some improved eye contact and more comfort in speaking. She was understandably very shaken at the memory she had uncovered. He had presented to her some difficult and possibly time-consuming tasks to complete prior to their next session, and she had not completely balked at the suggestions.

It was only their third session together, but he was already sensing the start of a therapeutic bond between the two of them. Anna was accepting his suggestions and was actively participating in the sessions. He knew that this was advantageous as it usually led to more effective therapy. He hoped Anna would view their sessions as a good, albeit anxiety-provoking, use of her time.

Dr. Ellis stopped writing, stood, and walked to his window. He gazed out through the small opening in the curtains, not really focusing on the people walking on the sidewalk below. He slowly stroked his chin while he was thinking. He was aware that he shouldn't speculate about what might happen in future sessions, but he always did.

What potential terrors would they uncover in the missing middle portion of Anna's lost memory? Would she be able to produce details that would help the police identify and eventually catch her assailant? How would she react if and when a specific suspect was presented to her?

Lastly, he wondered how to approach that epiphany that he stumbled upon in the session today when they were discussing why she had stopped dating. He was making assumptions about her remaining memories. If he was correct, they were likely to be a major challenge for Anna to process and accept.

He hoped she would emerge in good emotional shape after this ordeal. He wanted her therapy to succeed, but uncertainties to rival the threats of Scylla and Charybdis still lurked in their perilous journey ahead. He did, however, allow himself a moment to be quietly engulfed in bliss.

He was glad she'd come to him, as he knew he was the best person to assist Anna in retrieving her missing memories. He was planning to help her arrive at all of the answers. This professional success is what he lived for, and this could be the case of a lifetime for him. If he could just get help with that personal issue he was a little concerned about, he might then have achieved his goal of becoming the best therapist he could be. Everything was looking up for him.

CHAPTER 6

THURSDAY PM, WEEK 2

Anna had several errands to do after her appointment, which helped keep her mind off the session. She stopped at the independent bookstore, where she loved browsing their clever displays, and bought the newest Rebecca Yarros novel. She next went to the bakery. Though the glass display case was fairly empty by that time, the aroma of cinnamon buns and cupcakes still filled the air. She decided on croissants for the morning. Finally, she went to the family-run dry cleaner, where the pressed clothes scent relaxed her as she waited for her laundry.

By the time she had completed these tasks it was late afternoon. When she arrived at the police station to tell the detectives about her session, she was connected with Detective Smith, who told Anna that she had to leave for an appointment, and Detective Williams was out. They made arrangements for Anna to return at 7 p.m. to see Detective Smith.

Since Anna had some extra time, she decided to pick up dinner for her and Sonia. She texted Sonia to find out what she wanted for dinner from The Heidelberg, their favorite spot. While she awaited Sonia's response, Anna's mind rambled. Would she tolerate her new memories? What else had happened to her that night? Who attacked her? And how would she tolerate the meeting with Detective Smith?

As her mind was sorting through these thoughts, she saw the return text from Sonia. She asked for bacon and cheddar skins and a Cajun chicken sandwich with German potato salad. Anna went online and ordered spinach and artichoke dip plus a vegetarian chef salad for herself, as well as Sonia's items.

She drove to Ninth Street to hunt for a place to park that wasn't too far from her destination. When she finally reached The Heidelberg, she walked past the large plate-glass window that gave the patrons a view of the edge of the university.

She entered and passed the many rows of wooden tables, filled with mostly student diners, to reach the pick-up counter. She eagerly grabbed her package, whose aroma gave rise to visions of a massive consoling hug. Despite her tense session earlier, she practically floated to her car and headed to the safety of her home.

Detective Smith arrived at University Medical Center for her scheduled appointment. She was there to check in with Hannah's mother. They had made arrangements to meet in the ICU waiting room.

When the detective got there, the relatively small room was filled with families in various states of sadness. There were single people, couples holding hands and consoling each other, and extended families standing and sitting in groups. Many were in tears, and there were people from multiple demographics, but there was a sense of shared suffering.

As the detective entered the room, Hannah's mother rose from her chair. She was thin, fiftyish with graying hair, and she sported minimal makeup. She wore a casual cream blouse, jeans, and sneakers. She wasn't crying, but she looked haggard. The detective greeted her, and they moved out of the waiting room to the hallway to speak.

"How are you holding up, Mrs. Carey?"

"It's very tough, Detective. There's so little progress. It's just an eternal waiting game."

"How is Hannah?"

"No different. They still have no idea when she might wake up or how she'll be when she does. She breathes on her own, but there are no other reactions. They have to do everything for her, including pounding on her back to help her clear the secretions in her lungs that the suction tubes can't reach. Hannah's such a wonderful, caring person and a well-loved teacher. I can't stand seeing my beautiful daughter like this."

She took a minute to compose herself, then continued. "Do you have any kids, Detective?"

"I have a seven-year-old son."

"I hope nothing remotely like this ever happens to him. No mother should have to go through this."

"I'm so sorry that you have to endure this, Mrs. Carey. I want you to know that we're working very hard on finding the monster who did this, and we have some leads so there's hope, though I can't give you any guarantees. We'll let you know if anything more concrete arises. Are there any questions I can answer for you?"

"No, but I thank you for your frequent visits. I feel as if Hannah isn't forgotten. I can also sense that you care. You're a good person, Detective Smith."

"Thank you for saying that, and I'll stay in close touch. I sincerely hope that things improve soon with Hannah."

They shook hands and the detective headed out, resolved more than ever to learn the identity of the depraved serial attacker and bring him to justice. This was crucial for her.

Sonia arrived at the apartment she and Anna shared, still wearing her work outfit of tight-fitting scrubs. She greeted Anna, then she saw the takeout containers and moved in their direction.

"Hey, I heard something interesting at work today, honey," said Sonia, while she helped to unpack the food Anna had deposited in the kitchen. The kitchen featured a small L-shaped counter at the front corner of the apartment, with a separate island-style counter opposite it that Sonia was working on.

"It's not much, but I overheard a client and another aesthetician talking. What I heard is that the woman was badly assaulted but never told the police. That made me wonder if she could've been attacked by the same asshole who came after you."

Anna had taken utensils to the small, dark brown, wooden dining table in the living area just off the kitchen. Light-gray fabric chairs surrounded the rectangular table. Framed photographs and colorful artwork reproductions hung on the living area wall near the table, with a Hufflepuff banner prominently located in the center of the display.

Anna spoke excitedly. "That's really interesting. If there's any chance that was the person who attacked all of us, she would be the fourth victim, and she might be able to identify him. That would be fantastic. Do you think you can find out anything more?"

Sonia had her beer and Anna's water ready, and the roommates had taken the food to the table. Both Anna and Sonia eschewed plates in favor of eating directly from the takeout containers.

"I'll talk to my coworker to see what I can learn, and I'll get back to you."

"Thanks so much, Sonia. So, in my session today, I recovered more memories, and I need to go back to the police station later to tell the detective about them. Can you drive me, then wait and bring me home? I'd feel safer that way and I'd really appreciate it," Anna said expectantly, in between bites.

"Of course. Do you think there'll be any hot cops on duty tonight, to make the trip more worthwhile for me?"

"I don't really know. It might surprise you to hear this, but I was stressed enough the two times I've been there that your dating life didn't really appear on my radar."

"I'm shocked by that news. It's always on mine," Sonia replied, with that huge infectious grin of hers.

Sonia finished her beer and looked as if she was craving a second one. "I guess I should hold it to one beer tonight since I'm driving you to the police station," she chuckled.

"Good thought. Are you up for hearing about today's memories?"

She nodded as she continued to eat, and Anna filled her in on the new memories of the day.

"So, this rando just decided to cop a feel, and you remember being okay with it?" Sonia asked incredulously.

Anna took on an almost wistful expression. "Well, I was very drunk, but in the memory, he was gently massaging my boob, and it kind of felt nice at first. It wasn't rough or painful like I would've expected it to be from some pervert."

"You mean like the pervert who threw you into the trash cans so hard that you blacked out?"

"Yeah, good point. The images don't match up, do they?"

That comment brought the conversation to an abrupt halt. They finished their meals and went to their respective rooms to change.

Anna was still thinking about the incongruous messages she was getting from today's memory. She also had a painful flash from her past that she knew the police could never learn about if they were to believe her memories of the attack. She was in a confused and worried state as she donned jeans and a modest, casual, yellow short-sleeved top.

Sonia emerged from her bedroom with a tight green tank top from Shein and very tight jeans, accompanied by heels. She and Anna looked like they were headed to two completely different destinations, but Sonia was usually dressed for the chase when they went anywhere. They took Sonia's car, a used, sporty red Mazda that was seven years old, like Anna's car, but was missing the dog slobber in the back seat.

At the station, the desk officer called to the back, and Detective Smith emerged almost immediately. Anna stood to go back to the offices with her and turned to give Sonia, who was stretched out on the lobby bench, a thankful glance.

Anna walked beside the detective as they went back to her office. She realized how much more relaxed she was than she thought she'd be now, thanks to Sonia's joking nature and her deep concern for Anna's well-being.

Once they reached the office, Detective Smith sat at her desk and offered Anna the seat next to the desk, which faced the detective. Anna didn't notice any personal pictures on the detective's desk, then realized that was probably a safety precaution because of the type of people who could be sitting in this chair. "Thank you for seeing me so late tonight."

"That's okay—my family is used to it. Is that your roommate who brought you here?"

"Yes, that's Sonia. She's going to take me home after we talk, unless she picks up someone in the lobby first and goes home with him," Anna said with a laugh.

"Let's hope her judgment is far better than that! So, tell me how you're doing."

"I'm doing okay. I got some new memories today that were from the start of the attack." That statement prompted the detective to take out her notebook.

"I was out in the alley, but I didn't remember getting there. I was so foggy and I was more drunk than I ever had been before. In fact, I stopped drinking alcohol after that night. I assumed that being that drunk had caused me either to do something stupid or to be unable to prevent what happened, even though I didn't know what actually did happen."

Anna's gaze then shifted to the floor. She told the detective of her falling and being caught, of the hand massaging her breast, and of initially feeling as if she were in a dream.

Anna sat up straighter and made eye contact. "Then I seemed to wake up out of the dream. I had a 'what the hell' moment, but I was still in a fog and not thinking clearly. I realized that what he was doing wasn't right, but I was so out of it. Before I could say anything, he pulled his hand out of my dress. His hand was white and clear and had no tattoos. That's all that I remembered."

Anna was shaken by repeating this memory. She noticed that during her retelling of it, Detective Smith's jaw appeared rigid, and her eyes were glistening slightly with apparent empathy. She had been more reserved in their previous meeting, and Anna wondered what was responsible for the change.

The detective slowly replied, "That seems like a difficult memory to process. I'm so sorry that happened to you. Would it be okay if I asked a few more questions about this memory?"

"I guess so."

"Did you get any impression of whether you knew him or where he appeared from?"

Anna sat up and felt less anxious. "No, I didn't."

"You stated that he withdrew his hand from your dress before you could say anything. Did you get an impression that you were about to say something to him about his actions?"

"I'm not sure, but that phrase 'before I could say something to him' was actually a part of the memory I recalled today."

"Okay, this next question I'm very sorry to have to ask, Anna. You said he started rubbing your breast and you didn't react at first. Can you clarify what you mean by that?"

Anna shrank back in her seat. She had been dreading that question.

"Oh, gosh, it's so uncomfortable to say. When he touched my breast, it was more of a gentle massaging than a rough grab. I told Sonia I felt that it wasn't the kind of touch that I would've expected from a stranger taking advantage of me. Plus, I was in that dream-like state, and I think I initially felt it wasn't actually happening but was just in my imagination. Then I realized what was really going on, and it was awful."

The detective flashed an empathic glance, then continued. "Okay, what about the hand that you saw. You said you saw no tattoos. Which hand was it, and were there any other identifying marks or scars?"

"It was his right hand, and there were no other marks that I saw. I didn't see any rings either."

"And what did you mean when you said the hand was clear?"

Anna glanced away and furrowed her brow as she searched for more detail from the memory. "I could actually see part of his forearm along with his hand. His forearm wasn't hairy. His hand was clean and looked soft. It wasn't rough like what I might have expected from a mechanic or someone who worked with their hands. It had no wrinkles or age marks either."

The detective leaned back. "Well, I can tell that this was a lot for you, but it's important. We now know his race, a suggestion about his age, and that he had no identifying features on his forearm or hand. Along with his approximate height, we're beginning to collect some concrete information, and maybe you'll come up with even more later. This is really helpful, and I'm beginning to get more optimistic. I want to reiterate how brave it is of you to be undergoing this difficult and painful process."

Anna thanked her as they stood and walked out together. Sonia was still sitting on the bench and was scrolling through her phone.

"May I meet your roommate?" asked Detective Smith. Anna nodded and introduced them, and they shook hands.

"It's nice to meet you, Sonia. That's a beautiful yin-yang wrist tattoo."

"I'm glad you like it," said Sonia. "I have the sacral chakra of sensuality and sexuality on my other wrist," she said as she grinned and displayed her inner left wrist.

"Sonia's very inhibited and modest, as you can tell, Detective," said Anna.

The detective laughed and they all said their goodbyes. As the roommates left the station, Anna said, "I have a feeling that things are beginning to pick up on finding the attacker now. And if you can learn anything more at work about that woman who was assaulted, it could be just what we need to really get somewhere."

"I'll do my best, honey."

Detective Smith returned to her office. She was determined to work hard to find answers for Anna. She jotted down several thoughts she had gathered from tonight's meeting in order to share them with her partner.

She wrote that Anna had mentioned being very drunk, which made her feel foggy. Additionally, she mentioned that part of the time she felt like she was in a dream. The detective recorded her impressions that these statements might indicate that Anna wasn't fully aware of what was happening to her.

The detective wrote that Anna had still not unearthed a memory of any sexual penetration that would have explained the male DNA that was recovered on her exam. She marked down and underlined the new clues about the attacker: white male, probably not too old, no identifying marks on his smooth right forearm or hand. She also noted Anna's uncertain responses and posited a question. *Doesn't it seem as if every time we get new information from Anna, we end up with even more questions than answers?*

Finally, she didn't jot down the last fleeting thought she had. Her partner must not learn about that significant and related event in her own background, which had the potential to influence her thinking on this case.

CHAPTER 7

FRIDAY, WEEK 2

D r. Ellis relaxed in his apartment on what was for him a rare Friday afternoon off. He loved his apartment, which included two bedrooms and large picture windows with a view of the local park. He had the luxury of a large kitchen and a rain shower in the master bath. The furniture was modern, and a seventy-five-inch LED-screen TV dominated the wall in the living room, so the apartment contained everything he needed. He knew he could afford a nice house, but he wasn't interested in the maintenance.

He checked the time on his favorite Invicta watch. He wasn't a person to try impressing others with a Tag Heuer, even though he could afford one. He noted that he would soon need to leave for his appointment with the doctor. He had very recently scheduled it, but he wasn't completely sure about this appointment. He was having an issue that he was hoping to eliminate, but the idea of undergoing therapy himself was troubling.

After he changed clothes, he left his apartment and rode down the elevator to the parking garage that his high-end apartment provided. He located his nearly new silver Chevy Malibu and climbed in. He enjoyed driving this car as it had an impressive look, but it also signaled to everyone that he was down-to-earth and was committed to buying American.

He reached the medical building, then proceeded to Dr.

Wilson's office. It had a small waiting room that contained two chairs and a kiosk for self-registration. Dr. Ellis checked in, which notified the doctor that he was there. He sat in one of the chairs and grabbed an outdated copy of *Sports Illustrated* off the small table that was between the chairs. He was merely skimming the magazine, since he found it difficult to get interested in March Madness four months after its conclusion.

A short time later, the inner door of the waiting room opened and Dr. Wilson appeared. "Good afternoon, Dr. Ellis. It's nice to meet you," the doctor said, while ushering his new patient into the inner office. Dr. Ellis was immediately impressed. He noted that if his own office was a familiar old song, Dr. Wilson's office was a dramatic Puccini aria.

The wall to the right sported nearly floor-to-ceiling, magnificent mahogany bookshelves filled with impressive-looking volumes. In front of the bookshelves was a matching mahogany desk with a striking desk chair behind it. The wall facing the entrance to the office featured a large window, with plush, light-purple velvet curtains open to admit an almost heavenly glow. The wall to the left sported expensive original artwork, and it offered an exit door to a side hallway so that the entering and leaving patients could maintain their privacy.

The carpeting was a beautiful and calming shade of light ecru. In the center of the room sat a plush wingback chair facing right and a similar chair facing left. A third chair was up against the wall to the left. Each chair was covered with a soft, duck-egg blue fabric that exuded serenity. The temperature in the room was perfect, neither warm nor cool.

Dr. Wilson even looked the part, wearing a tailored light-gray suit with a light-blue shirt and tie and dark Cole Haan shoes.

His ebony skin blended well with the outfit. He motioned for Dr. Ellis to take the chair facing the wall of bookshelves, as Dr. Wilson sat opposite him.

"How has your day been, Dr. Ellis?"

"You can call me Ted, Doctor. It's been easy since I only had a half day in the office."

"Good for you. Let me begin today by inquiring if you have a specific reason for asking to begin therapy with me."

Dr. Ellis was sitting up straight with a moderately stiff posture, but he smiled as he said, "Maybe my Oedipal complex. Or maybe we should start at the very beginning. In the beginning, I was born, but I have no memory of that event. I presume that means it was a traumatic birth, and I developed dissociative amnesia."

Dr. Wilson frowned. "I see. Are we going to get all of the psychiatry and memory therapy jokes out of the way today?"

Dr. Ellis was surprised at himself that he was having trouble being serious. "I'm sorry, Dr. Wilson. It's not you. I originally made the appointment to start seeing you due to some odd dreams and nebulous feelings of unease. They were bothersome enough to me that I was worried they would interfere with my performance at the office. I decided to seek help dealing with them so I can be at my very best for my patients. But I must admit that actually talking with you is really difficult for me, hence the attempt at humor to defuse the tension I felt.

"I know it's a common practice among psychiatrists to seek therapy for themselves, but I've never considered doing so before. I know that we counsel our patients to avoid this feeling, but to me it seems that wanting therapy means that I'm somehow inadequate. And yes, I do know how ridiculous it sounds for a psychiatrist to admit that."

"I'm sorry you feel that way, Ted. Do you think you're able to set aside your worries about therapy and proceed with the session now?"

Dr. Ellis relaxed his posture and slid back in the chair.

"Yes, I guess so. Actually, putting my original sarcasm aside, starting at my birth is reasonable. I never liked the name I was given. I guess my parents named me after a character in a TV show. That sounded flattering until I had a chance to see my namesake in reruns of *Leave It to Beaver*. Theodore also seemed like a pretentious name for a kid. The nickname Teddy was okay at first but was too childish when I got older, and it took a while to get the other kids to call me Ted.

"I often fantasized about changing my entire name when I became an adult. Unfortunately, Lance Mannion was already taken by a *Cheers* character that I wished I'd been named after. I had some unhappy times with my name when I was younger, but that was the least of my emotional problems at that time. I had another problem that was much more serious."

Dr. Wilson took out a notebook, crossed his legs, and began to jot down his thoughts. "Can you tell me about that problem?"

Dr. Ellis was instantly sorry that he had mentioned the issue. He had never told anyone this embarrassing story before and hadn't intended to share it today. He hadn't really thought through what seeing Dr. Wilson would mean. This was going to mean real therapy and opening up. His patients were supposed to do this, not him.

"I guess so. About the time when I was nine years old, this other problem arose. My parents developed the bright idea to have a means of visibly identifying when any of the children were being disciplined. They bought a miniature doghouse and four small dogs. Each child had their name painted on one of the dogs. The doghouse really only fit one dog, so whichever child was in the most trouble that day had his or her dog placed in the doghouse with somber formality.

"I was the oldest of the four of us. The younger kids were given some leeway, so the older siblings were in trouble most often. And the bulk of the disfavor fell on me. I would estimate that three-fourths of the time it was my dog in the family doghouse."

Dr. Ellis paused, clenched his fists, and became red in the face. His speech grew harsher as he continued.

"To make it worse, the doghouse was prominently placed on the edge of the counter that everyone passed when entering the kitchen. Each night at dinnertime, the new dog of the day was ceremoniously announced, and the dogs were changed, if need be. Then this abominable display stayed that way until the next night at dinner. I saw that doghouse every time I entered the kitchen for a meal, a snack, a drink, or to fill my water bottle.

"And it wasn't just me. When my friends and playmates came over and needed to go to the kitchen for anything, they saw it. When my friends' parents were over to pick them up, they saw it. When relatives came over, they saw it. I felt that for most of my youth I was the laughingstock of everyone I knew. I was overcome with humiliation almost every time I entered the kitchen. That humiliation continued for years.

"I also felt like I was the biggest disappointment in my entire family when my dog was selected for the doghouse. And if that wasn't enough, the indiscretions that put me in the doghouse were minor. I didn't use drugs, get drunk, or shoplift. I didn't slug my siblings or get into fights at school. I made the doghouse for not making a sports team. I made it for getting minor reprimands from a teacher. I made it for losing my lunch money."

Dr. Ellis collapsed back into his chair. His muscles were shaking and he had become pale. Relaying that story had taken a toll. Although he presented an outer facade of supreme confidence, he was aware that underneath resided a layer of insecurity due to his childhood difficulty.

Dr. Wilson appeared amazed at hearing this textbook tale of bad parenting. He seemed somewhat taken aback about how he should follow up.

"How in the world did you deal with that, Ted? What coping mechanisms did you utilize?"

Dr. Ellis curled his lips into a sneer. "I used the wonderfully effective coping mechanism of leaving for college and never coming back."

"What about before you were able to leave for college?"

Dr. Ellis leaned forward and relaxed his expression. "I made life plans. To counter my sense of being a huge disappointment, I made plans to demonstrate success to my parents. I made plans to become a successful doctor so that I no longer would sense that disappointment. I also studied constantly so I could be sure to achieve my goals."

"Was that your primary motivation for going to medical school?"

"Honestly, yes. Sure, I enjoyed learning about how the body and mind work once I was studying medicine. But I enjoyed even more knowing that I'd have a career that wouldn't disappoint anyone."

"Your coping mechanisms sound exhausting."

"They were and still are. But they aren't always successful. For instance, a few months ago, I received a thank-you letter from a grateful patient. But instead of enjoying it, I obsessed about how good it would feel to flash the letter in the faces of my family members and the multitudes who had marched past that doghouse over the years. I didn't cope well that day."

"Maybe we should work on devising a strategy for you to stop obsessing on the disappointing treatment you suffered in childhood. Instead of dwelling on the negative, we should reorient you toward the positive. Tell me specifically about your self-esteem. What contributes to maintaining it?"

Dr. Ellis perked up at that question. It was a good topic for him as he could talk about success, and not about feelings.

"I believe that all of my self-esteem stems from the good that I perform. Currently, I have a job that helps people and earns me great respect. I know that I've truly helped many of my patients, and I need to continue doing so. I've also worked at the food pantry in town twice a month for years now. I donate to several charities. I'm selfless in offering to cover for my colleagues when problems arise for them.

"From the doghouse story I shared, you can deduce that by the time I finished school and could leave home, my emotional state had plunged to the depth level of the Mariana Trench. Fortunately, I later discovered that earning good grades in college, with hopes of becoming a doctor, helped to improve my state. Those factors were still not enough for me to completely escape the daily humiliation I had felt growing up, however.

"I was only able to really cope in life once I developed a deep personal conviction that I'm a very good and successful person. I count on my sense of this virtuousness very much, and I know that I can absolutely never allow myself to lose it."

Dr. Wilson looked up from his note-taking. "What keeps you from focusing on that self-esteem, rather than obsessing about your childhood, when you receive good news?"

Dr. Ellis developed a puzzled expression. "I don't really know. On most days, I sit in my personal therapist chair, which has always provided me strength and meaning, and I know I'm a good person. But the days with great successes can inexplicably lead to my obsessing. Those are the times that I want my family to know that I'm not the disappointment that I assumed they saw me as. Without them acknowledging my success, I feel as if I don't have closure."

"How is the feedback from your family about your successes and the good that you do now?"

Dr. Ellis struck a neutral expression, as if he was explaining a simple concept to a patient. "I actually have very little contact with them. When I said I was never coming back after college, I meant it. I don't return home for holidays. I rarely speak with my parents, and I only speak occasionally with my siblings. I have my own life now, and I'm never in the doghouse in that life."

Dr. Wilson had a concerned expression and folded his hands over his notebook in his lap. "Would you consider talking to them more and sharing your successes with them now? Maybe you'd find that they didn't really perceive you as a disappointment."

"I think I'm afraid that if I share what I feel are tremendous accomplishments, and they don't react with the appreciation that I expect, I'd feel even worse than I do now."

"So, who do you share accomplishments with now, Ted? Who are the confidants that supply you needed emotional support?"

That question surprised him. It wasn't something that he spent time contemplating. After a few seconds of thought, he replied, "I would honestly have to tell you that most of my emotional support is internal. I talk with the other doctors at work, mostly about patients, but I rarely socialize with them outside the office. I have contacts on social media, but I consider them acquaintances, not friends. I attend church off and on, but I'm not close to the minister.

"All of these contacts are people I suppose I could talk with about problems if I felt the need for extra support, but I've never felt the need. And I don't generally share my successes. I would classify myself as a loner. I think I must be an INFJ or INTJ on the Meyers-Briggs scale."

Dr. Wilson leaned in slightly. "What about romantic relationships, particularly long-term ones?"

"I've been a loner there also."

Dr. Ellis paused, then laughed at the joke he made at his own expense. "No, wait, that didn't sound right. I didn't mean to imply that I only participate in self-love. I've had several sexual relationships, but most of them were brief, some no longer than one night. I've never had a relationship last longer than a few months."

"Do you have any insights as to why that is?"

"That might be a long discussion that we should save for another session."

Dr. Wilson nodded, then opened his notebook. "That's reasonable. I'd like to address one more issue today. When talking about self-esteem, you mentioned both success and being a good and virtuous person as the main contributors to your self-esteem. How do you define those two ideas?"

Dr. Ellis took a minute to think. Dr. Wilson certainly wasn't tossing him any softballs today. "I'd say success is being a doctor, having my patients get better, and achieving respect. I guess being a good person is having a job that helps people, being charitable to my colleagues and others, and always being viewed as having done the right thing."

"It seems like much of what goes into both definitions comes from elements of your profession, and not from your personality, the true you. That might be something for you to think about more and for us to explore further in future sessions."

Dr. Ellis thought, *Great, more deep issues to discuss*, but he replied, "Sure. We can do that."

Dr. Wilson shut his notebook. "Okay. We've talked a lot, and this does seem like a good stopping point for today. Is there anything else you wish to talk about now before we adjourn?"

"No, I think this is good for today."

"To recap, we uncovered a great deal today. I think you should reconsider your lack of contact with your family. You should think about any steps you could take to avoid your obsessions with the negatives in your background. We have plans to talk about your lack of long-term relationships at the next session and talk further about the sources of your self-esteem. We also still need to address your original complaints. I look forward to seeing you next time to work on these issues."

Dr. Ellis thanked Dr. Wilson and left by the special side exit door. It was odd and a little unsettling being the patient who was leaving and who needed to maintain privacy. He was used to being the doctor who was in charge and not needing to worry who saw him.

He proceeded down the back hallway and made his way quickly to his car. Once he got home, he decided to avoid thinking about his session with Dr. Wilson and plan his activities for the evening.

He sometimes prepared simple meals for his dinners, but takeout or delivery were frequent options. He decided that he needed to relax for the night and just order a pizza with the works. He had beers in the refrigerator and would find a good action movie to watch. As it was too early to place his delivery order, he allowed his mind to wander.

He first reflected on his patient Anna, and how well he felt that her therapy was progressing. She was a pleasant person, and her case fascinated him. He tingled like a schoolboy dreaming of his new crush when he conjured up pictures of himself being the one to help her completely unblock her memory. He craved successes like that as they really validated him.

In his reveries, he visualized the front-page news story that highlighted his role in helping her identify her assailant and bring justice to all of the victims. Of course, he realized that could never happen, as his role required him to remain behind the scenes. This knowledge didn't prevent him from daydreaming, however.

He also contemplated his next session with Dr. Wilson. He didn't tingle excitedly with those thoughts. Today's session held some positives. It felt good that someone was aware of the dog-house story and of how incredibly much it had affected his entire life. He also knew it was probably good for him to share his deep need for constant success at work.

On the other hand, Dr. Wilson had asked him to consider increasing contact with his family, which he was not ready for. He also still needed to discuss his dreams and his recent unease.

And they were supposed to talk about his relationships next time. That might be a complicated discussion. It might expose some minor wounds in regard to his lack of a life partner at this age. But there was nothing overtly negative concerning his dating history, for the most part.

The question was whether he would mention his most recent

dating experience from last year. The one he'd never mentioned to anyone. The one that could lead to his possibly being viewed in an unflattering light. The one that caused him to wonder if he'd possibly not done the right thing for the first and only time in his adult life.

CHAPTER 8

TUESDAY, WEEK 3

I n the morning, Dr. Ellis arrived for his bimonthly shift at the local food pantry. He sauntered through the small distribution area that consisted of a few metal tables in front of a counter that spanned the width of the room. As he passed through the area, he received hearty greetings from other workers. He had been volunteering there for a long time.

He went behind the counter and to the storage area in the back and took up his position stacking and unloading boxes. His partner today was Malcolm, also a regular. Malcolm was dressed in worn-out jeans and a T-shirt, and his black hair was in short dreads. He had a three-day stubble on his face. They were in a moderately sized storage room filled with shelves stacked to the ceiling. The side wall consisted of a large garage door that was opened when deliveries arrived.

"Yo, Ted, how ya doin'?"

"Good, Malcolm. How are you?"

"I got food in my belly and my bus pass for the month is paid for so I'm ridin' high today."

"Good to know."

"I also like that I get to work with you today."

"Why is that?"

"'Cause you's a hard worker, Ted. Some of dem other stiffs just go through the motions. It's like they is here just to impress their people. But you's different, Ted. You get it."

"Thanks for saying that, but I might not be as selfless as you think. You're right that I'm not here to impress anyone. But I can't take credit for being here only to help others. I do get a self-satisfying sense that I'm a good person for helping here, and that motivates me. I'm certainly not going to claim that I'm another Mother Teresa."

Malcolm threw Dr. Ellis a "Who dat?" look, then replied, "Well, I like you, and from what I see you's here for the right reasons."

"Thanks. That means a lot. Now let's get some food to the people who need it today."

"Aight!"

Anna was enjoying her day. After she walked Milo, she took a refreshing three-and-a-half-mile run past the numerous businesses and apartment buildings in her neighborhood. She always felt in wonderful shape and was light on her feet the remainder of the day after a run. At work in the morning, the numbers for the previous month arrived. The number of patient visits was higher than anticipated, and the financial receipts were also above expectations, so the month was a marvelous win-win.

At lunch, the office observed the birthdays for the month with a party for Tammy, Jovanna, and Earl in the large break room. The tables were completely covered with food, drinks, and plates, and the room was filled with happy staff. Anna loved these potluck parties, which they were able to institute again a couple of years ago, once the COVID restrictions were lifted.

For today's party she prepared vegetarian lasagna and a delicious apple, walnut, endive, and arugula salad. She always brought a vegetarian entree and a healthy salad or side to counter everyone else's contributions.

She recognized that most of the staff delighted in the gastronomic orgy of meatballs, fried chicken, pizza, donuts, cake, and cookies that clearly were de rigueur for these events. But she noticed that people were starting to enjoy her salads more, so maybe she was helping to improve their nutritional choices. Plus, with the plentiful options available, she was able to satisfy her clandestine cake cravings during these parties.

Along with enjoying the food, Anna had a delightful time talking with the staff and the doctors. She enjoyed getting to know everyone better, and she felt especially pleased that the doctors, particularly the younger ones, treated her almost like a peer. She also enjoyed that everyone was happy during the parties, so no one brought up complaints or gossip.

After the birthday celebration ended, her good day continued. Her therapy was scheduled in the afternoon, and she was able to devote time to reviewing a major contribution that she was hoping to share. On her run this morning, she'd remembered something tremendously important to bring up to Dr. Ellis. She was surprised to realize that she was really looking forward to this upcoming session so she could divulge this revelation. Once it was time to leave the clinic for her therapy, she was nearly walking on air.

When she reached the psychiatry practice, the process of getting back to Dr. Ellis's office proceeded as smoothly as gliding on fresh ice. The doctor was waiting for her with his typical pleasant smile. He welcomed her as she took her seat.

"Good afternoon, Anna. How are you feeling today?"

"It's been a good day, Doctor, and I'm feeling upbeat about our session."

"That's great news. Let's begin by addressing your tasks from last time. Were you able to get to them?"

Anna was making good eye contact and was as positive as Dr. Ellis had ever seen her. "Yes. I spent some time on them."

"I'm interested to hear your thoughts. Please go ahead." Dr. Ellis leaned back but kept his pad and pen at the ready.

"Well, you first asked me to think about what it's like having new memories of my assault. As I thought of that issue, it became somewhat of a metaphysical conundrum, as my college philosophy professor would say," she offered with a smile.

"I used to think my past was just a bunch of stored memories waiting for when I wanted to recall one of them. Now I wonder if my past is really more a set of experiences that helped turn me into the person I am now.

"That thought made me worry that this awful new part of my past might change who I am in a negative way. But I'm hoping I can have some control over this relationship and maybe limit the negative changes."

Anna neglected to add what she had also been frequently thinking about. There was one major negative part of her past that she hadn't shared with Dr. Ellis and wasn't planning to, no matter how much it might be contributing to who she was.

"The things I've learned from these memories have also helped me understand my actions of the past two years. I've been completely avoiding bars, which I thought was just because something bad had happened when I went to one. Now that I've started to get back the memory of that trauma, I'm beginning to understand the real reasons why I changed my routines."

"I have to say, Anna, that I'm impressed with your response

to all of this. You really took the initiative to deliberate on the issues that arose during the last session."

"Thank you, Doctor."

"How have you done on your second task? What were your thoughts and responses to the specific new memories that arose in our last session?"

Anna leaned forward. She wasn't anxious, and she felt like she was explaining an answer to a friend rather than her therapist.

"When I think of those memories, the big question in my mind is: Why didn't I initially fight when he put his hand on my boob? I know I was very drunk and not thinking clearly. But even so, it seems as if some primitive reaction should have taken over to make me respond by lashing out.

"Plus, when talking with the police, I've noticed myself thinking that they might be doubting some of my memories. It seems to me wildly incongruous that I'd be okay with someone fondling me, when later the same man violently threw me into trash cans and knocked me out. If it seems that way to me, what the heck are the police thinking?"

"I certainly can't answer what the police are thinking. Have you thought about whether those new memories can explain your reluctance to be dating?"

Anna paused and frowned with thought. That wasn't a subject she'd spent much time on, or even one that seemed very important to her now.

"Just briefly, but the inappropriate boob touching is the only memory, it seems, that my mind could have associated with dating. I don't see how that was traumatic enough to be the memory that completely scared me away from relationships."

Dr. Ellis recalled his epiphany obtained during their last session. He knew there was real potential danger to Anna in locating the rest of her memories of that night. He gave no verbal reaction, but his expression changed to one of mild concern. Anna wasn't sure how to react to this expression, and they both remained silent for several seconds.

"This wasn't in my plans for today, but maybe we should address this critical question, Anna. Are you still committed to continuing the search for the remainder of your memories from that night? And if so, what's motivating you now for this search?"

Anna wasn't expecting those questions, though to be fair, they had crossed her mind. She frequently worried about what overwhelming and unexpected terrors her unfound memories might contain. Those worries hadn't dissuaded her from continuing this process, however. The more she learned, the more adamant she felt about needing to procure all of the answers.

She'd also noticed a change in her approach. Initially, she was seeking answers only for the benefit of the police and the other victims. Now the benefit seemed more for her in learning what had happened.

"I definitely want to continue. I think I really need to find out everything that happened that night. I'm also focusing more on identifying and capturing my attacker. He has to be punished."

"Thank you for answering. I think it's important that we clarified your feelings at this point. My purpose is to help you attain your goals, so it's important for both of us to know if they've changed. Let's continue now. Can you tell me if you were also able to try the mindfulness exercise?"

Anna sat bolt upright and she leaned forward. The body language of her arms and legs became very open and accepting. Her expression brightened and she began speaking a little more rapidly.

"Yes, and that's the most exciting, but troubling, thing that I have to tell you about. When I was running this morning, I was working on the mindfulness. I wasn't able to come up with anything to help find the missing part of my memory. But while these thoughts were swirling around my head, a memory from well before the attack surfaced. I remembered that a few months before my attack, I was worried that I had a stalker.

"There was a man I saw several times in the grocery store I go to, and at Seoul Taco, where I often got takeout food. The first couple of times that I saw him at the grocery, I ignored him. But after I noticed him several times at Seoul Taco, I began to think he was stalking me. He wasn't anyone that I recognized from my neighborhood or office. He was usually dressed in what looked like a work uniform of some kind.

"At the grocery, I never saw him in the middle of the store, only in the checkout line. He always carried one of those hand baskets with just a few items. He sometimes got in line behind me, even when I was in the line with a clerk and he could have gone to self-checkout. He was quiet and looked like a loner. He never spoke to me and never approached me. He never followed me out of the stores, that I noticed. But he always stared at me with a really creepy expression, which freaked me out.

"When this memory popped up today, I remembered that he appeared to me to be about five foot ten, which is the height of my attacker. That made me wonder if he could be my attacker. The more I thought about it, the more I worried about him."

Dr. Ellis appeared intrigued. "When you first began to worry that he might be a stalker, did you go to the police?"

Anna recalled those worrisome days. She told the doctor that her friends had convinced her not to go to the police since the man had never followed her or approached her. They had argued that the police were unlikely to do anything, and that the man sounded more like a creep than a traditional stalker.

"Your friends probably had some good points. How did this situation end or become resolved?"

"I stopped going to Seoul Taco for takeout. I changed the times that I went to the grocery. After making those changes, I never saw him again."

"That's certainly an important story, and it shows that your mindfulness exercise produced helpful results. Do you think you'll be telling the police about him now?"

Anna sensed an increased energy in the room. She exuded excitement and practically yelled her response. "Yes! I'll be meeting with them later today, and I'll certainly mention him and describe the stalker vibe that I got from him. I really get the impression that he could be the guy who attacked all of us."

"Since we're on the topic now of a possible suspect, are you worried that your assailant is still out there?"

Anna sat back and frowned. "Yes, I do. Since the police first came to me, I've had a low level of underlying fear. It hasn't significantly worsened in the last two weeks, though after today it might. Having a specific suspect now makes it more fearful, even if I haven't seen this man anytime recently. It would be really wonderful if the attacker could be caught."

Dr. Ellis put down his notebook. "Well, it's getting late, Anna. Would it be okay if I asked you, before we end today, what happened to the other women victims?"

Anna sighed. "The police didn't tell me any details. They only said that both of them were attacked in a nearly identical manner to my attack, and that they hadn't gotten any useful information from them, for the horrible reasons I've already told you about."

Dr. Ellis was quiet for a bit after hearing Anna's reply. It seemed as if he could feel the intense tragedy in this situation.

"We've discussed a lot today. If you have nothing else you would like to talk about now, let's make a plan for next time. I won't give you any assignments in between sessions this time. At our next appointment, would it be okay if we attempted the hypnosis again, and tried to unearth that missing piece of your memory of the attack?"

"As you know, I'm terrified about that piece, but we should go for it. I know we haven't found any strong clues as to who the attacker is yet. I also think it will help me to know ahead of time when we'll be trying the hypnosis. I noticed before that I get anxious when I'm surprised by the sudden announcement that we'll be using that technique."

"That's good for me to know. We know that the less scary mindfulness technique is a good option for you too. But let's continue to make plans at the end of each session in order to avoid any hypnosis surprises in the future."

Anna smiled slightly. "That's a great idea. I also hope that we won't need too many more of these sessions—no offense."

"None taken, Anna. That's a sentiment I hear expressed often in this office. We'll obviously see about the total number of appointments needed as we gather more of your blocked memories. For now, I'll plan to see you Thursday."

"Thanks, Doctor, I'll see you then."

Anna stood during this last exchange, and she left the office. When she exited the clinic, her stride was more normal and confident than her rushed exit was after the first two sessions.

While walking to her car, she speculated about the talk she was going to have with the police. She certainly wasn't going to bring up the discussion she had in today's session concerning whether her memories were accurate or not. Given her background, that discussion could lead down a very dark and dangerous path.

Otherwise, she was ecstatic about being able to offer the police a suspect whom she thought was a strong possibility to be the attacker. She hoped that this might provoke some real momentum in the investigation to find the horrible person who had been committing these crimes.

She also reviewed her feelings about the session today. She was gradually becoming more comfortable with Dr. Ellis and with the sessions. It was becoming easier for her to talk and actually share her emotions. She was seeing the point of his questions and felt progress as a result, but she still worried a great deal about the potential for unearthing some very traumatic memories in future sessions.

Finally, today was the first time she had visions of the sessions ending in the foreseeable future. Everything was going about as well as could be expected. She thought this might be a good time for her to call her parents since she was in a good frame of mind about the therapy. She resolved to see how she felt about making that call after she met with the police later. She permitted herself a smile as she began driving away.

Once Anna had left, Dr. Ellis's thoughts kicked in. Anna was handling these sessions increasingly well. This offered a good prognosis for being able to accomplish the plans for the therapy. He saw no major obstacles to them being able to eventually attain their goals. He was upbeat that Anna seemed to be more positive during today's session. He was becoming more optimistic that he would be able to help her produce answers.

He wondered whether a setback might occur when, and if, Anna recovered her remaining memories of the attack. He expected that these last memories would be the most terrifying of all for her, though they might answer some of her questions. He anticipated that the next session, with the planned hypnosis, would be very enlightening. There could be powerful and dynamic revelations.

He was primed to help Anna find the memories she needed in order to solve the case, and to add to his therapeutic successes while doing so. The next two days couldn't pass quickly enough for him!

CHAPTER 9

TUESDAY PM, WEEK 3

Anna arrived to confer with the detectives. She was becoming very comfortable at the police station, a sentiment that she never imagined would have ever appeared in her thoughts. Today she was even looking forward to talking with the detectives, given her promising reflections from the morning run. The usual desk officer on duty recognized her and immediately called back for the detectives. He then informed her that one of them would be out.

Detective Smith appeared soon, looking as stunning as ever. She greeted Anna and escorted her back. She mentioned that Detective Williams was at the station, so Anna would be meeting with both of them in a small room. Although Anna was more comfortable with just Detective Smith, the issue was less important today since she didn't have sensitive information to reveal.

When they reached the room, Anna, who was giddy with anticipation, observed that Detective Williams seemed a mere mortal compared to Detective Smith's Aphrodite. The mortal greeted Anna and shook her hand. "It's good to see you. Please sit down and tell us what you have for us."

The detectives sat on one side of a small table with Anna opposite them. She quickly composed herself. "I finished my therapy session a half hour ago, and there's one new memory that I want to tell you about. This isn't about the attack itself. While I was thinking about the attack, I flashed back on an older memory. Almost a year before the attack happened, I was convinced that I had a stalker. I'd completely forgotten about him until this morning when I remembered him during my morning run."

The detectives did a subtle double-take when she mentioned her run, but neither one interrupted her. Anna explained the situation to the detectives and told them why she thought he was a stalker. She explained that her friends had talked her out of mentioning him to the police at the time, and she pointed out that after she changed her routines, she never saw him again.

"The reason I'm bringing this up today is that when the memory popped up, I remembered that the stalker was white and about five foot ten like my attacker. Also, when I used to see him, he always leered at me with a really creepy expression. When I thought about all of this today, I realized that he might be the person who attacked me."

Detective Smith asked if she had any other reasons that made her suspect that he might be the attacker.

"Just the creepy feeling I got from him. It seemed that he could be the kind of guy to attack women, and he seemed particularly interested in me."

Detective Williams asked Anna to describe him. She noted that he was average weight, was about thirty years old, and had medium-length brown hair and a thin mustache.

"Is there anything else about him or his actions that you think we should know?" asked Detective Williams.

"No. That's all I remember now."

After glancing at her partner, Detective Smith took over. She expressed her concern but pointed out that they would need the possible stalker's name in order to look into him at all. She said they also would need more reason to worry about him in order to investigate him in depth.

Every inch of Anna's body sagged, and her mouth formed a silent "No." She was so excited that she'd unearthed a true suspect, but she was being told that nothing might come of it. The detectives clearly sensed her disappointment.

"Let me offer this option, Anna, and see if you and Detective Williams are okay with it. We still have the video of the bar from the night when you were attacked. We could at least view that and see if anyone matching your alleged stalker's description was seen there that night. If so, that would place him at the scene, and we would be free to look into him in more detail. How does that sound?"

Detective Williams replied, "That's doable. But your description of him would fit a lot of men in this town. Can we get you to sit with a sketch artist and create a picture that might help?"

Anna shot forward and became more energetic as she grasped onto this lifeline. "Yes, I'd be happy to."

Detective Smith replied, "I'll find out when we'll be able to get you together with our artist, and I'll call you to arrange a time."

"That's great, Detective. I look forward to hearing from you."

"Good. I can walk you out now." As she escorted Anna out to the lobby, the detective said, with her usual empathy, "Don't lose hope. We'll do the best we can with this information. We're working very hard on this case. We're anxious to help you and the other women."

"Thank you, as always, for your concern, Detective."

Detective Smith walked back to the office to confer with her partner. He greeted her with, "I see you took the silent hint that I wanted you to be the bad cop for once, Audra. I don't like always being the guy who the victim hates."

"Sure. I don't mind throwing you a bone this time. After all, I'll always be the good cop in the end." Another woman might have batted her eyes while delivering that line, but that was definitely not her style.

She continued. "Anyway, Anna needed a dose of reality to accompany her hopes. It's an interesting development that she remembered this man, but the odds that this creeper would intentionally find her in that alley are pretty low. Plus, we really think our attacker was an opportunist who didn't target any of the victims.

"And besides, the creepers usually just creep; they don't act. I'll take the onus to arrange the artist for Anna. Then I'll take a good, long look at the bar video after we obtain the sketch. Maybe something will come up. At the very least, we'll have done our best for her to get what answers we can. Anna's a nice young woman, and I feel for her with everything she's endured."

"You're a good person, Audra."

"And don't you forget it!"

Detective Williams said, "Never. By the way, since Anna mentioned her running, do we need to consider whether our assailant is targeting runners? I don't know if Monica was a runner, but maybe we should check."

"Good idea, boss. You're always thinking."

"And don't you forget that!"

The meeting with the detectives didn't go as well as she had expected it to. The high Anna was on earlier in the day was disappearing like the sun over the ocean horizon at the end of the beach day. The detectives seemed to think that her stalker was unlikely to be her attacker, which severely deflated the optimism she had about finally discovering a suspect. Although she still held out hope that her stalker was the guy, she wasn't sure what to think about this turn of events.

She needed dinner so she headed to a small deli that she loved. It had narrow aisles and shelves packed to the ceiling, giving it the atmosphere of an old mom-and-pop place. There was always a pleasant aroma coming from the sandwich toppings. She picked up an entrée-sized Greek salad, loaded with banana peppers and feta. She wasn't excited about her meal, but she hoped to see Sonia at home later. She hadn't talked with her since remembering the stalker during her run, and she looked forward to hearing Sonia's insightful thoughts.

When she reached their apartment building, the only available parking spots were near the back of the moderately sized lot. She left the car, grabbing her deli bag and her large Avalon Mist Kate Spade tote. As she headed through the partial shadows of the building toward the front entrance, she had an eerie feeling that she was being followed. She stopped and furtively glanced behind her but didn't see anyone.

When she started walking again, she could swear she heard footsteps almost matching hers from behind. She saw no one else in the mostly sunny parking lot, and she began to sweat much more than the outside temperature called for. She felt tremulous and was afraid to turn and look again, so she picked up her pace.

The matching steps she thought she heard behind her seemed to increase to match hers. It seemed like a race now. She unsuccessfully tried to calm down by realizing that it was daylight and the area in front of her building had a lot of foot traffic at this time. She finally reached the apartment building entrance and found herself praying that another resident would be in the lobby.

Fortunately, a kindly looking middle-aged man was waiting for the elevator. When she reached him, she felt comfortable enough to turn and look behind her, but no one else had entered the building, and she couldn't see anyone out on the street. Had she really been followed, or was her mind starting to play tricks on her as a result of her worries about the attacker? This would be a disturbing new trend if it continued.

At her apartment, she put away the salad and dropped her tote. She changed to shorts and a tank top for her walk with Milo. She grabbed his leash and they headed out. She never felt afraid while walking with Milo. She felt protected by him because he had always been able to sense how Anna felt about someone. With any of her friends or family, he was happy to see them. If Anna ignored someone, Milo did too. But if they passed a stranger that Anna was wary of, Milo could sense her uncertainty.

In those situations, he instantly began barking and growling. On this walk, Anna saw no one who worried her or appeared to be following her, so it was an enjoyable and stress-free walk for both of them. When they arrived back at the apartment, Anna fed Milo and thanked him for protecting her.

She called Sonia and learned that she would be arriving soon. When Sonia entered the apartment, she informed Anna that she had a date for dinner, but they could talk while Sonia got changed. Sonia popped into her room, the smaller, second bedroom of their unit, and was out a short time later, wearing only a baby blue thong and matching lace bra. "Why don't you come into the bedroom while I get ready, and we can talk there, honey?"

Anna followed her into the bedroom.

"So, can I gather by this part of your outfit that this isn't a first date?" Anna said with a smile.

"Of course not. These are my second date undies."

"If this is for the second date, what do you wear on a third date?"

"Well, all I can tell you is that my third date lingerie set is illegal in thirty-eight states," Sonia replied with a smirk.

She added a satiny blue floral minidress to the outfit, then started to provide some brief attention to her hair and makeup. "Tell me about your session today. Anything exciting come up?"

"Actually, it did. Do you remember when I thought that I had a stalker a few years ago?"

"I sure do, honey."

"Well, on my run this morning, the memory of that stalker suddenly popped into my head, and I remembered that he had the same height and coloring of my attacker. That made me wonder if he was the man who attacked me, so I told the psychiatrist, and then the detectives."

Sonia stopped applying her makeup and turned toward Anna, saying, "Do you think he could be the guy?"

"I certainly thought so this morning when I remembered him. I also said that to Dr. Ellis. But when I told the police, they seemed to dismiss him as a possibility. They said they would have me work with their sketch artist to get a picture of him, but they didn't seem optimistic."

Anna pointed out that the experience was very disappointing, after she had expected all day that she was going to bring a real suspect to the police.

"I'm so sorry," replied Sonia, as she turned to the mirror to continue readying herself for her evening. "But speaking of suspects, I did get a little more info for you today about that spa client who was attacked. I learned that it happened three months ago, and she said she was raped. I'm hoping to get even more details for you if I can."

Anna's attention perked up. "Thanks for getting that. I feel awful for her, but I wish she would come forward as she might know something valuable. Keep me posted. In the meantime, I'm going to go in for the sketch when the police arrange it. After that, they plan to look at surveillance tape of the bar with the sketch in hand, so maybe something will turn up. Ever since I thought of the stalker this morning, I've been convinced that he could be my attacker."

"Or maybe the video will show them how I totally failed you that night, honey. They'll see that I left you early that evening for that booty call. I'll never forgive myself. If I'd stayed with you all night, I would never have let you go out to that alley alone. I might not even have let you get so drunk. In any case, you would never have been attacked if I'd been a better friend. I'm so sorry."

"I wish you'd stop saying that. You didn't make someone attack me, and I don't blame you at all. You're a wonderful friend. Enough talk about that. You go out and have a great time tonight.

"But be really careful. When I was walking in from our parking lot after work, I had a sensation that someone was following me. I never actually saw anyone, but it freaked me out that there could've been someone out there. Please watch out and don't let anything happen to you. As for your date, I hope he doesn't have a heart condition, or he might not survive the night."

Sonia stood and laughed, but then immediately choked up and developed a serious and concerned expression. "Thanks. I love you. I bet that you weren't actually being followed. And don't you worry, nothing will happen to me. In terms of my date, we'll have to see."

After Sonia left, Anna scrolled through her phone while eating her salad. She remembered that she had decided to call her parents tonight. She wondered how they would handle the updates. She also had several other thoughts leaping madly through the sun-scorched veldt of her mind. Was someone really following her from the parking lot earlier? Was there any chance that the stalker would be a viable suspect? What about the person who attacked the spa patient? When would the attacker be caught so that she could stop dealing with her daily fear?

She shook her head to clear those thoughts. She should call her parents now. No more stalling. She moved to the soft gray sofa she and Sonia had purchased as one of their few joint expenses for the apartment. They had gone with the plain gray, as no Boston terrier fur shade options were available at the discount store. Milo jumped on the sofa to curl up beside her.

She settled in and went for her father's cell first. After he answered, they spent some time exchanging pleasantries, and she filled him in on her therapy and some of the memories she had regained. She avoided telling him that she'd remembered the stalker, as she hadn't shared that issue with him when it occurred. He was worried enough about the parts she had revealed to him.

"I'm so sorry, honey. Is there anything we can do? Send you food, send you money, persuade you to move back home?"

"You know I love my job and my friends here, Dad, so I don't have any plans to move back."

"Okay, honey. Then let me leave you with an observation about my herb garden this year. Did you know the quality's been really up and down due to the weird weather we had?"

"No, I didn't, Dad."

"Yes, it was the best of thyme, and the worst of thyme."

Anna groaned. "Really, Dad? Charles Dickens must be turning over in his grave now. Bye."

Anna was surprised that she got through that call without her father chastising her for agreeing to the therapy. She was sure her father would have scolded her if she had mentioned the parts of her recalled memory that she purposefully left out. She was glad the call ended on a good note. Now it was time to call her mother on her cell. Her mother would receive all of the details except for the breast grabbing.

"Hi, honey. I was expecting your call when I heard your dad talking to you. What have you learned in the therapy?" Unlike her father, Anna's mother was not much for chitchat and was diving directly into the heart of the matter.

"I'm great, Mom, thanks for asking. And how are you?"

"I'm sure your dad gave you the updates, so you can just give me the details of your therapy."

Anna sighed and thought, *Okay. Straight to the point then.* She explained to her mother the memories she had unearthed during her therapy sessions so far. Her mother seemed concerned and had a few questions.

"Do the police have any suspects yet?"

"Not really. I remembered today that episode with the stalker that I told you about three years ago. He was white and about the right height, so I told the police about him today. They're going to look into it, but they didn't seem to think that he's likely to be the attacker."

"That's too bad. Well, as we've talked about before, you need to realize that getting really drunk isn't responsible behavior and isn't good for your safety. Do the police seem to be taking you seriously?"

"Yes, they do, Mom. They seem very concerned for my welfare."

"Do they know about your issue in high school with lying to the police?"

"You could have gone this whole conversation without mentioning that episode, Mom. They haven't brought it up, so I doubt that they're aware of it."

"Well, I still don't understand why you did that, honey."

"Maybe we should talk about something else."

"I hope you know that I'm so proud of you for undertaking this therapy in order to help catch the animal who's preying on women there. It's so like you to stand up for other women."

"Thanks for your support, Mom. By the way, I didn't mention the stalker to Dad, as he might freak out if he knew."

"I won't talk to him about that. You know you could always move back here if you wanted. For your safety, of course."

"I know. However, I have high hopes that the attacker will be identified and caught and then you won't have to worry about my safety."

"Parents always worry. When, or if, you get to have your own kids, you'll learn that. Thanks so much for calling, honey. We miss you."

"I miss you, too, Mom. And thanks, as always, for the pressure to have children. Good night."

Anna felt relieved. That went better than she'd expected. She was scolded about the alcohol, and her mother brought up her significant indiscretion in high school, but otherwise it was not bad for a talk with her parents. She planned to wait for any truly major developments before calling her parents again to talk about this. She started to get ready for some streaming while in bed.

Hopefully she could find something very attention-grabbing to block out her thoughts. No crime shows, of course. She didn't want her daily fear level about the attacker who was still out there to increase. Her last thought before settling in to let the screen take over her consciousness was an odd query, however. Was it weird somehow that every one of the people in her life whom she was close to used the identical term of endearment for her?

On the other side of town, Gerald, who liked to be called Gerry, sat down to his dinner. It was late for him, because he'd stopped at a bar on the way home from his work as the day custodian at the mall. Gerry didn't usually stop at the bars since he was saving up money and he could get beer much cheaper at the stores. But it was a special day, and he rewarded himself. The reward didn't carry over to dinner, though, as his consisted of two frozen burritos zapped in the microwave.

He sat at his tiny kitchen table that was held together with duct tape. His apartment was small and a little dingy, and his decorating style would best be described as Broke College Student, though Gerald was in his early thirties. The only kitchen appliances that he used were the refrigerator and microwave. His meals had the commensurate nutritional value.

He had a small TV, but not a computer, which is what he was saving for. Watching porn on the small screen of his phone was too limiting. Life was already tough enough living in a college town, with the multiple coeds he was surrounded by all day at work stimulating his salacious thoughts.

This brought him back to his big day. He saw her today. The young woman whom he'd first noticed at the grocery store about three years ago. At that time, he'd noticed that she was as gorgeous and desirable as a college student, but a little more mature, which was a plus.

Today her hairstyle was different, and he didn't recognize her at first. He still looked, though, and when she turned her head, he realized who she was. When he used to watch her in the past, he stared too much, and she eventually caught on. Fortunately, she didn't notice him today. But he saw her and was able to follow her briefly without being spotted. She was now back in his life, and he planned to do everything he could to make sure she stayed there, where she belonged. It was a great day.

CHAPTER 10

WEDNESDAY, WEEK 3

Detective Smith spent a portion of the late morning at the insurance company offices where Monica's friend, Stacy Palmer, worked. She'd made an appointment to get some further information about Monica. The detective met Ms. Palmer in her private office, which contained a desk and desk chair, two comfortable chairs for clients, and numerous files and shelves. Ms. Palmer wore a rose blouse and light-gray dress suit. The detective told Ms. Palmer that she was hoping for assistance in filling in details they hadn't previously collected.

Ms. Palmer replied that she had been Monica's best friend, and that Monica told her everything. She had answered several questions a year ago, but the detective asked for more details about Monica's relationships. Ms. Palmer said Monica had a healthy sex life, and in the three years prior to her death, she'd had several short-term relationships.

She said most were men Monica had met at her gym or at a bar, and a couple were one-night stands. She said Monica, who worked at the university and was fairly intellectual, had a type that consisted of well-educated, successful, kind men. Monica told Ms. Palmer every detail of her sex life. She said none of the men were overly kinky, possessive, or misogynistic, and none pestered her after the relationships ended.

The detective then inquired about the night Monica was assaulted. Ms. Palmer said she hadn't spoken to her that day and didn't know of any plans Monica had for that evening. Ms. Palmer picked Monica up at the emergency room after the assault and her medical evaluation. While they were on their way to pick up Monica's car at the gym, a drunk driver ran a red light and struck the passenger side of the car where Monica was sitting.

Ms. Palmer told the detective that she'd lost consciousness in the crash and sustained a severe concussion. She developed amnesia for the period just prior to the crash, which her doctors told her was common with her degree of head injury. As a result, she remembered nothing of the conversation she and Monica had during the drive, so she wasn't sure if there had been anything significant said.

She further noted that her pre-accident amnesia had been total for almost a year, but in the last two weeks, some memory was returning. She was beginning to remember the crash, but nothing of their conversation before that.

"I want you to know, Detective, that Monica was a wonderful person whom everyone really adored. She was kind to everyone. She didn't deserve any of this."

"I'm so sorry for your loss, Ms. Palmer. Here's my card. Please call immediately if you regain any memory of your conversation with Monica that evening."

On her way back to the station, Detective Smith stopped at one of her favorite places, Chicken Salad Chick, and picked up a healthy lunch to go. She took it back to the office and settled in for paperwork while she awaited the afternoon meeting with her partner.

In the very early afternoon, Detective Williams arrived and joined his partner at her desk. He had just finished a typical lunch out, which was a barbequed brisket sandwich with fries and a root beer. His partner had worked through her lunch, a common practice for her. Doing so enabled her to get home earlier to her family on some days.

"Hey, Audra. Are we ready to review the latest on our case now?"

"Sure."

Detective Williams went first. He'd spoken with Monica's parents over the phone. They said Monica was very independent. The conversation suggested that Monica was not overly close to her parents. They had nothing to add to what they had told investigators the year before.

Detective Smith then shared with him that she had talked with some of Monica's friends, who all said that Stacy Palmer was the one to speak with. She told her partner about her interview with Ms. Palmer earlier that morning, and noted what she'd learned about Monica's relationships. Detective Smith related that Stacy still had no good memory of their drive back from the ER due to a concussion she'd received in the crash. She did learn that Monica wasn't a runner.

Her partner replied, "That's too bad that she has no memory of their talk. That might have given us some helpful details. But at least we got to the questions that needed to be asked to make sure Monica's report was complete. What else were you able to do?"

"Anna came in first thing this morning and we obtained the sketch of her alleged stalker. This afternoon I'll go through the CCTV footage we have both for the bar and the gym where Monica was attacked and see if I can spot him in either video. Anna was cooperative and highly focused during the sketch session, but I could tell that she'd lost some of her optimism that her story would be helpful in catching the attacker. I also reviewed

Anna's case reports in detail, again, and I wanted to share an interesting observation from the officers.

"Although Anna had a rape kit performed that night and semen was seen, she never mentioned anything that indicated to the officers that she was aware that she'd been raped. It appears as if she had then, and still has, no understanding that she was sexually assaulted.

"She also seemed to have no idea of why she'd decided to stop drinking alcohol after that night. I imagine that some part of her mind remembered enough of the traumatic event to warn her against drinking, but not enough to remember the specifics of what had actually happened."

"Wow, that's interesting. When I've seen Anna, she hasn't talked about those things. I knew she didn't remember the details of that evening, but I guess I didn't know that she wasn't even aware that she'd been sexually assaulted. That's a lot to take in."

Detective Smith said, "So anyway, I'll go through the footage from the bar and from the gym and look for the alleged stalker. I'll admit to you that I'm not expecting to find anything significant. I think I'll enlist some help for that video review, as it will be time-consuming."

"Sounds good, Audra. Let me know if you find anything."

Detective Smith replied, "Will do, boss," which caused Detective Williams to roll his eyes.

After that, Detective Smith tracked down one of the junior officers and asked if he had some free time that afternoon. When he said he did, she located adjacent computers for the two of them to use. She loaded the video files of the nights of the attacks on Anna and Monica. She gave the officer the rationale for reviewing the tapes.

She placed him in charge of reviewing the footage from outside of Monica's gym, and Detective Smith took the footage from the front of the bar where Anna had been. Detective Smith made a copy of the sketch they had obtained that morning from Anna's work with the sketch artist and gave the copy to the officer. Since Monica's attack had occurred just before 11 p.m., she suggested that the officer start checking the gym tape recording starting from 9:30 and continuing through midnight.

At the other computer, Detective Smith put the sketch down to her right and called up the video from the bar. The call to the police that night had occurred several minutes after midnight, and Anna had initially arrived at the bar between 7:30 and 8 p.m. Detective Smith reviewed the tape beginning from 7 p.m.

Soon after that point, Detective Smith realized the difficulty of her task. She was looking for a man who was about five foot ten and about age thirty, with medium-length brown hair and a thin mustache. Men leaving the bar were mostly seen from the back, so she stopped paying much attention to those leaving. She quickly noted that many of the men entering the bar fit the general description in terms of height and age.

So far, none she had seen sported a mustache that resembled the one in the sketch. Though she was paying less attention to those people who were leaving, she noticed Anna's roommate exiting the bar at ten o'clock. The detective jotted a note to herself to ask Anna about Sonia that night. Detective Smith had progressed through the tape to about the 11 p.m. time when the junior officer joined her.

"I finished going through the tape within the time frame that you gave me. I didn't see anyone who seemed to fit the sketch. There were a few men who I only saw from the back and who had the same approximate height and hair color, so I couldn't exclude them. None were acting suspiciously. Is there anything else you want me to examine from that tape?"

"No, that was it. Thanks for your help."

"Sure. I actually have nothing else to do now, Detective. How about if I sit with you and give you a second set of eyes on this tape?"

Detective Smith was aware that too many of the officers in the station had a second set of eyes on something other than their work whenever she was around, and she wondered if that was his motivation. This was an issue she'd been dealing with since she'd joined the Department, though it was better since she made detective. It wasn't universal among her male colleagues, though, and she decided that she'd appreciate some help.

"Sure, that would be great. Pull up your chair."

They continued going through the tape from the bar. It was fairly routine until just after midnight when they could see reflections from the flashing lights of the patrol car that had responded to Anna's attack. There was a minor commotion outside the bar after that, but it settled down after several minutes.

When it was getting close to 1 a.m. on the tape, they still had located no one who fit the description and who had a thin mustache. Detective Smith was preparing to end their review when they reached the hour. Suddenly, the officer told her to stop the tape.

"Did you see something?" the detective asked.

"I think so. Can you rewind it just a little?" he eagerly asked. The detective complied.

"That man leaving the bar. The one with the KU jersey. I think I saw him on the tape from the front of the gym. I remember because not a lot of people have the guts to advertise their

Jayhawks loyalty in this town. If he's the same man that I saw, he was in the vicinity of both attacks."

"Do you remember when in the tape you saw him?"

The junior officer was moving quickly and replied in an excited voice, "I think it was near the time of the attack. Let me call it up for you and check."

Detective Smith watched as the other officer took some time to scroll through the tape on his computer. "Here it is, Detective. See him walking, by himself, past the front of the gym. This is at 10:45 p.m."

Detective Smith looked very closely at the image on this tape. Then she went back to her tape of the bar and stared at it. This clearly was the same man, wearing the same jersey, and he was a white male who appeared to be about five foot ten. He was at the scene of both attacks, and he was there at or near the time of each attack. That seemed to be too much of a coincidence, and it constituted opportunity.

"This is wonderful work, Officer. I'll have to run this by Detective Williams tomorrow, but this could be the evidence we were hoping for. We can see that he left the bar alone, but I'm also going to review the bar tape tomorrow to see when he entered the bar, and with whom."

The other officer beamed at the praise. "Thank you, Detective Smith. And thanks for letting me work with you."

Detective Smith realized the junior officer would be the envy of his buddies, now that he had received praise from the detective they often drooled over like a pack of lovesick puppies. She passed over that unsavory thought, then jotted down a few more notes next to the one she had made about Anna's roommate.

Detective Smith was smiling and whistling to herself like a Vegas buffet customer who had grabbed the last of the crab legs when she finally left the station to go home. She had been expecting nothing to come of the CCTV footage review today, but their surprise finding seemed like the lucky break they had been hoping for. There would be some real surprises for Detective Williams when he reached the station the next day. He would learn that they needed to go Jayhawk hunting.

CHAPTER 11

THURSDAY, WEEK 3

I t was time for Anna's therapy. On Tuesday, she had looked forward to the session with Dr. Ellis, but not today. She didn't have any exciting news of a possible suspect today, news that the police downplayed anyway. Without such news, Anna resigned herself to the unpleasant task of focusing the session on seeking further memories of the attack. Memories that could reveal what other horrible things her attacker might have done to her, and what led to him throwing her so violently into the trash cans. She shuddered with these thoughts.

When she arrived for her appointment, the smiling faces of the office staff, who knew her so well by now, were unable to brighten her spirits. All of her optimism from Tuesday afternoon's visit had vanished like Miami Beach sunbathers before a rapidly approaching storm. When she was finally called back, the path to Dr. Ellis's office felt like a long walk down the jail corridor to her cell. The supposedly calming wall art transmogrified into bars on the cells she was passing. The aide ushered her into Dr. Ellis's room.

"Good afternoon, Anna. How are you feeling today?"

Anna took her usual seat. She made eye contact, but her hands were in her lap and her expression revealed uncertainty. "Not so good today, Dr. Ellis."

"Can you explain that for me?"

"Well, I was really demoralized when I saw the detectives after our last session. They decided that the stalker that I remembered wasn't a good suspect for the attack. They agreed to take a sketch of his appearance from me and review the video from the bar on the night of my attack to see if he appeared in it, but they weren't optimistic. I haven't heard anything from them yet.

"Also, my fear about the attacker still being out there has gotten worse. I think part of this is from having a specific suspect for the first time. Another reason is that Tuesday afternoon, I thought I was being followed in our parking lot from my car to my apartment. It was a scary feeling, even though I didn't actually see anyone. I guess I'm a little spooked now.

"And I know we'll have to try uncovering more memories today. After what I remembered during the last hypnosis session, I'm terrified of what we'll find today."

Dr. Ellis displayed his most empathic expression. "I'm sorry that the police minimized the possibility of your stalker also being your attacker. I know that you were looking forward to finally having a viable suspect. Tell me more about the feeling that you were being followed."

Anna looked intently at the doctor with a haunted expression. "It was really scary at the time, but since I didn't see anyone, it's hard for me to say how real it was."

"Then hopefully it won't happen again. Is there anything else you wish to bring up before we try exploring more memories today?"

"No, that's all."

"Okay. Well, as you know, we had planned for you to try recalling the middle portion of your memory of the attack. I think hypnosis is our only option for this. Do you think you're ready to try it now?"

"I guess so."

"Let's begin then. I'm sure that you're familiar with the process by now." Dr. Ellis left his chair to dim the lights, then returned. "Please try to relax. Sit back in the chair and close your eyes. Let your arms relax on the chair arms, and let your whole body try to sink back into the depths of the chair." Dr. Ellis waited a minute and observed Anna's reactions to see how well she was relaxing. Then he proceeded with his usual hypnosis method.

At the conclusion of his relaxing words leading her down a nearly endless sloping hallway, he said, "Clear everything out of your mind. Once everything is out of your mind, recall the alley memory. The man's hand has just left your dress. What do you see?"

Anna's eyes remained closed. Her body was limp at first, then she sat up quickly as something came to her. "I can see the alley, but everything else is behind me. His hand is out of my dress now, and I wonder what he's doing. He's still holding me around the waist with his left arm. After a few seconds, I can feel his right hand reach under the bottom of my dress. Oh God, he grabs my underwear and yanks them down." Anna's body became rigid and she leaned forward.

"Then he lifts my dress up above my waist and starts moaning, and for some reason I freeze, and I feel completely unable to move. He continues moaning and he bends me forward over the nearest garbage can."

Anna's hands were clutching the top of her head at that point, and she was practically shrieking as she continued. "Now I realize what the hell's happening. Oh my God, oh my God! He's inside me! That disgusting pervert stuck his prick inside me. He's still moaning and he finished in seconds. Oh my God, he raped me!"

Anna opened her eyes. She was red-faced, and a wall of tears cascaded down her cheeks. She looked toward the doctor. "I feel so disgusted and dirty. He raped me. That bastard actually raped me. When we started this therapy, I knew there were lots of potentially awful things that I might find out had happened to me that night, but I never imagined this. What the hell am I going to do?"

Although Dr. Ellis expected Anna was likely to eventually uncover a memory like this, he still felt bad for her. His prior epiphany that her memory block had probably erased knowledge that she'd been sexually assaulted was proven correct. She was fully experiencing this assault for the first time in her consciousness. This had to be extremely traumatic for her. He needed to be as gentle as possible.

"It's horrible that this happened to you, and I certainly can't comprehend what you're experiencing. I assure you we'll work together to help you get through this. Are you able to say any more about the emotions that are running through you now?"

"I remember telling you that I hated the new image of that night that I had in my mind after our early sessions. Well, that image was just a glimpse of unhappiness compared with the picture of total terror that I have now. This new image is life-altering. I've seen stories about women who'd been sexually assaulted, and I always felt so blessed that nothing like that had ever happened to me."

Anna's thoughts briefly diverted to an incident from her youth at that point, but she decided to suppress those thoughts and continue on her current path. She looked like she had a horrible taste in her mouth that she wanted to spit out.

"I just don't know how I'll ever be able to feel good about myself, knowing that horrible experience is part of my life and my past now."

Dr. Ellis became emotional. "It shouldn't be a question of feeling good about yourself, Anna. What happened wasn't your fault. You're still just as good a person as you would be if you hadn't had this terrible experience. You may find that you need to actively work on maintaining your self-worth. Obviously, that doesn't mean you should feel happy or even okay that this is a part of your past. Also, it doesn't mean that it will be easy to get over this new realization."

Anna was painfully aware of that point due to that awful experience from her teen years.

The doctor rose to turn the lights up as he continued, "Women deal with sexual assault in a variety of ways with a variety of successes. You might want to consider seeing a female therapist who specializes in this issue, once we're done with the memory therapy."

Anna stared at him with an expression of horror. "Done with it, Doctor? My God, aren't we done with it now?"

"I'm afraid not, Anna. I expect there's still more of that memory. I imagine you stopped today due to the shock of what you uncovered, but there's still the part that links what you just remembered to the moment that you were thrown into the trash cans. And it's possible that the remaining memory could carry some clues to the identity of your attacker."

Anna was beside herself now. More therapy? Wasn't this enough? Wasn't this sufficient pain? Was there a chance of even worse memories? "I really feel that I need some time to digest all of this."

The doctor was back in his chair now. "I understand completely. You can get back to me on that. I think that we need to attempt some closure today concerning your new memories. I know that you've had no time to think about this yet, but what are your first impressions?"

Anna frowned, and her eyes had a dull sheen. "Well, I understand now the reasons why I don't drink alcohol or go to bars anymore. And I think I know why I haven't dated since the attack either. I'll need to do a lot of reflecting about that part of my life. We also really need to find out what awful person did this to me."

She began to tear up. "It seems like it's too hard for me to talk any more about this now. I'm too upset."

Dr. Ellis leaned forward and spoke softly. "I imagine you'll be analyzing this over and over again. I'm not going to suggest any tasks for you, as you should discover what thoughts and emotions present themselves to you without any specific direction. You're going to need support too. Who do you think are the people you would at least consider sharing these memories with?"

That question struck a real nerve with Anna. The most prominent event in her past, the incident in high school she had thought about earlier, was something that she had never shared with anyone. Was the knowledge that she'd been sexually assaulted something that would be easier, or even harder, to share with people she knows and loves? She was taking quite a while to answer as these thoughts were racing wildly through her brain.

"I sense that you're having troubling thoughts on this question. Sometimes the difficult emotions that your mind keeps returning to are the most helpful things to share during therapy. Do you think you're ready to share any of them now?"

"Actually, I was thinking about an issue that happened during high school. It was something that I decided at the time not to share with anyone. Thinking about that decision made me wonder whether I should share any of my current experience."

Dr. Ellis perked up with apparent interest. "Do you feel comfortable sharing anything concerning that high school issue now?"

Anna was immensely unsure about opening up. Most of the details no one knew. She had never before had any related experience that would make her consider telling anyone about it. But this trauma was related and was completely dominating the forefront of her brain. If ever there was a time to share this story, it was now. The idea of telling it was rapidly gaining a momentum that she eventually found impossible to stop.

She blurted out, "I was thinking about an incident from my senior year in high school. I've never told anyone this story before. It's about my best friend, Madison." Anna paused as if having second thoughts.

"Can you tell me about it?"

Anna was still conflicted, but she spoke rapidly as if that was her only chance to actually get the story out. Her eyes were focused more on Dr. Ellis's chest than on his face. "This happened a month into our senior year. Madison had a very busy weekend planned and told me she might not have time to get together or even talk the whole weekend. I tried to reach her Sunday night, but she didn't answer my calls.

"When I saw her Monday morning in class, her look was somewhere between sad and zombie-like. When I was able to get her alone and talk to her, she wouldn't tell me what was wrong. She also had multiple excuses as to why we couldn't get together after school. It went on like that for most of the week. She finally agreed to come to my house one day when she learned that no one else would be home. I begged her to tell me what the problem was, and she finally broke down crying and told me.

"She said she'd been raped over the weekend. She said it made her feel dirty and worthless and embarrassed and ashamed, and it was by far the most horrible thing that had ever happened to her."

Anna's speech slowed a little and she looked pensive. "It struck me how significant it was for Madison to say that. Her older brother had gone through childhood lymphoma and was thought to be dying at one point, but fortunately he rallied and got better. Her parents went through a nasty divorce due to her father's affair with a Reiki instructor from the chiropractor's office—a woman who'd previously worked as an escort.

"The father ran off with her and rarely saw Madison and her brother after that. With his reduced financial contribution, and the bills from the lymphoma therapy, Madison's family was very strapped for money. When Madison said the rape was much worse than any of those experiences, it hit me how unbelievably bad it must be for something like that to happen to someone."

Dr. Ellis had stopped taking notes, and he was stone-faced. "That seems like it was a very powerful experience. It can certainly explain why your brain blocked your own memories."

Anna was leaning forward and appeared on high alert. She stared directly at the doctor and continued, speaking rapidly again. "Oh, you haven't heard the worst of it yet. I asked Madison if she'd reported the assault or told her mother, and she said she hadn't. She had no answer when I asked her why she hadn't done so.

"I also knew that she wasn't on birth control as her mother thought that would encourage sexual behavior, so I brought up that issue. She said she hadn't been on her period that past week-end, so pregnancy was a possibility. She wouldn't tell me who'd raped her either. I begged her to report it, but she said she couldn't.

"She kept making excuses about why she couldn't get together after school. When I saw her at school the next week, she was really depressed. I suggested she see her minister or a school counselor or a doctor, and she had reasons why she wouldn't consider seeing anyone. I talked with her every day at school about doing something or telling somebody besides me, but she always refused.

"The following week, she looked even more depressed. She was thinner and looked like she hadn't been eating. She missed school one day, which was something she never did. Finally, on Friday, she missed school again. In the early afternoon, we had an emergency school assembly, and we were told that Madison had committed suicide the night before."

Anna sat back and was on the verge of crying again. She paused briefly, looked down, then spoke through a trickle of tears.

"I was devastated. My best friend was dead because someone had raped her. And if that wasn't enough, I felt partly to blame for her death. As far as I knew, I was the only one, besides her rapist, who knew what had happened. I was the only one who was aware of how severe her despair was. Although I'd tried to convince her to seek help, I felt that I hadn't tried hard enough."

Anna briefly broke down, then gathered herself. Her brow creased and her facial muscles contracted as if she were in pain. She stared ahead but still not directly at the doctor, and her speech slowed.

"I realized, unfortunately too late, that I was the only one who could have helped her, and I didn't help my best friend as much as she needed. Even after she'd taken her life, I could have told someone about the rape and maybe obtained some justice for her. But I chose not to tell anyone, mostly because I was incredibly ashamed that I hadn't gotten her the help that she needed. That was the darkest moment of my life."

Dr. Ellis's emotions were raw following that story. His admiration for Anna and what she had endured grew exponentially after hearing it. He strongly felt a need to be able to help this young woman. He knew she would need a great deal of support now.

"That was a completely overwhelming story, Anna. How do you feel about having shared it with me today?"

Anna had fallen back in the chair. A small ring of sweat was visible at the top of her shirt. She replied with a determined expression but a voice that was like a sigh.

"I realized as I was telling it that, as you said, this disaster was the reason why my brain preferred amnesia to remembering the rape. I'd developed such a powerful personal fear of rape from Madison's tragedy that I guess my mind wouldn't let me realize that the same thing had happened to me. If I hadn't told this story to you today, I might never have completely figured out that relationship."

"That's good insight. You're going to need some time to process all of this, Anna. While you sit and begin to recover, let me suggest some next steps."

He spoke with a commanding voice. "I'll pass on to you the names of a couple of sexual assault therapy specialists. I think you should strongly consider seeing one of them. You're going to need as much support as possible processing these new memories, so consider sharing this with someone you trust. It's too much to keep inside you.

"I think you should have at least one more session with me, but not specifically to go after any more memories. You might find that the rest of the memories will tumble out now that you seem to have broken the seal on your amnesia. If they don't, you could try to focus on that remaining part of your memory with a mindfulness exercise. If you still don't recall any more memories of your attack by the next session, we can discuss one more appointment for hypnosis for that purpose.

"You should also spend some time working on feeling good about yourself. I'm sure that a sexual assault counselor would say the same thing, but you've revealed, and discovered, today two dramatic events that you indicated have made you feel negatively about yourself. It's important that you realize you have no reason to harbor such bad feelings about these situations. I strongly encourage you to think of some ways to help you counteract any such feelings."

Anna was uncertain how to proceed. She felt surprisingly relieved that she had shared her story about Madison with someone, but she was totally devastated to realize that she'd been sexually assaulted. She also thought briefly about the parts of the story that she had purposefully left out, which seemed to be a wise decision.

She was unsure whether or not she wanted to tell anyone else about this new memory, or whom she would tell. Would she feel better and more supported if she shared it, or feel even worse about herself if multiple people became aware of what had happened to her? There were so many unknowns.

"We can go ahead with another session, Doctor. Please send me the names of the other therapists, but I need to check my insurance and learn whether or not I can see two therapists at the same time."

"Okay. Is there anything else you want to talk about now?"

"No. I still have to decide how much of today's session I want to share with the police. I'll wait and see them tomorrow so that I have the night to think about it. I can't express how much of a disaster this entire situation really is."

Dr. Ellis leaned forward with a concerned expression. "As I've said before, I'm so sorry that these tragic events have happened to you and been a part of your life. In addition to what I've already mentioned, please let me know if there's anything else I can do for you. I'm always here for you."

Anna thanked Dr. Ellis and rose haltingly from her chair. She left slowly, with her head down and without any apparent trace of hopefulness this time. Dr. Ellis did, indeed, feel sorry for her, but he was pleased with the breakthrough they had made today. She would experience some very negative emotions concerning her sexual assault, but it was important for her to become aware of what had happened to her.

She should see an assault counselor, but he'd be upset if her insurance said she could only see one therapist at a time. He hadn't totally finished helping her. She still possessed many unresolved fears. More importantly, despite all they'd uncovered, they still hadn't found anything to indicate who her attacker was, which was the primary reason for the therapy. Hopefully, clues to his identity would be revealed with further therapy.

His personal needs then kicked in. He realized that he also hadn't yet achieved the full success and recognition that he'd been expecting from this case. The recognition that he deeply craved.

CHAPTER 12

FRIDAY, WEEK 3

Anna had arranged an early morning meeting with Detective Smith. She was exceedingly thankful that she could have this difficult meeting without Detective Williams being present. Anna had been soul-searching all night and had reached a decision to reveal to the detective everything from her session the day before. She knew it was important for the case, and she knew Detective Smith was on her side. These thoughts still didn't eliminate the dread she now felt.

As Anna approached the front desk, the desk officer, who knew her well, called back for Detective Smith. The detective was cheerful as usual when she entered the lobby and gestured for Anna to accompany her back to the office. Anna wished she could feel even partly as upbeat.

"How has your day been, Anna?" Detective Smith asked as they walked back.

"Today's been okay so far, but yesterday was a disaster."

"I'm very sorry to hear that. You can tell me about it once we reach the office."

Anna had to hand it to the detective. She was always personable, always pleasant, and to her, always approachable. When they reached the office, the detective offered Anna the chair by the desk.

"What would you like to share with me today?"

Anna was calm as she began. "I apologize if I seem reluctant. Yesterday, I remembered what happened after the man took his hand out of the top of my dress, and it was horrible. He began moaning and he yanked my underpants down. Then he lifted my dress, bent me over the nearest garbage can, and then he…he stu… He stuck his prick in me and raped me. He finished in seconds."

Anna trembled with that statement, dropped eye contact, and began having body-racking sobs. Detective Smith located some tissues for her. She waited a bit before responding to Anna's new memory. "I'm really sorry to drag out this painful memory for you, Anna. Was there any more to it that you need to tell me?"

Anna's eyes were still somewhat downcast, but they also flashed with disgust as she replied that there was nothing more.

Detective Smith leaned in toward Anna. "I'm so sorry to have to ask these questions after hearing that awful memory. These aren't meant in any way to demean you. If you're able to continue now, can you tell me if you recognized the voice by the moaning, or would you recognize it if you heard it again?"

Anna recovered enough to answer but was still despondent. "I didn't recognize it by the moaning as anyone I knew. I was so traumatized by that memory yesterday that I didn't initially pick up on this next part. But last night I realized that I got a definite sense that I'd recognize something about the voice if I heard it again. I don't know if he said something I would recognize or if I would recognize who he is by his actual voice, but I know I'd recognize something."

"I'm also very sorry about this next question, but did you cry out, scream, fight, or tell him to stop?"

"When he jerked my underwear down, I completely and immediately froze. It felt like I was truly paralyzed, either with shock or fear or maybe both. Then it all happened and was over so fast, I don't think I had time to fight. The only thing I can say is that I'm sure there's more to the memory that I haven't recalled yet."

"Do you remember wanting him to stop or not go through with his actions?"

"Oh, I desperately wanted him to stop. I didn't want it to happen. I realize now, after regaining that memory, that I was raped, which is something that I always assumed I could never, ever tolerate." Anna shook with anger, but her face was blank with a sense of hopelessness.

The detective replied very gently. "I have to tell you, Anna, that since we had the police report from your attack, we knew that semen was discovered on your exam in the ER. Detective Williams and I also noticed that you had never told us that you were a victim of sexual assault. We wondered if that was part of your memory block, and that you truly were not aware that it had happened to you."

"The rape wasn't part of my memory prior to yesterday's therapy session. I don't even have any memories from the ER visit. I was only aware that I'd been physically attacked and suffered the concussion and bruising. I should tell you that during my session yesterday, the doctor and I talked about an incident that probably caused me to suffer the memory block. I'll spare you most of the details.

"My best friend in high school was raped during our senior year. She was so embarrassed and disgusted by it that she committed suicide a couple of weeks later. I felt terrible for her and her family, and I was so devastated by it all that I told myself I could never allow anything like her rape to happen to me. I guess that when it did, my subconscious shut down my memory of it." Anna pointedly left out the damning information that she was the only person who was aware of the rape.

By then, the atmosphere in the room had become suffocating, and every element of joy had abandoned the office. The distressful information from Anna caused Detective Smith, who was always in charge of her emotions, to feel Anna's loss personally. She placed her hand gently on Anna's arm.

"I'm so sorry to hear about the loss of your friend. In light of this information that you shared, I certainly understand the development of your memory block. And it's imperative that we capture your assailant."

"Thank you, Detective. This is a horrible situation."

The detective leaned back. "Since you apparently remembered almost nothing you were told in the ER that night, I want to share some information related to your attack. The semen recovered from your exam after the attack was sent for analysis, but the DNA didn't match any in the system. Your exam showed no trauma to your vulva or vagina. Also, it's standard practice to treat for some STDs and test for others in your situation. You would've been contacted if any results were positive.

"Again, I can't tell you how truly sorry I am that this happened to you. Please feel free to talk to me at any time about any aspects of this. I'll fill Detective Williams in about our talk when I see him later. Do you have any more therapy sessions scheduled?"

Anna had recovered from her emotional state related to describing her memory. She was in control as she replied, "I have one for next Tuesday, but I don't expect much will come from that one. I'm hoping that the session after that will help me locate that part of my attacker's voice that I believe I might be able to identify, if I don't get any visual clues."

"We'll look forward to seeing if you can at least get that voice memory, as that would really be helpful. I hope that today gets a lot better for you. We're working hard on this, Anna."

"Thank you, Detective. Before I go, I want to ask about the video review to look for my stalker."

The detective tried to look hopeful for Anna. "I've gone through the video thoroughly. There are some interesting and hopeful findings that we need to follow up on. That's all I can tell you at this time, but I think I'll have more answers for you the next time we talk."

The detective walked Anna out to the lobby. She threw her a very emotional departing glance, which caused Anna to sense that for some reason the detective truly did understand her situation, in many unsaid ways. That made it even more imperative to Anna that the police here not learn about her actions with the authorities in Chicago. That had to remain her permanent secret.

That was when Gerry's day got much better. He was lurking across the street from the police station, where he had been surprised to see Anna as she left the building one day earlier in the week. Anna exited the station and stopped to raise her hand up to block the sun. The glare made it hard for her to see much detail, and she was unable to see anything in Gerry's direction. Anna grabbed some sunglasses from her bag and headed off toward the parking lot.

She was still just as beautiful and desirable as Gerry remembered. He watched her climb into her blue Kia. He saw her pull out into the traffic and drive away, noting her license plate number in the process. He was unable to follow her today, since he was on foot and she wasn't, but now he knew that this was a good place to secretly and longingly observe her. He would also watch for blue Kias when he was walking the sidewalks, since he was now able to identify her car.

It would soon be time for him to get to his job. He'd still enjoy watching the coeds shop, especially given the scandalous shortage of material that their summer outfits contained. However, today he'd seen his dream woman again. The sighting brought back some especially thrilling memories from his past. Oh, the dreams he'd have tonight!

Dr. Wilson prepared for his late afternoon appointment with Dr. Ellis. It had been added on after a cancellation. One of the potential topics for the session was Dr. Ellis's insubstantial relationship history. Although this was a common topic for patients of Dr. Wilson, it still posed a strain on him, due to the fact that his partner had recently left him.

He and Julius had been together for three years, but Julius decided that he needed to live in a state with complete acceptance of same-sex relationships and marriage, so he moved to Maryland. Dr. Wilson didn't want to leave his thriving, established practice and his patients, so he remained here. Since then, the irony of talking with patients about reasons why they couldn't sustain long-term relationships was quite glaring for Dr. Wilson.

Dr. Ellis arrived for his appointment, still in his work clothes—a tan blazer, brown-and-white striped shirt, and khakis. After he signed in, the office door opened almost immediately, and Dr. Wilson signaled for him to enter the inner sanctum.

"Good afternoon, Ted. I'm pleased that this time worked out for you."

Dr. Ellis was never quite sure how to address another doctor who hadn't specified a moniker, so he merely smiled and said,

"Good afternoon. I'm happy to be able to see you today."

"I'm glad that you seem to be in a better frame of mind for this session. Have a seat. Do you want to start with the topics we identified during the last session, or shall we begin elsewhere?"

"We can review some of the prior issues first. I'm not ready to talk about increasing interactions with my family yet, though."

Competence and command were now exuding from the consummately professional Dr. Wilson as he began the discussion. "How is the problem of not being able to concentrate on your successes?"

Dr. Ellis relaxed in his seat with his arms resting on the chair arms. "I haven't found myself in those situations this week. But after our discussion of last time, I've felt better about myself and my success. I think that unburdening myself about my background has helped me feel that I can minimize the obsessions. I've also had great patient successes this week, which has furthered my self-esteem and put me in a veritable palace of positivity at this point."

Dr. Wilson smiled. "Kudos to you. I suggest we continue on to address the major remaining issue from our last session, which was to review your relationship history. Are you prepared for that discussion today?"

"Sure, we can do that. You've already heard the basic overview. As far as details go, in high school I did no significant dating. I think it was due to the lack of self-esteem from my family issue. That led to a slow start in college for me in terms of relationships. I'm also a little shy, and with that trait plus my slow start, I didn't experience much real intimacy until my adult years.

"I've had several relationships over the past fifteen years. Some have been romantic, and some purely sexual. In terms of the latter, I would estimate that I've had around ten sexual partners.

I'm very motivated sexually, and I believe the nexus of that motivation with my underlying shyness has resulted in a high number of relatively short relationships. None have lasted more than a few months. A couple of my sexual experiences were with women I met at bars and took home, usually with no follow-up contact."

Dr. Ellis knew there was much more to that topic than he was willing to share with Dr. Wilson for now. He still felt some misgivings related to his last one-night stand a year ago, but he wasn't yet ready to tell anyone about that evening.

"The obvious follow-up query has to be, why do you think none of those relationships have lasted or have progressed any further?"

Dr. Ellis had to ponder that for a moment. "I would have to say that most of the time they ended for one particular reason: because the relationship wasn't progressing. The decisions to end them seemed to always be mutually acceptable."

"So something must be keeping your relationships from becoming serious. What do you think it is?"

Dr. Ellis had to admit to himself that he was concerned about the lack of serious commitment in his love life, but he hadn't spent much time contemplating the reasons. "I don't have an obvious answer."

"Do you and the women you date share the deeper parts of yourselves at some point, Ted?"

Dr. Ellis smiled. "Well, *they* certainly do, but that's something that I tend to avoid. I talk in vague terms about my successes, but I avoid profound discussions of any topic."

Dr. Wilson shifted in his seat and looked as if he disapproved of that response. "You're a psychiatrist. I'm sure you're aware that a prime basis for a strong relationship is sharing all, or at least large portions, of your background and who you are. Why don't you do that?"

"Given what I had to endure in my youth from my family and others who were close to me, I don't trust people to act reasonably or kindly with any knowledge they might learn about me. So, I avoid sharing, as that seems the safer way to go."

"That plan is almost certain to guarantee that you'll have great difficulty developing any strong, serious relationships. Are you interested in such a relationship?"

Dr. Ellis developed an uncertain look. "Well, yes, I definitely want to find someone to partner with and accompany through life."

Dr. Wilson softened a little. "What kind of person are you seeking for that endeavor?"

"I haven't really identified a list of characteristics that I'd like my ideal woman to possess."

"Let's take this approach, then. Do you have a celebrity crush?"

If he were anyone else, Dr. Ellis might have been embarrassed about his answer. But he had spent a great deal of time in therapy with a wide range of men, and he knew what they were like and what their guilty pleasures were. He sat forward and smiled.

"For years, my celebrity crush has been adult film star Aidra Fox. Now I know what that might make you think, but I assure you that I don't have an addiction to adult movies."

If Dr. Wilson was nonplussed about any portion of this response, he didn't show it at all. "What is it about her that attracts you?"

"I love her face, her body, her great smile, her long curly hair, and the fact that she's always positive and uncritical toward the people she's with."

Dr. Wilson said, "Granted, adult movies are not usually known for their tremendous depth in character development, as far as I'm aware, but you primarily mentioned physical features. Is that mostly what you look for in a woman?"

Dr. Ellis threw his palms out toward the doctor. "No, not at all. I want someone who appreciates me for who I am and for my successes. I want someone who'll support me. I want someone who respects me."

"How will a woman become able to appreciate you for who you are if you're unwilling to let her in to learn who you are? How would"—Dr. Wilson paused to glance at his notes—"Aidra Fox appreciate you for who you are?"

Dr. Ellis blushed at the sudden realization that he'd been wildly unrealistic to think that any woman would fall for him solely due to his successes and his profession. That someone would be really attracted to him without knowing more of his personality, background, and even flaws.

He surprised himself by replying in a meek voice, "I can see your point. This seems to also go along with what you were saying last time about my self-esteem. Maybe I'm too focused on my job and successes in the job. Maybe I'm afraid to let women know who I am because I'm afraid of rejection. Focusing on my job seems to be a safe way to avoid being rejected."

"That's good insight, Ted. You might spend more time reflecting on that topic. Would you like to discuss anything further today?"

"I don't think so. Thanks for adding on this session at a time after I was finished with patients."

"I was happy to do so. I look forward to seeing you at our next session at the usual time. Maybe we can discuss your original worry about unease at that time."

They both stood, and after they shook hands, Dr. Ellis headed toward the patient exit. He felt a little chastised, and his self-esteem felt mildly damaged. He would need to reflect more on the sources of his self-esteem and whether he should reexamine them. And though his dating style was not harming anyone, with the possible exception of his last one-night stand, it was an area of non-success for him. He knew that he needed to feel success in everything he did.

He could certainly work on some changes in his love life. He could think about revealing more of himself to the women he dated, though not the doghouse story, which was too embarrassing. He could spend time contemplating what kind of person he truly was and whether that was something he was willing to share.

He was definitely seeing some benefits to these sessions, to his surprise. Hopefully the next session might help him discover the source of his unease. He thought about it often but was still at a loss to explain it. It was a mystery that needed to be solved.

CHAPTER 13

MONDAY, WEEK 4

The day started off with high hopes for the detectives. They had their first big break in the case. They were going to interview Mr. Joe Friedman. After some extensive police work over the weekend, Detective Smith had identified Mr. Friedman as the person spotted on video at the scenes of both Anna's and Monica's attacks. She reviewed how the investigation had progressed.

After informing her partner of the exciting find on the video reviews, Detective Smith had spent time on Friday combing through the bar video from the night of Anna's attack. She found the image of the man now known to be Mr. Friedman entering the bar wearing his KU jersey. He arrived with a second man, a taller blond-haired man wearing a Missouri football jersey. They both appeared to be about thirty years of age. The taller man left the bar alone just before 11 p.m. Detective Smith had printed the best image she could generate of the two men and took it to the bar early Saturday evening.

The bar was sparsely populated at that time, and the lighting was dim and the music loud. There were several rows of booths and tables in the front of the establishment, and a long bar with a full-length mirror behind it on the back wall. Restrooms were to one side, and a hallway led to the rear of the building on the other side. After asking a server, the detective discovered that one of the bartenders working that evening had been employed at the bar for four years.

She had approached the tall young man with a dark beard who was cleaning glasses behind the bar to inquire whether he recognized either of the men in her printed image. The bartender eyed her up and down as if she were his lifelong fantasy finally come to life. "Please tell me how I can make your evening better," he inquired in his smoothest voice.

Detective Smith never entirely got used to this type of annoying behavior, but she knew how to deal with it. She subtly slid open her jacket to reveal her badge, and again she offered the bartender the image she had of the two men in question. "You could make my evening wonderful if you can identify either of the men in this picture," she replied with a confident smile.

The bartender did a double-take, but he regained his composure enough to continue his attempt at a superior air. He reluctantly took his eyes off the detective to examine the image. After a few seconds, he provided an answer.

"The man in the Mizzou shirt is Mack Gibbs. He's here a lot. The one in the KU jersey I recognize, but I don't know his name. Now I don't suppose you'd like a drink to go along with that information?" he asked, while leaning forward on the bar and regaining his slick demeanor.

"Not while I'm on duty, thanks. For now, I just need to chat with both of these men and ask a few questions."

The bartender replied with a smirk, "Okay, but maybe you should consider returning sometime when you're off duty."

Detective Smith replied that she definitely wouldn't be seeing him at any time when she was off duty, then left.

On Sunday, she'd tracked down Mack Gibbs at his apartment. She flashed her badge and told him that he wasn't in any trouble but that she had a few questions for him. She showed him the image from the bar and asked about the other man in the picture. He told her the other man was Joe Friedman. She asked Mr. Gibbs about Mr. Friedman.

His reply was that he had met Mr. Friedman at a bar and they hit it off. They spent time together occasionally, at bars and sporting events. He stated that Mr. Friedman was an actuary with an insurance firm in town, and he seemed to be a nice guy. He asked what the inquiry was about. The detective replied that she was unable to discuss it with Mr. Gibbs.

That led to today. Detective Smith searched through police records and found that Joe Friedman had no criminal record of any kind. It was time for her and Detective Williams to find Joe Friedman at the workplace she had traced him to and get some answers out of him. She was ready to head for the insurance office as soon as her partner arrived.

Detective Williams strode in a few minutes later, his rugged, fit appearance seeming to contradict his notoriously poor eating habits. He found Detective Smith so that they could begin their day.

"Are you ready to head to the insurance office, Audra?"

"I'm all set. I have no idea what to expect, though."

"I understand. Let's go. I'll drive."

"Okay, Mr. Macho. I guess on the trip there I could utilize the leisure time to do my nails," Detective Smith replied with a plastic Stepford Wives smile.

"Do you give your husband this much grief?"

"I'll never tell."

The detectives went to the insurance office, and after identifying themselves to the receptionist, they asked to speak with Mr. Friedman. They were directed to his office on the second floor. That floor included several open cubicles on one side of the floor and a row of glass-walled offices on the other side. The detectives knocked on Mr. Friedman's office door and were waved in by the lone occupant of the office, a clean-cut, handsome, brown-haired man appearing to be about thirty years old.

He had the coat of his well-pressed suit neatly hanging over the back of the desk chair. He stood and smiled as he walked toward the detectives. "Hi, I'm Joe Friedman. Brenda from the front desk notified me that you were on your way up. What can I do for you?"

Both detectives presented their identification and offered business cards. Detective Williams took the lead. "We just have a few questions for you. Can we sit?"

He replied in the affirmative while gesturing to the room's two chairs.

"What's this concerning?" he asked as he sat behind his desk.

"In a nutshell, we have video footage of you in the vicinity of multiple crime scenes, and we have questions about your activities on the dates of the footage."

Mr. Friedman couldn't have appeared more shocked if they'd told him his pants were on fire. After regaining his composure, he asked, "Are you here to find out if I witnessed anything, or do you think I had something to do with whatever crimes you're referring to?"

"We just want to find out if you remember anything about the dates in question," replied Detective Smith.

Mr. Friedman countered with, "I don't think I should answer anything without my lawyer present."

Detective Smith adopted a stern posture. "We usually only receive that answer from people with something to hide, as we just have a few simple questions. Do you have something to hide, Mr. Friedman?"

Mr. Friedman stood as his hands trembled and his face red-dened. "No, I do not, but I don't like the direction this is taking, so I must insist on not speaking further without my lawyer."

"We need to talk today. Please call your lawyer now."

A shaken Mr. Friedman flipped through the directory on his phone and placed a call. Detective Williams mouthed to his partner, "At least he doesn't have the lawyer's number on his favorites list." Mr. Friedman reached his lawyer, spoke briefly, then hung up. "I can be at the station at 1:30 with my lawyer. I insist that you leave my office now." His attempt at taking command of the situation, although noted by the detectives, failed worse than a science nerd asking the head cheerleader for a date.

The detectives reminded him to bring his calendar, thanked him for his time, and exited his office. It was apparent by their scurrying to appear busy that the entire office staff had been intently wrapped up in the spectacle that had just concluded. The detectives headed back to their car.

On the way to the station, Detective Williams asked his partner her impressions of what had just transpired. "I hesitate to say this, but we might actually have found our man, Derek. We really need to hear his account of those nights. At the least, it moves him to the head of a very short suspects list. Also, I must say that I vastly prefer suspects who say 'Go ahead, I have nothing to hide' to those with the one-word vocabulary, 'lawyer.'"

"You're preaching to the choir," replied her partner, throwing a fist bump for emphasis.

When Mr. Friedman and his lawyer arrived at the station that afternoon, they were taken to a large interview room. The detectives sat on one side of the room's table, and the visitors sat on the other. Detective Williams began by asking everyone to state their names for recording purposes. He began the interview.

"As we briefly mentioned in your office, Mr. Friedman, we'd like to ask you about your actions and what you might have observed, or done, on three particular nights in question. Have you brought a device containing your calendar?"

Mr. Friedman's shoulders were slumped forward, his eye contact minimal, and his voice shaky. Despite the rather cool temperature in the room, the sweat under his arms was prominent. "Yes, I have."

The lawyer added, "Are you charging my client with anything at this time?"

Detective Williams replied, "We aren't charging him. We're just interested in having some questions answered about those nights. It would be a bad look, however, if your client declined to tell us anything about the nights in question."

The lawyer turned to Mr. Friedman. "For now, you can proceed, but look at me for direction prior to answering."

The remainder of the interview proceeded without objections from the lawyer.

The detectives asked about the night of Anna's attack. Mr. Friedman said he didn't remember the evening, but his calendar showed that he went to the bar with Mack. When Detective Smith pointed out that Mack left early that night but Mr. Friedman stayed until 1 a.m., it didn't jog his memory of the night. No one could give him an alibi for the time after Mack left. He remembered no women in the bar who'd interested him. When the detectives asked, Mr. Friedman didn't appear aware of the bar's back exit to the alley.

As for the night of Monica's attack, Mr. Friedman noted that he'd attended a sports-themed game-watching party that his work had arranged at a different bar. That party began at 8 p.m., but he couldn't remember when he left. He said his colleagues, Terry and Leslie, could probably indicate his departure time. He stated he walked home from the bar alone, but he didn't remember passing the gym that night or noticing anything suspicious near it. He didn't remember when he arrived home.

Concerning the night of Hannah's attack, Mr. Friedman said he'd eaten dinner out and then attended a softball game that Mack had played in at the fields near the park. That information caused glances to flash between the detectives. Mr. Friedman noted that the game started at 9:30 and lasted about ninety minutes. He sat by himself, and no one there could support him with an alibi. He drove to and from the game and talked with Mack after the game.

Finally, he was asked about gun ownership, and he said he owned a handgun that he kept locked in a drawer at his apartment.

Detective Smith said in conclusion, "Thank you for your time and cooperation, Mr. Friedman. We'll let you know if we need anything else in the future." Mr. Friedman trudged out slowly and unconfidently, with his lawyer following.

The detectives looked at each other with flat expressions. Detective Williams spoke first. "What do you think?"

"First, I think I'll send one of the officers immediately to Mr. Friedman's office to talk with Terry and Leslie before Mr. Friedman can invite them to suffer any sudden memory lapses." She left the interview room and returned shortly thereafter.

"That's done. To answer your question, it was interesting to learn that he was near the park at the time of Hannah's attack, so we've placed him near all three crimes at the exact times they were committed. He doesn't have an established alibi for any of the three assaults. He fits the physical description of being white and about five foot ten. He also owns a handgun, and I noticed that he has smooth, white-collar hands."

"Is that a new adjective from you?" asked Detective Williams with a grin.

"I'll ignore that, Derek. On the flip side, after hearing him today, I think it's unlikely that he's our serial assailant. On the night of Anna's attack, he wasn't seen leaving the bar until nearly 1 a.m. I doubt we missed him twice, leaving and returning, in our video review. I also doubt that he left by the alley door, which he seemed surprised to learn about, attacked Anna, came back in through that door where many people could have seen him, then hung around until 1 a.m.

"And as for Monica's attack, I doubt he took his gun to his work event. Unless he left the event quite early, he had no opportunity to retrieve his gun prior to the time of the attack. And even though it would be a great alibi, sneaking out of the softball game crowd to go after Hannah—and then returning to the game after the attack— would take some balls. Overall, it seems highly improbable for him to have been able to accomplish everything reported in the attacks."

A dejected-looking Detective Williams replied, "Unfortunately, I think you're right. I'm not a fan of coincidence as an excuse, but we might have to let it slide this time. Finding a guy with the right description who was at each scene seems like way too much to just be a coincidence. But I agree that some of the facts of the attacks don't fit with his movements. He also didn't look guilty. He'll definitely need to stay on the suspect list due to the overwhelming opportunity factor, but we need to keep on searching. We can always come back to him later."

His partner said, "I'm afraid that I agree with you. Unless the officer discovers something suspicious when talking to Mr.

Friedman's work colleagues, we have much more work to do on this case."

In the evening, Anna arrived at her apartment having reached a conclusion. She would share with Sonia her memories from the last therapy session. Anna still had much remaining stress to endure, with the search for her assailant having been unsuccessful so far, and she knew she would need strong emotional support. She was closer to Sonia than anyone. She also expected that Sonia wouldn't judge her, since she never had before.

Sonia had late clients, so she arrived after Anna, who was ready. "Can we talk, Sonia?"

"OMG, are you breaking up with me? Did you find a room-mate who'll pay you more for the rent? Did you find a hotter roommate? Oh wait, that's not possible."

Anna smiled at the realization that even when she had serious problems, Sonia always made her feel better. "No one's breaking up with you. I want to tell you about my last therapy session."

They sat at the dining table and Anna gave Sonia the condensed version of the awful new memory she had recalled.

Sonia looked incredulous. "So the bastard didn't just cop a feel—he raped you?"

"He sure as hell did. When I talked with the nice detective after my session, she told me that I'd been examined for evidence of sexual assault in the ER that night, and they found DNA from his semen."

"Eww, gross. I'm so sorry. I never knew. When I picked you up from the ER that night, no one told me."

Anna had a forlorn expression. "And between the alcohol, the trauma, and my memory block, I didn't remember any of that information, or really anything that happened in the ER that night. And if they gave me any paperwork, I lost it."

"How are you handling this now?"

Anna sat back and sighed. "Not too well. I've been raped and I need to deal with that. Plus, the bastard who did it hasn't been caught and is still out there attacking other women. I'll be talking with the doctor tomorrow about my feelings, but I'm really going to need your support."

Sonia gave Anna a wonderful, deeply enveloping hug. "You know I love you and I'm here any time you want to talk about this. Just like you've helped me in the past, you'll always have my support, honey. I'd do anything for you. I wish I could hunt down your scumbag attacker myself and give you the satisfaction that he's caught."

"The way things are going, you might have to."

Detective Smith had finished dinner and playtime with her son. Her husband was putting their son to bed in the upper level of their split-level home, and the detective was sitting in their small home office, which had built-in bookshelves and a good-sized computer desk. The room was filled with family pictures. She was contemplating Anna's case and background, with its similarities to her own history.

In her sophomore year in high school, Audra had been molested. She was always considered attractive, and she had developed early, which made her an unfortunate target for predators. Her tormentor was a married and widely adored theater adviser.

He was often backstage during dressing changes. One day he cornered her alone, after school, and managed to grope her breasts. He later apologized, and she assumed it would never happen again. But two weeks later, she was again alone with him, and he forced her against the wall and slid his hand into her jeans and over her underwear. She begged him to stop, but he continued long enough to achieve his perverted goal. She ran home in tears to tell her mother.

The two of them complained to school officials the next day, but without physical evidence or a history of complaints from any other students, her molester went unpunished. This was one of the factors that led Audra to enter the police academy, so that she could help bring people the justice that she had never received.

This tragic background helped her to understand and to empathize with Anna. It also made her even more invested than she normally would be in finding the culprit responsible for the series of attacks. In the privacy of the office, she softly voiced her thoughts out loud.

"I've got to work as hard as I can to get complete closure for Anna and the other women—closure that I really never got for myself. I just have to succeed for them."

CHAPTER 14

TUESDAY, WEEK 4

D etective Smith arrived early at the station, as she often did in the summer, expecting a typical day. But she immediately noticed that there was a general buzz that was unusual at that time on a weekday morning. It was more than the usual noise increase during shift change. Shortly after she arrived, one of the overnight junior officers approached the detective at her desk.

"Good morning, Detective. My partner and I worked an assault case last night that you and Detective Williams need to hear about. Do you know when he's coming in? I need to stay until he arrives and brief the two of you."

"You've gotten my interest, Cynthia. Let me call him."

She called her partner, who said he could be at the station in fifteen or twenty minutes. While they were waiting, the junior officer asked Detective Smith if she could get some advice. She said her partner had been a little adversarial when questioning the victim overnight. He'd asked whether she was telling the truth, and whether her attack was from an ex-boyfriend. He'd come across as not being on the woman's side.

"What do you suggest I do if something like this happens again, Detective?"

"Well, particularly if you're working with someone of equal rank, you should feel comfortable speaking up for the rights of our women victims. It's okay to disagree with your partner in a situation like that. You can always come to me to back you up if you feel you need it, but that's not a great long-range plan.

"But your question gives me an idea. We should consider starting a formal support group for the female officers on the staff. That could provide help in lots of areas, such as advice, confidence-building, and training, as well as support. I'm going to try and look into that possibility when I get a chance."

The young officer thanked the detective and was still chatting with her when Detective Williams arrived. The three of them went to a small room, and the officer began reviewing her evening.

"I know you're working on the serial sexual assault cases. We took a report last night that might be related. Let me tell you about it."

She said at 1:30 a.m. they'd received a call from a movie theater employee who said that she'd been attacked. The officer and her partner drove to the employee's apartment to take her statement. The victim's name was Gwen, and she was a twenty-one-year-old college student working a summer job.

Her story was that she'd been walking to her car after the last shows at the theater had ended. Her car was parked in the back of the theater, a requirement for employees. She said there were only a couple of cars in that area, which had only minimal lighting. The area had no cameras that she knew of.

As she neared her car, she could hear footsteps behind her. She was spooked and was afraid to turn and look. She thought the footsteps were closing in on her, so she began running. Just as she reached her car, she felt someone grab her from behind. He shoved her hard up against the car door. She could see that he wore dark, surgical-style gloves, and she had the impression that he wore a stocking cap. He showed her a gun in his right gloved hand and whispered the words "Drop your pants now, bitch."

She stated she was initially too terrified to move or even make a decision about what she should do. She started crying and then, before she could act, she heard another car in the lot start up and she saw that light was coming from headlamps behind her somewhere. That seemed to frighten her attacker, who smashed her into the car door, threw her to the ground, and ran.

The detectives looked at each other with alarm as the officer finished her summary.

The employee noted that by the time she stood up and looked, her attacker had run away. She saw a shadowy figure disappearing behind a dumpster at the far edge of the back corner of the theater. The other car that had started its engine had turned and left the lot. She was terrified of being alone with the attacker, whom she thought was possibly still nearby and could return, so she got in her car and quickly left. After getting home she cleaned up, calmed down, and made the 1:30 call.

Detective Williams asked, "Did you get any more information from her when you questioned her?"

"She didn't know who'd started the other car. When she was smashed into the car and thrown down, she apparently didn't hit her head very hard and was mainly left with multiple body bruises. We encouraged her to go to the ER for exam and treatment, but she declined due to expense.

"We saw no facial or scalp lacerations or bruises. She denied confusion or headaches. We took photos of the multiple bruises on her arms for documentation. We asked about her feeling of safety, and she said a friend of hers was coming over to stay with her. We remained with her until the friend arrived. She said there was no one she knew who might have wanted to harm her. We plan to go to the theater tonight and make inquiries about the other car."

Detective Smith chimed in, "Was she able to give a description of the shadowy figure?"

"She mentioned that she only had that brief glance, but she said he appeared to be of average weight, not too tall, and he wore a head covering and dark clothes, including what looked like a light rain jacket. She said it was too dark to say anything about his race."

Detective Smith said, "Thanks so much for this, Cynthia. We'll interview Gwen ourselves later. Please let us know if you learn anything from the employees you talk with tonight."

After the officer left, the detectives looked intently at each other. "This sounds exactly like a Monica situation, Derek. It worries me that our serial attacker isn't waiting for another year to go by. Unless one of the other movie theater employees noticed something helpful, or we get more out of Gwen, there may be no useful follow-up to this report, unfortunately. We certainly need to be on alert for another attack at any time now. Maybe you should talk with the chief about reconsidering a warning to the public."

"That's a good point. I'll talk with him about it tomorrow after we get the report from the employee interviews tonight."

"Thanks, I have a really bad feeling about this."

The detectives had arranged to interview Gwen in the early afternoon. They arrived at her apartment, which was in a small two-story building. The apartment had a small living and dining area separated from a smaller kitchen by an island. The walls were painted white, and the simple furniture consisted of a small dining table with chairs, a sofa and two sitting chairs, and a TV on a dresser.

Gwen had a calm expression, but her body and voice were shaking. She was mildly overweight, blonde, and of average height. She was barefoot and was wearing black Mizzou sweatpants and a pink Sabrina Carpenter T-shirt. There were visible bruises on her arms. After making certain that she felt safe, the detectives interviewed her.

She reiterated that she knew no one who would have wanted to hurt her. She had no worrisome ex-boyfriends and no enemies. When asked about the whispered command to drop her pants, she said she might be able to recognize the voice if she heard it again, but she wasn't too confident about it. She said she wouldn't recognize him by sight.

She couldn't tell where in the parking lot area he had come from. She said that although he showed her the gun, she was terrified at the time and didn't know much about guns, so she could only say that it was a handgun. She wasn't aware of any other theater employees who had been attacked or bothered in the parking lot recently.

She said her arms were in front of her when the man threw her at the car, so she had no significant head trauma but had bruises on her arms and chest. Detective Smith asked if she could document the chest bruises if Detective Williams stepped out of the room, and Gwen agreed. When that was finished, the detectives asked if she would listen to a taped voice to see if she recognized it, if they located any suspects, and she agreed. They also arranged for her to go to the station later and look at gun pictures to see if she could recognize the gun that was used.

On their way back to the station, the detectives concurred that this was very reminiscent of Monica's attack, and that there was a good chance it was committed by the person they were looking for. This would make a fourth victim and a significant decrease in waiting time between attacks. They also agreed that they were unlikely to get any crucial leads from Gwen's attack. So far, the case file they had was filling up with multiple attacks but minimal useful evidence.

CHAPTER 15

TUESDAY PM, WEEK 4

Anna had a good day at work. She first led a staff meeting, and everyone agreed that they were progressing in the right direction. Staff was very happy, which delighted Anna. In addition, the day went well with no complaints from the patients— or the occasionally needy doctors. She left the office in time to attend her 3:30 therapy session.

She was not totally dreading her time with Dr. Ellis today, as no hypnosis or attempts at memory retrieval were scheduled. Nevertheless, she expected significant discomfort due to the issues she still needed to talk about in follow-up from the last session. When she arrived at the offices, she didn't have to wait long to be called back. As she entered the doctor's room, she noted him to be sitting comfortably in his chair, brown blazer open with a white dress shirt with narrow brown stripes. His eyes were focused on her approach.

"It's nice to see you today, Anna. Please take a seat and tell me how you're feeling after that difficult session last time."

"That's a loaded question. As you might imagine, wild thoughts have been whirling around my head, kind of like the tornado that circled around Dorothy. Learning about my rape, remembering Madison's rape and suicide, thinking about my actions in both instances, and wondering if I should tell anyone about this…all have been almost constantly on my mind."

"It seems as if there's a great deal to discuss today. Where would you like to begin?"

Anna noted that she felt surprisingly composed despite all the recent turmoil. Her posture was neutral, neither relaxed nor on edge. Her face was stern, and her voice quiet but steady.

"I suppose with the realization that I was raped. I know I haven't fully processed it yet. Currently, I wouldn't say I feel ashamed, embarrassed, or dirty, as some women mention on TV after suffering a rape. But I do feel less happy, and somewhat damaged. When the mental image of the few disgusting seconds he was inside me pops up, I'm completely grossed out by that image.

"I don't feel like I'm a completely different person, but I sure wish it hadn't happened, and it's almost always on my mind. I think I should talk with one of the sexual assault counselors you mentioned at some point, but I want to catch the guy who did this first. By the way, I contacted my insurance company, and they'll only pay for one therapist at a time. I hope we can finish our work discovering who did this to me and the other women soon. Then I'll look into the assault counseling."

"That sounds like a good plan for the time being, as long as you feel comfortable with it. Are there any other new feelings that you wish to share today?"

"Nothing major. In retrospect, I'm very glad I was on birth control. I also decided to tell Sonia everything, including Madison's story, as I needed someone besides you who would support me through this without being judgmental."

Anna paused, then crossed her legs, clasped her hands together, and leaned forward.

"I'm still worried about my reactions to the assault when it was happening. I remember that I was fairly drunk, that I completely froze when it was happening, and that I desperately didn't want it to happen. But it bothers me that I don't remember any attempt on my part to stop what was going on. I know there's still some of the memory of that night that hasn't been revealed yet, and that might show some fighting on my part. I mean, how does it make me look if I didn't struggle at all?"

"I'm not an expert on sexual assault, Anna. When you finally see a counselor specifically for that issue, you might learn that your reaction was not uncommon. I also don't know what it means to the police that you haven't yet located any memories of resisting. For now, I would suggest that you try not to dwell on the topic."

"I'll try."

"Are there other new thoughts or emotions concerning your attack that you feel you should share today?"

Anna uncrossed her legs and sat more upright. Her expression became more somber.

"There's one change I've noticed. I told you last week that I was moving away from primarily just wanting to find the person responsible for the attacks in order to help the investigation. I mentioned wanting to know more details now.

"Well, after learning more of the details, I'm also becoming much more interested in knowing exactly who this horrible person is that raped me. I don't mean identifying him to help the police, but learning whether it was someone I knew or a total stranger? I must know who he is."

She could have pointed out the many other things she wondered about. Who from her previous life could have done this? Why did this evil person choose her? And the most worrisome: Which of the people passing her on the street each day might be the person who attacked her?

Dr. Ellis had a concerned look. "That sounds worrisome. Do you wish to do anything to address that feeling?"

"Nothing except to catch him."

"Have you felt any other reactions to your attack?"

Anna knew that although she felt really bad, she wasn't as devastated as she'd expected. She'd always had an image in her head, based on Madison's experience, that being raped would be the end of her life as she knew it. The realization was absolutely horrible for her, but it didn't reach the depths that she'd imagined.

Still, Anna's shoulders slumped and her mouth was pressed in a tight line. "Yes. I'm sure you want to know about my reaction to understanding that I was actually raped. At first, I worried that I'd want to consider suicide like Madison did. Fortunately, that hasn't happened. As I thought about it more, I realized that our situations are different.

"For one, she was younger than me. But more importantly, I'm positive that Madison was raped by someone she knew and probably trusted. She had to deal both with being raped and with being emotionally abandoned by someone she liked.

"Also, Madison was immediately aware of her rape, but I basically learned about it two years after it happened. I think this time frame is the reason why I feel a little less devastated than many victims do. I didn't experience the actual rape last week; I only experienced the two-year-old memory of it.

"I realize that for the last ten years I carried a voice in my head that screamed out that being raped would clearly make me want to die. But I didn't know that it might have been a combination of the rape, the person who did it, and the greater and immediate awareness of the terror she experienced that caused Madison to do what she did."

Anna paused. She was looking at the floor and wringing her hands. She wasn't crying but her face drooped, and her eyes were dull.

"Why did you say that Madison was raped by someone she knew?"

Anna looked up with a puzzled expression. She paused before replying. "I guess I didn't tell you the whole story last time. These are also details I've never told anyone. After Madison's death, I tried to be an amateur sleuth. I figured it wasn't a stranger who attacked her, as that's something she definitely would've told everyone about. I knew who she was scheduled to spend time with during the weekend she was raped, so I tried to figure out who did it."

Anna then grimly painted a picture for the doctor of how Madison had spent that weekend. She had a Friday night movie date with her longtime boyfriend. They'd done a lot sexually, but Madison was still a virgin, and there may have been tension on the date as the boyfriend was pressuring her for more. The date presumably went okay, though, as Anna had seen the two of them together after that weekend, and Madison was sad but not angry or bitter with him.

Madison had a private study session with the advanced math teacher on Saturday morning. It was scheduled to be in a small study room in the mostly empty high school. The teacher was young and attractive, and some female students referred to him as an MTILF. Anna had heard some of the really loose girls talking about letting him get into their pants, though she didn't know if that had ever happened. The teacher did clearly enjoy it when girls wore short skirts or showed cleavage. He'd also shown a lot of attention to both Anna and Madison due to their math interest.

Then Madison attended a Saturday afternoon and evening family picnic that her mother's family held annually. It took place in a large outdoor park and was supposed to have ended well after dark. Two potential attendees were worrisome. Madison had been attracted to her older cousin when she was fifteen, and she thought the feeling was mutual. She said she'd grown out of it by her senior year but didn't know if he had. She also had an uncle on her mother's side whom she thought was pervy.

On Sunday afternoon, she was scheduled to go on a church youth group outing. It took place in a group of small cabins in an isolated area of the woods outside of their suburb. She'd told Anna that the leader of that group was a young stud whom the church girls all swooned over, and Madison was unsure how pure his intentions were.

"Doctor, I was aware of all of these possibilities, but I had no way to narrow it down, other than to exclude her boyfriend. I decided to give up my investigating. I was convinced that one of the others had raped her. And any of them could have caused her to feel that she'd been betrayed."

As she concluded that saga, Anna sank back in the chair and looked like she had just completed a marathon. She was a little surprised at herself for telling the doctor all of that, but not at all surprised at the additional and damning information she had withheld.

Dr. Ellis felt overwhelmed. He knew that Anna could really use a warm hug now, but of course, not from him. He settled for a verbal caress. "That's a lot of unsettling information. Again, I'm so sorry that you had to endure all of that."

Anna frowned. "Thanks, Doctor. Going over all of this has also made me feel even worse that I didn't do more for Madison. I didn't understand what she was going through. I was the only one who could have done something for her, and I didn't. Since our last session, I've been kicking myself for not telling anyone what I knew after her death either.

"You and I and the police are all trying to find out who assaulted me and the other women. Back then, however, I did nothing to help discover who her assailant—really her murderer—was. I was kind of a shit."

"Anna, you were just a seventeen-year-old at the time. You shouldn't expect to have had the maturity to deal with that awful situation at your age. Please don't beat yourself up about this."

"Well, I do. I couldn't even get it right when I did try something."

"What do you mean?"

Anna looked away and waved her hand in a gesture of dismissal. "Oh, nothing. It doesn't matter now."

"Whatever you're thinking about was significant enough that you referred to it."

"It's really hard to talk about."

"So is everything else in here. Why don't you try mentioning a little of it and see how things go? You can always stop if it's too much."

Anna withdrew a little and looked like she might be expecting the third degree, or a beating with a rubber hose. She wished she hadn't said anything. But something inside her decided that she had held on to all of the details of this tragic story for way too long, and this was the one place she could safely admit to her egregious past actions.

"I guess. Please don't think less of me, Doctor. This is stuff that no one except my mother has ever known, and she wasn't aware of the rape. After Madison died, I was unbelievably angry at the person responsible. Since my sleuthing was unsuccessful, I felt I had to do something. I was so mad. I'm not proud of what I decided to do. I know now I should've gone to the police.

"In my mind, I had four possibilities for who could have raped Madison, and I had no access to the two family members on the list. I decided to go after the most convenient of the two people I could reach. I'm really ashamed of my actions that I'm about to tell you about." Anna paused with her head bowed, and her speech slowed.

"I scheduled a couple of one-on-one sessions with the math teacher, and I wore low-cut tops to try and tempt him. I hoped that wearing those outfits would stimulate him into some inappropriate action, but it didn't. So, after the second session, I decided to tell my mother that the teacher had groped my breast under my shirt and bra during that session, and that we should go to the police."

Anna's entire body cringed. "As you might imagine, that claim morphed into a huge production. It was he said, she said, with no way to prove anything. In my corner was my history of being a model student, and the fact that the teacher was known for leering at female students. In his corner was his history of never having been accused of anything more than just staring, and his being so well-respected.

"After a huge investigation, the police concluded that there wasn't enough evidence for them to proceed with charges. The school administration concluded that they had no reason to discipline him, but no reason to disbelieve me, so they encouraged him to transfer the next semester. At the time, I wondered if his willingness to transfer meant that he was the person who'd assaulted Madison.

"After he left school, I became a real pariah, but I knew I was leaving for college soon. Since I was a minor and no formal charges were filed, there was no public record of the complaints, so the incident didn't follow me. I later confessed to my mother that I'd made everything up, though I didn't tell her why. Since the teacher had already transferred by the time of my confession, my mother decided to keep that information to herself."

Dr. Ellis leaned forward and spread his hands apart. "You really went through the wringer. How have you felt about the situation in the years since?"

"Honestly, I thought there was a real chance that he'd been the one to rape Madison, so I didn't feel at all bad about doing it. And I felt so angry and helpless at the time that I was happy to actually do something. More recently, though, I've felt negatively about myself and the kind of person that I was at that time. I realize that I should have just gone to the police after Madison's death."

"Are the police here aware of this full story?"

Anna recoiled. "My God, no, and I don't plan to tell them. I've only mentioned what happened to Madison, but nothing about the sleuthing or the accusation. I was clearly raped two years ago, so I didn't invent that story. Imagine how they would wonder about my credibility if they knew this whole story. It would be a real problem if they learned about my claim that the teacher had groped one of my breasts, the same thing that happened to me during the assault."

Anna was completely spent at that point, and it was obvious to Dr. Ellis. He needed to end the session.

"You've unleashed a lot of emotions and information today. You have a lot to think about going forward. We should plan for more hypnosis during our next session, so that we can help you uncover that missing portion of the memory that you alluded to earlier today. I think we can conclude for today, unless there's more that you'd like to discuss."

"No. That's quite enough."

Dr. Ellis stood then. "Okay, Anna. I hope you can continue to process the many disturbing memories and emotions that have recently surfaced for you, with the insight that you've demonstrated so far. As difficult as everything has been for you, you're doing amazingly well." Dr. Ellis felt bad for Anna's pain but was very impressed with her ability to open up. He hoped that much of the success was related to his abilities and support. This made him feel like the proud parent of a gold-medal-winning offspring.

He was basking in the glow of this therapeutic high as he watched Anna slowly leave. *If she can just find that one missing memory in our next session,* he thought, *life will be awesome.*

CHAPTER 16

WEDNESDAY, WEEK 4

A nna decided to go to the police station in the morning, mainly hoping for an update from them concerning the video review. When she arrived and entered the familiar lobby, the officer at the desk called back for Detectives Williams and Smith before Anna even asked. She wryly smiled as the thought struck her that being instantly recognized at a police station was certainly not an item on any memory board that she'd ever constructed for herself.

She was ushered back, and both detectives were waiting for her at a table in an interview room. Detective Williams was wearing his rumpled blazer, and Detective Smith wore a crisp blue top and dark pants with her signature belt buckle.

"Good morning, detectives. I had a therapy session yesterday. I didn't uncover any new memories during the session, but I still wanted to talk with you. I'd like to know if there've been any new developments in the case."

Detective Smith took the lead. She told Anna that the stalker wasn't seen in the video, but that another person was seen both at the bar and at the site of the attack a year ago. She noted that they had extensively interviewed him and others aware of his movements, which seemed to clear him.

"At this point we have no reason to suspect either him or your stalker to be viable suspects. I'm sorry."

Detective Smith glanced at her partner and received a brief nod from him before she continued. They had decided not to mention the Monday night attack to Anna as they were not yet certain that it was related.

Detective Williams spoke up. "We want to know where you do your running, and at what time of the day."

"I always run in the mornings. Before that woman was assaulted this summer, I sometimes ran in that park where she was attacked, but now I just run in my neighborhood."

"During any of your runs in the park, did you notice anyone following you, stalking you, casing you out, or watching you in any way?"

Anna suppressed a laugh. "Detective Williams, virtually every young—or I guess even not so young—woman who runs in a sports bra receives glances, looks, stares, leers, and creepy ogling from males of every age. My roommate Sonia, if she were a runner, would probably smile back and wave at them, but most of us ignore them. Even so, I think I would've noticed if any one person was regularly paying particular or worrisome attention to me, and I didn't."

Detective Smith, herself a world-class authority on men's stares, looked as if she felt her partner's chagrin, but she smiled at Anna's brilliant answer. She followed with "Thanks for that answer. Have you had any other memories that might shed light on who it was that attacked you?"

"No, I haven't, Detective. However, as I told you before, there's still an idea in the back of my mind that there's another part of the memory that hasn't yet been uncovered. I'm very optimistic that when I do uncover it, it will reveal a definite method to identify my attacker's voice. I can't seem to bring that memory to my consciousness, but I'm certain that the memory exists."

"It would be phenomenal if you could uncover that memory."

A junior officer knocked and entered the room. He signaled for Detective Williams to accompany him into the hallway. The detective excused himself and left.

"Is there anything else you wanted to say?"

"Since it's just us now, I had something else I could share. It's not flattering for me, but you've always made me feel very comfortable." Anna proceeded to tell Detective Smith briefly about her sleuthing after Madison's rape, though not about her false accusation or about her decision not to tell the police what she knew. The detective expressed her understanding of Anna's actions, which made Anna feel even more comfortable with her, but even less likely to reveal her indiscretions to the detective.

"If there's nothing else, we'll look forward to seeing you after your next session. Hopefully you'll uncover that crucial memory you're looking for. And Anna, I really do sympathize with what you're going through, more than you know."

After Anna had left, Detective Williams returned to the room.

"Cynthia's partner located the employee who had started his car in the lot behind the theater Monday night," he said. "He didn't see Gwen, the attack, or the guy running away, and he also said he didn't hear anything. Gwen came in and tentatively identified the gun she saw as a Sig Sauer 226 yesterday, but she wasn't too confident, so that's all the useful evidence we have from her attack. At least she wasn't hurt too badly. I guess we might never know for sure if she was a victim of our serial attacker, though it seems very likely."

"We've got to catch a break somewhere, Derek. This is becoming more and more frustrating."

Joe Friedman sat at home ruminating about his disaster of a week. It had only been two days since the police had arrived at his office to interview him, and his career and good standing were already on life support.

Everyone at work was aware that he'd been questioned by the police. The all-glass offices had allowed the entire staff to witness the scene. Only a few colleagues were aware of his afternoon trip to the police station, but they all saw the police officer interview Terry and Leslie while he was away.

As a result, the rumor mill blew into the office with hurricane force on Tuesday morning. Leslie had researched the date that the police had questioned her and Terry about and discovered that a sexual assault had happened on that date, not too far from their office event that evening. No matter how much good standing one has built up over time, an association with a sexual assault can bring it crashing down with haste.

Many people were shunning Joe at work now. Even Joe's friend Mack was no longer eager to talk with him. The only bright light was that Terry and Leslie's recollection of the time frame when Joe left the event was in accordance with Joe's response to the police. That time frame apparently satisfied the police that they didn't have to further pursue Joe as a suspect.

Joe had done nothing, other than to be in the vicinity of two crimes completely by coincidence, yet his reputation was being unceremoniously dragged through the thick mud of innuendo. It wasn't right or fair. Life was so bad for him now that Joe might have to move to another city. The innocent shouldn't have to suffer like this.

Detective Audra Smith and her family had finished a dinner, prepared by Audra's husband, consisting of a steak salad accompanied by corn on the cob and watermelon. After dinner, they played cornhole in the backyard. Later on, Audra's husband got their son ready for bed so that Audra could go to their shared office and focus on the case.

She'd been so excited initially when she and the young officer assisting her had found one person fitting the description of the attacker, who was conclusively seen on video in the vicinities of the first two attacks. Audra had sent an officer to talk with Mr. Friedman's two colleagues about the event, which took place the night of Monica's attack.

The colleagues, who were in charge of setting up and tearing down for the event, both confirmed that Mr. Friedman had arrived shortly after 8 p.m. and had left the event after 10:30. This meant he wouldn't have had time to collect his gun from his home before the attack on Monica. That information, plus the video from the bar the night Anna was attacked, essentially put the kibosh on him as a viable suspect.

Even though he was no longer a serious suspect, Audra had learned today that the mere hint of being linked to a sexual assault had caused significant problems for Mr. Friedman at his workplace. This information had also made its way to the station brass, resulting in a mild reprimand from the chief, focused more on Audra than her partner. This continued a pattern of less favorable treatment for female officers—treatment that she'd been a party to before.

She knew that they had needed details about Mr. Friedman's movements on the night of Monica's assault. They couldn't have obtained that information without interviewing his coworkers, which set the rumor mills in motion. She believed that the chief should have realized that they needed to investigate him and backed them up.

Audra also had done some digging into the case of Anna's friend Madison. She was trying to discover whether whoever had raped Madison had eventually come to justice. But instead, she found a reference to a teacher relocating from Anna's school after rumors of inappropriate actions with a student, and no reference to Madison having been raped or even assaulted, which seemed odd.

Given Anna's discussion of her attempts to learn who had raped her friend, this brought up other possibilities. For instance, Anna might have been involved in spreading the rumors in order to seek justice for her friend.

If she had, Audra wouldn't approve, but she would understand Anna's desire to do something like that, after what Audra had endured in her youth had gone unpunished. But would the officers who had initially interviewed Anna after her assault have completely dismissed her if they'd been aware of the possibility that she'd spread rumors in the past? And could Audra fully trust Anna now?

Audra's partner and superiors had also never been informed of the molestation in Audra's background. Bringing it up now was certainly off the table as that would risk them worrying about her objectivity in their cases.

Audra had to bypass these issues and begin to focus on the next steps. They had been offered two suspects so far, one from Anna and one through good old-fashioned police work. Since neither suspect seemed viable now, they needed to enlarge the suspect pool. The report of Gwen's attack behind the theater on Monday night hadn't helped much. They only had a possible ID on the gun used—and her statement that she might be able to recognize his voice.

Their assailant had been very careful to avoid leaving crime scene evidence in the three linked, completed attacks, other than his DNA in the semen. Audra had written notes in her case book that maybe he'd been suspected of sexual assault in the past, without having had DNA collected. She made plans to search for anyone locally with such a record, and for any unsolved rape cases that had common threads to Anna, Monica, and Hannah's attacks.

She also jotted down that she and Derek hadn't attempted any profiling to identify the type of individual they should search for. She would plan to talk with him soon about forming such a profile. The chief hadn't approved a media release when Derek asked today, so it was still up to her and her partner.

They needed to find the culprit to prevent future attacks, and they needed to procure the justice for the victims that Audra was determined to achieve. Tomorrow she would begin the records search. Maybe Anna would come up with the method of identifying her attacker that she seemed certain resided in her remaining memory of that night. Although the week had started unsuccessfully, there was hope for the final two days of the week. They couldn't let these attacks go unpunished.

Anna's day had been very busy, so she had little time to focus on her worries. The distressing thoughts finally began to intrude on her consciousness during the drive home. She continued to sense that there was some method of identifying her attacker that existed in the remaining unrecovered memories of that night. Her mindfulness techniques had so far been unsuccessful in unearthing that identifier.

She also continued to feel stress about the lack of viable suspects for the attacks. She was increasingly worried about what kind of monster her still uncaptured attacker was. As a result, she was constantly on the alert when she was out in public.

Many daily activities were increasingly unnerving for her. Even Detective Williams's idea, initially dismissed by Anna, that someone might be spying on her during her runs, was now taking root in her mind like the weeds that force their way through minuscule cracks in the sidewalk.

Sonia had texted Anna that she had late clients scheduled and not to wait for dinner, so Anna decided to take Milo to the dog park. It was a large park with open spaces interspersed with mature trees. When they arrived, Milo almost immediately began playing with one of his dog pals. Anna talked with the dog's owner, the idle chatter providing a welcome relief to her worries. It was a beautiful summer day, so they remained there for longer than she had planned.

Once she got home, Anna nuked a frozen Amy's vegetarian Mexican casserole for herself and enjoyed it. Then she remembered that she needed to grab some items from the grocery that she'd promised to bring to an early morning work meeting the next day. Simultaneously, Anna received a text from Sonia that she wouldn't be home until dark, but that she had an idea she was excited to share. Anna realized that she'd better head to the store immediately, as she was hesitant to be out too late by herself.

It was dusk when Anna arrived at the large store, so she hurriedly grabbed a small cart and began to motor swiftly through the mostly vacant aisles. Her progress was slowed by some items that she needed being out of stock, forcing her to replan her route through the store. When she'd finally located everything, it was getting fairly dark outside as she reached the checkout station. She fit her purchases into two bags that she could carry, and she began a power walk toward her car.

As soon as she left the store, her neck hair began to stand on end, as she again caught the eerie feeling that she was being followed. She was absolutely convinced that she heard footsteps behind her this time. She accelerated her pace, while realizing that due to the moderately heavy bags she held in each hand, she lacked effective self-defense ability.

The footsteps behind her sped up with her, magnifying her fear to desperate proportions. She sensed that it would be even worse if she turned around to look behind her, so she further picked up her pace.

She also was silently cursing herself that she'd parked far from the entrance so that she could obtain additional exercise. As her foot speed and her panic increased, she saw she was very close to her car. Just before she reached it, a white SUV passed her and pulled into the parking space adjacent to hers. A tall man with a pleasant expression got out of the car, and she knew she had to take advantage of this good fortune.

"Hi," said Anna, who continued rapidly. "It sure was a great day today. Do you also park this far out so that you get extra exercise?" Anna had opened her door and tossed in her bags as she spoke.

"Yes, I like the extra steps, particularly in the nice weather," replied the stranger.

"I'm with you. Have a nice evening," said Anna, as she closed the door, locked her car, and started the engine. No one was parked in the space in front of her, so she tore off. As she drove down the lane of the parking lot, she searched for the person she was sure had followed her out of the store, but she saw no one. She set off for home, glancing in the rearview mirror to ensure that no cars were following her, but there were no signs of that occurring. She was incredibly spooked by the night's events.

Gerry was at the grocery on a mission to restock his freezer with burritos and maybe grab some tasty philly steak and cheese Hot Pockets while he was there. He had a shock when he started to enter one last aisle and caught sight of his dream woman. His heart began performing Simone Biles-style somersaults. The beautiful woman, his woman, was concentrating intently on the K-Cups display, so she didn't notice him.

He ducked behind the end of the aisle and carefully followed her throughout the store. He was surprised when he spotted another man who was also following her through the store. The other man was about Gerry's height and age. He was wearing a dark-colored thin rain jacket over his T-shirt and jeans, and he had on a ball cap. Gerry continued to bring up the rear of this stalking parade as he watched his crush check out.

The other man waited until she'd finished, then he carefully followed her out of the store. He pulled gloves out of his jacket pocket and slid them on as he was leaving. Gerry hurried through the self-checkout aisle with his provisions. He quickly ran out of the store and scanned the parking lot. It was dark with several cars present and with numerous shadowed areas, but there were enough lights to enable him to examine the entire lot.

He didn't see his dream woman or the man who was following her. There was a tall guy just entering the store, and a car driving away in the distance. He watched for a couple of minutes more, then headed morosely to his bus stop.

His shopping trip had an exciting beginning, but it ended with him worrying about his favorite person. He would consider returning tomorrow, somewhat earlier, in order to keep an eye out for her. It would be a trip for his benefit, and maybe for her safety.

When Anna arrived home, due to the late hour, the only parking spots were near the back of the lot. This wasn't ideal, but she hadn't been followed from the store as far as she was aware. She jumped out of the car, grabbed her bags, and sprinted to the building entrance.

She hadn't sensed anyone following her, and she was able to jump immediately into an elevator. At her floor, she hurried to the apartment and let herself in. She was still trembling as she found Sonia standing in the kitchen, staring unhappily at the meager contents of the refrigerator while holding the door open.

"You look like you just saw all of the ghosts from the Haunted Mansion simultaneously, honey. What's going on?"

Anna related her certainty that she was followed out of the grocery, and said how frightening it was. She mentioned the man who had pulled into the space near her, which helped her to be able to leave safely.

"I'm so sorry I wasn't home earlier so that I could've gone with you. I keep failing you," Sonia said, with an exaggerated pout, as she closed the refrigerator door.

"We've discussed this before. You're not solely responsible for my safety."

"Well, maybe I can help you out now, honey. I thought of another possible suspect!"

"Really? Let me put my things away so I can concentrate on what you have to say. Maybe that will help me calm down." Anna's arms trembled mildly as she stashed some of her purchases in the refrigerator and others in a bag for the next day. She took a deep breath and slowly exhaled, which stopped the shaking. She sat on the living area sofa, and Sonia came over and sat beside her. "Okay, let's hear it. What, or who, have you come up with?"

"Do you remember Brian from three or so years ago? The three of us often went out to the bars together, and we always had a good time."

"Of course I remember him."

"Well, he's about the right height for your attacker, and I remember that he had the hots for you."

"I don't think so. I certainly never noticed that."

"Oh, yeah. I could tell by his looks and his comments when he was near you. And did you notice how possessive he was of us, or at least you? Remember how upset he got when we made plans without him for our usual nights?"

Anna scrunched her face into a quizzical but thoughtful look. "Actually, I'd totally forgotten about that, but yeah, he was almost angry if we went out without him. And there was one night he wanted to get together but you weren't available. I told him we couldn't go without you, and he got really mad at me for not agreeing to go out alone with him."

"See what I said. Well, what really struck me today was that he totally disappeared from our lives after your attack."

Anna paused again. "OMG. I never noticed that before, but you're right. Although I certainly had no interest in going to any bars after that night, he never called me to ask. I guess it didn't register since I wasn't looking to go out. So I assume he never called you either?"

"No. If you remember, he used to call us all the time. With helping you through the trauma, I didn't notice his lack of calling then either. But thinking about it now, it seems very suspicious that he happened to stop immediately after that night, doesn't it?"

Anna had a look of sudden understanding. If her life were a cartoon, a lightbulb would have suddenly appeared over her head.

"Yes, it does. Now that you've pointed it out, that timing is suspicious. How are you going to follow up on this?"

Sonia's eyes and face glowed with excitement. "Well, remember I said that I might have to do the investigations for you. I haven't figured out all of the details, but I'm going to track Brian down and find out why he stopped calling."

Anna had been increasingly having feelings that something had to break soon on the case or she would go crazy. Maybe this was the opportunity. "I'll be really interested to learn what the story is with Brian. You know, you might be very effective in this spy role."

"Thanks, honey. I really want to do whatever I can for you. I'll let you know any findings as soon as I uncover them. I'll start my sleuthing soon. I'm sure I'm going to help you find out who attacked you."

CHAPTER 17

THURSDAY, WEEK 4

S ince Anna had a busy afternoon scheduled at work, her therapy session had been set for the very end of the day. As she headed for her session, she realized that she had mixed feelings about it.

She presumed she'd made it past the most terrifying portions of her memory, but there could still be some unpleasant surprises left. She hadn't yet found out what had led her attacker to injure her by throwing her into the trash cans. She hadn't yet seen her attacker, and if that was part of her remaining memory, it could be horrifying. But she was also looking forward to finally unearthing some, hopefully tolerable, way to identify her attacker.

When she arrived at the office, she was greeted warmly by the staff who knew her so well. What a summer it was. At both the police station and the psychiatry office, it seemed like every employee had Anna ensconced on the speed dials of their recognition.

She had a short wait in the reception area after checking in, so she had time to flip through a copy of *Cosmopolitan*. In doing so, she learned that she had been quite remiss in not focusing on the *Cosmo* portions of her life recently. When her name was called, Anna strode briskly down the hallway to Dr. Ellis's office. She was prepared for today, or so she thought. When she entered the office, she was greeted warmly.

"Good afternoon, Anna. How are you feeling today?"

"I'm generally in good spirits, Dr. Ellis. How are you doing?" Anna shook his hand firmly.

"I'm doing well. Thank you for asking. Please sit down. What's put you into your good spirits today?"

Anna smiled and spoke with authority. "I'm looking forward to finding that missing piece of the puzzle. I hope to finally discover a method of identifying my attacker."

"We'll definitely get to the hypnosis for that purpose in a little bit. First, do you have anything new to report?"

Anna frowned slightly. She didn't want to delay her expected treasure find for the day. She wanted to move forward, and quickly. But there were some apprehensions that she could review. "Well, to begin with, last night I had the impression that I was being followed again. This time it was when I left the grocery store, and it was dark.

"Like the earlier time I thought I was being followed, I didn't see anyone. I definitely heard footsteps, though. Fortunately, someone pulled into the parking space next to my car, which gave me the cover I needed to safely get in my car and leave. Even without seeing anyone, I was convinced that I'd been followed. It was very scary, and I decided I should never again be caught out after dark alone."

Dr. Ellis leaned in a little. "I imagine that was really frightening. Did you want to talk some more about those fears?"

"No, I'm better today, so I don't think we should spend time on it."

"Were there any other recent worries that you wanted to talk about?"

This next one had surprised Anna. Dr. Ellis noticed her face and upper chest were flushed as she discussed it.

"There's one more. I've been worrying about Glen, who we discussed when we were talking about my relationships. He's the man who wanted more sexually than I was ready for during our last date. The one who kept pestering me afterward. When we discussed him during our early session together, my mind immediately dismissed him as the attacker or as a current threat. Now I'm not so sure.

"As I'd mentioned, he made extremely creepy remarks to me at the time. Since I now frequently find myself having the feeling that I'm being followed, the term *creepy* is in the front of my brain. As a result, Glen recently popped up in my mind as a possibility. I can also see him as the type of person who could be evil enough to have assaulted me and the others. And he's the right height. There's nothing else concrete, but I think I want him to be on someone's radar as a potential suspect."

The doctor leaned back. "Have you ever mentioned him to the police?"

"No, I haven't. It's only been very recently that I've begun to wonder about him like this. Do you think I should bring him up to them?"

"If you truly feel that he could be the person who attacked you and the other women, I think you should."

Anna took on a thoughtful expression. "Okay, Doctor. I'll think about it."

"Are there any more worries that you'd like to discuss before we move to the hypnosis for today?"

"No. I'm ready."

Dr. Ellis's voice transformed to assume a powerfully soothing tone. "All right, Anna. You know the drill. Sit far back into the chair and let the plush arms and back envelop you. Relax your arms and legs. Close your eyes and relax your facial muscles. Drive all thoughts out of your consciousness."

Dr. Ellis began his typical description of a long hallway intended to fully relax her. By the conclusion of his recitation, Anna had melted into the back of the chair and appeared as if she were in a trance. "Bring your mind back to the night in the alley now. You realize that you've just been sexually assaulted. What's happening now?"

After a few seconds, Anna rapidly sat bolt upright in the chair.

"It's coming to me. I can tell that something really significant just occurred, but I didn't quite get a picture of it." Her forehead crinkled and she frowned.

"Now I'm starting to fight. I'm swinging my arms wildly. I can't tell if I'm trying to get loose from his grasp, or attempting to hit him, or both. I continue to fight, and I can sense his anger. Shortly after that, he grabs my right arm with his hand, and he violently throws me into the trash cans. Then I hit the cans and blacked out."

Anna opened her eyes. They darted around as she grimaced in terror.

"What's passing through your mind now, Anna?"

"Actually, several things. I'm definitely as certain now as I think Hermione would be going into an exam at Hogwarts that there's a part of the memory that will help me identify the attacker. It occurred just before the fighting, but I couldn't quite grasp that part of the memory today. It's really frustrating that it hasn't come to me yet. I feel like I desperately need to locate it.

"I'm also sensing more terror. Recalling these memories so often makes it more obvious how really awful the man is who attacked me, and he's still out there."

Her entire body then relaxed, and her face brightened. "But I'm also sensing some relief."

Dr. Ellis was puzzled by that pronouncement.

"I can tell that surprised you. Well, the relief comes from finally realizing that I did offer some resistance. I had mentioned to you before that it bothered me that I didn't complain when he grabbed my boob, and that I didn't immediately fight when he jammed his prick in me. Now I know that I did fight back, and I'm thrilled that I'll be able to tell the police about it.

"I don't know how much time went by between his penetration"—Anna spat out that word with extreme disgust—" and the time I began fighting. There could have been only a few seconds between the actual rape and my arms flailing, which would mean I fought almost immediately. There also might be some more extensive fighting in the remaining memory. In any case, I know I've found some vindication with this memory."

"What other concerns do you have?"

Anna leaned back in the chair. She'd thought about this a lot, and she was fairly clear about how she'd like to proceed.

"I know that meeting with a sexual assault counselor in the future will be very important and helpful. I think that my terror feeling now is due to the knowledge that the attacker is still a danger, rather than being related to what memories might still remain. The sensations of being followed are a problem, though. I'd love to hear any recommendations you have about that issue."

"When your attacker is caught, I imagine the feeling of potential terror will disappear. In the meantime, have you ever considered obtaining personal protection, such as pepper spray or something similar?"

"With everything else I've had to worry about, I guess I hadn't thought about it, but that's a really good idea."

Dr. Ellis straightened up and assumed a commanding presence. "Why don't we wrap this up now and create plans for our next session? Locating that one last piece of the memory is the objective. Between now and then, use the mindfulness technique to concentrate on placing yourself inside the memory that you've recalled. See if that stimulates you to find the crucial missing part that you're sure is there. If that doesn't work, we'll use hypnosis again next time. And remember, the police might have found a suspect by then."

"I sure hope so."

"Good luck with your discussion with the police. I'm impressed with your ability to handle everything. Between the memory revelations, your past history, the knowledge that your attacker is still at large, and your worries about being followed, you're managing an enormous load. I can't imagine most young women navigating all of this as well as you have, Anna."

"Thank you, Doctor. That's helpful to hear. I'll see you Tuesday. Have a good weekend."

Anna stood and left. Despite her fears and her recent discoveries, after receiving the doctor's strong praise, she was walking with force and resolve. Her worries yesterday about desperately needing a break in the case were beginning to be at least partly replaced with a sense of increased optimism, and she was looking forward to the next session. She'd found some vindication in today's memories. Even the simple recommendation to obtain pepper spray was reducing her apprehension.

Dr. Ellis was beside himself with pride. Anna had shown really good progress and had tolerated so much. She had reacted with the expected fear, disgust, and despondency, but had dealt with all of those emotions. She was stronger than he'd expected she would be.

This had been as good an outcome as he could have imagined. They just needed to locate that clue to the attacker's identity, a clue that Anna was certain the remaining memory contained. If they could find that, this would be the best case of Dr. Ellis's career. And it would validate his belief that he was the best therapist for Anna. Although he knew that he needed to avoid focusing solely on clinical success as a basis for his self-esteem, this case would be his holy grail. Life couldn't get much better.

Anna found her car and drove away from the psychiatry offices. This was a later session than usual, so she decided she would need to wait a day before going to the police station. She had time on Friday morning that she could devote to a meeting with the police.

Anna felt wonderful that she had unearthed that memory of resisting the attacker. This would be great to share with the police and with Sonia. Anna decided to make their dinner tonight a celebration and obtain the ingredients to prepare her spaghetti puttanesca sans anchovies. It was a safe time now to go to the grocery, even without any pepper spray. There would be a large before-dinner and after-work crowd, and the sun was still high in the sky.

The Columbia rush hour traffic (Anna wondered if that was an oxymoron) did nothing to impede her journey to procure the ingredients for gastronomic pleasure. When she arrived at the store, she located a very close parking spot between two other vehicles. It was bound to be safe.

Anna glided smoothly through the store aisles like an Ice Capades star crossing a glistening, well-frozen stage. She easily located everything that she needed, so the expedition was quick and painless.

As she was leaving her final stop in the pasta aisle, she wondered if she had sufficient olive oil at home. She quickly whirled around to head in the opposite direction, and her mood plunged faster than the Millennium Force rollercoaster at Cedar Point amusement park. Her stalker was at the other end of the aisle, creepy thin mustache and all.

He jumped quickly behind the endcap of the aisle, but Anna could tell that he'd been watching her. Was he the man who'd followed her the previous evening? Was this abomination happening again? Anna whirled back and raced to the front of the store. She went to the far bank of self-checkout stations, as that location provided her a view of the ends of every aisle. She scanned her items while maintaining most of her concentration on watching for the stalker.

She once thought she saw him peek out of the end of an aisle, but she wasn't certain. She placed her bags in her cart so that her hands would be readily available if needed for threat response. She left the store, and this time she turned to look behind her every few seconds, but she wasn't followed by him or anyone else. She continued to watch while unloading her bags into her trunk and while pushing her cart to the corral.

She never saw him again, and she escaped the parking lot safely. When she reached her apartment, she was fortunate to find a parking spot near their front entrance. She had an easy, mostly worry-free run to the entrance with her purchases. Her dinner with Sonia was now going to be more of a strategy session than a celebration, though the food would still be savory.

Sonia arrived over an hour later, providing Anna time to walk Milo and prepare the puttanesca. She also cobbled together an iceberg wedge salad with ranch dressing, plus bacon bits for Sonia. An aroma of garlic bread escaped from the oven, and along with the puttanesca fragrance wafting from the stove, produced sensory sensations suggestive of the famous Campo de'Fiori in Rome. A chocolate lava cake she'd gotten at the store completed the menu.

"Are you trying to seduce me with delicious food again, honey?" asked Sonia as she waltzed in.

"No, I just prepared a celebration dinner since my session today was worthy of a minor party. It's also a thanks for your plans to begin investigating on my behalf."

"I hope you won't be disappointed that I haven't really dived fully into the Brian investigation yet."

"No worries. I'm not expecting immediate results."

Sonia perked up. "But I did get some more details about that spa client who was raped. She was on an internet date when it happened, and the guy used a fake name on his dating site, so the client doesn't even know who he is. My coworker said she wouldn't be able to give me any more details, though, and the woman still isn't willing to tell the police."

"Thanks for all the time you spent following up on that lead. Since she was on the internet date, it's a much different situation than what happened to me or the other women. I guess it's probably not related. We could always come back to it later if it seems important. Besides, between my therapy sessions, getting followed last night, and what happened tonight, there's a lot going on that could help us find my attacker."

"So, tell me what you've got. If you're okay with me not changing into one of my many Dior gowns for dinner, I'm ready to eat and listen to you now," Sonia said with a smile.

Anna chuckled and placed everything on their table. As they prepared to eat, Anna summarized the memories she'd regained in her session, focusing on the realization that she had fought back. She also informed Sonia that she didn't yet recall the portion of the memory that contained a method of identifying her attacker.

"I knew you were a fighter, honey. You'll get that other part soon, with the way to ID your attacker, I'm sure."

"Thanks, and I still need to tell you about tonight. When I stopped at the grocery to get the ingredients for your dinner, I saw the stalker watching me."

Sonia finished a large gulp of her beer and replied, "You mean that creeper from three years ago? No freaking way!"

"Yeah, it was him. He was peeking at me from the end of an aisle, so I know he was following me in the store."

"Do you think he was the scary perv who followed you last night?"

Anna had a fork full of food, but her hand paused halfway to her mouth as she thought. "I don't know, but it's possible."

"What happened after you saw him?"

"I got out of there and watched closely, and he didn't follow me."

Sonia had been smiling while savoring her lava cake, but her expression changed to one of anger. "Well, he's damn lucky that I wasn't there with you. I'd have beaten the crap out of him. What are you going to do?"

"I'm going to tell the police about this tomorrow and see if they can see him on the store camera from yesterday. You know, it was so creepy seeing him, but with my worry about being followed last night, this is good timing. I hope the police will get something useful on the store video, and maybe there'll be a real break in the case, finally."

"I'm still going to do my masterful investigation of Brian for you. I plan to start in the next day or two."

"Thanks, but I'm a little more worried about my stalker now. This is all so hopeful. I'm almost positive that by next week the police will have something useful, and then at my next session I'll discover a way to conclusively identify who my attacker was. It's all coming together fabulously now."

Anna raised her water glass. "Bon appétit!"

CHAPTER 18

FRIDAY, WEEK 4

Anna began the day with a run through her neighborhood of apartment buildings and a few scattered businesses. The morning was beautiful and the temperature a perfect sixty-seven degrees for her. She wore the sports bra and running shorts outfit she'd discussed with Detective Williams. There were a surprising number of other people outside. Most were either other runners, power walkers, or dog walkers. A few appeared to be dressed for work, presumably headed for shift jobs or other businesses that started early.

Anna didn't usually pay much attention to people she passed while running, but now she was. She watched them closely, but no one appeared to devote special interest to her. No other runners followed her through her route. No one she passed looked scary. The would-be Ted Bundys were apparently all sleeping in today. The rational part of Anna also realized that all of the attacks in the current assault spree had occurred at night.

After completing the rest of her morning ritual to prepare for the day, Anna headed to the police station. When she arrived, Detective Smith came out to the lobby to escort Anna to an interview room. Detective Williams was already there seated at one side of the table in the small room.

"Good morning, Anna," said Detective Williams. "I hope your day is starting off well."

"Yes, Detective. I had a wonderful run this morning, which involved absolutely no creepy men ogling me," Anna teased.

Detective Smith responded as she smiled, "That's great. Do you have any news from your therapy session yesterday that you wish to share with us?"

"Yes I do, plus something else too."

"Okay. Let's hear what you've got."

Detective Smith sat next to her partner, leaving the other side of the plain table for Anna. After Anna sat, she leaned in with her arms resting comfortably on the table.

"I regained some new memories yesterday. First I got a sensation I've shared with you before, that I know without a doubt something occurred that can help identify my attacker. I just couldn't quite get the details of it yesterday, and I don't know if it was visual or something I heard. The memory I got started immediately after that point. I began to fight. I was flailing my arms at him, and I could sense his anger. After I fought for a while, he grabbed my arm hard, then he violently threw me into the trash cans."

Detective Smith replied, "You'd mentioned the anger previously. Did you get any sense of what provoked the anger?"

"No, I'm sorry but I didn't."

"Did you get a sense of the duration of time that you fought with him?"

"It seemed brief, but I can't say anything more than that. I do feel much better knowing that I finally fought back."

The detective glanced at her partner, then turned toward Anna with a serious expression.

"I agree that's good, Anna, but we need to be up front with you. Previously you mentioned your apparent nonchalance at his touching your breast, and your inability to remember any verbal stop commands that you might have uttered. These memories could be a little problematic. But, technically you would need to give some form of consent, or the action is still sexual assault. A prosecutor would focus on that.

"You also indicated that you were very drunk and in a fog. So you might have been unable to make reasonable judgments, or even to give valid consent, and no one should've taken advantage of you even without you saying no. You were definitely sexually assaulted, Anna. It's just that proving it in court, assuming we can ID your attacker, might be a very stressful experience for you."

Anna's expression was still upbeat. "I understand, Detective. At least I feel better knowing that I did eventually begin resisting. I also hope that the final piece of the memory will explain more about the fighting and the anger, in addition to uncovering the way to identify my attacker."

"We very much look forward to your remembering that last part, as I'm sure you do too."

"More than you can know, Detective. I also have two other important stories that I need to share with you today."

"Please go ahead," said Detective Williams in a hopeful tone.

Anna hated to relive her fright, but these were important events to tell the detectives. She shifted in her seat and clasped her hands together. "I want to tell you about some worrisome incidents from the past two nights. Both occurred at the grocery store."

She told them about her sensation of being followed out of the grocery on Wednesday night, and of seeing the stalker staring at her in the aisles last night.

Anna leaned in toward the detectives. "Because of what happened the last two nights, I want to ask if you're able to view video from the store's cameras. You should be able to see someone following me out of the store two nights ago. You should be able to identify my stalker entering the store last night. He still looks the same as in the sketch we had drawn, by the way. Please tell me that you can do this and help answer some of my questions about being followed."

The detectives eyed each other with optimistic expressions. Detective Smith said, "I can ask if the store manager will agree to let me view the videos without a warrant. Often people are very cooperative in situations such as this, particularly if we're not trying to imply any fault on the part of the store. If the manager isn't cooperative, however, I can't guarantee that we would have sufficient justification to obtain a warrant."

"Anything that you can do would be great, Detective. I know my stalker was there last night, watching me, and I'm 99 percent positive I was being followed out of the store by someone on Wednesday. I'd love to know who that was."

"I'll definitely check into the possibility of viewing those videos, then get back to you. I also should mention a related issue. You know that we located a person of interest when reviewing the bar video. As I told you, we interviewed him and effectively cleared him as a viable suspect."

Detective Smith frowned. "Unfortunately, the process of us investigating him has caused some negative effects on his life. It was unavoidable, but as a result we have to be very careful in the future. We don't want to unduly cast suspicions on anyone who has a low likelihood of being a real suspect. Therefore, we can only proceed if we have strong reasons to do so."

"I understand, Detective."

"Good. About what times were you at the store the last two nights?"

"It was about 8:15 or so Wednesday and 5:30 yesterday."

"We'll check and let you know. In addition, I'm looking into records of locals with sexual assault accusations or convictions. Maybe this guy has committed other similar crimes, which might help us identify him."

"That sounds great. Thank you for continuing to pursue this actively. My next session is scheduled for Tuesday afternoon, when I hope to discover that identifier for you."

Detective Smith stood and indicated that Anna could see herself out.

Anna had much to be hopeful about now. Her next session could produce the key memory. The store cameras could identify her stalker and follower. Detective Smith's records reviews could produce helpful results. With so many options available, one just had to come through.

After Anna left, the detectives conferred. "Two young women being followed in dark parking lots this week with one attack similar to Monica's. This seems really ominous, Audra."

"I agree. If we locate video of someone following Anna Wednesday night, it will be very interesting to see if the suspect fits with the minimal description we have from Gwen, and if we get a good look at him. We also really need to catch this guy as this seems to be quickly getting out of hand."

Dr. Ellis arrived at Dr. Wilson's office and signed in. He sat and was pleased to note that the magazine selection had improved considerably. He selected a *Travel + Leisure* and enjoyed the articles concerning tropical getaways. The ocean-view villas with personal butlers and individual pools were enticing, but they reminded him of his single status.

While he was dwelling on that issue, Dr. Wilson opened the door and invited him in. As he entered, Dr. Ellis found himself wondering whether the presumably more affluent Dr. Wilson had ever been to one of those exclusive resorts. It didn't seem prudent to ask.

They exchanged greetings, and Dr. Ellis sat in the exceedingly comfortable chair. He imagined that it would be as easy as finding a Waffle House in the South to get someone relaxed and hypnotized in this chair.

"How are you doing today, Ted?"

"Very well, thank you."

"How would you like to begin?"

"First, I want to thank you again for your advice of last week. I took the initiative to sign up for an online dating service this week. I've spent some time flipping through the available profiles, but I haven't messaged anyone yet. I find I'm actually getting excited about the possibility of entering into a relationship in which I can share more of myself. I'll let you know in the future how the experience turns out."

"That's very good to hear. What else would you like to share?"

"If you remember, I told you that I initially arranged to start seeing you due to some feelings of unease. We haven't talked about those yet, so I was hoping to begin today."

"By all means. Please elaborate upon these feelings."

Dr. Ellis leaned in toward Dr. Wilson.

"I believe they might stem from some dreams I've been having. I've been regularly having a sex dream involving Aidra Fox, who I mentioned to you last week. In this dream, I see her, and we embrace. She's wearing a sexy and very short red dress. I recognize the dress from one of her videos. After we embrace, she says, 'Thank you.' She then drops her dress and takes off my clothes.

"After that we fall onto a bed. We proceed to have the most incredible lovemaking of my life, culminating in simultaneous whole-body convulsions. I actually get pictures of Mt. Vesuvius erupting violently in this dream as if this were a comedy movie with visual props. But then I get a sudden feeling of unease or of being unsettled. After that the dream ends."

"When did this dream first occur?"

"I don't really remember. Maybe about a year ago."

"Do you have any idea what this dream represents?"

Dr. Ellis leaned back, spread apart his arms, and had a puzzled expression. "I have absolutely no clue. I don't remember when I first saw the video in which she wore the red dress. Perhaps it was shortly after that when the dreams began. Other than that possibility, I'm at a loss to explain it. I've never had any other similar sex dreams."

Dr. Wilson continued with his most concerned therapist voice and appearance. "How about the unease that you mentioned? Is this solely an unease you perceive immediately after your dreams, or does it permeate your daily life also?"

"The unease isn't limited to just the day after I have the dream. In fact, there's often a faint hint of unease hovering, hummingbird-like, in the background of my consciousness. More recently it's occasionally popped into the foreground, and I sometimes worry that it might interfere with my performance with my patients. That's one reason why I wanted to discuss it with you. I can't definitely tie the unease to the dream, although the unease didn't seem to start until after the dreams began."

"Is there anything else going on that you feel might contribute to the unease?"

Dr. Ellis immediately thought about that last date he had, which still weighed heavily on his mind, but he wasn't about to tell Dr. Wilson anything about it.

"Nothing I can think of. I don't think it's related to the childhood trauma and self-esteem issues."

"Is there anything specific you'd like to try in order to address this unease? Do you feel that a mindfulness exercise would help?"

Dr. Ellis knew that he wasn't thrilled with being the patient who was asked to try these exercises, instead of the psychiatrist in charge who recommended them. Still, he was interested in understanding the source of the unease. He also would feel better and more in charge if he suggested the specific exercises to try.

"I suppose that when I awaken from the dream, or sense unease during the day, I could try an exercise to see if any cause is suggested."

"That sounds like a good plan. Additionally, you could be mindful of the exact degree to which the daily subconscious unease is affecting you."

Dr. Ellis adopted an optimistic expression. "All right. I'll try both of those strategies. I think that's a good start to addressing these concerns. Thanks. I'll also let you know if anything happens with the online dating service. I guess I'll see you in two weeks for our next session."

"I look forward to it, Ted. I hope you have an enjoyable couple of weeks."

They shook hands, and Dr. Ellis let himself out of the office. This session had gone well, though they hadn't discovered if the unease was definitely related to the recurrent dream.

It seemed odd to him that the sex dream ended in an unsettled manner. He was concerned that the dream might relate to the unsettled feeling that he continued to have about his last sexual encounter a year ago. Maybe that was making the unease worse for some reason.

Perhaps he should bring up that last encounter in their next session, if it seemed appropriate. Perhaps.

CHAPTER 19

MONDAY, WEEK 5

D etective Smith sat at her desk in the station expecting a busy day. She'd had promising findings from her review of the videos of Anna's recent trips to the grocery store. She planned to return to the store today and see if any of the employees recognized pictures she had made from the videos. She also needed to complete her review of the area's sexual assault records.

The detective had spent considerable time reviewing the store videos. She initially had no problem gaining access to them, thanks to a helpful store manager who was happy to bypass any problematic privacy issues or store policies. She first reviewed the Thursday night tapes. She was able to find a good image of Anna's alleged stalker entering the store.

His appearance was similar to that in the sketch Anna had assisted in producing. He wore a work shirt and long pants. The time stamp showed that the man had entered well prior to Anna, so he hadn't followed her to the store. He also wasn't seen following her out of the store. The store manager who had helped her didn't recognize the stalker.

She had then reviewed the Wednesday night video, which contained both surprising and chilling findings.

Detective Smith had located Anna entering and leaving the store, wearing shorts and a T-shirt. She also found images of the stalker, wearing a short-sleeve work shirt and shorts, entering and leaving the store. Anna had said she hadn't seen her stalker on Wednesday, so finding him on that night's video was significant. As in the Thursday video, he had entered well before Anna, indicating that he hadn't followed her to the store.

When Anna exited the store on Wednesday, it appeared that she truly was being followed. A man wearing a ball cap, dark athletic pants, a black raincoat-like jacket with a hood, and gloves was seen walking a few steps behind Anna.

The cameras only covered the store's entrance and exit area, so the two of them left the camera feed while she was still being followed. Almost immediately after that, a car entered the lane that Anna and her follower had been walking on.

A minute later, a man in shorts and a polo shirt appeared at the bottom of that lane. That seemed likely to be the man Anna had mentioned—the person who'd parked next to her. About the time he was entering the store, the stalker could be seen leaving the store and scanning the parking lot. After he completed his scan, he slowly headed left on the sidewalk that fronted the store.

The detective knew that a bus line had a stop in that direction, so it was likely that the stalker was a bus rider. If that were true, it would've been impossible for him to have stalked Anna to the store.

Detective Smith noted that the man in the athletic pants and jacket never reentered the camera zone. She also noted that his appearance was consistent with the vague description they had from Gwen about her attacker.

The detective had then reexamined the video footage for people entering the store earlier. She located the man in the athletic pants and jacket, who wore his cap but wasn't wearing gloves when he entered the store. The facial image was poor due to the ball cap, but he was white. The cap was a black Mizzou cap.

He seemed to be about the same height as the stalker. He didn't appear to be following anyone in particular into the store, and he entered well before Anna. The manager didn't recognize that individual either.

Detective Smith had obtained copies of the tapes and had still pictures made at the station of the two men in question. She knew that she needed to uncover the identity of the person who had followed Anna. His actions on Wednesday evening had been ominous. He could also be the person who'd attacked Gwen. This might be the big break they needed.

She planned to show these images to as many store employees as possible. Since all of the action had been late in the day the previous week, her plans were to make her visit in the late afternoon to catch employees from the later shift.

While awaiting that later hour she completed her records search. A review of all reports of sexual assault in the area in the past three years yielded no helpful results. Her search for local residents with any accusation or conviction for sexual assault also produced no one who fit their profile and wasn't currently incarcerated. She and her partner would need to visit the grocery store later if they hoped to get any significant information today.

A while after that, Detective Derek Williams was driving back to the station. He was alone, so his thoughts first drifted to the pastimes he enjoyed such as fishing and watching sports. He tried the radio, but since he was in a city vehicle, he was unable to enjoy the Sirius XM soul stations he loved. The poor listening choices forced him to concentrate on his case.

He had interviewed a Stephens College student in her apartment. She had been assaulted two nights previously. He was called in because the investigating officers labeled it as an out-door attempted sexual assault at night, similar to the cases he and Detective Smith were investigating. The officers thought it might have been committed by the same man. The detective initially worried that they might have another in the enlarging pool of victims of their serial attacker.

According to the report, the student, Sydney, who was twenty years old, told the officers that she was walking back to her apartment just before midnight on Saturday when a man jumped her from behind. She'd worn a white Alo crop top and a short white skirt that night. The attacker wrenched at her top and ripped her underwear, but he didn't pull down her skirt, fondle her, or touch her genitalia.

The attacker had slapped her hard, but she wasn't seriously injured, and she declined medical help at the time of the attack. She told the officers that her attacker didn't mention or display a gun. She noted that he'd verbally threatened her in what she thought sounded like a fake deep voice. She heard loud voices coming from a block or so away shortly after the attack began and said that her attacker ran when he heard the voices.

She'd been carrying a large designer tote, which held her wallet and laptop. She was on her phone at the time of the attack, and the phone was dislodged from her hand when she was hit. The tote and laptop remained at the scene, but she couldn't locate her phone afterward. The male officers who were called to the scene that night made the assumption that Sydney had been the target of a sexual assault that was interrupted, so the attacker took her phone so that the night wasn't a total loss.

Detective Williams had viewed this crime report and the related photos before speaking with the victim. He initially noticed several worrisome similarities to the other attacks they were investigating. Sydney was of average height and physically fit and had medium-length dark hair. She'd said she could tell that her attacker was white. She'd stated that he wasn't very tall. The attack and his touching of her underwear were done from behind, and it occurred outside late at night.

The notes taken at the time of the attack revealed that the location of the rip in her underwear was not near the right spot to have provided the attacker easy access to her genital area, however. They also showed that the wrenched top was not in a good location to have provided access to her breasts. The assault was on a sidewalk that was not nearly as secluded as the locations of the other attacks they had been investigating.

The detective pondered the similarities plus the other details, then put it together to reach a different conclusion from that of the responding officers. He wrote down that the clothing disruptions might have been a counter-measure intended to suggest that sexual assault was the objective of the attack, when in fact the goal was something else.

The objective wasn't theft, as the wallet, tote, and laptop would have been much more valuable than her phone. And if the attack had been meant to scare her, why take the phone? The detective speculated that the attacker may have been interested in something specific on Sydney's phone.

Detective Williams had been able to interview Sydney in her apartment. It was located in an older building that had been renovated. The apartment had a clean, modern kitchen that was off the living area. He saw a balcony outside a fashionable French door. The sitting area was cluttered with papers, books, and clothes strewn everywhere.

Sydney was thin and well tanned. Her hair was nicely done, and she was dressed in a form-fitting designer top and crisp white shorts. She moved some clutter and sat on the sofa while the detective took a chair. Sydney was calm and composed for the interview.

She responded to the detective's questions by stating that she was frightened at the time of the attack and noticed only a few details. She said the attacker wore a ski mask, but she was still able to tell that he was white. She didn't recognize anything about him. When he ran away, she saw that he wore jeans and a long-sleeve black shirt. She said she had no enemies or ex-boyfriends whom she was worried might have attacked her.

The detective asked Sydney if there could have been something damaging or embarrassing to someone on her phone. She said there wasn't anything like that, but she was hesitant and wasn't at all convincing with her reply. He pushed again and got the same answer.

The detective was left with the impression that something was off in this case. The many incongruencies made him continue to question the labeling of Sydney's attack as a sexual assault, which could be lumped with the other cases he and his partner were investigating.

He decided that he would need to return and talk to her at a later time. He needed to get her to open up about the possible presence of something significant in the messages or pictures on her phone. She seemed to be holding something back.

When he returned to the station, Detective Williams met with his partner. She informed him of her findings on the video reviews and of the plan to return to the grocery later in the afternoon for more interviews. He said he would accompany her, and he filled her in on his investigation of Sydney's attack.

He mentioned his theory of a simulated sexual assault being a countermeasure to cover up the real reason for the attack. He also pointed out that this assailant wore clothes different from those described by Gwen or seen on the grocery video.

After that he went to his desk to work on the report concerning his interview of Sydney. He left the conclusions open pending another visit with her later in the week. If this had been an attack by their serial assaulter, it would be the third attempt in a week by him, and that would be extremely concerning. But the detective made some personal notes that he believed something else was going on. He wrote that this incident almost certainly wasn't related to the other assaults.

In the late afternoon, the detectives drove to the grocery store where Anna's incidents of the prior week had occurred. They located the evening manager and showed him the pictures of the stalker and the person in the hat who had followed Anna. The manager didn't recognize either of them but suggested that the detectives talk with Lillian, one of the long-term checkout staff.

Lillian wore an apron over her T-shirt and jeans, and she appeared to be about fifty, with many streaks of gray coursing through her dark hair. She didn't recognize the person who had followed Anna, but she did recognize the stalker. She told the detectives his name was Gerry and he worked the day shift as a custodian at the mall. She said he seemed like a nice guy. The detectives thanked her and went back to the manager.

They asked if they could show the second image to the other employees. The manager agreed, and he took them around to everyone else working that shift. None of them recognized the man in the hat and jacket.

The detectives then went straight to the mall. They located the management offices and showed Gerry's picture to the supervisor on duty. They said that he might be a witness to something important and they needed his contact information. They informed the supervisor that Gerry wasn't in trouble and that this matter shouldn't reflect negatively on his employability. The supervisor produced the contact information and told them Gerry had gotten off work at 4:30.

The detectives thanked him and headed to Gerry's address, which was in an older and slightly rundown apartment building. When they located Gerry's unit, there was a subtle aroma of microwaved burritos emanating from it.

They knocked, and Gerry opened the door. He wore a uniform and had the previously described mustache and straggly brown hair. His facial expression displayed surprise and some uncertainty, but not fear. "Hello," he said tentatively.

Detective Williams introduced himself and Detective Smith, confirmed that they were at the correct apartment, and asked if they could come in.

"I guess so, but what's this about?"

The detectives stepped into his apartment. They took note of the minimal furniture, some of which appeared to be directly out of the dumpster-diving collection. The apartment was clean but disorganized. There were no stalker photos of Anna adorning the walls.

Detective Smith took the lead. "We want to talk with you about your trips to the grocery last Wednesday and Thursday. We identified you from entrance and exit photos those two evenings. Do you remember those trips?"

Gerry silently and slowly nodded in the affirmative.

"Let's talk about Thursday night first. Did you recognize anyone there that night?"

Gerry assumed a 'kid caught in the police flashlight at Lover's Lane' look. He appeared paralyzed and didn't immediately reply.

"Let me help you out here, Gerry." Detective Smith produced the image of Anna entering the store. She continued in a stern and authoritative voice. "This woman says that she saw you there that night, and that you were inappropriately staring at her. She said you've done that before. Now I know you want to cooperate with us, so let me ask again. Did you recognize anyone there that night?"

Gerry lowered his head and nodded again.

"Were you following her, Gerry?"

"No, I wasn't. I don't follow her. I was just at the store shopping, and I saw her."

"You said that you don't follow her. That sounds like an admission that you've seen her before—is that right?"

Gerry sheepishly nodded a yes.

"Can you tell us about the other times, please, Gerry?"

Gerry replied defiantly. "Well, she's so pretty and sometimes you notice a pretty girl. There's nothin' wrong with that. I seen her in the past in that grocery, and a takeout place, but I never followed her or bothered her."

"Okay, Gerry. Then please tell us about last Wednesday evening. Did you see her in the store that night?"

"Yes, but I didn't think she saw me. I'm not the one you need to worry about, though."

The detectives flashed concerned looks at each other. "What do you mean?" asked Detective Smith.

Gerry replied more rapidly and confidently. "When I seen her that night, I seen that there was a tough-looking dude following her. When I seen that, I started following both of them. I'm pretty sure that they didn't see me. When she checked out with her food, I seen that he was still following her. He didn't buy nothin'. I rushed up to check out with my food and tried to watch.

"When he started to head outta the store, I seen him grab some gloves from his jacket pocket and put them on. If you ever watched any cop shows you know it's a terrible sign when the bad guy pulls on some gloves. So as soon as I finished paying for my stuff, I ran out of the store. I couldn't see either of them in the parking lot. All I seen was some car leaving the lot, and some tall guy coming in the store, so I left.

"I worried about her the next day, and I was real relieved when I seen her at the grocery the next night."

Detective Smith continued. "Did you recognize the tough-looking dude?"

"No, I never seen him before."

"What made him look tough, Gerry?"

Gerry appeared thoughtful. "I couldn't see him too well, but he had a mean look. He was wearing a ball cap to hide his face, and that's not a good sign. He also had on a jacket and jeans, and it was hot out that night. All that gave me a bad guy vibe."

"How tall would you say he was?"

"He was about my height, so five ten or eleven."

Detective Williams took over then. "Thank you for answering our questions, Gerry. This has been very helpful." He handed Gerry his card. "If you see the tough dude again, please give us a call, or tell someone like a store manager to call the police."

Detective Smith stepped in. "Also, Gerry, you need to stop staring at that woman, or any other women. It's not a nice thing to do, and women are bothered by that behavior. Can you promise me that you won't do anything like that again?"

"Okay, I won't," he said quietly, with downcast eyes.

Detective Smith then asked Gerry what he was doing on June 28 of this year, and in July two years ago.

"I went to Branson to see my mom on June twenty-eighth this year 'cause that's her birthday. I think two years ago I couldn't see my mom on her birthday, so I went down for a week sometime in July instead. I don't remember what else I was doing then."

The detectives asked if they could call his mother for confirmation and he got her number for them. Detective Williams took it and told Gerry he was going to call right away. After four rings the call was answered.

"Mrs. Kiner, this is Detective Williams from the Columbia police. I don't want you to worry. Gerry's okay and he's not in trouble. We're with him now and he's helping us with a case. We had some questions he said that you could answer for us."

"Put him on, then, so's I know this is legit."

Detective Williams handed Gerry the phone and he spoke briefly to his mother, then handed the phone back.

"Mrs. Kiner, we're checking on a couple of times that Gerry said he left Columbia to see you. When was the last time he went to Branson to be with you?"

"On my birthday, June twenty-eighth. He done went back to Columbia that Sunday."

"He also said he saw you two summers ago in July, but he couldn't remember when it was that month."

She expelled an exasperated grunt. "Hang on. My executive secretary's not here so I gotta check the calendar on the fridge myself." There was a moderate pause. "He was here from July tenth to the eighteenth that year."

"Thank you very much for your help, Mrs. Kiner. Gerry's been very helpful to us in our case. Good evening."

The detectives thanked Gerry and left, conferring as they walked away. "First of all, Audra, we can eliminate Gerry as a suspect. He has alibis for both Anna's attack and the most recent one, so he's out."

His partner replied, "Additionally, did you glance at his hands? They were not white-collar hands."

"True dat. I got a gut feeling that the tough dude is our guy. He's white, the right height, and your description of his actions leaving the store Wednesday had 'assault in the dark parking lot' written all over them. I still feel that all of these attacks were random, making it a crazy coincidence that he would follow Anna last week."

"That brings up an issue I've been thinking about, Derek. We haven't yet produced a profile of the type of person we're searching for."

They reached the car and got in to continue the conversation on their drive, with Detective Williams behind the wheel. His partner turned to him and began speaking.

"It seems that this must be a fairly intelligent person, as he's been very careful to leave no evidence at the scene, other than the semen. He must also know his DNA isn't in the database. Prior to this month, his attacks have been fairly spaced out in time, so he can control his impulses.

"Although intelligent, he has degenerate instincts, so he may not be highly functioning. He also apparently has a type, liking fit young women. He's strong enough to be able to control and assault the women. What do you think?"

"I think you're on the mark, Audra. He's likely well educated, fairly young, and he either works out or has a job requiring heavy exertion. I doubt he's a successful white-collar type like Joe Friedman, though we can't rule that out."

Detective Smith replied, "We should keep this profile in mind when any potential suspects come up. We really need to find out who he is ASAP. It seems like he was on the prowl twice last week, so he's a serious threat now. Those recent parking lot incidents are ominous, and I sense we're running out of time."

Detective Williams surprised his partner with his droll rejoinder. "Yeah, I agree. We need to do our Holmes and Drew thing quickly and well."

CHAPTER 20

TUESDAY, WEEK 5

Detective Smith was at her desk working on the case. They finally had a viable suspect in the string of sexual assaults and beatings: the man seen following Anna out of the grocery. Unfortunately, they couldn't identify him.

There was a good chance he was also the person who'd attacked Gwen, but they couldn't identify him from the information they had after that attack either. This case had to be really frustrating for the detective. As she was working through this quandary, her telephone rang. When she picked it up, the desk officer informed her that she had an incoming call.

"It's a Stacy Palmer for you, Detective. She seems anxious to speak with you."

"Thanks. Please put her through."

"Stacy, this is Detective Smith. How are you today?"

"I'm fine, thanks. I have some important news for you, Detective. Yesterday, I regained some memory from the car ride with Monica the night she was attacked."

"That's great to hear. Do you think any of the memory is relevant to our case?"

"Yes, that's exactly why I called. I didn't remember a lot, but then we hadn't been driving for very long before the crash.

"There was one significant thing that Monica told me. She had a favorite necklace that she wore everywhere she went. She said she was wearing it that night, but didn't notice until she left the ER that it was no longer on her. When she noticed it was missing, she said she had a vague recollection that the attacker had taken it from her."

"That's really important information. Are you able to describe the necklace?"

"Yes. It was a Tiffany rose gold *oui* necklace."

The detective looked down as she jotted her notes. "Okay. This is crucial, Stacy. We need to prove, as best as we possibly can, that the necklace was Monica's, in case we locate it. Do you know where she got it or who gave it to her?"

"She bought it as a gift to herself. She wanted something that made her feel really good about herself but that wasn't obviously super expensive. That's why she chose the *oui* necklace instead of her first preference, which was a necklace that had the word *Rock* spelled out in diamonds."

"Do you know about when and where she purchased it?"

"I would say she got it about two years ago. I don't know if it was online or at a store."

"Okay. Now for the really important question. Do you have a picture of her wearing it?"

"I'm sure I do, as she always wore it."

The detective smiled to herself.

"Would you please do me a favor and search through your pictures for the best one of her wearing it? I'll give you my direct number and you can text me the picture. If we find someone who has the necklace, or who sold it, we need proof that Monica did own and wear that particular necklace. It would have been ideal if that had gone into the police report the night of her attack, but we can still work with this information."

"I'll search through my pictures as soon as I can, Detective. I'll text you the best image that I have. I really hope this helps."

"If the person who attacked her still has the necklace and shows it around, or if he sold it, this could be the lead we need to bring him in. I'm very sorry that you needed to recall such painful memories, but I'm thankful that one of them is potentially helpful. Thanks so much for calling."

"You're welcome, Detective. Please get this bastard."

"We'll do our best, Stacy. I'll look forward to your text."

Maybe the day's earlier frustrations were going to vanish. This could be the slipup from the attacker that the detectives needed so they could find him. Detective Smith would share this news with her partner later. The day was starting off very well.

Anna had another marvelous day at work. The clinic had a resident from the medical center working with them for two weeks. The staff and the doctors usually looked forward to residents joining them, which happened about eight weeks each year. Although there were exceptions, most of the residents were kind and treated the staff well. The staff especially appreciated weeks like this.

The resident working with them now was Dr. Luke Sterling. He was young and had Brad Pitt looks with a Tom Hanks personality, so the staff were perpetually in a superb mood. They liked him almost as much as they had liked Jennifer, the last resident who had worked with them. Having a pleasant resident made managing the clinic seem as easy as finding a Girl Scout selling cookies in early March. Everyone helped each other and never thought of complaining. Anna didn't have to worry about leaving for her therapy.

When she arrived at Dr. Ellis's office, Anna waited only briefly before she was called back. She had an eager bounce to

her step. Although she had mild fears about how she would identify her attacker in her memories, she greatly anticipated uncovering those crucial, final portions of her memory and finding that
ID. She could barely contain herself with that anticipation. She
entered Dr. Ellis's therapy room feeling like a Heisman winner
striding to the podium.

"Good afternoon, Doctor. How are you today?"

"I'm doing very well, and it appears as if your day has been
more than satisfactory."

"Yes, it's been great, and I'm excited about our session."

"That's excellent. Please have a seat."

Anna no longer worried about her seat being the closest to the
exit door. She was quite comfortable in this setting now. She didn't
even mind how dark the room was, which usually was off-putting
to her rather than calming. She was happy to be here. She noticed
that Dr. Ellis seemed equally happy to be here, and she was glad he
was invested in her care and had helped her to this point.

"We have several issues to review today. Do you have anything new to bring up before we discuss the prior issues?"

"No, nothing new. Fortunately, I haven't been followed
again. I'm mainly excited about the possibility of coming up with
the last of my memory today."

"I'm well aware of that. Let's begin with a brief review of
some of the issues from last time. Did you acquire any pepper
spray or other personal protection yet?"

Anna was smiling and sitting forward. It seemed like everything they needed to talk about today was positive. "Yes. I bought
it over the weekend, and it's in my purse now."

"That's good to know. Have you made a decision about
whether to share with the police your worries about Glen?"

"I want to bring him up at some point, but I'm going to hold off on that for a bit because the police are looking into some other leads, and my roommate Sonia is too."

Dr. Ellis raised his eyebrows. "What's Sonia investigating for you? Is that her area of expertise?"

Anna laughed at that assumption. Sonia would have been thrilled if she'd heard the doctor's question. "No, Sonia's an aesthetician, but fancies herself an amateur sleuth. She remembered another man from my past who also might be a suspect.

"He was only a friend, so you haven't heard about him from me. She remembered some things about our friendship that are worrisome. She plans to look into various aspects of his life and see if she discovers anything that makes him more of a suspect. If she finds something troubling, I'll tell the detectives about him."

"I see. Sonia sounds like the baker and caterer who help police solve crimes in some of the Hallmark shows. The two of you are actively examining all of the angles. You also mentioned that the police are looking into some leads. What are they working on?"

The session was going fabulously for Anna today. Another positive to discuss. The difference for her between the earlier sessions and now was immeasurable.

"They hope to look at the video footage from the grocery on the nights that I was followed and that I saw the stalker. I haven't heard from them yet about that. I'll be seeing them later today and might get some good news from the video review, if they were able to complete it."

Dr. Ellis smiled broadly. "I see there's a great deal of activity occurring in regard to searching for your assailant. It's encouraging to know that so much is happening in the investigation. How does all of this activity impact the terror you've been feeling at times?"

Anna furrowed her brow. Finally a difficult question, but she could put a good spin on it. "On the one hand, I still get flashes of wondering who exactly the assailant is, wondering if he knows me, and worrying about how to avoid him. The pepper spray helps reduce the terror somewhat. Plus, with all the possibilities I mentioned, I'm increasingly hopeful that a suspect will be identified and captured soon. If I can uncover the memory that helps me to identify my assailant today, I suspect I'll feel even better."

"We'll certainly try our best to uncover that memory. Are you ready for your hypnosis?"

Anna practically jumped out of her chair with enthusiasm. "I'm more than ready. I'm in launch mode and all systems are go."

"Okay then. I'll take that as an enthusiastic yes. You know what to do, Anna. Slide back in the chair until you're resting against the seatback. Relax your arms and legs. Relax your neck muscles. Try to empty all thoughts from your consciousness and close your eyes. Take slow, deep breaths."

Dr. Ellis then verbally led Anna down the hypnosis hallway. He concluded with, "You're back in the alley. Remember what's happened so far. You felt paralyzed and frozen, and then you were sexually assaulted. What happened next?"

Anna first scrunched her closed eyes, but then her mouth formed a frightened *O* and she began to sweat. She spoke rapidly.

"I felt like a large block of ice had been encasing my whole mind and body, and it suddenly thawed, which let me be able to express myself. I shout 'No, no!' and I start to straighten up. He immediately reacts, saying 'Shh, now shh!' with a harsh, terrifying, and controlling tone. I shout 'No' even louder, and then he becomes very angry and viciously grabs me.

"Everything's happening at the same time. I'm shouting 'No!' while he's grabbing me and getting angry and while I'm starting to fight. It seems like my arm flailing is an attempt both to get away and to hit at him, but I don't know if I landed any blows. This all happens very rapidly, and then he throws me into the trash cans. This whole section of the memory probably took place in a time period of twenty seconds or less, I'd guess."

Anna raised her eyelids during the last portion of that recitation. She turned her head slightly and focused her deep, soulful, and thankful green eyes upon Dr. Ellis.

"I'm so grateful that I finally have all of my memory back. I think I've remembered all of the trauma I suffered that made me develop the amnesia. I also finally have the ammunition needed to identify my attacker, as I'm sure I would definitely recognize him saying that 'Shh' phrase."

When Anna finished, Dr. Ellis seemed momentarily mesmerized by her recitation, and his eyes seemed unfocused while gazing at her. He quickly regrouped before responding.

"That sounds wonderful for you. Can you now fill me in on how you feel emotionally after locating this final memory?"

Anna was sitting forward. Her eyes sparkled, and she was gesturing with her hands. There was an electricity in the room.

"There are so many emotions. I feel so much relief that I've recovered the whole memory now. At times I worried that we wouldn't be able to unearth all of it, and I'd be left constantly wondering, like viewers after the last episode of that TV show *Lost*. That worry is now gone. I'm also relieved that I don't have to dread any more hypnosis sessions.

"And finally, I can work with the police to identify my attacker now. I was certain that an ID, probably a verbal one, was somewhere in my memory, and we found it today. The tone of his voice saying 'Shh, now, shh' feels unique, and it also chills me to the core. I know without a doubt that I'll recognize that voice if I hear him say that expression again. I previously said that I didn't think I'd recognize his moaning, but that one phrase he spoke is embedded in my brain now."

Dr. Ellis looked very happy for her. "It seems as if you're going to have a monumental meeting with the police later today. Between your newfound identifier and their potential video review results, it's bound to be dramatic."

"I certainly hope so. I'm very optimistic now, but I have my reservations. I've had a few meetings with them in the past when my expectations were crushed. We'll see how this meeting goes."

"What are your feelings concerning continuing with our meetings?"

Anna relaxed into the back of the chair. "I'd like to continue, if possible, just until there's a good suspect. My issues of dealing with the sexual assault will be long-term, so I think I can wait for a bit before starting with a sexual trauma counselor."

"I understand. We can keep our scheduled appointment for later this week, then. We won't need any more hypnosis. I'll be very anxious to hear the results of your discussion with the police today. This was a very positive session, Anna. You've been handling the mass of emotions coming from all aspects of your attack, along with the uncovered memories, brilliantly. I'm proud of you, and you should be very proud of yourself. You did it!"

Anna had the feeling that she had just completed a dramatic journey with more ups and downs than a dinghy sailing through a hurricane. "Thank you, Doctor. If my attacker can just be caught, this will be nearly over. I very much appreciate all of your help to this point." Anna stood to leave.

"You're most welcome," replied Dr. Ellis, who stood and extended his hand.

Anna took the proffered hand with gratitude, then left the room. She knew she shouldn't become too excited when thinking about meeting the police, but she couldn't help it. She would be able to identify the attacker now. This was the ultimate goal of her agreeing to attend these therapy sessions. The sessions succeeded. Plus, the police might have some important news from their video review. It seemed as if today's meeting with the police couldn't possibly disappoint her.

She had continued to frequently wonder who her attacker was. Was it Brian? Was it Glen? Could it still be her stalker, or was it a complete stranger that she didn't know? They couldn't get to this answer fast enough for her. But at least the likelihood that they would answer this question was much greater now than it was even a few days ago. She smiled with this thought.

Dr. Ellis was beside himself with excitement. Anna had achieved the goal of finding a method of identifying her attacker through their therapy together. They were successful together. His earlier daydreams were coming true.

He was going to conclude his best and most satisfying case ever. He had visions of being the hero standing boldly atop a low hill, with bright rays of sunshine flooding down on him. Sure he'd planned to reduce the amount of his self-esteem that was derived from his patient successes, but he couldn't help himself now. If the police could just locate a suspect for Anna's voice confirmation, he'd feel overwhelmed with this achievement.

So why was something nagging just a little at him now? What in the world was it?

Anna left Dr. Ellis's office and drove immediately to the police station. When she entered the lobby, she noted that the desk officer wasn't familiar to her, so she had to inform him of the reason for her visit. She didn't receive the VIP treatment that was usually accorded to her there. After a short wait, Anna saw Detective Smith coming out to escort her to the offices in the back.

They greeted each other pleasantly and shared small talk on the walk to the interview room they would use. Detective Williams was waiting there and greeted her also. Anna sat at the table opposite the two detectives.

"What do you have for us today, Anna?"

Anna's smile beamed at them.

"I hope you remember that I've mentioned several times that I was convinced there was a way, which I hadn't yet remembered, for me to identify my attacker. Well, today was the day. I remembered it. Let me tell you like it occurred in the memory. I had told you previously that I felt frozen and unable to move or speak while he raped me. I don't know if the frozen state was due to fear, shock, uncertainty, or something else.

"Today I remembered that as soon as he withdrew"—Anna grimaced awkwardly at that word—"the frozen state vanished. I immediately shouted 'No, no,' and then several things happened at once. He angrily said, 'Shh, now, shh.' I began flailing my arms as I had mentioned before, and I shouted 'No!' again. Then he got even angrier. That's when he grabbed me hard and threw me into the trash cans.

"I know with absolute certainty that I would recognize him saying that 'Shh, now, shh' phrase. I also verbally expressed my opposition to his disgusting actions twice. I realize that this opposition occurred after his assault. I think the delay was due to my frozen state. Also, I physically expressed my opposition by the arm flailing I'd mentioned to you before. I got the feeling that the flailing was an attempt both to strike at him and to get free."

The detectives glanced at each other with optimism in their expressions.

"Wow, there certainly was a lot of detail in that memory you recalled today," replied Detective Smith. "Let's first focus on the phrase you mentioned. Why do you think you could recognize your attacker saying that, but not recognize his moaning as you stated before?"

"It was his tone of voice and something in the way he said it. It seemed very unique to me, and very macabre. Because of those qualities, I feel it was imprinted indelibly on my brain. I know that sounds odd, since a day ago I wasn't even aware of that memory. But I believe that the memory was always there and was never going to leave. It just needed to be found."

"It's good to know that you're so certain," replied Detective Smith. "In terms of voicing your opposition to the attacker, it's still a little of an issue that it was done late during the attack."

Anna's expression became puzzled. "Isn't it important that I never said yes or encouraged his actions?"

"Absolutely. We haven't talked about this before, but do you recall making any verbalizations at all prior to saying no?"

"No, none."

"No moaning, sighing, or any sounds or words that might suggest to him that you were okay with everything that was happening."

Anna tensed up. "Definitely not."

"That's very important to know. You mentioned the anger again today. Could you pinpoint the cause of his anger with this memory?"

"I had the impression that he got angry because I was resisting. So, getting back to identifying the attacker, is there a way to do a voice ID lineup?"

Detective Williams chimed in with some enthusiasm. "Voice IDs can be done. They aren't considered as valid as visual IDs. They can be one piece of evidence, but aren't ideal as the only or primary evidence. We don't do them in a lineup. We usually tape people in an interview room and have you listen, in real time or later."

Detective Smith said, "That discussion provides a good segue into our video findings. After reviewing the grocery video, we have news, but I'll leave it to you to decide whether it's good or bad."

She told Anna about the video findings of someone definitely following her, just not her alleged stalker. She informed Anna of the alibis her stalker had. She told Anna that the store images weren't great, but they planned to look at mugshots to see if any resembled the images. She slid over to Anna the best picture they had of the person who had followed her.

"You're right, Detective, I can't see his face well. I can't say that I recognize him from this picture."

Despite relaying that message, she also couldn't rule out the possibility that it was Glen or Brian on the video. She was already worried about Glen, and ever since Sonia had injected the Brian possibility into her thoughts, visions of him flashed through Anna's brain at regular intervals. Now with her stalker no longer being a suspect, she felt even more worried about these two men from her past, but she was still uncertain about identifying them to the detectives now.

Detective Williams took over. "Let me get back to the voice ID you asked about. There's only one realistic way to use that in your situation. If we come up with a good suspect, we could have the person read your phrase in our interview room while record-ing it. We would play it for you later and hope that you could conclusively identify him by his voice."

"Thank you, Detective. I just hope that we can eventually find a suspect. I sincerely want to listen for and positively identify the bastard who said that phrase to me."

"This was a good meeting today," said Detective Smith. "I feel we have more potential to locate your attacker now than we've ever had before. We don't like to give guarantees, but I feel really optimistic." The detective was directing positive vibes toward Anna. "I assume that you aren't expecting to recall any further clues to your attacker in any upcoming sessions?"

"That's right."

"Well, thank you very much for your initial decision to agree to the therapy, which seems like it was successful. Hopefully we'll speak with you soon with some results, Anna."

As Detective Smith walked her out to the lobby, Anna thanked her for being so supportive through this tragedy. Anna pointed out that a lot of her optimism and ability to handle every-thing was due to the kind feelings and strong support she'd gotten from the detective. The detective thanked her as she left, then returned to her partner.

"Are you going to review the mugshots, Audra?"

"Why is it that I'm always rewarded with the time-consuming tasks?"

Audra knew her partner was not part of the problem that she and other female members of the force felt as far as prestige and assignments, but she had to push a little. It was a constant frustration.

"Protocol. You're the junior member of the team."

"All right. I'll get to it soon. I'm not sure how we're going to get viable suspects to attempt getting a voice ID from Anna or from Gwen, though. Maybe the information about Monica's necklace will lead us somewhere. Otherwise, we might need some new information to just fall into our laps."

CHAPTER 21

WEDNESDAY, WEEK 5

D r. Ellis had another new patient on his schedule this morning. He had no information about her reason for the appointment. He was only aware of her name, Alex, and her age, twenty-five. He hoped her story would be interesting and worthy of his expertise.

The young woman was escorted in by the female office assistant. The patient was on the shorter side, with a plain face, a plain style to her brunette hair, an unremarkable figure other than being slightly overweight, and an unassuming demeanor. If you checked the dictionary under 'mousy,' you might find her picture. The glasses she wore were even quite plain.

She wore a green midi dress and white sandals. She carried a simple white purse that was not from a designer label, and she wore a simple mall-kiosk watch with a white band. She had no other jewelry. She had on minimal lipstick, and her fingernails were not painted.

When she first saw Dr. Ellis, her facial expression changed from timid to worried. Dr. Ellis introduced himself and indicated that she should sit in the comfortable chair across from his therapist chair. She glanced around the room, then tentatively sat, and her mouth contracted in a grim expression as she watched the assistant exit the room and close the door.

Dr. Ellis began. "Good morning. I'm Dr. Ellis. Shall I address you as Alex or as Ms. Templeton?"

Her answer was whispered so softly it was almost inaudible. "Either is okay. I'm confused, though. I thought I was going to see a Dr. Linda Keller."

"Dr. Keller had to leave the practice suddenly due to family issues. Her scheduled patients were all reassigned, and you should have been informed of the change. I'm very sorry if you weren't. I sense that you might not be comfortable with the switch. Would you like to discuss your worries?"

The patient avoided making eye contact. "I, well, I was really hoping to see a woman psychiatrist."

"Unfortunately, with Dr. Keller leaving, we have no women on the staff now. We're a small group. We're in the process of recruiting a new female group member, but that process usually takes months. If you're only interested in seeing a woman for your therapy, we can cancel today's session without charge. There are other practices in town with female psychiatrists. What's your preference?"

The patient was tearing up and grabbed some tissues from her purse. She replied with a shaky but more audible voice. "My insurance only covers two practices. The other one that's covered didn't have an appointment available with a woman for six months. I really don't think I can wait."

Dr. Ellis replied in his most gentle voice. "Let me offer this option, then, Ms. Templeton. Would you consider seeing me for one session today to find out how tolerable it is for you? You may change your mind at any time."

"Well, I really want to talk with someone about my problem now." She paused for several seconds before continuing. "I...I guess we can try it."

"Okay. Why don't we start slowly, and you tell me at any time if this becomes too uncomfortable. What's the reason for your visit today?"

It seemed as if Alex was attempting to sink deeper into the chair, to the point of vanishing completely. "Something horrible happened to me last year. I was…" She paused, and her speech volume became very low again. "I was taken advantage of. Thoughts of it have gotten worse for me recently. They are really affecting my work and my life outside of work now."

"What else are you able to share with me about this issue?"

Her eyes widened and reeked of desperation. She replied slowly in a monotone but with normal volume.

"I can't seem to get through an entire day at work without these thoughts intruding and making me lose my concentration. I have bad dreams at night and lose sleep because of them. The loss of sleep makes me work less efficiently. It's noticed by my boss and coworkers, but I can't bring myself to tell them the reason for the changes."

"What's your profession?"

"I'm an office assistant. It's sort of a glorified secretarial position."

"When did your thoughts begin to worsen?"

She paused briefly before replying, "Earlier this summer."

Dr. Ellis leaned in with a kindly expression. "I know this is the really difficult question for you, Ms. Templeton. Are you willing to describe the traumatic event to me? Are you willing to tell me what you mean by being taken advantage of?"

The patient recoiled and looked as if Dr. Ellis had suggested she jump out of a plane without a parachute. For a moment she appeared frozen and unable to speak or move. Finally, she replied, "I suppose I'll have to explain what happened, as I really feel that I need some help now. I'm so ashamed and embarrassed about it, though. I hate these feelings, and I worry they'll worsen if I talk about it at all."

The doctor leaned back. "Just take your time and tell me as much as you feel able to."

She bent her head down and spoke directly into her lap. "I haven't dated a lot in my life. It certainly hasn't been as often as I'd like. Last year I decided to try and be more proactive about dating. Reluctantly, I joined one of the online dating sites. I didn't reach out to any men but waited for them to contact me. I've been rejected enough in the past to know that if I made the first contact it would lead to more rejection.

"I had a few responses, but most of the men didn't seem interested in continuing contact. I was invited on only one date. That was just for coffee, and when it was over, the man didn't ask for my phone number. My experience to that point was really discouraging."

She slowed her pace of speech. "Finally, I met someone who appeared nicer and more interested. His profile picture was attractive, and he was well educated. We had some similar interests, as we were both hikers who also liked to canoe on some of the rivers in Missouri. We messaged for several days, back and forth."

She ceased talking and looked as if continuing would be nearly impossible for her.

"Please go on, Ms. Templeton."

Her hands began fidgeting, and she continued to stare into her lap. "He, uh, suggested a date at a nice restaurant. I was excited, but also worried and unsure, as he was much more attractive than me. We agreed to meet at the restaurant.

"I should've picked up on the first red flag when I got there. He was already seated and he waved. He was nice-looking enough, I guess, but he wasn't the person that I saw in his profile picture, and he was a little shorter than he listed.

"When I got to the booth, we exchanged names to make sure we were each meeting the right person. He then immediately gave a somewhat plausible explanation for his deception. He told me his actions weren't a Cyrano de Bergerac story or a catfishing scheme. He said that he was being very careful because of his job.

"He said that since so many people have access to the profile picture, he didn't want to chance someone sending his real picture throughout social media, possibly attached to negative comments. I accepted his explanation." She abruptly stopped as if that was the maximum she could relate at one time.

Dr. Ellis could see that he would need to tease it out of her. "Then what happened?"

"Well, we continued with our meal, and it was an enjoyable date. He was well spoken. He was considerate enough to be interested in my life, and we spoke mostly about me. I guess that should've been another red flag.

"Anyway, our meal was very good and he didn't encourage me to drink too much. He held my hand, which made me blush. I have to admit I was thrilled with the attention I was receiving from someone many women would be excited to be with. He paid and I was happy to see that he was a good tipper."

She hesitated, then became even more somber in her recitation, which was still directed at her lap.

"When our meal was over and it was time to leave, we walked outside together. I didn't know what to expect next, as all kinds of thoughts were racing through my brain. Would he suggest a short walk holding hands? Would he ask for my number? Would he ask me on another date? Would he hug me? Would he kiss me?

"None of those thoughts matched his actual plans, though. He asked how I'd gotten to the restaurant, which seemed odd to me.

When I said that I'd driven, he asked from what part of town. I was really confused then, but I answered. He said that he lived within a long walking distance from the restaurant, but he'd taken an Uber so he could be fresh for our date. He said that he'd like to see me home, as a gentleman always sees a lady safely home after dark.

"Since my car was there, he asked if he could ride with me for my safety. He said that he'd be able to walk home from my area of town. He said that even though it would be a long walk, he'd be cheerful from our date. It all sounded so good...maybe too good."

She looked up then and said, "Doctor, you know those cartoons where someone has a devil giving advice on one shoulder and an angel on the other? This was just like that, with a common-sense angel on one shoulder and a devil-may-care one on the other. I really have no idea why I ignored the common-sense angel. I told him I'd be glad to drive him to my house and then he could walk home.

"When we reached my house and parked, we both got out. He said he'd just walk me to my door for safety. I got strong warning signals from the common-sense angel, but fantasies of a good night kiss from the devil-may-care side, so I agreed.

"When we reached the door, he grabbed my hands with his, looked into my eyes, and thanked me for a wonderful date. He started to turn and leave, but then he asked if he could just use my bathroom before his long walk home. The warning signals became ear-piercing, but again I ignored them and invited him in."

The patient lowered her gaze back into her lap before continuing. She appeared to be composing herself for the next portion of her recitation. There was a significant pause, and Dr. Ellis interjected, "Are you okay with continuing?"

"I'm not sure if I can bring myself to actually say what happened next. It was so awful and devastating."

After another long pause, she seemed to gather the minimal strength she needed to continue. She appeared to be nearly in a trance, and she was glassy-eyed. Her hands were gripped tightly together.

"When he came out of the bathroom, where he'd been for a long time, he was a different person. He was kind of wild-eyed and agitated. He grabbed me and forcibly carried me into the bedroom. I fought and started to yell.

"That's when he threatened me with severe injuries, or worse, if I continued to resist him or yell. He turned me around and unzipped my dress and yanked it off. He yanked off my underwear." Alex was very tearful as she was barely able to continue. "He apparently pulled down his pants, then he entered me from behind like a filthy dog. I was shaking and crying and feeling helpless and hopeless."

She broke down to cry some more, then wiped her eyes. Dr. Ellis grabbed her some tissues during that time, then he sat back down.

"The only other thing I remember is a small sense of relief, as it felt like he'd put on a condom before assaulting me. When he finally got off me, I didn't even look to check for the condom. I didn't want to look in his direction for any reason. I just lay there bawling my eyes out. A short time later I heard my front door close."

She stopped talking as massive sobs engulfed her and took over the room. It was a couple of minutes later before she was able to speak again. She reported the last part hurriedly.

"I was mortified, horrified, and incredibly ashamed. I didn't know what I was going to do. I didn't know how I was going to go about my normal life after that. I was too ashamed to tell any of my friends or my parents. I was too ashamed to call the police.

"I figured I wasn't going to get pregnant or get an infection since he'd used the condom. Otherwise, I had no plan and no response to being assaulted." She looked completely defeated and near collapse after finally finishing her highly emotional description of the events.

"I'm so very sorry that this horrible tragedy happened to you. Why don't you take a moment to recover, and I'll grab some water for you."

Dr. Ellis took a bottle of water from his mini refrigerator and brought it to his distraught patient. She thanked him and they sat briefly while she consumed a few sips. Dr. Ellis then softly continued. "If I may ask, when did this occur?"

Alex looked down in her lap again. "It was in May of last year."

"And since then, you haven't told anyone what happened that night?"

"No. Not a word to anyone."

"How were you able to handle all of this initially?"

She raised her head but glanced around the room while she replied, "I tried to just accept the shame, and my part in letting it happen, and live day to day."

"Ms. Templeton, you must understand that you had no part in that assault occurring. No matter what you might believe about your judgment and decisions during that night, nothing was your fault. Everything that happened can be blamed entirely on the subhuman animal who assaulted you. This understanding should be an important part of any long-term healing plan for you."

Dr. Ellis was shaking as he finished saying that, but he gathered himself together and paused to let his advice sink in. "Now, with that being said, how did the last year go for you?"

Alex spoke in a soft voice. She was making some eye contact.

"I think I forced much of that night's events into my subconscious. I don't know if that was denial or if I was suppressing the memories. I haven't tried dating since then, but otherwise I was able to get through most days without the image of that evening bothering my daily routine. I couldn't enjoy romantic movies, but for the most part I tried not to dwell on that night."

"You mentioned earlier that your thoughts of that night resurfaced and worsened recently. Why do you think that happened?"

"I know exactly why. The worsening happened immediately after I heard about that woman who was attacked while running through the park. I wondered if it was him."

"Do you have any reason to believe the person who attacked you also attacked that woman recently?"

Alex was sitting more comfortably as she replied in a normal volume, "Not really, but the idea of an unwanted assault made me immediately think about him."

"You earlier mentioned troublesome dreams and thoughts intruding on your concentration at work. What happens in the dreams and what specific thoughts are interfering with your days?"

"It's the same in both. I have nightmares that recreate the attack and the terror it caused me. During the days, I have flashbacks about the attack. My attacker knows where I live. If he also attacked that woman recently, then he's still acting on his ugly desires, and he might come after me again, even though I always keep everything locked now." She shuddered.

"Do you have any ideas as to what might help you reduce the dreams and flashbacks?"

"I suppose if he were caught it would help immensely."

"Does that thought make you want to consider going to the police now with the details of your attack?"

She stopped for a few seconds before replying. "I think I'd be too embarrassed, both by my decisions that night and by waiting for over a year to report it."

Dr. Ellis tried to exude as much empathy and confidence as possible with his reply.

"I'm sure that many sexual assaults go unreported for many reasons. I'm also sure that the police are well aware of the non-reporting. I assume that they would be more likely to appreciate you reporting a crime than they would be to chastise you for the wait time in reporting it. Plus, as you've pointed out, the best way for you to be rid of your nightmares and flashbacks is for your attacker to be caught."

"I just don't know. I wonder how much help I can be to the police. I'm fairly sure he didn't use his real name with me."

"What led you to that conclusion?"

She paused a few seconds, then replied in a regular pace of speech and while making fair eye contact. "Several things. After my initial shame and fear diminished somewhat, I got very angry about the assault. This was out of character for me, but I attempted to track him down. I got on the dating website, and his profile had been removed. He'd given me his name as Todd, but he never mentioned a last name.

"I remembered that when I got to the restaurant for our date, the hostess checked the reservation, and it was for a Todd Scott. I searched Facebook and Instagram for that name, and I couldn't find anyone with his picture. I searched for anyone in the Columbia area with that name and found nothing. He hadn't given me a cell number or an email address. I decided that everything I thought I knew about him was a lie, and I had no way to find him.

"So I'm not sure how much help I could give the police. I could pick him out of a lineup, but I don't have a way of locating him to be in the lineup in the first place. I didn't see a car that he was driving, and he paid the bill in cash, so I didn't see a credit card. He's essentially a ghost."

Dr. Ellis was vexed at this situation. It wasn't going to be easy to help her. "Let's consider some potential options to reduce your fears and help you get through your days. You could decide to go to the police and hope that they can locate your assailant based on your description of him. You could try to comfort yourself with the fact that even though he knows where you live, he hasn't chosen to attack you again, so you're likely safe.

"You could carry around a personal protection device. You could see a sexual assault counselor, if your insurance will cover that. You could attend a support group and get advice from others in your predicament. All of these are possible approaches for you to take. Maybe you should take some time to consider them and decide which, if any, seems best for you. Also, remember that more than one can be an option."

The shy Alex Templeton reemerged as she clutched her purse tightly while replying. "I guess those are all methods that might help my anxiety, Doctor. I'll spend some time thinking about them. I can't really run the options past any friends or family, since no one knows about my assault."

"Why don't you also consider calling your insurance company and ask about coverage for sexual assault specialists? A call like that wouldn't be entered into your record, so you would still maintain privacy concerning the attack."

"Okay. You've given me a lot to consider. I don't know which way I'm leaning now, but I feel like this session has helped. We've talked about my fears, and you've given me some possible ways to deal with them. It feels like just telling this to someone will help me somewhat.

"I don't want to schedule another visit with you if that's okay. This one was traumatic enough for me. It was one of the hardest things I've ever done. I surprised myself that I could tell you so much about that night."

She appeared completely spent, but her shoulders were held high, and she made good eye contact.

"I think your plans are appropriate. Maybe just talking about this will reduce your dreams and the intrusive thoughts at work. Let me give you my office phone and email. That way if you want to run any future thoughts or ideas by me, you don't need to spend the time or expense of an office visit.

"You're welcome to reach out to me at any time. You should be aware that the contact information I gave you is for the office, so if you send me a message over a weekend, I likely won't respond until Monday." Dr. Ellis handed her his business card.

"Thank you very much for this information, and for listening to me today, Doctor. I'm glad that I stayed and gave this a chance."

"You're quite welcome, and I sincerely hope that this will reach a good conclusion for you. Have a good day."

They shook hands and the patient left the office. Dr. Ellis reflected on this session. He hoped this new patient would take her story to the police. There was a significant chance that her attacker was the serial rapist who had attacked Anna and the other women, the man the police were searching for. If so, Alex was the only person who could give a visual identification.

He knew that he couldn't push her toward this plan of action. He could only encourage her to reach her own conclusions. She didn't seem nearly as strong as Anna, so going to the police would be very difficult for her. But what strength she did have might end up being the only hope for justice in this situation. He took even this small possibility as fuel for optimism. The chances of finding Anna's attacker were certainly better today than yesterday.

CHAPTER 22

WEDNESDAY PM, WEEK 5

Detective Smith was in her office. This was her planned time for reviewing mugshots and the accompanying information. There was a new and very viable suspect for the serial assaults, and they needed to learn his identity. The man's actions as seen on CCTV, when he followed Anna out of the grocery store last week, were reminiscent of virtually every gruesome unsub depicted on *Criminal Minds*. There wasn't a clear picture of him, however.

The detective had a copy of the best image with her, but it was unlikely that any of the pictures she had grabbed to review would be recognizable as the man in the image. The hat he wore and the angle of his face limited the ability to identify him.

When she sorted through the mugshots, her suspicions were confirmed. All she was able to do was whittle the list down to a group of white males the approximate size of the suspect, to be available for future use. She further reduced the size of the list to twelve by eliminating men with tattoos on their right hands.

It was some progress to have this list, but not much. She randomly formed six-packs of the shots for use later if they ever had a victim who saw enough to possibly pick out their suspect, which didn't seem too likely at this point.

She then received a text message that brightened her day. It was from Stacy Palmer, and it was a close-up of Monica wearing the necklace she'd lost when she was attacked. The detective had what she needed to start her search, and she would go to the local pawn shop in the morning to see if it had been turned in. Maybe this would be the break that they needed.

Sonia waited anxiously in the small independent spa for her scheduled special client to arrive. The spa had a front reception and waiting area with large plate-glass windows overlooking the street. Behind that area was a hallway going to the back of the building and passing six treatment rooms, three on each side.

Sonia was in her room, wearing her uniform of tight-fitting black scrubs. After extensive sleuthing, she had located this special client and decided she needed to get to know the young woman. Sonia delivered an envelope to the woman's workplace. It informed her that she had won a free facial and dermaplaning at the spa, and she should contact Sonia to schedule it. The woman replied and the scheduled time was now.

At that moment, as if on cue, the young woman was escorted into Sonia's treatment room by the receptionist. The room contained a reclining chair, a cupboard, a small sink with a large, attached counter, and Sonia's stool. The woman was a slightly overweight, attractive blonde of medium height. She had hazel eyes, and her hair was styled in an attractive shag. She wore a ribbed coffee-brown Shein tank top and a short cream skirt, along with brown sandals. She had a colorful flower tattoo on her left upper arm extending to her shoulder.

"Hi, I'm Sonia. It's great to meet you. You're Chloe, right?"

"That's me. It's nice to meet you too, Sonia. I was, like, sure surprised to learn I'd won this free facial. I don't remember entering any contest."

"Don't worry about how that happened. Let's get to your free service. You relax and we can chat while I work on you."

Chloe sat in the treatment chair and they began. During the chat Sonia learned that Chloe had moved to Columbia from Springfield four years previously, and she was happy with the move. She worked as a waitress in a nice restaurant in the small downtown area, and she enjoyed her job. They exchanged other pleasantries, then Sonia moved on to the interrogation portion of the facial.

"How's dating been for you here, dearie?"

"When I first moved here, it was hit or miss. Then about a year ago I met a great guy and, like, we really hit it off. We've been dating ever since, and I'm pretty happy."

"So, tell me about this guy. Is he a real hunk?"

Chloe smiled. "He's attractive, but I wouldn't call him a hunk. He's very nice and considerate."

"Tell me more. I want all the deets!"

"Well, his name's Brian, and he has a good IT position, so he's able to, like, really treat me well when we go out. We get together several times a week now. It's very nice."

"Chloe, you shouldn't be settling for nice. You should be demanding raw animal magnetism served with a heaping side of heart-pounding romance!"

Chloe blushed at that statement. "I guess the relationship could be a little better."

"Then let's get straight to the main question. How's the sex?"

Chloe was slow to respond. "That's one area that could be better. I feel that I'm, like, a little more reserved than most women my age, but even by my standards the sexual part of our relationship started slowly. We dated for over six months before he finally was willing to have sex. I wondered if something was, like, wrong with me.

"Eventually I got the impression that his slow moving was because he was still carrying a torch for someone else. That idea didn't make sense to me because, like, he said he hadn't dated anyone seriously in over three years, and he'd never been engaged or married."

"But when it finally started, how was it?"

Chloe frowned and said, "You know, it wasn't that great. At first, he seemed to be, like, just going through the motions. Sex was quick and he always finished, but I usually didn't. And it didn't seem to be that exciting for him.

"After a few weeks of this I talked to him. I told him that most of our relationship was great, but the sex had to improve. After that he was more attentive, but, like, I kept getting the feeling that even during our wildest times together, he was still carrying that torch.

"The sex got better for me, but it still wasn't great. I jokingly came up with song titles that described it. I told a friend that it improved from, like, "The Twelfth of Never" to "Halfway to Heaven," but it remained stuck there." Chloe frowned and her face twisted. She leaned in and whispered softly to Sonia, even though they were in a private room. "He also insists on doing it doggy style. That's not so enjoyable for me, and I wonder if he likes doing it that way so he won't have to face me since he's thinking of someone else."

"Okay, it was great that you told him what you wanted. But it still seems like you're letting him control what happens. Does he ever get super aggressive or violent with you?"

Chloe looked taken aback and replied, "No, never anything like that."

"That's good, Chloe. But you really need to let him know more how you want it," Sonia said with emphasis.

"Thank you, Sonia. That's great advice. You're, like, so easy to talk to. I never would've shared these details with anyone else that I'd just met."

"Bartenders, hairdressers, and aestheticians are the world's best listeners and advice-givers, dearie. By the way, you said the sex was one area that needed to improve. Are there others?"

"Just that I overheard him talking on the phone to his brother once. He said, 'No one here can ever learn about that time.' When I asked about the call he said I must have heard it wrong, but I'm sure I didn't. I know he's keeping something from me, but I don't know what it is and that worries me."

Sonia frowned and said, "It seems like that's something you really need to find out about."

Sonia also learned that Brian never mentioned any friends except some work buddies, and he denied carrying a torch for anyone when Chloe had asked. She learned that the two of them get together some weekdays and every weekend night unless Brian was traveling for work.

"I really enjoyed our talk. I really hope your relationship improves, Chloe. Oh, that reminds me. When you first came in, I thought you looked familiar. Did I maybe see you with your boyfriend last Wednesday night? I was out at a couple of the bars then."

"No, we weren't together last Wednesday. That must've been someone else."

"Well, I know you now and if I ever see you two out together you have to introduce us. Maybe I can straighten him out a little for you," she said with a grin.

Chloe laughed. "Thanks again for everything today. I'd, like, love to run into you when I'm out with Brian. You wouldn't really get me in trouble by complaining to him, though, would you?"

"No, I'd be on my best behavior, but that's not saying much. Have a great rest of your day, and I'll call you to come in for another treatment soon."

Chloe wore a very cheerful expression as she headed toward the exit. The session had gone even better than Sonia could have expected. She was able to gather all of the information that she hoped for, and more. She'd have a very detailed update for Anna tonight.

When Anna arrived home that evening, Sonia was waiting with a meal she had picked up at Sophia's. The aroma from this takeout feast enveloped the entire apartment in a fragrant olfactory mist. Even Milo was stunned into wistful inaction by the scent. Anna was piqued to learn the reason for this pleasurable surprise.

"I can tell that something is, literally, in the air. What gives?"

"You just take Milo for his walk, honey, while I put our meal together. Then I'll share my news while we eat."

Anna did as instructed, and while she was out, Sonia pulled out a nice Merlot for herself and fresh lemonade for Anna. She laid out the place settings and spread the feast on their small but cozy table by the kitchen. She was excited for Anna's return.

"We're back," announced Anna a few minutes later. "I'm ready for some great food—and some more good news on top of what I told you last night about my new memories and the grocery store video findings."

They both sat and began eating. Sonia was beaming and couldn't sit still or hold it in, so she began. "I was able to finish my investigation. I've got so much to tell you.

"This is about Brian, of course. I started with a Google search of his name for any major changes in his life in the past two years. I didn't find any job changes or news stories about him. Then I reviewed his social media. He'd actually blocked me from Facebook, which seemed suspicious. I found that I still had access to his Instagram posts. He only posts occasionally, but there were still several pictures to review.

"He had vacation and football game pictures, but there was no sign of a relationship until the past year. At that time a blonde began showing up in his posts. Between then and now she showed up more and more. The posing suggested a relationship that was getting more serious. I followed up by reading through all of the comments under the posts of the two of them."

"Wow, you were so thorough."

"Thanks, honey—anything for you. Now let me continue to my triumphant conclusion."

Sonia sped up her recitation. "Between the comments and the mentions to her account, I was able to figure out the girlfriend's name. I also had one of my young coworkers, who loved doing this by the way, follow the girlfriend on Insta. With all of this clever spying, I learned where she works, and I sent an envelope to her workplace telling her that she'd won a free facial with me at the spa. She took the bait and called. I paid the spa so when she checked in no one would tip her off.

"I saw her today. Her name's Chloe and she's very nice. I was my usual chatty self, and I was able to get her to tell me everything, and I do mean everything. Here's the scoop. They've been dating for a year. They didn't have sex for the first six months because he was smitten with someone from before. Even after they finally started having sex, he wasn't fully into it, like he really wanted someone else. Also, Chloe said Brian only likes the sex position where he's behind her.

"I learned they weren't together last Wednesday, and he's never mentioned us. Chloe also overheard him on the phone talking about something shady from his past. So, the important findings are that he might have a shady past, he could've been your follower on Wednesday, he stopped calling us immediately after your attack, and he doesn't mention us. Also, he's carrying a torch for someone, and he likes to strike from behind. In conclusion, sensual sleuth Sonia has struck success!"

"So smooth, Sonia," said Anna, as they laughed together.

"So, what do we do with this amazing information that I collected, honey?"

Anna took on a puzzled expression.

"That's tricky. From what you learned, there are a lot of reasons to suspect that Brian could be my attacker. The police showed me a photo of the person following me last week, and it wasn't clear, but I thought it could have been Brian. The police also told me the last person they investigated was cleared, but he suffered real backlash because he was investigated. I wouldn't want to put Brian through that unless we were pretty sure he was my attacker. But I don't want to let a real suspect get away either.

"I appreciate what you learned, but I'm not sure what to do. For now, I guess I want to think of this as really suspicious, but not definite. If anything points even a little more toward Brian in the future, I'll tell the police then. I will share this with Dr. Ellis first, though, and get his take. I sure wish we knew what Brian was hiding from his past."

"I do too. Maybe I'll try to see Chloe again. How are you handling your memories and all of the suspects?"

"It was super scary seeing the pictures of that person following me out of the grocery. But other than that, I'm more confident and upbeat. The police are trying to track down my follower, and we can recognize Brian and know to stay away from him. Also, I've got the phrase I can positively identify my attacker with now.

"I feel like I've turned a corner on my memories and my past, and the investigation has turned a corner in terms of suspects. I'm really hopeful now. Something major is bound to happen soon."

CHAPTER 23

THURSDAY AM, WEEK 5

Detective Williams arrived at Stephens College to work on Sydney's case. He tracked her to an eleven o'clock class on her schedule. He leaned against the wall as he waited in the hallway outside the room for the class to end. He planned to approach her with the follow-up questions he had after Monday's interview. He located Sydney in the small group of exiting students when the class ended. Sydney wore a multi-colored Ft. Lauderdale T-shirt and white shorts and had her black Tory Burch tote with her.

"Hi, Sydney, Detective Williams. Do you remember me from Monday?"

She smiled at him. "Yes, Detective. Do you have any news for me? Has anyone found my phone? Have you found out who attacked me?"

"None of that yet, Sydney. I need to get some more information from you that should help us answer those questions. Can we go sit somewhere?"

She agreed and they found a wooden bench in a fairly private area that was shaded by several well-placed trees. The foot traffic wasn't busy since it was summer session, and the student population was small. The temperature was warm, but the weather was partly cloudy with a nice breeze, so it wasn't too hot for sitting outside. Sydney sat with her hands in her lap and looked intently at the detective.

"I want to go over some questions I'd asked you on Monday, Sydney. Despite the physical trauma that you suffered, it's possible that your attacker was after something on your phone, rather than intending to sexually assault you. So, I need to ask you this again. Is there anything on your phone that could've been embarrassing, or legally threatening, to anyone? I don't mean embarrassing to you, but to someone else."

She responded with some hesitation. "I really don't think so, Detective."

"Let me suggest some possibilities you might not be thinking of. Did you have any email or text messages that might have been an issue? For instance, someone may have told you about something they did that was illegal. Or someone may have told you about an affair they had with a teacher or someone who was married."

She replied confidently. "No, I definitely don't remember anything like that."

The detective leaned forward a little. "Now I'm not trying to embarrass you or get you in trouble with this next question. We'll only be going after the person who attacked you. Did you send or receive any emails or texts with any teachers or married individuals in which the messages could have implied an inappropriate relationship?"

Sydney recoiled a bit and replied with a disgusted look. "No way, Detective."

"I'm sorry I needed to ask that question, Sydney. I'm just trying to get to the bottom of this for you. Did you have any pictures on your phone that could have been embarrassing or a problem? For instance, did you take any pictures, even if accidental, of anyone who could have been doing something they shouldn't have been doing?"

"Not to my knowledge."

"Okay, last question. Did you have any nude or partially nude photos on your phone, of anyone other than yourself?"

The detective had struck a nerve. Sydney was either struggling to find the correct response or deciding whether to divulge what she had held back before. She took a minute to reply. She glanced down, then looked back at the detective, who had leaned back.

"I think college is different now compared with back in your time, Detective. We're much more open about our bodies. Two of my close girlfriends and I have shared our nude selfies, tasteful ones of course. But I don't think either of them would have any reason to steal my phone to erase those pictures. And there's no pictures of us all together, in case your mind went there, just the individual pics."

"Were there any other nude photos on your phone?" the detective asked, while flashing his best "I'm as chill as any of you youngsters" expression.

Sydney hesitated while she thought for a minute, then her eyes widened as she replied, "Actually there was one. One of the two friends that I mentioned texted the other two of us a nude selfie that her boyfriend had taken. I guess she thought that we'd either be impressed or jealous when we saw a picture of his junk, you know?"

"Was that picture just a close-up of his genitals, or could you see his face and recognize him?"

"It was a full body shot, so you could see his face."

The detective leaned forward with an excited look. "Did you have that saved to any storage you could access without your phone?"

"No. It was on a text, and I really wasn't impressed enough with his junk that I wanted to save it."

The detective's shoulders sagged but he replied with a hopeful tone. "I should really find out who that man is. This could be the reason that someone attacked you and stole your phone. Do you know his name?"

"No. I'm sorry, I don't."

"Who's your friend who forwarded that picture?"

Sydney's eyes flitted around, and she paused briefly before replying, "Will she get in any trouble?"

"No. We're not going after anyone for sexting, I promise. I just need to find out if that man could have attacked you in order to erase that picture."

"Well, I'd really like to catch the lowlife who came after me. My friend's name is Sofia Morgan. She's a student here too."

The detective stood and gave a slight smile. "Thank you, Sydney. I'll talk with her, and if it turns out that her boyfriend was the culprit we'll let you know. Thank you for your honesty today. I realize it can be tough to answer our questions."

The detective then gave a brief lecture on the dangers of sextortion that was intended to convince her to have more careful practices in the future, after which he left.

He had obtained Sofia's contact information from Sydney and immediately headed to her address. No one was home at her apartment when he arrived. He would have to return to complete his investigation later. His hunch had indeed been correct. Sydney did have something compromising on her phone that might have been the motivating factor for her attack. He would need to get further answers from Sofia Morgan soon.

Detective Smith headed to the local pawn shop to find out if Monica's necklace had been pawned. She entered and looked around while the man who was the store's single customer completed his business. The shop had relatively full glass display cases on both sidewalls and down the middle of the store. Along the back wall was a combination counter and display case that extended the width of the store. The side walls had larger items hung on them.

When the one customer left, the detective addressed the older-looking man with the rumpled clothes and thinning gray hair who was working behind the counter at the rear of the store.

"Good afternoon. I'm Detective Smith," she said, displaying her badge. "I'm here to inquire about a specific item that was involved in a crime and might have made its way here. Are you the manager?"

"Owner, manager, bookkeeper, and janitor," replied the older man with a smile. "John Smith at your service. No relation, I assume."

"Really? John Smith, at a pawn shop?"

"I can show you my license if you don't believe me. A lot of people have this name. It's quite popular. In fact, 100 percent of people currently in this shop have this same glorious last name."

"Good one, Mr. Smith. Let me first ask about your procedures here. What type of surveillance do you have?"

The manager pointed over his left shoulder. "We have a camera on the counter. The tape is erased after a month."

"What about records of your transactions?"

"We keep those for five years. Customers who pawn items have to show us their driver's license. We don't ask for that level of ID for buyers."

"Do you ask for proof of ownership from people who bring items in?"

"We don't generally get things valuable enough to require that level of record keeping. We already have the licenses—and the camera IDs for a month. This usually manages to discourage sales of products from theft. It also enables us to cooperate with law enforcement, at least if they come to us in a timely manner. What specifically are you asking about?"

Detective Smith pulled out her phone to show Mr. Smith the picture of the necklace in question. She enlarged the picture to just the necklace before displaying it to him.

"Do you remember receiving a necklace like this?"

Mr. Smith leaned in and looked at it briefly, then replied to the detective. "You're a little late on this one, aren't you? This came in several months ago. I remember because it's about as high-end an item as we ever receive. I still have it because most people who come here to shop aren't looking for something at that price level."

"May I see it? I don't have a warrant to take it. I just want to make sure it's the same as in the picture."

"I assure you it is, but I'll fetch it from the safe for you. Wait here a minute."

He went into the back of the store and reappeared a short time later. He had the necklace in a box and showed it to the detective. It looked identical to the necklace in the picture.

"Can you get the record on this transaction, please, Mr. Smith? I'll need the seller's name because this necklace was stolen."

"Sure. I'll just put this back in the safe first. It will take me a few minutes to find the record." He left for the back of the store again.

Detective Smith spent the wait time browsing through the store. The watches, electronics, and bracelets in the display cases were of no interest to her, and she didn't think her husband or son would be interested in any of the sports equipment hanging from the walls. Mr. Smith eventually returned with the information.

"I received the necklace from a Dennis Rogers. Here's the address from his license. He brought it in on January 24. I remember that there'd been no jewelry thefts mentioned in the paper near that time that would have made me even more suspicious than I already was."

"Thank you very much for this, Mr. Smith. You're a credit to your name! This may be extremely helpful to us, though if it is you'll probably lose your merchandise to the evidence vault at the station. I'm sorry for your loss if that happens."

The owner smiled and spread out his arms. "What, no reward money?"

"Not at this time, but you never know what might happen. Have a good day. And please don't sell that unless you've heard from me that it's okay to do so."

"I assure you I won't, Detective."

The detective left the shop with a triumphant spring in her step. This could be the really big break they'd been searching so long for, and she was pleased with her role in uncovering this suspect. This should help her get more respect at the station. More importantly, she had her own deeply personal reasons to help get justice for the multiple women who'd been assaulted.

She drove immediately to the address her namesake had provided her. It was a two-story apartment building with fading yellow paint on the walls and mild rust on some of the railings. The building itself wasn't in the best shape either. She was hoping to confirm that Mr. Rogers still lived there so she located the manager's unit, but no one was in. She would have to locate the manager another time for that confirmation. If she got it, they could be one big step closer to solving their case.

CHAPTER 24

THURSDAY PM, WEEK 5

Anna entered the increasingly familiar police station in the late afternoon. She even received waves from a couple of the officers. It reminded her of the theme song from that old TV show she'd watched with her father. She remembered it going something like, you wanted to be at the place where everyone knows your name.

The desk officer had seen her and called back already, and he told Anna that Detective Smith could see her. Anna was such a regular that she was allowed to walk back unescorted now. As she did, she was startled to see a man who represented an unwelcome blast from the past. He was not much taller than her, had brown hair, was wearing a blue dress shirt and dark gray dress pants, and was carrying a binder.

"Glen? I haven't seen you in years. What are you doing here?" Anna said in an accusing tone.

The man pulled up next to her. He slowly eyed her up and down, then he smirked while replying, "Why Anna, I could ask the same of you. Are you here to see your parole officer?"

"Gee, and I wondered why I never missed you these past three years. But really, why are you here?"

The man puffed up his chest. "Don't you remember? I'm a reporter. I'm here on a big story. Of course, I can't tell you anything about it. Media confidentiality, you understand?"

Anna shuddered with the creepy vibe she got from him, and she waved her hand in a dismissive gesture. "You just continue with your delusions of grandeur, Glen."

"Gee, that's a good one. But if this story pops, Anna, I'm in line for a big promotion."

"Wow, I'm so happy for you that I might self-combust with joy. Bye now."

Anna turned and strode confidently down the hallway to her destination. She didn't look back at him. When she reached the back area, Detective Smith stood up from her desk and was ready with a smile for her. "How are you today, Anna? I wasn't expecting you."

"And I wasn't expecting the shock I just received. I really need to ask you about it."

Anna contorted with angst and disgust as she pointed toward the station lobby and raised her voice.

"I just saw the reporter Glen Hammond headed out of the station. He and I have a history, and it's not good. We dated for a while, and on our last date he practically forced himself on me. It was ugly and scary for a few minutes before he backed off. I've even spoken to my therapist about the possibility of him being my attacker because of how scary and creepy he was. And he just creeped me out again here."

Anna took a deep breath and relaxed a bit.

"You should also know that there's another person from my past that I've worried about. I recently talked with both Sonia and my therapist about him maybe being my attacker. Because of the problems you told me that the person on the bar video had after being investigated, I didn't want Glen or this other person to suffer the same consequences. But both have physical features and other reasons why they could be considered as suspects."

Anna sat up straight and tensed her body. "Now I have to seriously wonder about Glen. He wouldn't tell me what case he was here working on. I'd be very worried if I found out he was asking about me."

"I can assure you that he wasn't inquiring about your case. Furthermore, due to what you just disclosed to me, I'll make sure he never gets any information about your case. We'll watch him closely."

"Please do. I'm really concerned about him. Thank you so much, Detective."

"I gather that's not the reason you're here, though."

Anna's posture softened. She said she had come in to see if there were any updates from the detectives.

"Nothing major, but we did get another very promising lead today that I'm following up on. At this point it's too early to tell you anything about it and I don't want you to get your hopes up without good reason, but I'm really optimistic about this."

"Thanks, Detective. Every possibility counts. Thank you for talking with me."

"Of course. Any time, Anna."

Anna turned and headed to the front entrance of the station. Detective Smith sat down at her desk to write herself a reminder to share the information about the reporter, Glen, with her partner when she saw him. Activity on their cases was surging like customers flocking to a half-off sale on Black Friday. The days were certainly going to be busy, and possibly quite productive, from now on.

After Anna arrived home she walked Milo, then she prepared a meal she'd ordered from HelloFresh. She also laid out some lemon bars she'd gotten at the bakery. Sonia was in a bright mood when she arrived a little later.

"Hi, honey. Isn't it a great day? I'm still thrilled with my investigative work from yesterday. Monk, Castle, and the whole of Scotland Yard have nothing on me. I really need to think of this as my new side hustle. How much do you think someone would pay for my services?"

"I'm really thankful for your work on my behalf, but let's not get carried away. Besides, I have another new development for you."

They sat down at their dining table to the meal as Sonia asked what the new development was.

"Do you remember me telling you about Glen, the guy I dated three years ago? The one who didn't want to let me go?"

"Was that 'I can't live without experiencing the physical expression of our love' Glen?"

"I guess you do remember."

Anna then furrowed her brow and spoke more brusquely. She told Sonia about running into Glen in the police station and the uncomfortable exchange that followed. She mentioned her conversation with the detective, who assured her Glen would get no information on her. She let Sonia know how worried she was.

"So, in addition to my investigating, am I going to have to whack a few kneecaps for you too, honey?"

"You aren't from Jersey, are you?"

"No. I'm from the Florida kneecap-whacking side of my family." The friends laughed.

"Also, while I was at the station, the detective said she had a new lead, but she told me not to get my hopes up. So now I have that lead, Glen, and Brian all to worry about as possibilities. I feel like I'm juggling multiple suspects simultaneously, like those clowns do with balls at the circus."

Sonia smiled. "That's a fun visual I'm getting, with our boys being tossed around through the air. We're going to make sure this all works out okay, though. I promise."

"Thanks."

"And thank you for the delicious meal."

After they finished and cleaned up, Anna's worries kicked in. She'd mentioned her concerns about Glen to Detective Smith, who presumably knew him but didn't say anything about him. Then the detective told Anna of an important new lead she had. Anna wondered if the lead had a name attached. If so it surely wasn't Glen. And if all of that was true, some new thoughts occurred to her.

All along she'd been wondering if someone she knew, like Glen or Brian or her stalker, had attacked her. But if they had, then they must have attacked the other women too. Could any of them have done that? Were any of them capable of committing serial assaults on women? And if they weren't, maybe that meant that they hadn't attacked her either. Her head was spinning with these thoughts, all of which made her even more confused. She decided to put this on the back burner until she got more information from the police.

It was time to call her parents now. She needed to tell her mom something tonight. She went to her room for the call. Her room was small, but it had a tranquil and homey feel. She had soft lighting, and familiar knickknacks covered the top of her dresser. She enjoyed the soft pink comforter on her bed. The walls were painted a soothing shade of ochre. Her bedside table had a picture of her family, one of her and Sonia, and the phone charger. Being in this room felt almost like returning to the womb for Anna. Milo jumped up beside her.

She called her dad first, and they had the usual brief sharing of pleasantries, then said their goodbyes.

Anna then called her mother. "Mom, I have a few things to tell you about tonight. Are you sitting down for these?"

"What's going on, honey? What have you learned?"

She began by telling her mother that her therapy was basically over, and that she had found a way to ID her attacker, which she hoped would lead to an arrest.

"But I've also got something else important to tell you, which is the main reason I called. I've had several sessions with the psychiatrist. During them, several issues besides the lost memory have come up. One of these I need to discuss with you tonight. It's about Madison, and the lie I told to the police after her death. I never actually told you everything."

Anna then related the complete story about Madison's rape, including Anna's sleuthing and the reason why she'd made the false accusation about the teacher. She said she realized through her therapy that she needed to tell Madison's mother everything she had withheld before.

"I plan to call her tomorrow, and I didn't want you to hear any of this from her without hearing it from me first. By the way, the teacher I falsely accused was one of the five men that I know Madison spent time alone with that weekend, so he could have been her rapist."

Her mother, never previously at a loss for words, was stunned. After a moment she asked why Anna hadn't at least said something after Madison's death.

"Frankly, I was embarrassed that I hadn't made her tell anyone, and also really frightened that her mother might blame me for her death."

"Well, I guess I know now why you made up that lie. I never understood that." Anna's mother paused to collect her thoughts. She said she was disappointed that Anna didn't do more when that all happened but was proud of her that she was going to tell Madison's mother now. Her voice was choked with emotion as she finished talking. They hung up and Anna knew that the next night would be one of the hardest of her life. This was one Friday she was not looking forward to.

It was well after midnight when Jillian stumbled out of the bar and headed to her car in the mostly empty, dark parking lot located behind the bar. She could faintly hear strains of "Mr. Brightside" escaping the open windows on the backside of the place she'd just left. She hummed to herself as she searched for her car in the fog of her overly sedated brain and the darkness of the night.

As she searched, she noticed someone walking through the scattered cars left in the lot. It didn't really register until he veered in her direction, and she could see that he wore a ski mask and gloves. At that moment she finally spotted her beat-up Toyota and turned toward it. The man in the mask also headed toward her car. She was fumbling in her purse for her keys as she neared the car. The man was close behind her.

Just then a bright light strikingly illuminated the entire parking lot. Jillian turned, shaded her eyes, and saw that someone had come out a back door from the bar and propped the door open so he could take out empty beer cases. She then heard the man who'd been near her run out the back end of the lot. She got in her car and started it for the drive home.

She drove very slowly and erratically and finally reached her apartment. When she got inside, she heard her roommate complain about the noise she was making coming home that late. As she collapsed on her bed, still fully clothed, she could hear her roommate yelling out that she was going to rip Jillian a new one in the morning. Then Jillian passed out.

CHAPTER 25

FRIDAY, WEEK 5

D etective Smith arrived at the station earlier in the morning than usual. Her husband and son were sleeping in, so she had a quick bowl of oatmeal to go with her coffee and rushed to the station.

Her plans were to locate as much information as she could on the new suspect, Mr. Rogers, then reach the manager of the suspect's apartment building to help her get more information on Rogers and track him down. She also had to contact personnel from Tiffany about Monica's necklace. She was at her desk and had just begun to work on her tasks when her partner arrived.

"So, what kind of donuts are on today's menu?"

"Even when I get here early, I can't hide my breakfast from you, can I, Audra? Are you going to hassle me all day?"

"It's possible. On a more serious note, I have some things to run by you."

"Sure, shoot."

She told her partner that Glen Hammond had been in the office looking for information on both Hannah's attack and Sydney's attack. Anna ran into him and mentioned that the reporter had been physically inappropriate with her when they were an item in the past. Anna wanted to make sure that the reporter didn't learn anything about her attack. She also said that she had considered him as a possible suspect for her attack.

Detective Williams said, "He hasn't asked me anything about our series of attacks. The info you got from Anna is good to know, though. I'll be on alert in the future for any questions from him on our cases."

"More importantly, Derek, I learned some very useful information yesterday." Detective Smith filled him in on the details of her visit to the pawn shop, with the revelation that a Dennis Rogers had pawned what was almost certainly Monica's necklace. She outlined her plans for today to follow up on the necklace and on Mr. Rogers.

"Wow. That's fantastic work. Let me know if you need help with any of that follow-up. I sure hope this is our guy. We need to finally put away our one-man crime spree."

The detectives were interrupted by an officer who brought them some results that had just arrived. Detective Williams opened them and showed them to his partner. They were the DNA results from Hannah's vaginal swab, and they revealed no male DNA.

"That's unfortunate," said Detective Smith. "We know she was raped by the genital trauma that was present. Maybe the attacker knocked her unconscious at the outset and knew he had time to use a condom. In any case, this doesn't contradict our belief that the same man is responsible for all three rapes; it just doesn't prove it. But we're not catching enough breaks on these cases."

"I agree. Hopefully you'll strike gold when you find Mr. Rogers. We need some real success."

In the early afternoon, Detective Williams got a message from the front desk. They were putting through a call. A young woman was on the line. She told him that her roommate had come home late last night quite drunk. The detective wondered why the desk had sent this to him, as it wasn't starting off as a call a detective needed to take. As the woman proceeded with her call, she said when her roommate finally woke up, in the early afternoon, she told a worrisome story.

The roommate, whose name was Jillian, said when she was walking to her car in the dark parking lot of a bar last night, she saw someone coming toward her. She said he wore a ski mask and gloves. She apparently was so drunk that his appearance didn't worry her. She said a bright light suddenly shot out from a door in the back of the bar and the man ran from the light. Jillian got in her car and drove home.

When the caller heard the story today, she felt the police needed to be aware of it. She said Jillian could tell her nothing about the man except that he was of average height.

Detective Williams took down the caller's information and thanked her. After that he went to his partner to fill her in on this development. They decided to send a junior officer to check with Jillian and make sure there wasn't anything more that she remembered. The two of them agreed that these reports were getting way out of hand. If this was the man they were looking for, they had to find him quickly before he succeeded on one of his increasingly frequent attempts. He seemed to be getting desperate.

In the late afternoon, Anna left her clinic and headed to Dr. Ellis's office. When she arrived, she didn't have to wait long to be seen. She felt comfortable walking down the hallway to the therapy room, as nothing major was scheduled for today's visit.

Dr. Ellis was pleased to see his favorite patient. She was wearing a cream-colored silk blouse and black dress pants today, and she looked to be in a good mood.

"Good afternoon, Anna."

"Good afternoon, Dr. Ellis. Are you looking forward to the weekend?"

"I am. I have some fun planned. How about you?"

"I have a picnic at the dog park planned with some friends," Anna replied as she sat in her usual chair.

"That's nice. I'm glad you're planning enjoyable activities. That's a good segue into our session today. How are you doing in general and with your emotions?"

Anna appeared thoughtful. "Things fluctuate. Recently the days have been better than the nights, but in general, I'd say things are definitely improving. I think I'm dealing as well as possible with the rape revelation, thanks to you, Sonia, and even Detective Smith. I have periods of sadness and anger, but I find I'm mostly looking forward rather than backward.

"I'm also doing better because more significant action is happening on the police case, so the investigation seems more concrete rather than just hopeful." Anna informed the doctor of the video findings from the grocery, and of the detective speaking of an additional new lead. She didn't mention her own odd thoughts from the day before that had been stimulated by the talk of the new lead.

"That's really good news. Hopefully they'll locate a suspect soon. Let me pursue one thing you said. You mentioned that the days are better than the nights. Why is that?"

Anna grasped her hands together and developed an uncertain appearance. She hadn't necessarily planned to talk about this issue today. It made her uncomfortable when otherwise she was doing better. "Well, to begin with, the days are very busy so there's not much time to be worried. The other thing is that I've had some dreams recently that have made the evenings rough."

"Can you tell me about the dreams?"

"In the last two nights I've woken up with these dreams. I'm scared when I wake up. Not 'Freddy Krueger suddenly materializing behind me' scared, but I'm still frightened."

Dr. Ellis leaned forward and gazed thoughtfully at Anna. "What happens in these dreams?"

"They were identical, except that the person in them changed from one night to the other. In the dream, I wake up and someone I know is standing by my bed and leaning over me saying 'Shh, now, shh' with the exact same chilling voice that I remembered at our last session. Each time this happened, I woke up feeling certain that the person in the dream was the person who'd attacked me. But it was a different person in each of the two dreams."

"Who are these people that frightened you so?"

Anna stared into Dr. Ellis's eyes. "Two nights ago it was Brian. He's the person that Sonia's been investigating. He's a former platonic friend who often went to the bars with us. We initially considered him to possibly be my attacker because after the night I was attacked he suddenly stopped any communication with either of us. He also had been overly possessive of our attention in the past.

"Sonia's investigation found out that Brian still carries a torch for someone from his past, presumably me. She also learned that he only likes to have sex from behind, like what happened in my attack.

"After she shared this with me on Wednesday, I had the dream about him that night. I woke up feeling that there was a good chance he was my attacker. Also, the day before the police had shown me a picture from the store of the man following me. I remembered looking at it specifically to see if it reminded me of

Brian, but it was impossible to tell. So, after Wednesday night, he seemed to be a real possibility.

"Then last night, I had the identical dream, but this time it was Glen who was saying the phrase. He was the person who caused that bad ending to our relationship three years ago. I ran into him yesterday for the first time since that awful last encounter we had. He was at the police station and said he was looking into some recent crimes in his job as a reporter.

"Our interaction at the station wasn't very civil at all. That worried me, and then last night I had the dream about him. When I woke up it seemed to me that he was a good possibility to be my attacker.

"That made me think about the picture from the grocery video again. The more I thought of it, the more it seemed as if the height, the body type, and the posture of the person in the video were all similar to both Brian and Glen. My follower could have been either of them."

"Those are very interesting dreams, Anna. Do you think they occurred primarily because you'd talked about each of them in the day before the dream?"

Anna sat back and her body relaxed. "It's hard to say, Doctor. That would be the obvious interpretation. On the other hand, I've been spending time wondering what specific horrible person attacked me. So maybe my mind is either auditioning the options or coming up with the only possibilities available to me."

"What about the voices saying that phrase in each dream. You said that each time it seemed identical to the voice in your memory. I imagine Glen and Brian have different voices. Did the phrase seem more like one of their voices than the other?"

Anna paused briefly to contemplate that question. "That's an interesting question. Nothing else was said in either dream besides that phrase. In each dream the phrase sounded identical, like it was from the person who attacked me. I didn't notice it sounding like either Brian or Glen particularly. I don't think I can really answer you any more than that."

"How worried were you the next day after each of these dreams?"

"Not too worried. I was scared about each of them when I woke up from the dreams. But the next day I was focused more on wondering whether it would be worthwhile to look into either of them as a suspect in more depth. I don't remember being especially frightened of them during the day yesterday or today."

"You mentioned pursuing them as suspects. Did you bring up either of them to the police?"

"I talked with Detective Smith about Glen when I saw him at the station. I mostly asked her to avoid talking about my case with him, but I did say I'd thought about suggesting him as a suspect. I also told her that Sonia and I were considering another possibility, but I didn't give the detective Brian's name. Since then I've been focused more on wanting to hear about their new leads before I would suggest that they pursue Glen or Brian."

Dr. Ellis assumed a more relaxed position and briefly grinned. "I probably shouldn't ask this, but I'm curious. Do I even want to know how Sonia learned about Brian's sexual preferences?"

Anna chuckled. "I think that I'll let that remain a mystery for you, but it was a devious plan."

"Okay then. Now, assuming you haven't talked about or run into either of those men today, it will be interesting to see if you continue to have those dreams. If so, it would be telling if only one of the men you mentioned is in them in the future."

"That's a good point. I'll definitely pay attention to that."

"I want to approach one more topic today. You mentioned that this Brian had been a little possessive of your time in the past. You also had that relationship in college where possessiveness was an issue. Then there's Glen and the way that ended. This suggests a theme in many of your relationships. What are your thoughts about that?"

Anna's eyes drifted sideways and she raised her eyebrows. Even when she thought these sessions would be easy, they weren't. "I'd actually never thought about that until Sonia pointed out the possessiveness in Brian. I don't think I look for possessive men. Maybe I let them hang around too long after that trait shows up, though. I think this entire therapy experience has helped me think about a lot of issues like this. I'm fairly confident that in the future I'll stand up for myself more."

"That's good insight, Anna. You seem to be on a great trajectory. I'll be interested in hearing about any future dreams you have. Also, I hope to hear that the efforts of the police are as successful as you feel that they might be with their new information. Should we schedule one or two final sessions for next week?"

"Let's go ahead and put two on the calendar. I know you've heard this often from me, but I really believe we'll have most of the critical answers by the end of next week. I have a strong gut feeling about it this time."

"I sincerely hope that you're right. I'll send confirmation of two session times for next week."

"Thank you, Doctor. I'll see you next week."

Anna strode out with an air of relative self-assurance. She could tell that her confidence was improving through this therapy process. She noted that she could talk about those difficult dreams without too much anxiety. And despite previous setbacks in her case, she felt that the police were finally making some headway. She headed to her car with a smile on her face.

Dr. Ellis was confident also. In addition to all of the new developments that Anna brought up, he was aware of another potential piece of the puzzle that might be added soon. His new patient, Alex Templeton, had quite possibly been attacked by Anna's assailant. Since that man had used a fake name, the doctor even wondered if Brian or Glen could have been the person who'd attacked Alex.

He speculated that if Alex decided to go to the police, they might be able to track the man down. If that happened, Anna would have the opportunity to positively identify him as her attacker through the phrase she remembered. Then, all of Anna's terror and hard work would have been rewarded. He was excited thinking of the conclusions next week could bring. He realized that he was primarily happy for Anna this time, and not just for himself and his self-esteem.

Could it be possible that he was actually growing through this process?

With the exception of Milo's glorious company, Anna was alone for dinner. Sonia had another date, with a bartender this time. Anna nuked a frozen mac and cheese to go with her salad and fresh fruit. She enjoyed healthy eating as it helped her feel good about herself. Healthy food was comfort food to her. This was especially important tonight, due to the uncomfortable phone call she was planning to make.

After her meal she proceeded to her bedroom. She settled onto the bed to make her call. Anna had gotten the number for

Madison's mom from her mother, and she punched it in with trepidation. "Hello," answered the familiar, gentle voice.

"Hi, Mrs. Richards, this is Anna Jones."

"Anna! What a wonderful surprise. We haven't spoken in years. How are you?"

"Fine, I guess. I'm sorry that I haven't called in such a long time. How are you and Marvin doing?"

"Marv is very healthy and he's had no recurrence of his lymphoma. He finished college and is going to med school now. I'm so proud of him. I'm fine. It's just me and a couple of cats here now."

Anna decided to stop stalling. "I'm glad things are okay. I hope this call doesn't make everything too much worse for you. I don't know if my mom mentioned it to you, but I was attacked two years ago. Lately, I've been having therapy related to the attack. During the therapy, Madison's tragedy came up."

Anna hesitated. She hated what was coming. "The psychiatrist and I have had several long discussions, and I realized that I need to share some things about Madison that I never told you before. I'm so sorry." Anna paused briefly. "Mrs. Richards, two weeks before she died, Madison told me that she'd been raped."

Gasps, cries, and a shout of "What?" came from the other end of the conversation. Anna hurried on. She told Madison's mother about her interactions with Madison in the two weeks after her rape, and of Madison's demand that Anna not tell anyone.

"I'm so sorry. I failed her and I failed you. I should have told someone, but instead I listened too much to my best friend. I knew she was depressed, but I had no idea she was depressed enough to do what she did. I'm so very sorry." Anna stopped and burst into tears.

Mrs. Richards replied in a shaky and raised voice, "You didn't have the right to withhold this information from me, no matter what Madison said. You were seventeen. You had no right! So, who did this to her? Who raped my beautiful baby?"

"I don't know, Mrs. Richards. She wouldn't tell me or even give me a hint. All I know is that it happened sometime during the weekend of your family picnic two or three weeks before her death."

Anna could almost hear the gear wheels meshing in Mrs. Richards's mind as she desperately searched for answers to this new information. "I'm going to need some time to try and come to terms with this. I'm too angry and upset to think now."

Anna collapsed into an almost uncontrollable fit of tears. She wanted to crawl into a hole. She wasn't sure now that she'd done the right thing in telling Madison's mother about this. She managed to get out, through her wall of tears, "Okay, Mrs. Richards. I guess I should go now." Mrs. Richards hung up without a closing.

Although Anna knew she had to tell Mrs. Richards what she knew, this was an abysmal start to the weekend. She hoped that the remainder of the weekend would pass quickly. Detective Smith had told her there was a promising new lead, and Anna was looking forward to hearing about it next week. She was also hoping to get an opportunity to use her voice ID soon. Next week just had to bring her some real answers.

CHAPTER 26

SATURDAY, WEEK 5

Detective Smith had a busy Saturday planned. She was in the station early, and her goals were to get some information from Tiffany & Co. on Monica's necklace and track down Dennis Rogers.

A background search on Mr. Rogers that she had done the previous day yielded minimal helpful results. His driver's license listed him as thirty-one years old with brown eyes and a height of five foot ten. An internet search revealed that he'd graduated from Kansas State eight years previously. He majored in business. There were no references to any awards, scholarships, sports team participation, or distinguishing achievements in college. He'd taken five years to complete his degree.

His spotty record since showed no consistent history of employment. There was no record of marriage. No accolades were mentioned. Pictures revealed that he wore medium-length hair. His body habitus was consistent with that of Anna's follower at the grocery. His current listed address was the one from his license. During her social media search, the detective was unable to locate a Facebook or Instagram account for him.

Police records revealed that Mr. Rogers had two arrests for minor drug possession, but nothing of a more serious nature. His most recent misdemeanor was for possession of a moderate amount of pot twenty-one months previously. There were no listed accusations of sexual battery or violence of any kind. He had no outstanding warrants. The detective checked, and his was one of the twelve pictures she had saved in two six-packs after her initial mugshot review.

He didn't have the profile of a model citizen, or even a particularly productive member of society, but this wasn't the background of a hardened criminal. People who commit the crimes he was being considered for usually had more warning signs in their background than the detective had been able to find for Mr. Rogers. She'd been unable to locate the apartment manager so far in her quest to get more information on Mr. Rogers.

Detective Smith began her Saturday by reaching out to the Tiffany company. After several minutes and several phone transfers, she was connected with someone in authority. Detective Smith explained to the manager that she wasn't seeking to obtain any information on their customers. She said she just needed to confirm that a Monica Hadley of Columbia, Missouri, had purchased a *oui* necklace through their company.

The detective indicated that the information was crucial to helping them solve a crime. After that explanation, the manager told her that Monica had purchased that specific necklace from their company online about two years before. She also mentioned that it was not one of their most popular styles. Detective Smith now had the confirmation she needed that Monica had once owned a Tiffany *oui* necklace that was lost on the night of her attack, and which Dennis Rogers had pawned six months after the attack.

The detective's next task was to locate and speak with their suspect. She returned to his apartment building and proceeded to the manager's apartment. This time her knock was answered by an unkempt man who wore cutoff shorts, ratty sandals, and a filthy T-shirt. He looked fortyish, and he sported a two-day growth of beard.

"Hello. I'm Detective Smith of the Columbia police. Are you the building manager?"

The man salivated with his reply while he eye-fondled the detective. "Yes, I am. My name's Stu, and I guess this is my lucky day. Did you want to handcuff me and do naughty things to me, Detective?"

Detective Smith was quite used to handling this type of behavior, but it still was irritating to have to deal with actions that her male colleagues didn't have to worry about. "Harassing an officer of the law isn't an ideal way for this conversation to start, Stu. Let's begin again, okay? I have a few questions for you."

The detective asked about Dennis Rogers. She learned that he still lived in that building. She obtained Mr. Rogers's contact information from the manager, and she learned that the suspect worked construction jobs off and on and was occasionally out of town. She learned that none of the other tenants had complained about him, and none seemed to have befriended him.

"How would you describe Mr. Rogers, in terms of the kind of person he is?"

"He always pays on time. He's a loner. He seems really full of himself. I get the impression he feels he's getting a raw deal from society. He comes off very frustrated by this, and also angry at the world. He's never gotten angry at me or the other tenants, though, that I've heard of."

Detective Smith thanked him and returned to her car. She immediately got on her phone to call the number she now had for Mr. Rogers. When he answered she told him she had several questions for him. He replied that he was out of town for a job and asked the detective if he could just answer her questions on the phone.

When she said it needed to be in person, he said he would be returning to Columbia the next day. They scheduled an in-person meeting at his apartment for Monday at 10 a.m. As she ended the call, the detective knew that the pieces were starting to come together. The conversation on Monday would be crucial.

Audra's partner was on his way to speak with Sofia Morgan. When he reached her off-campus apartment, his knock was answered by a tall, thin, attractive young woman with black hair and a medium-olive skin tone and complexion. She was barefoot and dressed in an oversized silky top and designer shorts. "Good morning. I'm Detective Williams from the Columbia police. Are you Sofia Morgan?"

"All five foot eight of me," she replied, spreading her arms in a "Ta da!" gesture. "Am I in trouble for anything?"

"No, I just need to ask you a few questions. Would you mind if I come in?"

"No, that's fine."

The detective entered and closed the door. He noted that the furniture was new, modern, and plentiful and the place nicely decorated. It was a spacious apartment, unlike most student apartments he had needed to visit over the years.

"My questions might be sensitive, Miss Morgan. Do you have a roommate or anyone else with you in the apartment now?"

"No. It's just us. Have a seat."

The detective took a seat in an armchair that was not too close to the black leather sofa where Sofia had flopped down. "I'm here about your friend Sydney. She had her phone taken last week, and I had some questions for you about that incident."

"She told me about the attack. I thought she was sexually assaulted. You don't think I did it, do you?"

"Certainly not, Miss Morgan, but you might be involved. We think her phone was taken because someone wanted to remove some incriminating evidence from it. We think the attack was staged to look like a sexual assault in order to take the focus off the theft of her phone. Sydney and I discussed this in depth.

"The only thing she could think of on her phone that was embarrassing enough that someone might steal for it was a photo from you. By the way, I'm not talking about a selfie you would have taken, but one of your boyfriend."

Miss Morgan instantly got a faraway expression. "Oh that. Wow, that makes some sense."

"What do you mean?"

She sat forward and spoke with confidence. "He and I broke up several weeks ago. Then he showed up recently to talk. He said he's up for a promotion at work, and if that picture got out anywhere it would ruin his chances. He actually demanded that I delete it in front of him, which I did. He also asked about backup to the cloud, but I reminded him that I had an Android phone with no backup storage app.

"After that he asked if I'd sent the picture to anyone else. I told him I'd forwarded the shot to my friend Jo Jo, but I knew that she erased it immediately because she didn't want to take a chance on her boyfriend or parents seeing it. I said no one else had a copy except Sydney, and I knew she wouldn't show it to anyone so he didn't have to worry. Do you think he's the one who attacked her just to get that picture erased?"

"It's a definite possibility. I'll need his name so I can check on it."

She replied in an angry tone. "Absolutely. If that jerk attacked my friend, he deserves anything he gets. His name is Glen Hammond. He's a reporter."

The detective was able to conceal his shock at this news. He would need to inform his partner ASAP. "Thank you for talking with me, Miss Morgan. I'll look into this right away. Please don't tell Mr. Hammond about this conversation."

"I won't, Detective. Am I in trouble for sharing the photo?"

Detective Williams stood and replied, "No, but I'll give you some advice. Technically, sharing nude photos of someone without their consent is a crime. However, the bigger crime here is the attack on Sydney, so we'll just concentrate on that for now and let your actions slide. Please don't forward nude pictures of anyone else in the future, though."

She rose and escorted him to the door. "Okay, Detective. Have a good day."

"You too, Miss Morgan." Detective Williams headed back to the office to see if he could catch his partner in on a Saturday and share the surprising news.

Detective Smith was at her desk when her partner reached the station. For once, he had something major to share concerning their case. "I had a very productive day that I need to tell you about, Audra."

"What a coincidence—I had a productive day too."

Detective Williams continued in a much more animated manner than usual for him as he leaned against her desk.

"Always scooping me, aren't you? Well, here's my news. I hadn't told you yet, but when I reinterviewed Sydney, the Stephens College student I thought was hiding something in her first interview, she remembered a nude photo that one of her friends had sent her. The friend had texted Sydney a nude picture of her boyfriend. When I spoke with Sophia Morgan, the friend who'd sent the photo, I learned something very interesting." He paused for suspense.

"Okay, you have my complete attention."

"The nude photo was of our reporter, Glen Hammond. Not only that, but he'd recently told Sofia that he was worried about that photo getting out. Sofia let him know that only Sydney still had a copy.

"Now didn't you tell me that he'd been asking about Hannah's attack, but also about Sydney's? Maybe he doesn't care about our sexual assault cases, even Anna's. Maybe he wants to know where we are on finding out who attacked Sydney and stole her phone."

Detective Smith said, "That's interesting. It suggests Mr. Hammond was attempting to ingratiate himself into our investigation, possibly because he committed the crime. What's your next step?"

"I'll have a tough talk with our curious reporter. I'll try to see him Monday. Unfortunately, we don't have enough on him to be able to get a warrant to search for Sydney's phone, so I'll try to scare it out of him."

His partner replied, "Having seen him, I think you might be successful. Let me fill you in on my morning."

Detective Smith became more energetic as she spoke. "I reviewed the report of the officer who went to talk to that Jillian who thought a man might have been coming after her in the bar parking lot Thursday night. The officer said Jillian was about five foot five and slightly overweight with brunette hair. She admitted to being very drunk and not remembering much. She only came up with one new memory. The man was wearing a thin black rain jacket, and she knew the brand, since they sell that jacket where she works in the mall.

"The officer also took the initiative to check out the bar parking lot, and there were no cameras in it. That means it's the type of place our serial predator likes to use for his attacks, so it could have been him again.

"As far as progress with our new suspect, I went through our records, and Dennis Rogers seems to be his real name. He has two priors for minor issues. He's a college grad who seems to have taken the low road after graduating, with no steady jobs. His apartment manager said Mr. Rogers works in construction and feels he should be in a better place in life than he is. He certainly fits our profile. I got his number from the manager and called him. We have an appointment to meet at his apartment Monday morning."

"Do you want me to back you up, Audra?"

"No. I want to go in there being the primary detective as a woman. I hope it will either put him off guard or make him over-confident. I'll take a junior officer as backup, but I'll be in charge."

"What are you going to look for in his interview?"

Detective Smith smiled. "I'll glance around his apartment and look for a black Mizzou cap, a Sig Sauer that he denies owning, sexual assault gloves, or a rain jacket of the brand Jillian mentioned. I'll get a sense of who he is. I'll hit him up for alibis for all of the attacks including Gwen's, and for the night Anna was followed. I hope to put some fear into him. I'm also going to try and get him to come to the station afterward so I can make a recording of his voice to play for Anna."

"We're starting to get some real headway. Monday should be very interesting," said Detective Williams.

Anna enjoyed her picnic at the dog park with the other dog owners. They had taken possession of a large table under the shade of a small group of trees. Anna brought a penne and arugula salad tossed with cherry tomatoes and pine nuts, along with an extra cheese pizza from Shakespeare's. Everyone else brought their own delicious favorites, and the picnic was spectacular. Anna was even able to sneak some cake.

The dog owners had a great time talking, and the picnic plus the warm but not overly hot afternoon was a welcome escape from Anna's Friday evening call and her anxiousness about the upcoming week. When the picnic ended, Anna loaded Milo into her car and headed for home.

When she got there, she parked and grabbed the residue from the picnic, along with Milo's leash. As she reached the sidewalk in front of her building, Milo tensed up and growled. Anna looked around for the source of this displeasure and was surprised to see Glen approaching her on the sidewalk. She didn't tell Milo to stand down as Glen neared them.

Glen snarled at her. "That crazy dog never liked me."

"He's a great judge of character, and I should've paid more attention to him in the past. Are you stalking me?"

"You should be so lucky. I was just passing through this cheap neighborhood to reach the nicer end of town."

"Please continue passing then." Anna bent down to address Milo. "And good boy, Milo, very good boy."

After that brief, unpleasant interlude, they reached their building and went up to the apartment. Anna immediately reached for treats to reward Milo for his support. At that moment, Sonia sashayed out of her bedroom.

"Hi, honey. How was the picnic?"

Anna walked over toward Sonia.

"It was really fun. I wish I could say the same for our trip

home. Milo and I bumped into Glen on our way into the building. Fortunately, Milo had my back and growled at him."

"I've always loved that dog. Well, while you were out, I got
some interesting news."

Sonia filled Anna in on a conversation she'd just had with
Chloe. Apparently the discussion at the spa lit a fire under Chloe,
and she approached Brian about the worrisome phone conversation with his brother. After several attempts at denial, he finally
broke down and told her what the comment referred to.

When he was in college he was accused of sexual assault. He
claimed the accuser had made the whole story up to get back at him
for dumping her. There was no evidence, and no formal charges
were ever filed, but Brian didn't want that chapter of his life to follow him. He apologized to Chloe for keeping it from her, and Chloe
told Sonia that Brian seemed to be sincere, and she believed him.

"So, with that news plus your run-in a few minutes ago,
what are you thinking about our boys Brian and Glen now?"

"Well, I hadn't told you yet, but I told Dr. Ellis yesterday
that during the last couple of nights I've had scary dreams about
each of them standing over me saying 'Shh now.'"

"Whoa! Shut the front door. What do you make of those
dreams?"

Anna smiled. "Spoken like a true therapist. That's the kind
of question that Dr. Ellis asks. I know the dreams made me really
think that one of them might be my attacker. Dr. Ellis asked me
to pay attention to any future dreams and notice whether I focus
more on one of them than the other."

Sonia began gesturing with her hands. "So, are you telling
me I should open a combination PI and shrink office now, honey?
I could make a fortune with that."

"I wouldn't go that far. Anyway, it's really eerie that I've run into Glen twice in the last three days, and dreamed about him once, after having had no contact in three years. If I believed in omens, it would really make me believe that he's the guy who attacked me. I've gotten an attacker vibe from him ever since that last date we had."

"Should I start looking into him also, honey? You know what a great detective I am."

"Maybe you should hold off on that for now. I'm really expecting some major breaks from the detectives in the case this coming week. I just know something big is going to come up."

CHAPTER 27

MONDAY AM, WEEK 6

D etective Williams hoped to get Glen Hammond into the station that morning for questioning by pretending to be on his side. He called the reporter and asked him if he wanted to come to the station to learn more about the cases he was interested in. The reporter jumped at the chance and said he would be right in. The detective had hooked him.

When Mr. Hammond arrived a few minutes later, the detective asked the desk officer to wait one minute, then send him back. During that minute the detective turned on the voice recording device in the interview room. He quickly returned to his office so he could continue the apparent favorable treatment for the reporter.

"Good morning, Mr. Hammond. Thanks for being able to come in. It's good to work closely with a member of the press. I figured that before we start, I could show you some of the ropes while you're here, if you like."

The reporter, who was dressed casually in jeans and a light-blue polo shirt, replied with an actual squeal of delight. "Sure, Detective. That would be awesome."

The detective escorted the reporter down the hallway. They entered a room with a metal desk and chairs flanking the desk. One wall had a large mirror that suggested an observation area was behind it. "This is interview room one, Mr. Hammond, where the magic happens. Step in and have a seat on the other side of the table." The reporter took the bait.

"Let me show you something interesting. We have a case where we're trying to get a voice ID on the suspect. We plan to have him read a phrase that the victim might be able to identify. Then we see if there's any recognition. The phrase is printed on that piece of paper. Go ahead and read it and you can see what it's like on the perp side of the table," the detective said with a hearty smile.

The reporter picked up the paper and read, "Shh, now, shh." He had no reaction while reading it.

"What's it feel like sitting on that side?"

"I think I'd be intimidated if I were here for real."

"Why don't we use this room for our talk as long as we're here?" The detective sat opposite Mr. Hammond. "My partner said you were asking about my assault case at Stephens College the weekend before last, and also about the jogger who was attacked earlier this summer. Why are you asking about those two cases together?"

"I was thinking that we might have a serial sexual predator in Columbia now."

"Are you assuming the cases are related and were committed by the same person?"

"Yes, don't you, Detective?"

"No we don't, but why do you? What are you thinking?"

The reporter had an unsettled appearance, and he paused before responding. "Well, both women were attacked late at night on the weekend. Also, both were sexually assaulted, so it seems to be a good assumption.

"Actually, after I closely reviewed the recent case, the woman was more physically attacked than sexually assaulted. I've also been able to rule out sexual assault as the intention for the attack.

Therefore, the cases aren't similar." The detective watched for a telltale reaction to that statement and was rewarded with a startled look and dilated eyes on the part of the reporter.

"I wasn't aware of those details, Detective," said the reporter.

"Also, due to these conclusions, we have decided that we can release the first name of the victim to press members. Her name is Sydney, and she's a twenty-year-old Stephens student.

"Now, while you're here, Mr. Hammond, I'd like to ask a question I've always wondered about. Do journalists have ethics about reporting on someone that the reporter knows?"

Mr. Hammond shifted position in his chair and paused for a bit before answering, in a wary tone. "It's the decision of the reporter to decline the story if he or she is too close to an individual."

"Since Columbia is fairly small, I imagine that happens regularly. Do you know any Stephens College students, Mr. Hammond?"

"I dated a student from the college a while back, but otherwise I don't know any students there."

"Do you know any Stephens students named Sydney?"

The reporter gave a start, then made a face as if he were thinking. "No, that name doesn't ring a bell, Detective."

"So you never ran into or heard about a Sydney from the Stephens student you were dating?"

He replied brusquely, "No I haven't, so I should be fine working on the story. Let me take out my notebook. Can you tell me why you eliminated sexual assault as the motive for the recent attack?"

Detective Williams replied in a matter-of-fact tone, "There were some details I noticed that made it seem like there was a completely different reason for the attack. Hey, you didn't happen to be on the Stephens campus around midnight the Saturday before last, did you, Mr. Hammond? Maybe you were on a date and saw something that could help us."

He replied huffily. "I stopped dating that girl several weeks ago. And I went to the movies that night."

"Who did you go with?"

"I went by myself. I still have the ticket stub if you need to see it. I saw a late show of *Despicable Me 4*."

The detective's demeanor changed dramatically, from colleague to interrogator, at that point. "How convenient that you have a ticket stub as an alibi. Do you think anyone at the theater would be able to confirm that you were there for the whole show?"

The reporter shrank back in his seat. "I doubt it, but why would I need an alibi? Why are you asking where I was that night?"

"Because you've already lied to me twice, Glen, and I wanted to see how many more times you'd lie. Sofia Morgan told me that the two of you talked about Sydney a few days before her attack, so you definitely were aware of her, and you lied about that both times I asked. Why would you lie unless you had something to hide? Lying to a police officer is a real problem, Glen.

"It's very convenient that your alibi is that you went to the movies by yourself. I wonder if I could find an image of you on a security camera near the campus when you were supposed to be at the theater. What do you think, Glen?"

The reporter was sweating like a 10K runner in a Fourth of July race, and he wasn't replying.

"We're also looking for a phone that was taken from Sydney at the time of her attack. Do you think we could find it at your home?"

The reporter's voice cracked. "Why do you think that I had anything to do with this? You can't treat me like this."

The detective replied sternly and with authority but not malice. "You know very well why I'm asking these hard questions, Glen. You know what you did. And why hadn't we seen you in the station in months until just after Sydney was assaulted? It sounds like a classic case of a suspect weaseling his way into the investigation.

"Face it, you're in trouble, Glen. You've lied to the police, and your alibi is crap. Let me give you the best-case scenario. I'd be glad to ask the prosecutor for a plea deal on a misdemeanor charge of battery against Sydney if you cooperate and return the phone, then confess to attacking her. We could even keep it out of the news, and it might not affect your job. That's your best option, Glen. I suggest you think about it. You can reach me when you've made your decision."

Detective Williams stood and opened the door. The reporter hung his head and slowly trudged out. The detective followed him to the lobby and watched him leave. He would share news of this interview with his partner later. He returned to the interview room and shut off the recording.

At about the same time, Detective Smith and the junior officer pulled up to the address for Dennis Rogers. They went to his unit and knocked. The door was answered by a moderately good-looking man appearing to be thirtyish. His brown hair was well cut and in place. He had no facial hair. He wore very nice jeans and a green polo shirt. He wasn't smiling.

"Mr. Dennis Rogers?"

"Yes. Are you the detective?"

"Yes, I'm Detective Smith," she replied, carefully showing him her badge. "This is Officer Daniels. May we come in?"

"I guess," he grumbled. "How long will this take?"

"Long enough that we should sit."

"Okay, we can sit here," he replied, while indicating two folding chairs that were placed by a small circular dining table directly in front of them. Officer Daniels remained standing by the entrance door.

The tiny kitchen was on the right. Beyond the table was a small living room with a sofa, a TV, and a dresser that had a black Mizzou cap resting on it. A door on the left led to what the detective assumed was a bath and bedroom area. The walls of the living area were bare. There was leftover food on the kitchen counter and a few dirty dishes were in the sink. A coat rack near the entrance door was empty.

"What's this about, Detective?"

"I have several questions for you, as you're a subject of interest in an ongoing investigation."

"What investigation?"

"I'm not going to go into the specifics now, but I'd like you to answer the questions."

"Are you arresting me?" he asked, while he touched his hand to his chest and displayed a fake look of shock.

She informed him he wasn't under arrest and didn't have to answer her questions, but that it would be a bad look if he took that approach. She then asked if he had gotten into any trouble growing up.

He was clearly perturbed, but he answered. "Not with the law, just things like playing hooky and stealing an answer sheet once."

Detective Smith continued with an authoritative tone, asking how long he had been in Columbia and if he had gotten into any trouble during that time.

Rogers replied huffily, "I've been here three and a half years, and I assume you've checked me out so you know I've had two arrests for pot, including a bogus one two months before it became legal. That's all."

"What kind of work have you been doing since you arrived here?"

Mr. Rogers remained focused on Detective Smith and ignored the officer at the door. "Whatever I can get, but mostly construction jobs here and there."

"Do you enjoy that line of work?"

"I suspect few people really enjoy construction work, Detective. But I enjoy the pay."

The detective glanced around the minimalist apartment. "Yes, I see. It enables you to live in the lap of luxury."

Mr. Rogers let out a disgusted sigh. "Do you have anything to ask that's actually important, Detective?"

"Yes. Where were you on the night of Friday, June twenty-eighth, from 9:30 to 11 p.m.?"

Mr. Rogers answered immediately and without emotion. "I was out of town on a job in Springfield, Illinois. I remember because it was just before the Fourth."

"What dates were you there?"

"From Friday the twenty-eighth through the following Wednesday, July third."

"Where do you stay on a job like that?"

He replied in a sarcastic tone, "We're put up in a no-star motel. You know, that lap of luxury that I enjoy."

"Can anyone vouch for your presence there?"

"Yeah, my manager."

"I'll need the name and number of that manager before I leave."

Detective Smith asked Mr. Rogers about July 13 of a year

ago, and about the summer before that. He answered immediately about the past July, saying he was out of town most of
that month. He assumed he was gone on that specific date, but
he had no records of his jobs for that month to verify it. He
answered more slowly about the prior year, as if the question
surprised him, and said he had no recollection of what he was
doing then.

The detective then asked about the Monday and Wednesday
nights two weeks prior. Mr. Rogers had trouble hiding his surprise at those dates. He had an immediate alibi for the Monday
night, stating that he'd watched a movie on TV and mentioning
the movie by name. He asked the detective if he should describe
the plot for her, but she said he didn't need to.

He said he couldn't remember anything about the Wednesday
evening. Finally, she asked about the last few nights. He replied
that he was out of town on a job from Friday through late Sunday.
He said he was home by himself all evening, doing nothing in
particular, the nights before that.

"I have one last question, Mr. Rogers. Where did you get
this necklace?" she asked, while quickly opening her phone to the
picture she had taken at the pawn shop.

There was a significant pause before his answer, which was a
little shaky. "That? I found it on the sidewalk."

"Which sidewalk, where?"

"I don't remember."

Detective Smith took on a supercilious look. "You don't
remember where you found such an obviously valuable necklace?"

"I'm afraid not."

"Do you remember when you found it?"

"I believe it was last fall, or maybe at the end of the summer.

I'm not sure since it was a while ago."

"If you found it then, why didn't you take it to the pawn shop at that time?"

He replied immediately and confidently. "I waited a few months to see if anyone advertised losing such an expensive piece of jewelry."

"You're a prince of a guy, Mr. Rogers. Why did you take it in when you did?"

"I figured I'd waited long enough, and it was winter when jobs are scarce, so I needed the money. Is this why you're here? The person who lost this thinks it was stolen or something and finally wants it back now? I didn't do anything wrong. I just found it on the sidewalk."

"Huh. Well, to answer your question, the owner of the necklace was attacked, and the necklace was stolen during the assault. She has no interest in getting the necklace back now, since she's dead." Detective Smith watched for a reaction and saw a brief tell on the face of Mr. Rogers. He hadn't known she was deceased, and the knowledge upset him. She then asked if he owned a gun and he hesitated briefly, then said he didn't.

"Okay then. I have no further questions for you. Please find me that contact information on the manager for your June twenty-eighth job. Would you mind if I used your bathroom while you get that?"

He said that was fine while pointing to the opening on the left side of the apartment.

Detective Smith stood up and headed in that direction, with Mr. Rogers watching her every move. She did sneak a quick glance into his bedroom when she walked by. When she returned from the bathroom a couple of minutes later, she sneaked another glance to confirm what she first saw, then she took the contact information that he had for her.

"I'm going to write this discussion up as a statement from you about your recovery of the necklace. I'll need you to come by the station and read it and sign it if you agree with the statement. Can you come by this afternoon at 1:30?"

"I'll be there, and I hope we'll be done with this ridiculous harassment at that time. Am I going to have to give back the money I got for the necklace I found?"

"Not at this time. Goodbye, Mr. Rogers. Thank you for seeing me." The detective and the junior officer left the apartment without backward glances.

In the very early afternoon, Detectives Williams and Smith met in his office to share the results of their interviews. Detective Smith sat in the chair by her partner's desk. They were both upbeat.

Detective Williams detailed his talk with Glen. He concluded by saying that he had offered him a plea bargain if he would confess to attacking Sydney.

"I pressured him by pointing out that he'd made false statements to a police officer, although you and I both know that's not a crime. I told him to get back to me when he'd decided what to do. Between his lying, his sweating, his motive, and his fake alibi, I'm sure that he attacked Sydney. Unfortunately, I don't think we can nail him for it unless he confesses. By the way, I also got him on a recording saying 'Shh, now, shh' for Anna."

"Way to go, boss. I would've loved to have seen you in action with him!"

"Your turn now."

"Here's what I've got. I took Officer Daniels with me, and I talked with Dennis Rogers, who was willing to answer all of my questions.

"His alibi for Hannah's attack is that he was in Springfield, Illinois, for a job. I called his boss, who said he was there from Friday night through the following Wednesday, but she couldn't confirm when he arrived Friday. She gave me the name of the motel where he stayed. The helpful desk clerk at that fine establishment confirmed that he checked in at 2:45 a.m. So, he could have attacked Hannah, then had time to drive rapidly to Springfield to establish what he thought was a good alibi."

Detective Smith said Mr. Rogers didn't remember where he was on the dates when Monica and Anna were attacked, but he had that answer instantly prepared when she asked about the date of Monica's attack. She said he was more uncertain when asked about the night of Anna's attack.

"I saw a black Mizzou cap in his apartment, and a thin black rain jacket like the one Anna's follower wore, though I couldn't see the brand. It was hidden on a chair in his bedroom instead of being on the more obvious and visible coat rack. I also asked about the three recent nights women had been followed or attacked, and he had no reliable alibis, though he had a poor one already prepared for the night of Gwen's attack.

"So, just like you're sure about Glen attacking Sydney, I'm convinced that Dennis Rogers is our serial rapist. The problem is that we only have circumstantial evidence, and we need more. He's coming to the station later to sign his statement, so I'll get him on a recording saying Anna's phrase while he's here. Hopefully she'll recognize Rogers's voice, so we have something more concrete on him. Otherwise, we may need something to just fall in our laps."

"Well, that's great work, Audra. Your findings definitely top mine. You win."

"No, Derek, but if we can get the evidence we need, justice will win."

CHAPTER 28

MONDAY PM, WEEK 6

A nna had the afternoon off, so she was sitting on her sofa watching TV when a personal call came to her cellphone. She recognized the number as that of Madison's mother. She wasn't expecting a call from her and was hesitant to answer it, but she did.

"Hello."

"Hi, Anna. It's Madison's mom. Do you have some time to talk?"

"I guess so, Mrs. Richards."

"I'm sorry that I came on so strong in our last conversation. The news was really upsetting, as you can imagine. I've had time to think about it since. I want to see if we can track down the bastard who destroyed my Madison's life, and I'll need your help. I don't remember that weekend that you referred to very well after all of these years. But I imagine you do, since you agonized over it with Madison. Can you help me?"

When she answered yes, Mrs. Richards asked Anna to tell her how Madison had spent that weekend, which she did. She also asked Anna for her thoughts. Anna told her she thought it was someone who'd made Madison feel betrayed, and she doubted it was Madison's boyfriend.

"I could see it being the teacher since he was so close to both of us. I could see it being the youth minister, since you were a deacon of the church and Madison wouldn't have wanted your church reputation to have been damaged. And I could see it being a member of your family.

"Your brother, the pediatrician, always gave Madison creepy vibes, and Madison wouldn't have wanted to destroy the family or his practice by accusing him. Madison's older cousin was also a possibility in my mind. At one time she had a crush on him, so if it was him, she might have felt that she'd led him on, and it was her fault."

"Thank you for your honesty today, Anna. I'll talk with some people about what options we have at this late date to look into any of them. With luck, we can get some justice for Madison."

"I sure hope so, Mrs. Richards. Once again, I'm so sorry about my actions at that time. I'll never forgive myself."

"Goodbye, Anna."

At the police station, Detective Smith received a surprising call from the front desk. "There's a young woman here at the desk, Detective. She wants to report a sexual assault. Are you available to talk with her?"

"Absolutely. Please escort her back now."

A few seconds later, a shy and reserved-appearing young brunette woman was shown into her office. She was wearing a plain light-green blouse and a modest-length white skirt. The detective stood and extended her hand to the young woman.

"Hi, I'm Detective Smith. Please sit down," she said, while indicating the chair next to her desk. The detective took out her notebook.

"Hi, Detective. My name's Alex, Alex Templeton. I'm really nervous about being here, but I have an upsetting story I need to tell you. It concerns a crime you should know about."

"Please take your time. Let me know if I can do anything to ease your nerves. I'm on your side. You can start whenever you're ready."

Alex sat with a stiff pose and her hands in her lap. "I guess I should get right to the point. I was raped by someone I was on a date with. I don't even know his name since I found out later that he was using a fake name with me."

"Is this the first time you're reporting this?"

"Yes, I'm sorry."

"That's okay. When did this happen?"

"It was May 27 of last year."

"Did you seek any medical care after it happened?"

"No. I was sore, but I didn't feel like he'd really injured me."

The detective said, in her most empathic tone, "Please describe what happened."

Alex then slumped down and developed a somber expression, but she maintained eye contact. She described her date and how they ended up at her house. She mentioned that the man threatened her but didn't strike her, then raped her from behind.

She paused for several seconds, then continued. "I found out later that he'd used the fake name. I was so embarrassed that this had happened, and I didn't even know his name, so I decided not to go to the police then. He'd used a condom, so I didn't worry too much about pregnancy or disease, though I guess that was pretty naive."

Detective Smith asked, "Why are you coming forth now?"

"After that woman was attacked while jogging recently it made me wonder if it was the same man. That made me anxious that he might come after me again, so I went to a psychiatrist for the anxiety. He brought up the idea of reporting the rape so that maybe the person could be caught and I'd feel safer."

"You said you didn't previously report this crime. Did you tell anyone about it at the time?"

Alex lowered her head. "No, I was too ashamed."

"Have you told anyone since, prior to today?"

"Just the psychiatrist."

"Okay, what name did the man who assaulted you give, and how do you know it was fake?"

"Todd Scott was the name he used. I looked him up afterward on social media and Google, and no one with that name and his picture existed in this area. He'd also removed his online dating profile."

"Can you describe him?"

"He was white and had brown hair and no beard or mustache. He was about thirty years old and was five ten or eleven, and average weight."

Detective Smith instantly knew where she was going next. "Could you look at some pictures and see if you can identify him?"

Alex sat straight up, and her expression brightened. "Yes, Detective. I can do that."

"I'll be back shortly." The detective left the office and grabbed the six-packs of mugshots she had previously assembled. She brought Detective Williams back with her when she returned.

"Alex, this is Detective Williams. He'll just be in here while you look through the pictures. I need a witness if you happen to recognize anyone." She took out the first of the six-packs. "Take a close look at these pictures. Let us know if you recognize any of these men."

Alex looked very closely. "He's not in these pictures."

"Are you sure?"

"Yes, I'm sure."

Detective Smith laid out the second of the six-packs.

"There he is," shouted Alex immediately, pointing to one of the pictures. "That's the guy who raped me. Thank God. I thought you'd never be able to find him since I didn't have his real name or any contact info."

"Are you certain about this?"

"Absolutely, Detective. How did you come up with his picture for me to look at?"

"That's a long story we can't get into now."

"Well, anyway, thank you so much."

"The key question now, Alex, is this. Would you be willing to testify in court that he was the person who raped you?"

"That's a really scary thought, but I think I would."

"Thank you, Alex."

Detective Smith had Alex sign her name under the picture she'd identified. As she did that, the detectives looked intently and knowingly at each other. Alex Templeton had picked out Dennis Rogers instantly from the twelve pictures she was shown. Jackpot!

Dr. Ellis rushed out of his office and headed to Dr. Wilson's office for his end-of-the-day appointment. Within two minutes of his arrival Dr. Wilson opened the door to the inner sanctum and invited Dr. Ellis in. The experience entering the plush office was as commanding as always. This was the Taj Mahal of offices.

"Good afternoon, Ted. How has your day been?"

"It's been fine," replied Dr. Ellis, as his mind inexplicably drifted off to wonder what epicurean delights Dr. Wilson had enjoyed for his lunch while Ted was having his daily egg salad sandwich and an apple.

"Have a seat. Where would you like to begin?"

"Things have been going well with my practice. I've seen some interesting new patients that I feel I've helped. The one grand case that I briefly mentioned to you is coming to a close. The woman was a victim of a crime and is hoping to locate the unknown person responsible through memory therapy. We're making great progress, and it's likely that her therapy will end soon with amazing success."

"That's wonderful. What else would you like to address today?"

"Let's go over the issues from our last session. To begin with, I had a date over the weekend. I joined an online dating site immediately after our last visit, and I met a couple of nice women right away. I messaged with one several times, and we had the date Saturday. We met at a restaurant and had a great time. I didn't have or offer sex with her, just a good-night kiss. I shared some personal anecdotes. I really enjoyed it.

"We haven't spoken since that night, because I know that calling too soon suggests desperation, but I plan to call her in a day or two. She works at a local insurance company, and we have a lot in common. I really appreciate you making the suggestion that I change my dating approach. Thank you."

"That's really great news. I'm thrilled for you. I hope the good experiences continue."

Dr. Ellis enjoyed elaborating on his good news. As much as he had initially dreaded therapy, that part of it was good. He didn't enjoy talking about anything that was a negative in his life or detracted from his self-esteem, however. One of those topics was coming up now.

"Thanks. I should also tell you that I tried the mindfulness exercise when I sensed the unease. As far as I could tell, the unease seemed to be related to concerns about the ending of the dreams we discussed, although it was a weak association and might not be correct.

"I tried the mindfulness exercise after the dreams too. I've had the dream three times since our last meeting. After the first two of them, I got no clear suggestion as to a cause, although there was a nagging in the back of my head that it was related to something I should recognize.

"After the third, I finally sensed a reason for the unsettled feeling that occurs after the dream's literal climax. I don't know if this was the reason why I had the dream in the first place, but it seems to be why it had the unsettled ending. This reason involves my last date prior to the one this past weekend."

"Can you tell me about it?"

Dr. Ellis knew that he was about to reveal a real negative from his life. Telling Dr. Wilson the doghouse story hadn't been so bad, since he was a child and he took none of the blame. This story was different, though, as it reflected badly on him.

"That last date, if I can use that term, was approximately a year ago. It was one of those types of dates I'd told you about. I went to a bar immediately after work one night. I met a very nice woman shortly after I arrived. We were both there alone, and we really hit it off. As the saying goes, one thing led to another, and she invited me back to her apartment.

"We hadn't even had dinner other than bar snacks. Shortly after getting to her place, we had passionate sex. It was very enjoyable, for both of us as far as I could tell. She asked me to spend the night.

"That's where the unsettling aspect entered. We've discussed my unwillingness to get up close and personal with women. It always seemed to me way too personal to spend the night on a first date, and I was never comfortable with that course of action. I had the same feeling that evening.

"Even though I didn't need to be somewhere early in the morning, I didn't want to give out that much of a sense of closeness. That was despite it being a very enjoyable night, on more than just a carnal basis.

"So, I declined her invitation and prepared to leave, although it was only shortly past dusk. She seemed put out by my decision, but we parted on amicable terms. I honestly don't know if I would have tried to contact her again or not."

Dr. Ellis lost some eye contact and spoke a little slower. "Anyway, the unsettling part is this. Since she didn't have a sleeping partner that night, and I left early, she apparently decided to go back out after I left. All I know is that I read in the paper a couple of days later that she was in a serious car accident late that night and died shortly after the accident.

"When I read that I felt awful. If I'd stayed the night with her, she wouldn't have left and couldn't have gotten into the accident that killed her. In a sense, my unwillingness to get close to her led to her death. I truly felt responsible."

Dr. Ellis's face twisted into a hopeless look. "I even considered going to her funeral to apologize and give my condolences to her family, but what could I say? 'Hi parents, I boned your daughter who wanted me to stay overnight with her, but I didn't care enough about her to do that, so she died. My bad, but sorry for your loss.'

"Ever since then I've felt that it was the meanest thing I've ever done to anyone. Obviously, I didn't know she was going to be in the accident, but I felt as if I didn't do right by her. This has weighed on my self-esteem, which as you know is based on me always doing the right thing on every occasion. In fact, it bothered me so much that, until Saturday, I haven't been to a bar or dated since.

"After I had the most recent sex dream, that connection popped into my head. Maybe the dream is recreating that night. I had a great time, with great sex, then there was an unnerving ending. What do you think?"

"First of all, you know how this works. What do you think, Ted?"

Dr. Ellis's hope that Dr. Wilson might quickly dismiss his concerns and absolve him of any poor choices didn't seem like it was going to happen.

"I think it's likely that my worries about my actions a year ago are responsible for the unsettling ending to the dream."

"What do you think you can do about that?"

Dr. Ellis looked at Dr. Wilson with a hopeful expression and a wistful smile. "I wish I could get absolution from someone stating that my actions were okay and I wasn't responsible for that nice woman's death."

"As long as you still have questions about that night, I believe that you're the only one who could grant that absolution, Ted."

"Maybe my penance could be the requirement to be more considerate of the woman's needs in the future. I was clearly not considerate of that poor woman's needs a year ago."

Dr. Wilson looked thoughtful before replying. "This seems to be a question that will have to play out over time in your future relations with women. It might even be a reason to consider continuing to see me, possibly on an infrequent basis."

"That's something I could consider."

"Do you have anything else you'd like to discuss today?"

"No. I think this is plenty. I don't think I want to set up

another appointment soon. I think you've helped me find clues about the cause of my unease, as well as made good suggestions about my dating style. Let me see how it goes for me, and I'll get back to you if it seems reasonable to have another session."

"I think that's an acceptable plan. You know how to reach me. But keep in mind that it's easy to avoid the work needed to deal with your issues if you don't have anything scheduled that will hold you to your goals. Good luck with your penance, as you referred to it."

They both stood, and Dr. Ellis thanked Dr. Wilson and headed out the special patient exit door, once again wishing that he had that option available in his office. It was something he would surely love to utilize with certain patients. Ah, the life of the high-tier specialist.

He was content that he'd apparently discovered the cause of his recent unease. He hoped that just uncovering it would be enough to improve his daily outlook. He realized that talking about that date from a year ago might even minimize some of his guilt about his actions. He knew it would have been even better to get that total absolution from Dr. Wilson. But still, things were looking up for him.

Now on to bigger and better things. He would see Anna tomorrow, with hopes that everything would come together for her, and the resolution of her troubles would be effected this week. That was an outcome that he did need. Despite his recent growth in this area, his self-esteem was still largely tied to his clinical success, and after today it couldn't tolerate another blow.

CHAPTER 29

TUESDAY, WEEK 6

Anna had received a call from Detective Smith in the morning asking her to come to the station for an update. Anna was thankful that she'd scheduled her afternoons off for the week, so she was able to head to the police station at noon instead of having to wait until later. She wondered what the detective had for her. Had a suspect been identified? Had they found anything on the people she'd been worried about?

When she arrived at the station, she greeted the usual desk sergeant and informed him that Detective Smith was expecting her. Anna was ushered back to the office immediately, where Detective Smith was waiting.

"Hi, Anna. It's nice to see you. How are you doing?"

"Honestly, I'm really excited to find out what you have for me."

The detective smiled. "Well, let's not keep you dangling for too long. Come down the hall with me."

The detective led her to the interview room where the voice recordings were available. When they entered the room, Anna noticed that Detective Williams was waiting.

"Hi, Anna," said Detective Williams. "I'm joining you, as we need two witnesses to your reactions when you listen to our recordings."

Anna's excitement reached an intoxicating frenzy after hearing that. Was she going to be able to identify her attacker, finally? "What do you have, Detectives?"

"We have two voice recordings for you to listen to," said Detective Smith. "We'll play each one two times in a row, then ask for your reaction. Let me know when you're ready."

Anna remained standing as she replied forcefully, "I'm so ready."

"Here's the first one." The detective leaned over and played the tape of a man saying 'Shh, now, shh' twice. "Do you recognize this voice?"

Anna furrowed her brow as she concentrated. "Not really, Detective. That's not the attacker's voice, and it's no one I recognize."

"Let me play it one more time for you, Anna, just to be sure." The detective played it again.

"I'm sure. I don't recognize that voice."

"Okay. Let me play the second recording now." The detective pushed another button and again "Shh, now, shh" was heard.

"That one I recognize. That's Glen Hammond. But it's definitely not the voice I heard from my attacker. I'm very sure of that. I guess it wasn't Glen," she said, somewhat disappointedly.

Anna sensed that the detectives were very frustrated with the results of this test. Her earlier excitement had completely disappeared. "What does this mean?"

"We have some new, really promising information, Anna," replied Detective Smith. "If you'd recognized the voice today it might have clinched the case. As it is, we still have high hopes that we've identified a very good suspect. We'll be working diligently over the next couple of days on this, and we might have more for you by later in the week. Try not to be too disappointed, and I promise that you'll hear from us very soon."

"Okay, Detectives. Good luck, I guess." A quiet and frowning Anna trudged slowly out of the room to leave the station.

Detective Williams slumped his shoulders and sighed. "Well, we didn't need that ID to make the case, but it sure would've helped."

"I know. It would've been the nail in the coffin for Mr. Rogers. I'm going to hold off on getting a recording for Gwen to listen to for now. I'll go to the DA with what we have so far on Rogers and see if he agrees to go forward with warrants. We need to get this guy, Derek."

"You got that right."

A still disappointed Anna set out for the psychiatry office two hours later. She had changed clothes after the police station visit and had an earlier-than-usual appointment scheduled with Dr. Ellis. When she arrived, she was pleasantly greeted by the all-too-familiar personnel. She was almost surprised that she wasn't receiving invitations to their office parties by this time. After a brief wait, she was directed back to Dr. Ellis's office. She was calm and wore a neutral expression as she entered and sat down.

Dr. Ellis noted that Anna was dressed more casually than usual, in a pair of red shorts, a pink cotton top, and white sandals. He noted the neutral expression. "How are you today, Anna?"

"I suppose I'm a little disappointed."

"Why is that?"

"I had a meeting earlier with the detectives. I was expecting them to present some major findings, but that didn't happen. They had tapes of two suspects saying the "shh" phrase, but I could tell that neither one was my attacker. They seemed disappointed that I hadn't identified either of the voices as the person who was in the alley.

"After that failure, they said they had more information they were working on, and they expected more answers in the next day or two. Unfortunately, I've heard that story from them in the past, and so far no significant breaks in the case have actually happened. The frequent letdowns are super frustrating."

"I can understand your disappointment. Have they told you anything else about specific suspects?"

Anna sighed. "No. They usually hold back the details until they have a major finding, so I don't know what or who they're working on."

"Well, hopefully the next time they talk with you they'll finally have a good answer. What else has happened since our last session?"

Anna perked up a little. "I ran into Glen again. This time it was near my apartment. It was unpleasant, but I didn't get the feeling that he was stalking me. By the way, his was one of the two voices the police played for me, and I could tell when I heard it that he wasn't my attacker."

"That's interesting. Do you think that he's been cleared now?"

"He should be, but I guess I'm not totally sure. I wonder what the police think and what they have on him, since they decided to have him record the phrase. I'd love to know how they got him to do it."

"Speaking of Glen, what about your dreams?"

"I haven't had the dream of Brian saying 'shh' since our last appointment. I was pretty sure that Brian wasn't the second voice the police played for me, either. I had the dream of Glen saying that phrase one night. I worried about him the next day, but the taped voice trial seems to have eliminated him."

"Have there been any other developments since we talked?"

Anna glanced at the floor before resuming eye contact. She had a wistful expression. "I talked with Madison's mom twice. Each time was tough for me. The first call made me really cry. I let her know what Madison told me, and I went through trying to get Madison to talk with someone. It was a hard conversation, as Mrs. Richards blamed me for not telling someone at the time. That call ended on a very bad note.

"Yesterday she called me back and apologized a little. She seemed to be very interested in discovering who had raped Madison. I went through all of the possibilities for her. It was a less difficult conversation, and it ended better."

"I'm sorry that the calls were so tough for you, Anna. It was a very brave and mature action for you to take, and I applaud you for it."

Anna smiled minimally. "Thank you, Doctor. I felt I needed to make the call, but I didn't feel any relief from it. Could I have stirred up too much for her?"

"Only time will tell, but the intention on your part was noble. You've grown so much since I first met with you."

"Thanks, again."

"It seems like a lot has happened in the last three days. Was there anything else?"

"No. That's all I can think of."

"How are your emotions now after all of this?"

Anna perked up again and sat forward in the chair. "Surprisingly not too bad. I continue to worry that my attacker hasn't been caught, but that's no worse recently. I don't think I have to be concerned about Glen anymore, or even Brian, and that seems to make me less worried that someone is out there looking specifically for me.

"And despite all the false hopes in the past, I still look forward to hearing from the detectives, since they seemed so optimistic and the next meeting might finally produce real answers.

I'm less worried about being followed since getting the pepper spray. Overall, I'm kind of in a holding pattern."

"Is there anything else that you'd like to discuss?"

"I can't think of anything."

"Do you want to keep our final session on the books for Thursday?"

Anna had a slightly dejected look as she replied, "We might as well. The detectives said they expected to have something else for me by then, so there might finally be something important to talk about."

"Okay. Before you go, I wanted to ask something. When you arrived today, I noticed that you were wearing a vastly different outfit compared with what you usually wear for our sessions. Why the change?"

"I have sort of a staycation scheduled this week. I'm working until noon every day, then I have the rest of the day off to enjoy the end of summer. These are my hanging-out-at-home clothes."

Dr. Ellis smiled, and his eyes crinkled with happiness for her.

"I noticed that the colors seem different from your typical look too. Could this be a new trend for you?"

Anna sat forward and smiled while making great eye contact. "Not a new trend. But that brings up something else that might be worth discussing. When I picked out this outfit today, I realized that I hadn't worn red in over two years."

"Why not?"

"Well, you know that I stopped drinking alcohol, going to bars, and dating after my attack. Those were more or less conscious decisions that I was aware of, although I didn't know the reasons until our therapy. When I was looking through my closet today, it dawned on me that my subconscious must have made a decision not to wear red after the attack. So, I wasn't even aware of that decision until I picked out these clothes."

"Why do you think that your subconscious chose to remove red from your wardrobe?"

"I guess this never came up before in our talks, but when I was attacked, I was wearing a short, flashy red dress. I assume that's what caused me to avoid red."

Instantly an oppressive silence completely enveloped the room, stopping all activity. Anna saw that Dr. Ellis had abruptly adopted the bodily comportment of a James Bond martini; he was clearly quite shaken, but he had not stirred. He stared straight ahead with an expression that hovered between blank and shocked. She had the impression that he might have just had a horrible revelation.

After a long, silent period, the doctor slowly began to come out of whatever spell had taken him over. His eyes were glassy and unfocused. He cleared his throat before speaking softly, without making eye contact.

"That's, uh, an interesting decision your subconscious made, Anna. Your attack must have been very traumatic indeed."

"For sure. In fact, it was so traumatic that I also made another change after my attack that I don't think I ever told you about. I changed my hairstyle. I used to wear it mid-back length and curly, but I changed to the short bob I wear now. I thought that change might help distance me from the attack."

The stony silence returned with a vengeance after that statement. The air in the room became completely still. Anna felt chilled, and she sensed that icy fingers were crawling down the cream walls. She became intensely aware of her own breathing.

Dr. Ellis appeared to have gone into a complete stupor. Then he deteriorated even further. He stared at her with wild eyes. His hands began shaking, and he had taken on the color of a cue ball. He seemed completely unable to respond.

Anna had never seen him this taken aback by anything she'd said in prior sessions. She was at a loss as to how to proceed, and she couldn't imagine what she'd said to provoke this reaction.

For his part, following Anna's last disclosure, the horror Dr. Ellis had grasped from the sudden realization of his past actions instantly descended upon him like a heavy shroud. He had the life-altering recognition that he too had suddenly suffered dissociative amnesia two years ago, for a shocking reason that he now completely understood all too well.

Unlike Anna, however, his amnesia had now vanished totally and instantaneously. He couldn't believe he had made such a horrible, drunken mistake, which could now ruin him. His entire world and self-image were collapsing into him like a black hole in space. He had to sort out his emotions, while also taking quick action before this became completely obvious to Anna.

He shook his head in an attempt to clear it, then softly and uncertainly said, "I'm so sorry, I don't know what came over me. I think I suddenly felt ill. Maybe it was a bad batch of egg salad in my lunch. I'm glad we've essentially finished for today since I think I'm going to have to end our session now."

Anna looked confused and a little worried. "That's okay, Doctor. I sure hope you feel better soon. I can just see myself out and I'll plan to see you again on Thursday if you feel okay by then."

Anna rose from her chair, walked gingerly to the door, and left, after giving a parting glance to check on the doctor.

That's when Dr. Ellis truly felt physically very ill. He was extraordinarily thankful that his next two patients had canceled and he was through for the day, as he was sure that he couldn't face anyone else now. He had to process this quickly.

How was he going to proceed? How was he going to handle this newfound and abhorrent knowledge? How was he going to face himself in the mirror every day? How had he been so careless and stupid? And how was he going to save himself, his self-esteem, and his career?

He certainly wasn't going to seek advice from Dr. Wilson. He was on his own for this one, though honestly he'd been mostly on his own for a great many years. Maybe his loner status had helped prepare him for this, if anything could prepare a person for this situation.

His self-esteem was completely predicated on his inner knowledge that he was a wonderful person in all situations. If leaving his date last year early on the night that she eventually died had been a blow to his self-esteem, this was a nuclear explosion. No wonder he'd developed dissociative amnesia. His consciousness couldn't possibly have accepted what he'd done, and it was forced to erect an immediate blockade that night. Unfortunately, the blockade had now been blasted to smithereens.

He was at risk of moving into his own gigantic self-imposed doghouse for life. What should he do now—admit everything, or go into damage control mode? He wanted to run through his options, but he was too overwhelmed to think clearly. His addled brain only popped out one crazy notion.

Anna was already somewhat paranoid about being followed and about her attacker still being at large. Although she'd been stronger lately, if she managed to suffer those feelings of being followed a few more times, she might become worried enough to leave town before discovering all the answers. Should he do something along those lines? Was he that short on options? He knew that he desperately longed to continue with his current life and career, which wouldn't happen if the truth came out.

He decided that he needed to make reasonable plans, and knew he had to be more clear-headed to do so. He needed to go home and spend the night racking his brain for good ideas. He wasn't sure what path to pursue, but he knew that he was ready to fight for his life. He was in for a long night.

Anna spent some time shopping at an affordable clothing store after her therapy session. At the conclusion of this enjoyable pursuit, she started wondering about Dr. Ellis. She couldn't imagine why he'd begun acting so strangely near the end of their appointment. She didn't remember saying anything that would have triggered such a response in him. She hoped it was really something bad he'd eaten. Hopefully he'd be okay at their next visit. His sudden change was really bizarre.

As she was pondering that issue, she rounded the corner of the store and headed to the shadow-filled parking lot behind it. As she did that, the eerie feeling began again. Her neck hairs stood on end as she sensed she was being followed. She whirled around and no one was visible, but there were cars and dumpsters someone could utilize as concealment. She quickly reached into her bag but found that she had neglected to bring her pepper spray with her.

She turned back in the direction of her car and hurried to it. She thought she heard footsteps far behind her, but when she looked, she again saw no one. She nearly dropped her key fob as she fumbled for it, and she could feel the anxiety building up within her like lava bubbling in an awakened volcano. Her hands were shaking, but she finally managed to get the car unlocked. She jumped in and safely sped away.

She'd had a good couple of weeks, but this feeling now was maddening. She didn't know why this was happening to her and whether it was real or imagined. It had to stop.

Between the false alarm at the police station, Dr. Ellis acting odd during their session, and this scare while she was out, it had been a very unsettling day. She was glad to be going home. Hopefully tomorrow would be much better. Things couldn't possibly get worse, could they?

CHAPTER 30

WEDNESDAY, WEEK 6

D r. Ellis awoke in his elegant bedroom. Despite its modern furniture and beautifully painted light-blue walls, he had slept very poorly. His eyes were bleary and his hair a mess. It wasn't the dreams of Aidra Fox that had prevented a good night's rest. It was the residual from yesterday's revelation. He felt as if he were hanging by a tiny thread over the great abyss of the unknown.

He'd spent most of the night reviewing all of the options he could think of to deal with his new and horrible dilemma. He'd come up with several possibilities, though not all were great.

He could argue that he was very drunk and truly confused about who he'd seen in the alley, but it seemed unlikely that argument could redeem him. An apology would do even less. The forthright approach seemed like a bad way to go.

The best option seemed to be hoping that the truth never came to light to anyone except himself. No suggestion of his involvement had been made to this point, and Anna had recovered her entire memory. He mentally kicked himself for telling Dr. Wilson about the Aidra Fox sex dreams, as the doctor might conceivably at some point recognize what the dreams really represented. But if the doctor didn't connect the dots, simply keeping quiet seemed to be the best plan.

Then there was the option he'd come up with the day before. If Anna continued to get the sensation she was being followed, she might decide just to leave town.

An even better option would be if one of the many suspects the police had considered was eventually blamed for Anna's attack. And Dr. Ellis knew he had a great candidate for that role.

If his patient Alex Templeton would just tell the police about her rape, that could solve everyone's problems. The details of her experience suggested that she was very likely to have been attacked by the same serial rapist who had struck two other women in the past year. If she could identify him, there might be enough evidence to convict him of the other recent attacks. Then Anna would have to assume she was another victim of his. This possibility was giving him some real hope.

He could also suggest to Anna that she tell the police about Brian. If she did that it would be the third suspect she'd suggested to them, and she might wear the mantle of the girl who cried wolf in the eyes of the police. They might then have to completely ignore any future suspects that she threw at them.

He'd gone over all of those options repeatedly through his nearly interminable night, and he finally formulated what he thought were his best plans. First, he'd call Alex and suggest that she tell her story to the police. There was nothing but upside to that strategy.

Then, at his next session with Anna, he would strongly suggest that she present Brian to the police as a suspect. He would also suggest that she consider moving away from Columbia to avoid the mental associations with trauma that the city undoubtedly provoked, particularly after all of her episodes of being followed. This three-pronged set of plans seemed to be best.

Today his schedule called for reaching out to Alex Templeton. He was in his bedroom, and he had her phone number from her medical records. He felt it was acceptable to be calling her at 7 a.m.

"Hello?"

"Hi, Ms. Templeton. This is Dr. Ellis. I've been concerned about you and your well-being. I wanted to know how you're doing and if you've a made a decision about whether or not to talk with the police about your attack?"

"Oh, Dr. Ellis. Good morning. You're starting early. I guess I should have called you earlier this week. I decided to go to the police, and I spoke with a nice detective on Monday. When I told her my story, she got excited, and she asked if I would view some mugshots. In the second group of pictures that she showed me, I spotted my attacker. They know his real identity, and I got the impression that they're going after him. I'm really hopeful that he'll be arrested soon.

"I want to thank you for listening so comfortingly to me and giving me the idea of going to the police."

Dr. Ellis couldn't conceal his enthusiasm. "I'm so glad to hear that you were able to take that step, Alex, and that it seems to have worked out so well. I'm proud of your ability to accomplish that."

"Thank you for calling, Dr. Ellis. And thank you for being welcoming so that I was able to tell you about my tragedy without too much humiliation."

After such a horrible night, Dr. Ellis's day could not have begun any better. Not only did Alex go to the police, she had identified her attacker. Hopefully the police would charge him with the entire series of assaults.

He'd still plan to suggest that Anna bring up Brian so as to further discredit any new theories of hers. He felt like he was stepping back from the edge of that abyss now. He was really encouraged.

Detective Smith was excited for her day. She found a judge to sign off on a warrant to search Dennis Rogers's premises. She was in her office early and was prepared to head in that direction as soon as her partner arrived. As if on cue, Derek sauntered in. "Ready for our big day?"

"I'm so ready. I was thrilled when I heard that the warrant was approved. After several recent disappointments, I'm ready for success. I really want to find something in Dennis's possession with Hannah's DNA on it. We've got to get this disgusting POS and put him away."

"Audra, such language. You're getting more like me every day, which is a good thing of course. Should I bring you a box of donuts and a slab of brisket tomorrow?"

"If it would ensure that this dirtbag is going down, I'd take that every day."

The partners got in one car, with Derek driving. A car with two officers followed behind them. When they reached the apartment complex, one of the officers took a position behind the complex to prevent an escape, and the rest of the group presented to Rogers's apartment.

The doorbell was answered by Mr. Rogers, who seemed shocked at the size of the police presence. Detective Smith took the lead and showed him the warrant, and the detectives and one officer began the search, while the second officer was called to guard the door.

They spent nearly an hour searching every area of the apartment, but located no gun, no gloves, no mask, and no obvious sexual assault souvenirs. They did find the black rain jacket hanging at the very back of the bedroom closet, and they noted that the brand matched the one Jillian had identified her follower as wearing. They photographed the black Mizzou cap.

When it appeared as if they were nearly finished with the apartment, Detective Smith approached a rather smug Mr.

Rogers and said, "This warrant also says we can search your vehicles."

She flashed the warrant again. That seemed to push his buttons, and he became irate. He very grudgingly handed over his car fob.

Detective Williams and the other officer went outside to his silver Jeep Cherokee and searched it thoroughly. The interior revealed nothing of significance in the glove box, in the door side panels, under the seats, behind the visors, or between the seats. In the hatchback area, however, they were able to locate a ski mask hidden under the spare tire and a Sig Sauer 226 hidden in a false compartment.

The two detectives conferred and were in agreement. They had a gun that Mr. Rogers had denied having and that Gwen had said was the type of gun used in her attack. They had the sexual assault ski mask that was hidden in his trunk. They had a black rain jacket, which matched the brand Jillian had seen.

The mask and jacket would be tested for DNA; they hoped it would be positive for Hannah's. They didn't have DNA linking him to any of the assaults yet, but they briefly discussed their case against him. In addition to today's findings, they had Rogers's possession of Monica's necklace and the testimony from Alex Templeton. They agreed that was more than enough for an arrest and to hold him, hopefully long enough to get the DNA results back if they could get them rushed.

The DA would decide if they had enough even without waiting for the DNA results from the mask. If they could get a warrant for it, they would also collect his DNA to match against the semen findings from Anna and Monica. The detectives returned to the apartment.

Detective Smith began speaking as Detective Williams was pulling out his cuffs.

"Dennis Rogers, you're under arrest for the assault of Monica Hadley and the rape of Alex Templeton."

They read him his rights. Mr. Rogers, who had been complacent for the most part up to that point, became anxious after hearing the charges. His attempt at bravado, invoking the wrath of his lawyer toward false imprisonment, fell flatter than the coyote after being steamrolled by the roadrunner.

The detectives were fairly confident that his crime spree was at an end. DNA results could clinch the case and help put him away for a long time. If so, the streets were going to become safer. Detective Williams and one of the officers walked Mr. Rogers to the squad car, and the group headed back to the station.

Later in the morning, Detective Smith made her calls. She first called Alex Templeton and told her the good news that her tormentor was under arrest. She next called Anna and asked if she was available to come down to the station. Anna said she was off work at noon and could be there immediately after that.

Anna was accompanied by her roommate when she arrived at the station. Sonia sat in the lobby while Anna went back to see Detective Smith. She was surprised to see both detectives waiting for her in Detective Smith's office.

Detective Smith said, "Come in, Anna. I think we have some great news for you."

Anna sat in the chair beside the detective's desk and noticed the smiles from both detectives. This caused her to become a little excited.

Detective Smith continued, "We arrested a man this morning that we believe was responsible for the series of sexual assaults and attacks, including yours. He's white, five foot ten, and has no hand tattoos. We can't reveal any other details to you now, but he has strong ties to two rapes, and we're awaiting testing that could conclusively link him to all of the attacks. We won't have the results for a few days, but he's currently in jail and hopefully will stay that way, pending bail. You can feel safe now.

"You should also feel happy that the ultimate goal of your taking on the memory therapy was accomplished. The man responsible for the attacks is in custody."

Anna's brief excitement had abated by then. She wasn't smiling and her lips were pressed tightly together as she replied, "Thank you for letting me know this, Detective. I have a question, though. Was his voice the second one you had me listen to yesterday, besides Glen's?"

Detective Williams replied, "We won't be releasing any voice ID as evidence against him, so we can't comment on that."

"Well, if it was, I really don't think he was the one who attacked me. I'm sure that wasn't my attacker's voice."

The detectives glanced at each other and their moods clearly waned. Detective Smith said, "We have a great deal of other evidence against the person we arrested, including that which is still pending, and which could conclusively link him to your attack. We're very optimistic about this."

"His name isn't Brian, is it?"

"No. I can tell you that much, it's not."

Anna stood slowly and looked forlornly at the detectives. "Well, thank you both for everything you've done. I guess you should keep me posted in terms of the pending evidence. When will you know the results?"

"It will probably be a few days," said Detective Smith.

Anna's shoulders were slumped forward and her eyes were dull. "Okay. I'll try to stay hopeful until I hear from you again. Thanks for asking me here to tell me your news in person. You've both always been very good to me. I appreciate all of your hard work."

Anna trudged out from the back of the station and entered the lobby. Sonia rose to greet her with a million-dollar smile. "So, is it good news, honey?"

"Not really. Let's head out, and I'll tell you about it."

They left the station, and Sonia offered to treat Anna to lunch. They took the short drive to one of their favorite eateries. Anna said she would reveal everything at lunch, so the trip was silent, except for Sonia's colorful expletives at drivers she felt were not up to her level of driving expertise.

The small and cozy restaurant had the day's menu written on a large chalkboard on the wall. Most of the light came through the windows. Ceiling fans were slowly circulating the air. The tables were simple and constructed of dark wood. They were able to get a seat by the wall, so their conversation could be fairly private.

"What gives? Why the not-so-happy face?"

Anna replied in a matter-of-fact tone, "The police arrested someone they think is responsible for the attacks. The problem is that I don't think he was responsible for mine."

"Why not?"

"I don't think I've had the chance to tell you this yet, Sonia. Yesterday they asked me to go to the station and listen to recordings of two suspects repeating the 'Shh, now, shh' phrase. One of the voices was Glen's, and I could tell his voice wasn't that of my attacker. The other suspect didn't have a voice that I recognized, and I'm sure it wasn't him who growled that phrase at me in the alley.

"At the station today, they wouldn't confirm that they'd arrested the person with that second voice, but I could tell by their expressions that it was him. I told them I didn't think he was my attacker, but they kept saying that there was a lot of evidence on him. They weren't able to tell me any details of that evidence, so I don't know what to think."

"Do you think they arrested the wrong guy?"

"Well, I know by how slowly they've moved in the past that they wouldn't arrest anyone without good cause. I'm just fairly sure that he isn't the person who attacked *me*. It makes me think that maybe I was attacked by someone different from the person who attacked the other women."

Their conversation was interrupted by the server coming for their orders. Anna ordered a healthy entree salad without meat, and Sonia a somewhat less healthy double cheeseburger with the works, topped with potato straws, plus tiramisu for dessert. When the server left, they both leaned in and Sonia kept her voice at a low volume.

"Does this put our boy Brian on the radar again?"

"I don't really think so, because I'm fairly sure it wasn't his voice growling that harsh phrase at me either."

"So, what now?"

Anna sat back. "First, I'll run this by Dr. Ellis tomorrow for his thoughts. Then I'll wait to find out what evidence they have on the person they arrested. I just can't believe that the detectives are so excited by this but I'm not. I can't tell you how disappointing, and a little frightening, this is. I wonder if they're going to be putting away the attacker of those other women but leaving mine still on the streets."

When their food came, Sonia dove into her cheeseburger, but Anna just picked at her salad.

"Why aren't you eating, honey?"

Anna barely made eye contact as she replied, "I thought this was going to be over today, but now I'm sure it's not. This is really defeating."

"I'm so sorry. But now that there's an arrest, even if you aren't excited by it, do you think you can start to move on somewhat? Maybe start getting your groove on and even dating?"

Anna smiled. "You're so good for my mental health. I feel like I have been moving on and putting some of this behind me. I'm in a better place and I feel more like myself now. But I don't know about dating yet. And I know I won't feel completely back until everything is resolved and this is totally over."

"So, speaking of my new side hustle, the combined PI/shrink business, how about a takeoff name for it? I kind of like Sonia's Snoop and Shrink."

"No!"

"How about Pursuits and Psychotherapies R Us?"

"Really? You might have to work on this for a while."

"Okay, but I might be getting some help on the sleuthing side."

"What do you mean?"

"While you were with the detectives earlier, a nice, and really hot, officer stopped to talk with me. He took my number so maybe I can get a partner to help with my investigation business, along with other perks he might provide."

Anna sighed and stared at her plate. "It's good to know that at least someone had a successful time at the police station today, Sonia."

At the station, the detectives talked over their case in detail. They were happy that they'd found Dennis Rogers, but what they had on him so far was not a slam dunk in terms of a prosecution or serious incarceration time. "Let's go over where we are on Rogers and review any questions we have, Derek. That way we can decide if we have more to do."

"Sure. What are you thinking?"

"All we have on him for sure is the testimony of Alex Templeton. He'll argue that even though he lied about owning it, the gun model is common and the one he had can't be linked directly to Gwen's attack. He'll say that he found the necklace, that he didn't steal it, and maybe it wasn't even Monica's.

"But I don't buy his timing of finding the necklace, as he said he found it on a sidewalk long after the night she was attacked. I can't see such a nice piece of jewelry lying there for any length of time without someone picking it up. We also know that style of necklace wasn't popular and no other necklaces like that were reported stolen or lost, so it was likely Monica's. He has a con-cocted alibi for the night Hannah was attacked, which doesn't cover the time of the attack. Unfortunately, those flaws in his stories aren't going to convict him."

Detective Smith furrowed her brow as she continued, "I was really hoping to find gloves in his apartment or car that would still have Hannah's DNA on them. Without that, we have to hope that the ski mask has some of her DNA. She did sustain a lacera-tion on her scalp from the blow that knocked her out. If he lay in the correct position on top of her with the mask on, it could have picked up some DNA from her blood or sweat.

"If we can get a warrant for a DNA sample from him and it matches the male DNA from Anna's and Monica's vaginal sam-ples, we've got him. If the mask contains Hannah's DNA, we've got him. If none of the DNA matches, our case would mainly hinge on Alex Templeton. It really helps that she came in before any publicity about a serial rapist, and before Rogers was identified. But it would have been better if she'd said something to someone, anyone, a year ago."

Her partner said, "What about Anna saying that Rogers wasn't her attacker, after she heard the recording?"

"Yes, that really throws a wrench in the works. We know that some features of the attacks could suggest that Anna was the victim of a second attacker, if it wasn't for the same DNA being recovered from her and Monica."

Detective Williams replied, "There's the condom question, too. Rogers used a condom with Alex Templeton. He could easily have used a condom with Hannah since she was unconscious. That would explain the lack of DNA from her exam. Monica's attacker had a gun with him, and we know that perps who use guns can sometimes control their victims enough so they can use condoms. Maybe he was smart enough to use them."

Detective Smith responded with, "But there was no condom used in Anna's attack. Now that was a year before Alex and Monica were raped, so maybe it was Rogers, and he evolved. But Alex was raped before Monica. If it was Rogers for all of them, he likely used a condom in Monica's assault. Where would the DNA found in Monica have come from in that instance?"

"All good thoughts with no obvious answers, Audra, unless the condom leaked in Monica's assault but not in Hannah's."

"This is a real quandary, Derek. There's some minimal evidence that Anna might have been attacked by someone other than the person, almost certainly Rogers, who attacked the others. I just can't get past the same male DNA that was in Monica also. Are we missing something other than your leaky condom possibility?"

Before being able to pursue that thought, the detectives were interrupted by one of the junior officers. He told them he was instructed to pass on two messages.

The first was that Dennis Rogers had found someone to post bail for him, so he was being released. The second was that the hospital had left word that Hannah was beginning to show signs of coming out of the coma. She was nowhere near being able to answer any questions now, so they were not to come to the hospital yet.

"That's really great news on Hannah, for many reasons," said Detective Williams.

"I agree, but I can't believe that scumball Rogers found someone willing to post bail for him. At least for now I don't think the young women of Columbia need to be worried, however. With what he knows we have on him so far, even he wouldn't have enough belief in his own superiority to risk attacking someone now. I'm afraid I'll have to make Ms. Templeton aware of this bad news, though."

The good news of the morning hadn't survived the remainder of the day for Dr. Ellis. He fretted constantly, which served to wear down his morning elation. He had gone from the top of the mountain in the morning to barely above sea level now. This didn't seem fair. He was collapsed on his bed, and he had passed on dinner.

Sure, Alex had gone to the police and they'd identified her attacker, but how much would come of that, and would her attacker be accused of the other attacks? Would Anna be willing to offer Brian to the police as a suspect? Would any of her worries about being followed impact Anna enough that she might consider leaving Columbia? And if none of those hoped-for events happened, what lengths was he willing to go to in order to get himself out of this mess?

As his earlier joy now ebbed, he wished he didn't have to wait until the next day to press Anna on these issues. He wanted answers today in order to reassure himself that things would be okay. The waiting was killing him. He had barely noticed the string of patients he had seen through the day. He was sure he hadn't helped any of them.

He realized that being a loner hadn't prepared him for any of this. His past actions had left him now adrift alone in the shark-filled seas in a tiny lifeboat, with no help expected to come. It was going to be another very long and miserable night for him.

He wasn't even sure if he actually deserved to get good news. He certainly wasn't the person he had always thought he was.

But he held out a semblance of hope. After all, tomorrow was another day. Anything could happen.

CHAPTER 31

THURSDAY, WEEK 6

Anna left her apartment to travel to her final therapy session. Sonia was at work, and she'd made plans with Anna to have a celebratory dinner tonight in honor of the psychiatry sessions ending. Milo was sleeping on the apartment floor in an area where the warm sun shone through the window.

Anna had heard nothing more from the police about the man they'd arrested. She was no longer worried about Glen, her stalker, or even Brian. The day was starting off okay. Anna made sure she wore no shades of red today, to avoid upsetting Dr. Ellis. She hoped he'd eaten something other than egg salad for his lunch.

When Anna arrived at the psychiatry practice, she fantasized about walking back to Dr. Ellis's office through a double column of employees offering hand slaps, as if she were the star basketball player being introduced at the start of the final game. She made it back to his office without the benefit of that introduction, however. It was time to bring this journey to its conclusion.

In a way, she had more baggage now than when she started this trip, but it was somewhat tolerable baggage, and she was fully aware of it. She hadn't gotten all of the answers she'd sought, but she had recovered all of her memory. She had tolerated the process better than she might have expected, and she expected that her upcoming therapy with a sexual assault counselor would help further.

She noted that Dr. Ellis was seated more stiffly than usual in his grand therapist chair. Anna had always thought the chair was designed to look a little like a throne. She wondered if it had been chosen for the benefit of his self-esteem, or to establish the power dynamics in the room.

Dr. Ellis was also quietly pondering the end of their time together, but not with his usual approach to their sessions. He was no longer having fantasies of being the expert therapist to help Anna arrive at all of the answers. He had only one thought in mind today, and he was laser-focused on it. What concession was he going to be able to get from Anna?

"Good afternoon, Dr. Ellis. I hope you're feeling better today."

"Hi, Anna. I believe that illness has left me for the most part, so I am better today. Let's explore what's happened over the last two days, along with any new emotions that you might have."

"The big news is that the police have arrested someone they believe is the serial attacker."

She appeared to be ready to continue talking, but Dr. Ellis jumped right in. "That's fantastic news. I'm so excited for you. This is what we've been working toward. You can finally rest easy."

Anna held out her palms in his direction. "Whoa, not so fast. As far as I know, the person they arrested is the one whose voice didn't sound like my attacker. They wouldn't tell me what evidence they had on him for any of the cases, including mine.

"I'm feeling that maybe they were wrong about assuming one person was responsible for all of the attacks. I can see now that there's at least a possibility that I was attacked by someone else, and the police have no idea who that is."

Anna noticed that Dr. Ellis had an odd look when she finished talking. She couldn't tell if he was puzzled, unhappy for her, or upset for some reason.

"Are you sure about that? From what you'd told me previously, there seemed to be very strong reasons for them to conclude that there was only one attacker for all of you. I think accepting that they've finally located your assailant might, psychologically, be the best course for you. Everything could be over for you now."

Anna was surprised at that response. It was as if Dr. Ellis was not listening to her and was not accepting her conclusions.

"Maybe not. I'll only be able to accept that they're right if they find proof that he attacked me. They said they're waiting on other evidence, presumably DNA testing. Since they found semen in me, if he's not matched on those tests, I'll know he's not my attacker."

Dr. Ellis paused briefly, then said, "If that happens, would your friend Brian be a possibility? You had those two ominous dreams about him repeating the phrase to you, and you said Sonia had unearthed some good evidence that he could be your attacker. Perhaps you should tell the police about him if the DNA tests don't work out."

"I considered that, but I think it's very unlikely he's the one who attacked me. I'm almost positive that his voice was not the one who said that phrase to me. I wouldn't want to negatively affect his life with an accusation that's probably false. I'm done with going that route in my life."

"But I think you should explore all of the possible suspects so you can find the right answer."

"Well, I've already decided not to tell the police about Brian."

Dr. Ellis expelled a heavy sigh and appeared frustrated. "Has anything else happened since our last session that you want to talk about?"

"I did have an issue later that afternoon. I thought I was being followed once again, but I didn't see anybody. It was in a parking lot too, which is a real worry." Dr. Ellis was nodding as Anna related this event.

"Again, Anna? These things have happened way too often to you. I feel terrible that you have to put up with these continued worries. Have you ever considered leaving Columbia? I expect you'd feel completely safe if you moved to another town. What do you think?"

Anna wryly smiled. "This is going to sound like a bad joke. But, other than for being raped and constantly worrying about being followed, I love it in Columbia. My best friend is here, I love my job, Milo loves it here, and the weather is great. I'm also finally starting to put the past behind me and look forward to the future now."

"So, if the police don't connect the person they arrested to your attack, what next?"

"I'm not sure. There wasn't any other evidence at the time of my attack, so I don't know what the police could do. I wouldn't let it go, though. I went that route with Madison and look where that led. Now that I'm aware of everything that happened to me that night, there's nothing for me to lose if I keep on hunting for answers."

Anna was also thinking she should search other, newer avenues. Maybe she would press Sonia again on that spa client who was attacked.

Dr. Ellis was becoming increasingly worried. He furrowed his brow and shook his head. Anna had, in no time, rejected every concession he hoped he might get from her. Every easy way out of his dilemma was now seemingly gone. What was he to do? He had no plan for this scenario. He needed some time to think. He left his chair and began pacing the room while not making eye contact with Anna. She had no idea what to make of his actions.

"I just hate to see you waste all of your time and energy over this, Anna. You're young and have so much of your life left. It shouldn't be consumed with a futile search for your attacker. You deserve better."

Anna was very puzzled by the doctor's behavior, but she was sitting comfortably and responded in a calm voice. "I agree that I deserve better, Doctor, but we don't always get what we deserve, do we?"

"That's so very true, as I'm becoming painfully aware." Dr. Ellis stopped pacing briefly and looked toward the ceiling, as he wondered to himself if he'd just actually said that last thought out loud.

Anna was aware of being remarkably composed. "Are you sure that you're okay, Doctor? You don't seem at all like yourself. You're acting strangely and it's upsetting. I feel like I'm the one who should be asking you to share your emotions now."

Dr. Ellis stopped pacing, turned toward her, and glared as he replied in a harsh tone, "Oh shh, now, shh, Anna! I'm the therapist here."

TIME, QUITE SUDDENLY, STOOD COMPLETELY STILL FOR ANNA. She'd been rocketed back to the alley behind the bar. She immediately understood that it wasn't Brian, or Glen, or whoever the police had in custody who'd snarled those words on that awful night. She knew that as soon as she heard her doctor utter that terrible phrase.

Dr. Ellis was once again pacing around the room, primarily between Anna's seat and the exit. He appeared to be in deep thought, or maybe having an internal conversation with himself.

Anna desperately wanted to scream, and curse, and vomit, but she didn't have that luxury now. She realized she had to quickly move past the shock she'd just received. This situation was potentially dangerous. She had to find a way to get Dr. Ellis away from the door. She needed an exit strategy.

At the same time, Dr. Ellis's thoughts were as jumbled as the pieces of a collapsed Jenga game. They alternated between hoping for a solution to his dilemma and realizing his new truth.

He hoped that Anna hadn't recognized his revelation, and that the police would never have any reason to suspect him. His new reality was that the action represented in his dream hadn't taken place in a fantasy bed, but in a dingy alley. And the woman with the long brunette curls he'd encountered by chance two years ago was definitely not his longtime crush, as he'd drunkenly thought.

While this back and forth was going on in his mind, he wasn't paying much attention to Anna, but he eventually noticed that she wasn't talking.

"What's going on, Anna?"

Anna tried to keep the hesitation out of her voice. "We seem to be done for today. Maybe I should just go."

Dr. Ellis's voice was calm, as he replied, "No, Anna, no. I don't think you should go now. That wouldn't be a good idea at all."

For the first time since he had met Dr. Wilson, Dr. Ellis was glad that his office didn't have the fancy separate patient exit door that he'd once coveted. He only had one exit to protect here, not two.

"We should talk more. What's on your mind now?"

Anna worked hard on maintaining eye contact. "It's hard to

think while you're walking around. Maybe if you sat down in your chair, I'd be better able to answer your question."

"I like it better here. We can talk like this."

"But it's making me uncomfortable."

He replied with a sneer. "With all you've endured, I'm sure you can tolerate it."

This standoff continued for another couple of minutes, while Anna wondered if Dr. Ellis had figured out what she'd just learned. He didn't seem to realize that he'd uttered the fateful phrase as he said it. Why would he be aware of her new understanding now? But if he hadn't realized it, why would he be keeping himself between her and the door and telling her not to go?

The doctor started pacing again, this time in a small area directly in front of the door. He was mostly staring into space and wasn't paying much attention to her. This gave Anna an idea. There was a rule about no phones on in the therapy room, so Anna had always left hers in her bag on mute. When the doctor turned, she quickly reached in the bag, grabbed her phone, and jammed it between her leg and the side of the chair. In that location it wouldn't be visible to him where he was pacing.

On his next turn away from her, Anna texted Sonia: *Need help! Don't reply.* On the following turn, she texted again: *Call cops, at dr.* She had to hope that Sonia had seen the text and would figure it out and respond quickly with help. She also had to keep stalling.

"Doctor, you've always been so nice to me, but you're worrying me now."

Dr. Ellis stopped, smiled, and looked at her. He replied calmly. "I am nice to you. I'm always nice to everyone. There's no need to worry."

"I'd feel better if you'd just sit down and relax."

"No. I need to stand and use up some of my energy."

Anna was getting nowhere. Her mind was racing to search for a strategy. She settled on trying a different approach. "You know, maybe you're right, Doctor. Maybe I really should talk to the police about Brian. Maybe he did attack me."

She picked up the pace of her speech. "The more I think about it, the more I think this could be the answer. I should go to the police as soon as possible. In fact, I think I'll go right now with this idea so they can get started immediately."

Anna made a motion to get out of the chair.

The doctor was wary of this sudden change he was sensing from Anna. "No. You're not going anywhere right now. I need to figure this out first."

"Figure what out? The police can make the decision about whether or not to investigate Brian."

His voice became gruffer, and he started pacing again. "No. I need to decide what's best for both of us and what you're allowed to do."

Anna realized by his wording that it was becoming more dangerous for her by the minute. She thought briefly and decided on another gambit, which could backfire big-time if unsuccessful. Her only hope seemed to be keeping him talking until help arrived, if Sonia had even seen her message. She didn't want to think of the possibilities if she hadn't.

She felt surprisingly calm as she replied, "Dr. Ellis, how long ago was it when you realized?"

"Realized what?"

"You know, that you were the one who attacked me in the alley behind the bar."

Dr. Ellis stopped pacing and had the crestfallen look of

someone who'd just lost a winning fifty-million-dollar lottery ticket. He stared open-mouthed at her and eventually said, "I don't know what you're talking about."

"Then why are you acting terrified and keeping me from leaving the room?"

Dr. Ellis didn't know how Anna had figured it out, but she had. There seemed to be no hope left. He couldn't pretend anymore. Anna wasn't going to buy a denial from him. He decided he had only one way left to play it now. He had to appeal to her sense of reason.

"Okay, Anna. During our last session, I suddenly realized that we were both victims of dissociative amnesia because of what happened, and that I hadn't remembered that night either."

A suddenly enraged Anna clenched her fists and shouted at him. "Victims! Don't you dare try to call yourself a victim!"

Dr. Ellis attempted to defuse the situation. He said in his calmest voice, "So, help me understand. When did you realize?"

"When you said 'shh, now, shh' a few minutes ago."

The doctor staggered and nearly collapsed. He hadn't recognized his horrible mistake when it occurred. He instantly realized that without that foolish mistake, he might never have been discovered. He could have had a normal life. He deserved to be in the doghouse now. He knew he had to respond quickly with the only reply that instantly came to mind.

"You know this doesn't really change things. I've listened to you for weeks now state that you never said 'No' before the event occurred."

Anna replied, with a disgusted look on her face, "Don't try to downplay your guilt by calling my rape an event."

The doctor tried his most commanding voice. "No matter.

You never said 'No.' You said that massaging your breast felt pleasant. I have all of these statements in my notes. You didn't say anything about stopping until after it was over. You said you wondered if the police doubted the veracity of your memories. When I first caught you, you even said 'thank you.' I didn't really do anything wrong, and my notes prove it."

Anna was increasingly becoming more angry than worried. She raised her voice.

"First of all, I never said 'thank you' at any point—that's a lie. Second, I did eventually say 'No'. And even if you think you can make a ridiculous case that I allowed it and what you did was okay, I doubt that you want to go through a very public court battle to determine whether or not you're a rapist. You could kiss your career goodbye if that happened."

"What about you? Your name would be dragged through the mud too."

"I think I could take it better than you could."

Dr. Ellis had stopped pacing and was attempting to stare Anna down. Nothing was working. He hadn't realized that Anna had gotten so strong. He had nothing left but to grasp at straws.

He pleaded. "Is there any compromise plan we could reach? You now know what happened to you, so that worry is behind you. You've got all your answers. But if you don't say anything, my reputation remains intact. And you wouldn't have to go through the public humiliation of people hearing how little you resisted. You know I'm a good person. How does that sound?"

Anna practically spat out her reply. "Like I'd be letting another rapist go free. I already did that once with Madison. Never again."

Dr. Ellis was starting to become unhinged. The pleading look had vanished and was replaced by one of fear. He had a wild-eyed expression and his pacing began again, at a more rapid pace. Anna was truly afraid now, and she noticed herself beginning to sweat.

"Anna. I have a wonderful life here. I can't lose it. So I'm not going to let you take that away from me. I'm going to do whatever I have to in order to prevent that from occurring." He started shouting. "Do you understand me? Whatever it takes!"

The spell of that terrifying moment was broken by a knock on the door. The doctor responded promptly and forcibly. "Not now. We're in a private, confidential session. Go away."

Dr. Ellis headed toward the door in order to lock it. Anna, who'd been defiant a few minutes earlier, was now petrified with fear and her hands were clammy. Just before the doctor reached the door, it jerked open, and Detective Williams was framed in the entryway, with his hand on his firearm. In her highly emotional state, Anna had the unexpected thought that the scene resembled a superhero entrance, missing only the beams of light that should be shining in from behind him.

"Columbia Police." Detective Williams stepped in, with Detective Smith on his tail, her hand on her gun also. They both wore Kevlar vests. They instantly assessed the situation, noticing no weapons, no injured individuals, and that Anna wasn't being physically restrained. Anna had never been so happy to see Detective Williams.

"What are you doing? This is a private physician-patient encounter. You have no right to barge in here."

Detective Williams replied, "There were exigent circumstances, Doctor. We had reason to believe someone was in danger. We received a message that Anna had requested help."

"There's no danger here, is there, Anna?" a desperate Dr. Ellis said as he turned toward his patient with pleading eyes and with an arm extended toward her.

But while he was saying that, Anna was running to the side of Detective Smith. "Thank you so much, Detectives," she said, while pointing toward the doctor.

"He did it. Dr. Ellis was the one who raped me in that alley."

The detectives seemed stunned by this information.

"You can't believe her, officers. She has a history of lying to the police. I have it noted in my records. Her mother can even confirm the lying."

Detective Williams replied, in an attempt to take control of the situation, "I think it would be best if we all calm down. We should go to the station and sort everything out there."

"You can't haul me out of my own office in police custody. I'll sue you for damaging my reputation."

"If you relax and cooperate, we can all leave together in a pleasant group. There would be no reason to cuff you or imply that you were in custody."

After much grumbling, Dr. Ellis reluctantly agreed.

The group descended in the elevator and reached the building lobby. Two officers were there controlling the entrance to the office. When the procession, including the two additional officers, left the building, Anna spotted Sonia on the sidewalk and ran to her. She grabbed Sonia in a giant bear hug. "Thank God! I had no idea whether you'd seen my texts. I can't tell you how happy I am to see you. Thanks so much."

"I've always got your back, honey. You know that. I'd never let anything bad happen to you."

Detective Smith indicated to Anna that she should ride with the officers while the detectives took Dr. Ellis in their car. Anna asked the detective if Sonia could come with her to the station, and the detective gave her permission. In the patrol car, Sonia turned to Anna and said with a huge grin, "Don't worry. You're in good hands here. This is my new friend Jeff in the passenger seat, protecting us."

Jeff greeted Anna and gently asked if she was okay. Anna replied that she was as she thought that Sonia might have found a keeper.

In the short ride to the station, Sonia told Anna about noticing the texts when she'd just finished with a client. She carried the phone with her to a coworker's area and borrowed the coworker's phone to call the station. She relayed Anna's texts to Detective Smith, who said she'd rush immediately to the doctor's office. "How scary was it in there, honey?"

Anna seemed to relax a little. "It was pretty bad. I'll tell you the details later, but Dr. Ellis admitted that he'd raped me in the alley. They better put him away for a long time."

When they arrived at the police station, Anna was taken to one interview room and Dr. Ellis to another. Anna was interviewed by Detective Smith, and she gave a detailed account of her session with Dr. Ellis, including her recognition of him repeating the 'Shh, now, shh' phrase. She mentioned his veiled threats and his admission of guilt in committing Anna's assault.

When the detective asked about the doctor's claim that Anna had lied to the police, the story of the false accusation in Madison's case spilled out. Anna pointed out that she'd never lied during the current investigation. Her interview was brief.

In the other interview room, Detective Williams pointed out that Dr. Ellis wasn't under arrest and didn't have to speak. The doctor was shaky and sweating but was attempting to appear confident. He spoke up and didn't attempt to deny what had occurred two years ago in the alley. He explained why he thought he shouldn't be held at fault.

"I assume Anna has told you everything that she told me in our sessions. I put my hand on her breast, and she enjoyed it. She never said no or resisted prior to my having sex with her. She even said 'thank you' after I first caught her. Why would I think that any of my actions weren't okay?"

"Did you ask her if she wanted to have sex with you?"

The doctor shrank back. "Not per se."

"Did she give any kind of verbal indication that she clearly was interested in having sex with you in that alley?"

The doctor leaned forward. "Yes, when she said 'thank you' after I caught her."

Detective Williams had an incredulous look. "Do you think every woman who says 'thank you' to you is asking for or agreeing to sex?"

"Well no, of course not."

The detective stood and leaned over the table at the doctor. "Are you in the habit of forcing yourself on women who are very drunk and unlikely to have full control of their senses and judgment?"

The doctor sat up and raised his voice slightly, though it was shaky. "Well, I was really drunk too, so drunk that I legitimately thought she was someone I knew when I entered the alley and saw her from behind. It was mistaken identity. Don't those points make me not responsible for my actions?"

The detective threw up his hands and started pacing. "Being drunk doesn't excuse you from responsibility for your actions. And this other person you thought Anna was, is she a regular partner of yours that would have been thrilled to have sex with you in an alley?"

"You're twisting things around."

The detective stopped moving and stared at the doctor. "And what's your argument for why it was okay to violently throw Anna into the garbage cans?"

Dr. Ellis had a surprised and hurt expression and did not reply.

The detective stepped toward the doctor and calmly asked, "Why in the world didn't you say something when you began counseling the woman you'd sexually assaulted?"

Dr. Ellis looked excited to reply to this question and blurted out his response in a near manic pace.

"Okay, this is more evidence for my side. I'm such a good person that after I had sex with Anna, I suffered dissociative amnesia like she did. Because of the wonderful person that I am, my brain decided that I shouldn't have, and therefore couldn't have, done that to her. So it blocked the memories, and I wasn't aware of it when I began counseling her. A person who wasn't as good as I am would never have blocked out those memories." He sat back, appearing triumphant after his response.

"First of all, you didn't have sex with her—you raped her. And second, a person who wasn't as stupid as you are would've realized that admitting you shouldn't have done that to Anna was, in fact, an admission of guilt."

"No, no, you're twisting things around again."

"But for the record, you really didn't remember that night in the alley? You really weren't aware you were Anna's attacker while you were counseling her?"

The doctor dropped his head. "No. I knew none of that until this week when my amnesia for the night suddenly broke. In addition, I had no way of even recognizing her, as I only saw her from behind that night and her hair is very different now."

"Why didn't you tell Anna the truth when your amnesia broke?" The doctor turned away. "I guess I was protecting myself." The detective was still speaking in a calm voice. "From what? You just tried to argue that for many reasons you're not to blame. If you're not to blame, why not tell Anna?"

"You just aren't understanding my logic."

"How is this for logic? I just demolished every one of your arguments that your actions were acceptable. I think we're done now. Don't go anywhere, Doctor." The detective left the room.

The detectives conferred. After sharing their interviews, Detective Smith asked Anna about the doctor claiming she'd said 'thank you' to him. Anna pointed out that he had mentioned that to her in their session earlier, but that wasn't a part of any memory she'd gotten about that night. Otherwise, the stories basically agreed. The detectives decided to ask for a warrant for the doctor's DNA, which could confirm that he'd sexually assaulted Anna, even though he'd already admitted it.

They discussed the need to figure out how the doctor's DNA got into Monica if the test results were as expected. But they agreed that given the violent throwing of Anna into the trash cans, and the lack of admitting what he'd done two years ago once he realized it, they should have enough for the DA to agree to prosecute Dr. Ellis. They agreed they had probable cause to arrest him now, though they expected he'd get out on bail.

"After all of the questions we had as recently as yesterday, Derek, it seems as if we're ready to close the serial assault cases with not one but two assailants who'll hopefully come to justice. It's a great day."

Anna had joined Sonia on the bench in the waiting area of the station.

"Detective Williams told Detective Smith that the doctor isn't denying his actions, and they have a good case against him. It looks like this is finally coming to an end. I knew that other voice the detectives had on tape wasn't my attacker, and I was afraid we'd never find the real rapist. But just a day later and here we are, thanks to me finishing the therapy, the doctor's poor choice of words today, and you having my back.

"I'll tell you all the details later, Sonia, but we did it. After some really terrifying moments earlier, it all turned out okay."

"You can say that again, honey. And by the way, if you find yourself in the future missing the experience of being involved in an investigation, I have a great solution. You could become my second in command at Sonia's Snoop and Shrink. What do you say?"

Anna just smiled and smiled.

SIX MONTHS LATER

Anna had managed to find a seat at a four-person table at the busy Heidelberg, and she was waiting for her roommate. Sonia was parking the car, and it always took a while to find a spot in this section of town. Anna's thoughts veered away from the pleasing aromas she was sensing to a rehash of the past several months.

What an eventful year it had been. Beginning with the attack on that poor woman in the park, so much had transpired in Anna's world that it was hard to fathom it all. The visit from the police led to her seeking memory therapy, and it all poured out after that.

All of the concerns, the therapy sessions, the traumatic memories, the numerous suspects, the being followed, and the visits to the police station. It had been a wild and often terrifying ride. Along the way, Anna had learned a lot about herself. She'd opened up to Sonia, to her mother, to Madison's mother, to the police, and to a therapist who turned out to be her attacker from two years previously.

She discovered why she hadn't been dating, consuming alcohol, or spending time in bars. She learned about her failings, and she learned about the terrible things that had happened to her that her mind had suppressed. She also discovered many inner strengths, which continued to grow in recent months. This prolonged reverie was interrupted by Sonia's arrival.

"Finally find a spot?" Anna asked.

"Yes. I think it's near Upper Siberia. And the temp feels like it too. Is the frostbite still an inch thick on my face, honey?"

"No. You look ravishing as always."

Sonia sat and replied, "So, while we're waiting for the others, you said you had some news."

Anna sat forward and smiled. "Yes, this is exciting. First, Detective Smith told me that the woman who was attacked last summer is continuing to improve after waking up from her coma. She didn't remember her attack and she isn't expected to completely recover, but she will have a life. Second, I just heard from my friend Madison's mother, and they found the guy who raped Madison. He was convicted recently of raping someone else. Mrs. Richards learned about the conviction while she was attempting to track down each of the suspects.

"She visited him in prison and asked about Madison. Since the statute of limitations was up on Madison's assault, he was willing to admit to Mrs. Richards that he'd done it.

"I'm so glad that I told her everything. She was not only able to get closure but to also see that he ended up receiving punishment, even if it wasn't for what he'd done to Madison. Mrs. Richards will always be upset with me for not saying something back then, but she thanked me for helping her find the truth."

"Which one of the people you'd investigated was the perv who did it?"

"It was the youth pastor. I guess he convinced Madison that her mother would get in big trouble if he was reported, since she'd been one of the two main church leaders in charge of hiring him. He'd moved states twice in the past ten years, so the news of his conviction had never made it back to Chicago."

Sonia replied, "See, you had it nailed all along. You're going to be great as the second in command at the Snoop and Shrink."

Anna chuckled, but her mirth was interrupted by a couple wearing matching white ski jackets and jeans, moving in their direction. Sonia noticed Anna's glance and looked over and saw who was in Anna's sight line. "Chloe, Brian, how are you doing?"

The couple came up to their table, and Brian replied, "Really well, thanks. Although I shouldn't be speaking for Chloe."

"I second that emotion," said Chloe. "You know, Sonia, before our talk, Brian wouldn't have cared so much about my concerns. But, like now, my concerns are all he thinks about," she concluded, with a double wink for emphasis.

Brian blushed. "I'm also thankful, Sonia. When we ran into you early last fall, I was upset to find out how sneaky you'd been and that you thought I could have attacked Anna. But when you explained the situation I understood.

"And I'm sorry again that when I got so ill right around the time of your attack, Anna, it kept me from communicating. By the time I recovered, I was looking for new outlets. I can understand why you interpreted the timing as being related to your tragedy. I'm glad we cleared that up when I ran into Sonia. Maybe we could all get together sometime."

"That sounds like a good idea," replied Anna. "Sonia said so many wonderful things about you, Chloe, that I'd love to spend some time getting to know you."

Now Chloe blushed. "That would be great, and I think I can speak for Brian also. Give me your number, Sonia, and we can, like, make arrangements some time."

After the numbers were exchanged, Chloe and Brian went to a table on the other side of the restaurant. "You know, honey, things are turning out so well. We made up with Brian, your scumball attacker's in jail, the other attacker's in jail, Madison's attacker's in jail, and your stalker doesn't bother you anymore."

"I just wish I hadn't needed to go through that awful trial testimony to get here. I think I was actually prepared for it by all of the times I was questioned by the police, though. The difference is that I could feel that Detective Smith was on my side at the station.

"I never told you, but the detective told me, after the trial was over, that she'd been molested as a teenager and she sympathized with my situation. Anyway, I gained a lot of strength through the process, so I was ready to defend myself on the stand."

Sonia said, "You did great. I was so proud of you. Now in addition to everything else that's happened, we have two other wonderful changes in our lives to be thankful for."

As if on cue, two attractive men approached their table. They both appeared to be about thirty years of age, and were casually dressed in jeans, denim shirts, and North Face jackets. One was average height and fair-skinned with dirty-blond hair and a very muscular build. The other was a little taller with a darker complexion, jet black hair, and a thin, athletic build.

When they reached the table, they bent forward for quick kisses with their respective partners, but Sonia grabbed the blond man and made it a passionate and prolonged lip-lock. "You know how much I love PDA, Jeff."

She turned to Anna. "Can you believe our luck, honey? I meet this law enforcement hunk on one of your many trips to the police station, and he's tolerated me for six months. He also manages not to get intimidated by my insane hotness. Then I talk you into dating again, and you immediately find this jewel of a man. Diego, why don't you and Anna try the extreme PDA? It's good for you. I'm thinking of lobbying for it to become a new Olympic sport!"

Anna grasped hands with Diego. "That's only because you'd be a cinch for the gold medal, Sonia. Anyway, I think we're okay with a simpler approach. Besides, we wouldn't want to try to compete with you, as we know you'd win hands down."

"Who said anything about hands?" smirked Sonia.

They all laughed deeply before Anna continued. "Anyway, thanks so much for convincing me to get back into dating. It's been a great three months and things are constantly improving. I'm really happy now, and I'm so glad Diego is tall. I'm done for the rest of my life with men who are five foot ten." Anna gazed affectionately at Diego.

Sonia added, "So everyone's in their happy place, except for your parents. They'll never get you back to Chicago now."

"That's okay, Sonia. That's really okay."

Detective Williams strolled into the room where his partner sat at her desk. "Can you believe we're finally done with these assault cases, Audra? It's been a long haul."

"I hear you. The doctor caused some delays in his trial, with his high-priced lawyer, but justice finally prevailed. I understand that the jury was very sympathetic to Anna's side. It seemed natural that they would lean toward the more regular person, as opposed to the physician. I heard that Anna was a great witness too, and the jury loved her, as they should have."

Detective Smith smiled. "I'm also glad we didn't have to attempt to get records from the doctor's psychiatrist, which would have proven difficult. I wonder what the good doctor said in their sessions. Anyway, the DA said we wouldn't need them. I heard that the doctor's psychiatrist has moved to Maryland. Do you think it was guilt that he didn't suspect something about Dr. Ellis, or did he have other reasons for the move?"

Detective Williams replied, "Who knows? But can you believe that crazy twist in the case? The doctor met Monica in a bar, and they went back to her place for sex before she was attacked later that night. What are the odds? No wonder the DNA in the semen threw us off. At least the doctor had timestamps proving that he was entering records into patient charts at the time of Monica's attack, so we could keep Dennis on the hook for that one.

"I also wonder if the doctor tried the defense he gave us, that he confused Anna with an adult film star, so what he did was really okay."

Audra laughed. "Yeah. He tried the deluxe gift basket of excuses on you during your interview; a real potpourri of rationalization."

She was happy as she continued. "At least we ended up with a very strong case against our buddy Dennis. Finding Hannah's DNA on Dennis's ski mask was huge, and finding a trace of her DNA on the butt of the gun from Dennis's car was the clincher.

"Then we were gifted the icing on the cake when that call came in from the young woman, Tanya, who said that Dennis had raped her last spring. When she described the same fake ID scenario as Alex told me about, I knew we could use her testimony. Even though she hadn't gone to the police or a hospital, the fact that she told one of her friends and her aesthetician about it at the time really helped too."

Detective Smith had a satisfied look. "Those pieces plus Alex Templeton's testimony gave us more than enough to put him away for a long time. We didn't even need the evidence of Monica's necklace, though I think it may have helped. The streets of Columbia have been safer for months now. I'm also glad we could give closure to Monica's and Hannah's friends and families."

"Yes, Dennis was a real menace." Detective Williams chuckled lightly at his rare joke. "And he was getting more dangerous since he was continuing to get away with his crimes, while also becoming more violent. I'm glad we caught him when we did, thanks to your great detective work. One less scumball on the street."

His partner replied, "Thanks for the compliment, and thanks so much for your good words to the chief. That helped me feel like I could ask him to let me start that working group to support our female officers, as I had wanted to do. This will help us handle the bull we get on a regular basis from suspects and a few of the male officers. Hopefully it will also help us get more respect. At the very least it's going to be great for our morale."

"I'm glad for you, Audra. I wish I'd been able to do more about that creepy reporter, though. When he lawyered up, I knew we didn't have enough evidence to get him on the assault charge.

"All my hard work finding him on a street cam, wearing the clothes Sydney described when he was claiming to be at the movie at the time of her attack. I even tracked down that friend of his who bought the movie ticket that was his alibi, but the DA said everything was too circumstantial."

Detective Smith said, "Yes, it's been a really interesting few months. I'm so glad we were able to help most of those women, though. It was very important to me, personally, that we brought their attackers to justice. That really helped me to deal with some demons from my past, but that's a topic for another time.

"All in all, Derek, there was a lot of really good police work involved in solving our cases. But I have to say, given who Anna's attacker turned out to be, we never would have learned all of the answers to all of the crimes without the help of Anna's memory."

ACKNOWLEDGMENTS

I must give a great many thanks to the wonderful people who helped me in this process. Without their assistance this book would not have been possible. Thanks to Dr. Creagh Boulger, Seth Cooper, Bethany Mowery, Greg Murden, and Joanne Vickers for technical assistance. Thanks to Bethany Mowery, Chelsea Murden, Greg Murden, Kathy Pearson, and Joanne Vickers for manuscript review. Thanks to my publishing team, Emily Hitchcock and Clair Fink of Columbus Publishing Lab. Thanks to my wife, Linda, and many friends and neighbors for input concerning the book's title. Thanks to my daughter Chelsea for listening to me endlessly ramble on about issues with this book. And thanks, of course, to Roget, for frequent assistance. Finally, I need to give immeasurable thanks for support through this process to my family, especially my wife.

I also wish to acknowledge my mom. She started me on Agatha Christie and Asey Mayo books at a young age, and she gave me my first Sue Grafton novel. I know she would have been extremely proud to know that one of her children had written a mystery novel.

ABOUT THE AUTHOR

At a young age, Robert Murden was introduced by his mother to the marvelous world of mysteries. He became an avid mystery reader and fan, with favorite authors ranging from Agatha Christie to Sue Grafton to Shari Lapena. He developed the concept for this story over twenty-five years ago but had to wait until life changes provided him the time to put fingers to computer to complete it. He is a recently retired physician, who attended the University of Michigan and then medical school at the University of Missouri in Columbia, where this story is set. His training provided him with a strong background in psychology and counseling, which helped with the development of this novel. He lives in Worthington, Ohio, with his wonderful wife, Linda, and their adorable dog, Carousel.